Clare Morrall

Clare Morrall's first novel, *Astonishing Splashes of Colour*, was published in 2003 and shortlisted for the Man Booker Prize that year. She has since published the novels *Natural Flights of the Human Mind*, *The Language of Others*, *The Man Who Disappeared*, which was a TV Book Club Summer Read in 2010, *The Roundabout Man* and *After the Bombing*.

Born in Exeter, Clare Morrall now lives in Birmingham. She works as a music teacher, and has two daughters.

When
the
Floods
Came

CLARE MORRALL

SCEPTRE

First published in Great Britain in 2016 by Sceptre
An imprint of Hodder & Stoughton
An Hachette UK company

First published in paperback in 2016

1

A CIP catalogue record for this title is available from the British Library

ISBN 978 1 444 73651 9

Typeset in Sabon MT by Hewer Text UK Ltd, Edinburgh
Printed and bound by CPI Group (UK) Ltd, Croydon, CR0 4YY

Hodder & Stoughton policy is to use papers that are natural, renewable
and recyclable products and made from wood grown in sustainable
forests. The logging and manufacturing processes are expected to
conform to the environmental regulations of the country of origin.

Hodder & Stoughton Ltd
Carmelite House
50 Victoria Embankment
London EC4Y 0DZ

www.sceptrebooks.com

For Alex and Brian, Heather and Jon

I

It's a late afternoon in August. Dense clouds hover overhead, signposting an end to the suffocating heat of summer. I'm standing on the steps at the entrance to the Birmingham Art Gallery, looking out over the amphitheatre of Chamberlain Square, examining the neo-Gothic tower, which only partially resembles its online image. The pool at the base, where small fountains once bubbled charmingly and prevented the water becoming stagnant, is now filled with mud, home for a profusion of marigolds and nettles. Vicious brambles are snaking their way up the tower, gripping it tightly, claiming yet another conquest on their path to world domination.

The outline of the surrounding architecture, blurred by a cloak of moss, is pleasing.

In my head, I can hear Popi's voice, dark, quiet, typically grave: 'Roza, is this wise?'

'I really don't know. It can't still be against the law to be here.'

'We both know it probably is.'

'Well, nobody's going to enforce it, so what does it matter?'

'You should be guided by more than the law. Common sense should play a part.'

He's a Literalist. He prefers to think in the present. He'll occasionally go backwards, but refuses to go forwards. I've got no time for this attitude. I'm twenty-two. The future is ahead and I have no intention of missing any of it.

I'm wearing rose-coloured, skinny trousers that are wearing thin at the knees, trainers, a greyish velvet jacket worn smooth with age, and a brown woolly hat. I'd like a smarter jacket, but I make do with what I can get, these days. I can't summon the dedication of my sister Delphine, who spends hours, sometimes days, hunting for quality clothes. The frizzy wisps of hair that peep out from under my hat have been bleached to a shining blonde by the sun, while the rest of my hair is tied back into a single long plait that reaches to my waist. I've got good hair, inherited from Moth, light brown, thick and glossy. I've sewn two yellow felt flowers with orange centres on one side of my hat, but they won't stay upright. They're meant to be daffodils, but they're too droopy. More 'rest in peace' than 'the beginning of spring'.

I told Hector about this place when we decided to get engaged – it wasn't quite official at the time. We'd had the results from the Hoffman's test verified, not yet the fertility one, but it was good enough for me – and I wanted to offer him something personal. It was a password into the secret world of my mind, an invitation to understand me.

But he was shocked. 'I don't like you going there. It's not safe.'

Hector and Popi are going to hit it off splendidly. They are synonyms personified. Different appearance, same intentions.

'It's perfectly safe,' I said. 'There's never anyone else there.'

'Maybe you should ask yourself why.'

'I do ask that. But I can't think of an answer.'

He looked directly into my eyes, made his voice deeper than usual. 'Roza,' – he's not so impressive when he's being serious – 'you must promise me not to go back. Otherwise I'll spend my entire life worrying about you.'

Tricky. Should I refuse to promise or should I lie? I hesitated, watching the dismay gathering in his gentle eyes at the delay in my response. 'Very well, Hector,' I said.

He smiled then and leant over to send me a kiss. I watched his mouth pucker into an intimate round shape, surrounded by the soft wisps of unshaven hair, and approached the computer screen, pretending to kiss him back. It might have been more satisfying if he'd been a hologram, but my POD hasn't been functioning all that well recently, and he'd have been even less substantial as a holo. I don't like kissing air.

I'm lucky to have him. We're required to be married by the age of twenty-five. Safeguarding the next generation, says the government in Brighton. But it's hard to find suitable men when it's all done online – almost impossible, in fact, unless you're given an introduction – so I'm proud that I've been able to find Hector myself. He's clever, wordy. The formality of his manners delights Popi and Moth, and keeps me, Boris and Delphine endlessly entertained.

The statue of a man, the nineteenth-century economist, Thomas Attwood – I know this, I've read all about him on the History Mall on Freight – reclines on the steps opposite the art gallery, a bronze sheet of paper spread out on his knee, while the rest of his papers are scattered, apparently random despite their metallic rigidity, further up the steps. Attwood has broken the rules, done his own thing, by climbing down from his assigned position and proving himself to be an original thinker. The plinth where he should be perched remains empty, an insignificant block at the top of the steps. There's something satisfying about the fact that he never returns to his rightful place, never moves, never feels the need to read information from another sheet of paper.

The silence is enormous.

Moth has told us how it used to be, pre-Hoffman's, when the country was heaving. As a child, more than forty years ago, she came here once a year with her own mother, the grandmother I never met, for the German market. The floods were creeping across the country even then, claiming new ground after every cataclysmic storm, slowly furrowing out pathways for future expansion, but it was still possible to travel during the winter months.

To market, to market, to buy a fat pig.

There was a curious desire to think backwards in pre-Hoffman's times, Moth said, to recreate the world of the Middle Ages, as if it had been a period of boundless good cheer: dancers, men on stilts, jugglers, market stalls; crowds of cheerful people drinking steaming mugs of mulled wine, eating, talking, jostling, spending money. I've studied the scenarios on History, seen photos of adverts from old newspapers.

Home again, home again, jiggety-jig.

Nobody comes here any more. Or if they do, they know how to hide. Even the birds keep away, knowing that the overflowing bins, the discarded food, have all gone. Just occasionally, a flight of pigeons manoeuvres overhead in tight formation, banking steeply to one side, turning, soaring up and coming round into a giant circle, their wings flickering in the sunlight, their movements carefree but controlled. So someone somewhere still has a pigeon loft. But they never land or even come close to the ground, never show any curiosity.

For years, I used to cycle along the A456, the Hagley Road, with my brother, Boris, who's two years younger than me, and, when she was old enough, my sister Delphine, six years younger. When we reached the Five Ways roundabout, we would circle endlessly, examining the white barriers that blocked access to Broad St, convinced there was a way through to the city centre, a secret door somewhere in the apparently seamless construction. But they remained huge and pristine, travelling along the outer rim of the roundabout and then onwards, north and south, a small arc in the giant protective ring around the city. They were curiously beautiful, glittering in the sunlight, washed clean by rain and snow, impossible to breach. Purpose-built by men in contamination suits, sent by a government frantic with fear.

We once saw two racers in training on the roundabout. They swept past us, clad in tight-fitting black bodysuits, as sleek and shiny as their bikes, banking sharply as they sped round the inside of the curve, skilfully avoiding the potholes, slicing away every possible centimetre in their pursuit of speed. Pigeons on wheels. They disappeared into the distance of the A456, too fast to notice us. Delphine suggested afterwards that we should have thrown ourselves on the road in front of them, compelled them to stop, risked our safety for the sake of contact with other human beings. But they'd gone before we'd had time to release our breath.

Another time, several years ago, a group of three children on bikes, slightly younger than us, appeared on the roundabout, guarded with zealous vigilance by women, one for each child. Where had they come from? Did they all belong to the same family? The adults stayed close, on the lookout for danger, expecting to be obeyed, while the children chatted to each other with restless enthusiasm.

'Hey!' I called, waving my arms to attract their attention, excited beyond belief by their presence. 'Hello!'

They slowed down for a few seconds when they first saw us, equally astonished, delighted to acknowledge our existence, but the women closed in, a human barrier between them and us.

'Parvinder, please concentrate. Keep away from the barriers.'

'Yes, Mrs Atkins.'

'Walloo!' shouted Delphine. 'Over here! We're the Polanskis. Who are you?'

'Can we race you?' yelled Boris.

They turned their heads away and cycled towards a slip-road in the opposite direction, as if we weren't there. Why didn't they show more curiosity? Were they afraid of us? Had they spent so much of their lives obeying the adults that they'd lost the ability to act independently?

They carried on, in a direction unfamiliar to us, lurching dramatically from side to side as they picked up speed, past the redundant road signs, the twisted shapes that had long since lost their function and their words.

'Beat you home, Pikkanip!'

'Mrs Aggarwal! She called me Pikkanip!'

'Apologise, Ishani.'

'Sorry!' A voice trailing through the wind, lacking conviction.

'Let's follow them,' said Boris. 'We could find out where they live.'

'What if we get lost?' said Delphine. 'Popi said we mustn't go too far from home.'

'He didn't know about the children when he said that,' said Boris. 'We can't let them go.'

We trailed them for a while, keeping a respectful distance. I imagined arriving in front of their home, knocking on their door. Would they offer us drinks and biscuits? We could sit round a kitchen table and chat, exchange experiences, play a game, then invite them to our flat when we left. But when the children glanced back, they seemed to look straight through us, as if we didn't exist, and I started to wonder if we were invisible. We lost the confidence to smile or to wave at them. Were they just the product of our wishful thinking, a mirage, some kind of memory film that presented an image of people as they used to be?

After ten minutes, we started losing speed, uncomfortable in the unknown surroundings.

'We'll have to let them go,' I said, aware of our responsibility to look after Delphine, who was only eight. 'We'll get lost.'

We told Popi when we returned home, because it didn't occur to us not to. He and Moth exchanged frowns. 'You know, don't you, that you must never tell anyone where we live?' he said.

'Yes,' said Delphine, nodding vigorously, as if we met other children all the time. 'Of course.'

I remembered uncomfortably my plan to invite them back to our flat.

'But who are they?' said Boris. 'Where do they come from? Where were they going? Why haven't we seen them before?'

Sitting next to Moth when I was about five, singing quietly together:

'*Where do you come from? Where do you go?*
Where do you come from, Cotton-eyed Joe?'

Squeezed side by side in an abandoned one-person carpod, becalmed, unlikely to go anywhere, ever. 'What does "cotton-eyed" mean, Moth?'

Moth laughed. 'Do you know, I have absolutely no idea. You'd have to ask an American. They talk the same language as us, but you can never work out what they're on about.'

'But I don't know any Americans.'

'No, nor me.' She paused for a moment. 'It doesn't really matter if we understand them or not. We're never likely to meet any.' She had been a teenager at the time of the anti-pollution protests, celebrating enthusiastically when the laws were passed, delighted when the visitors from abroad stopped coming and the airports lapsed into silence, but less vocal when the economy failed. Now she thinks the laws were pointless, far too late to be of any use. 'It just made everyone feel better. Didn't stop the floods, did it?'

We pretended we were shooting up the M40 in our carpod, returning from the theatre in London. Moth made the sound of an engine for the sake of verisimilitude, a kind of gentle whine, like the whirr of the yoghurt-maker. One of thousands of vehicles, exactly forty feet apart, eighty miles an hour, on the road home. The past according to Moth: the fleeting presence of Cotton-eyed Joe; speed; home in time for tea.

The roads still slice across the land, routes to forgotten cities, promises of connection. They're crumbling at the edges – and in the middle – fatally perforated by water and frost, surrendering to the silent march of the weeds, cluttered with debris from the floods, but clinging on, the blood vessels of the old world.

One summer's day, about four years ago, I found the way through to the city centre. We'd been searching in the wrong place. While I was still on the A456, just before I reached Five Ways, I saw that a section of the metal fence along the right edge had collapsed, weakened by a hundred-mile-an-hour wind, the weight of a flood or the searing summer heat. And there was a road behind that I'd never noticed before. It sloped downwards, underneath the roundabout. Narrow, almost invisible, hidden by the waist-high grass, buddleia and rhododendrons that had grown up round the fence.

I veered to the side, towards the gap where the fence had broken, swerved through and entered the wilderness of the slip-road.

I had to dismount almost immediately, unable to negotiate the thick undergrowth on my bike. Within a short distance, as increasingly higher walls rose up on either side, all external sounds ceased and the plants began to thin. Darkness wrapped round me as I entered the underground section. The silence had a tangible quality, as if I could hear breathing, as if Boris, Delphine and our little sister, Lucia, were running along behind me, struggling to keep up.

Are we allowed? The whisper of Delphine's voice in my ear, excited, but hesitant, only just discovering the attraction of independence, still prepared to report back to Popi.

Go for it, Roza! No reservations from Boris.

Can I come? Lucia, just behind me, anxious to be in on the action.

Mud, deposited by constant flooding, had accumulated underneath the roundabout, replacing the vegetation: black, still and unknowable. I picked my way carefully, searching for the matted roots of weeds as stepping stones, trying to avoid sinking into the slime. I used the bike as a prop and kept going, through the lowest part, up the opposite slope into heat and sunshine.

Into the forbidden city.

I came to a halt. Ghostly buildings rose up, tall and hollow-eyed where windows had been blown out by fire, and the bricks of blackened walls were slowly eroding. Several of the buildings had sycamores growing through their centres, seeded into the mud, trunks forcing their way up through broken ceilings and roofs, onwards to the sky, pausing on the way to send their branch-like fingers into side-rooms, poke through empty window frames and out towards the sunlight. Their leaves shivered in the open air, excited by their release, the opportunity for photosynthesis.

I was amazed to find most of the infrastructure intact. Twenty years ago, in the aftermath of Hoffman's, the Brighton government sent out drones and zapped most uninhabited areas. They identified empty buildings, marked them on their computers, then crumpled them neatly. The debris was removed by sky trucks and the land was left to lie. A short-sighted policy, according to Popi, who rambles on about the lost opportunities of supermarkets when he's feeling nostalgic.

An unnecessary policy, according to Moth, who's a science teacher and understands these things. 'It was bonkers. Viruses have a limited life. You just have to wait for them to die out. If the government had acted more decisively in the first place, told everyone to go home and wait out the thirty-day incubation period, we'd have avoided catastrophe. But no, panic was more satisfying. It was like setting up a hosepipe by the garden gate to protect your fences, watching the sparks shoot over your head and land on your roof, while next door goes up in smoke. Typical blundering. Probably just as well most of the politicians didn't survive.'

'They were only trying to prove to the outside world they could manage a quarantine,' said Popi.

'Don't be ridiculous, Nikolai. The fire was ten miles down the road by that time.'

But Birmingham wasn't flattened. Other big cities – I know about London, Manchester, Edinburgh, but I'm not sure about the rest – have also been left upright, hidden behind more white barriers, as if someone somewhere made the decision that we should hold on to our history. Although Boris, who studies satellite images on the Geog Mall on Freight, says much of London is now under water, and therefore not preserving its heritage after all.

I'm not afraid of contamination. 'The virus can't survive long outside the human body without mutating,' Moth told us. 'So when all the people died, that form of Hoffman's died with them. It wasn't necessary to destroy all the food, demolish all those shops. They really should have waited.'

'Anyway,' Popi said, 'we're good. The Polanski genes have protected us.'

'I'm a McCracken,' says Moth. 'My genes are good too.'

And we can still have children. It's now thought that most Hoffman survivors weren't actually immune at all, but caught

9

the virus in the milder form that eventually spread to the continent and the rest of the world. They didn't know they'd had it until they discovered that they'd lost their fertility. Popi and Moth are part of a tiny minority with genuine immunity.

'A double first,' says Popi. 'Born with silver spoons in our mouths, without even knowing it. No idea why, but it's been useful.'

Understatement. Popi's civilised response to the world.

Why would he worry about me being here?

I turn away from my contemplation of Chamberlain Square, towards the heavy doors of the art gallery. I've been planning this for some time, wanting to see if any of the art still exists, but nervous about entering the building. I usually cycle the streets, study the architecture, create memories for all those people who didn't live long enough to inhabit their own futures, but I rarely go inside anywhere. I've recently made a decision, aware of my dishonest promise to Hector, and the short time before he arrives. If it wasn't true when I said it, maybe it should be in the future.

Popi, who's an artist, has taught me to think beyond the mundane. He's working on a giant sculpture, the image of a young girl who will look like me when she's finished, constructing it on the concrete playground beside Wyoming House, our tower block, between the traces of old roundabouts, see-saws and swings. Before starting the sculpture, Popi spent many months preparing a platform that could be raised during the winter, knowing that if his art isn't made secure while he's still working on it, it'll be washed away, cracked open by frost or blown over by a tornado. At the first suggestion of bad weather, he sets off the mechanism, and, from windows high up in Wyoming, we watch the child rising, past the lower levels, up and up, until it reaches the delivery bay on the 4th and tucks neatly into the cavity. Then Popi closes the weatherproof doors and waits for spring.

The sculpture has been growing steadily for years, like a real child, but the girl remains fixed at five years old, painted in brilliant, shining colours, coated in layers of varnish, heading inexorably upwards. Progress is painfully slow. I can't remember when he started on the feet, but for a while there were just two shoes, black with straps across the top fastened by vel, and white socks. Then came the legs, round and chubby, with a graze on the left knee. He's reached the shoulders and we're waiting for the head, but there's some concern that she won't fit into the delivery bay once she's complete. Popi will come up with something, I'm sure. If it's important to him, he can solve anything. We make fun of his ambition – Moth complains at the paints and varnishes left lying around in the hall – but we all know it's important.

His intention is to weatherproof it, leave it outside and let it expand and contract with the seasons, like the wooden beams that were used to construct old ships. It will be hard to watch it deteriorate, and there would always be the danger that it'll come away from its fixings. Maybe he'll eventually find a more suitable place for it than the abandoned playground, on top of Wyoming, perhaps among the solar panels, the turbines and the water tanks, with Edward the goat (who is female and should be called Edwina, but ended up with the male version of her name because we were all fond of the story about the three billy goats) and the hens, only visible from the sky. Then it can endure as long as there's someone to see it, a symbol of our family's refusal to follow the crowd.

Now I would like to know if any of the pictures from the past were saved, or if everything has to start again. I've seen plenty of images on the Art Mall, but Popi is contemptuous of online art. 'Don't be fooled,' he says. 'No smell, no tingle – you're only getting half the experience.

'Don't be so precious,' says Moth. 'It's not as if we've got a choice.'

Snowflakes start to flutter round me, as if slightly bewildered, not quite sure whether they are doing the right thing. I stare at them, annoyed. It's still August. It's not even that cold. The blizzards can't start this early. Why didn't the meteos warn us?

I'll have to go home. Nobody argues with the weather. It's the one rule that every member of the family respects. Remember Lucia, they say, without actually saying it.

My visit to the art gallery will have to wait for another time. Just before I leave, something catches my attention.

On the right pillar, on the inner curve, at eye level, someone has drawn with paint pencils a very small picture of a black and white cat.

2

The next morning, I wake in the darkness to the sound of nothing. Assuming it's still the middle of the night, I glance at the time on the ceiling – 9:00 – and sit up with a shock. Why hasn't Rex, my computer, woken me?

The automatic lights are now coming on, triggered by my movements, growing in intensity until they resemble daylight.

'Good morning, Roza,' says Rex. I've selected a macho tone for his voice because I enjoy the fact that I can switch him off in mid-sentence when he irritates me. It gives me a sense of empowerment. 'You might be interested to know that today's weather is—' I wave my hand in the direction of the sensors and he stops.

I swing my legs over the side of the bed, pause briefly to check that the temperature is correct, and put my feet on the carpet. The pile should settle comfortably round my toes, regulating itself to produce exactly the right amount of heat, but it doesn't. It's chilly. I search for my slippers with a sigh. Popi insisted he fixed it yesterday – he found a spare part in a flat on the 12th and spent two hours up here, fiddling around under the floorboards. But the parts would have been built at the same time as mine, with the same limits on their lifespan. They're probably all on the verge of multiple organ failure.

Who painted the cat outside the art gallery? Has someone else discovered my route through the barriers, or is there another entrance elsewhere? Does he or she know of my existence?

Normally I like to spend five minutes gazing out of the window before getting dressed. I've become an expert on the weather, watching cloud patterns from my 25th window, then checking details on the computer: cloud streets and cathedrals of *cumulus congestus*; dark and lowering *cumulonimbus*, with its promise

13

of drama; high streaks of fine *cirrus uncinus* in a blue sky; the cloudless shimmer of early summer mornings. I can follow the progress of storms as they form on the horizon, then roll across the countryside towards our home in Quinton, in the south-west region of Birmingham. They expand and batter everything in their path before pounding against the windows of my flat. The building sways with the wind, elastic as the reeds it was designed to emulate, bending rather than snapping. In particularly bad weather, I imagine we're in harmony with the elements, riding the clouds. I love this sensation of delicate balance, but I've wondered if the designers intended the movement to be quite as noticeable as it is or if it was just carelessly – possibly danger-ously – constructed.

We look out over the Woodgate Valley, which is now almost completely impenetrable. When I was a child, you could see the ordered rows of crops – potatoes, carrots, onions and fruit trees – stretching out for miles, but there are only small patches left now. They're tended by the last of the weeding machines, prun-ing machines, harvesting machines, which automatically shut down and head for raised platforms at the first hint of excessive moisture in the air. There used to be dozens of them, designed to read the weather like ancient farmers, recognise the harbin-gers of snow and rain, but now that the mechanism of so many raised platforms has failed, most have been swept away in the floods. Much of the produce rots anyway – not enough hungry mouths.

For years, Boris and I have sat together in the family flat, watching for signs of a visitor, longing for change, for someone new to enter our lives. There are four blocks of flats here, named after American states: Wyoming, Montana, Colorado and Idaho. They huddle together for comfort, halfway up the slope of the valley: not too close to the unpredictable stream (or torrent, depending on the season) that runs through the centre; not high enough to be subjected to the worst of the winds on the exposed ridge. Idaho and Colorado are visible from my window, with Montana just out of sight on the right, and I seem to have spent hours of my life examining them, wishing someone would appear at a window, someone who'll look back and wave.

There are people online, British women of all ages, who sometimes contact me or Delphine or Boris on Freight. They offer us food, clothes, anything we want, plead with us to cycle great distances to meet them, or to tell them our address so they can come and find us, but our parents have warned that we must never accept anything from these women, or give them any hints of our whereabouts – under any circumstances. They're searching for surrogate children. Desperation makes them dangerous.

'But let them down kindly,' says Moth. 'It's not easy for them.'

They're the lost parents. Maybe their children died, or maybe their ability to have children. They're unfulfilled mothers who are just yearning to perform their natural role.

Are there people who travel across the country, wanderers? *How many miles to Babylon? Three score and ten.* But it never happens. If anyone comes to stay, drops in for a night's rest on their way to somewhere else, they're not prepared to be seen. *Can I get there by candle-light? Yes, and back again.*

Could the person who drew the cat be a traveller, someone who might visit us? At last?

I select from my wardrobe a one-piece suit, faded blue with a few loose threads that I might sew in when I have time, and place it on my bed. Just as I'm pinning my plait up on my head, preparing to strip for the shower, Rex interrupts. 'Boris is here,' he says.

'Don't let him in,' I say. 'Tell him he has to wait.'

'Too late,' says Boris, as he appears at my bedroom door, grinning, his abundant dark hair flopping over his face. Moth finds hairdressing tedious – she loses patience halfway through, leaving him lopsided, reasonably tailored on one side, too heavy on the other – so I've taken over the responsibility. But it's not easy. As soon as you chop one section and move on, the first bit springs back up again. It's like Japanese knotweed before the beetles move in – it never pauses for breath.

'Rex! You're supposed to ask,' I say. 'You can't just let him in.' So now my concierge has started to malfunction and make his own decisions. But I'd hesitate to introduce spare parts. They might undermine his personality.

'Don't blame Rex,' says Boris. 'I told him you were expecting me.'

'He shouldn't have listened. You can't just walk in. I might not have been dressed.'

He grins, awkward, but determined not to be. 'No probs.'

It's hard to be annoyed with him as he stands there, tall, brimming with energy and good humour. 'Boris,' I say. 'There are probs. I need privacy. Can't you come back later? I'm in a rush.'

'You won't be going anywhere today.'

'I wasn't intending to. I've got work to do, and so should you.'

'Look outside.'

I gesture at the window. The shutters slide back to reveal fat snowflakes tumbling urgently out of leaden clouds, a steady stream of icy beauty. So that's why the alarm didn't come on. The computers are programmed for the past, assuming I go out to an office every day like their past owner, not realising I work from home. They've interpreted the weather and adapted. I wasn't expecting this. When yesterday's warning flurries didn't develop into a snowstorm, I'd assumed it had been a false alarm. 'How bad is it?'

'It's not going to let up for some time.'

I should still work, but I'm changing my mind. The first snow of the year is always special.

Boris laughs, a deep, rumbling chuckle. 'Come on, Roza. We can't work today. It's the Stair Game.'

We've both recently moved into flats of our own, one level above the family home, on opposite sides of the 25th, with plenty of space between us. There are four flats to a floor, two on each side, their front doors separated by glass partitions from a central landing that gives access to the stairwell. There are lifts, too, but we don't use them. Moth's law. Anyone who even contemplates putting a foot in a lift risks instant execution. At the age of six, Delphine got stuck halfway between the 18th and the 19th and none of us has forgotten the trauma. They'll have seized up completely by now – they need constant maintenance.

'I'm thinking about it,' I say.

I examine the situation outside. Snow is clogging up the shafts of the wind turbines on the neighbouring flats, accumulating on top of the water tanks, and triggering their shut-down. The snow's coming down too fast, and the energy stored from the solar panels is not managing to melt it yet, or suck it into the tanks. The systems have mechanisms to deal with snow, though, and they're still working. We won't run out of water or heating for the time being. Most of the shutters on the residential floors opposite are closed, as if there are people inside, as if they've woken up like me, looked out and gone back to bed when they've seen the snow. But it's only climate control doing its job. There's nobody there to override the computers.

You can see the shape of the streets from here, once house-lined, now fringed with encroaching forest, undulating easily with the natural contours of the land. I know the numbers of them all, even the B-roads. We like old maps in our family. Cloth parchments, almost weightless, covered with tiny coloured threads that go somewhere, head out, double back on each other, suggest unknown destinations. Some of the smaller roads have disappeared altogether, invaded by the shrubs that have crept out, uncontrolled, from abandoned gardens, indistinguishable in the snow. In the distance are the Lickey Hills, the shadowy dark shape of the Malverns beyond, then far, unknown places.

What's Hector going to do? He was meant to set off from Brighton long before the first snows but kept delaying, dealing with last-minute assignments. And now it might be too late.

I'm annoyed with him. When I told him about yesterday's flurries, he was ridiculously optimistic. 'It won't settle,' he said. 'It's far too early. You only have to smell the air.'

If he was Boris, I'd have told him to stop talking turnips. 'We'll see,' I said. 'But liberate your shovel. Just in case.'

'Stop worrying,' he said. 'Mr Weather or Not – that's my name.'

17

'Well,' I said. 'I suppose I might still let you marry me. Even if you're late.'

A sharp, tight wind dances between the blocks of flats, disrupting the flow of the snowflakes and hurling them against the automatic barriers at ground level. It won't be long before we're trapped indoors. Access denied until the snow melts. If the rain comes immediately afterwards, our enforced incarceration will start early this year. Then the only way out will be over the three-foot walls of the bicycle floor on the 1st.

Popi removed the scaffolding from his sculpture the day before yesterday – he has a better instinct for weather than Hector – after spending a morning examining the sky, but even he's been caught out. The headless child is still there, white and smooth on one side, coated with snow and thick ice. The bright reds, blues and greens of her skirt and jumper shimmer on her sheltered side, garish against the pale elegance of the background.

Moth and Popi are not entirely happy about my engagement to Hector.

'You need plenty of eye-to-eye before you decide,' says Moth. 'You can't possibly know if he's right for you.'

'There's no rush,' says Popi. 'Why not wait until he can give you a ring in person?'

But I don't want to wait. I'm not interested in choices or uncertainties. I want to grab him while he's there. I like him – I'm pretty sure I love him. My pulse accelerates when I talk to him. Our minds work in the same way. We've argued, forgiven each other, seen each other at our worst and our best. We fit.

But it's frightening to contemplate the intimacy, the loss of privacy. I sometimes wake abruptly at night, flushed and trembling, imagining he's lying alongside me, wondering what it will be like to share a bed, touch his skin, allow him to touch mine. Will I have to invite him into the privacy of my mind as well?

I'm worried about my lack of knowledge. Reading the O'Hara Manual of Sex online doesn't quite suffice. It tries – quite vividly, actually – but is that encouraging or undermining? What if I can't do it? What if I laugh at the wrong moment?

I can hear Hector's voice, even in his absence. 'Stop worrying, Roza. Think in clichés: the beginning of spring, fluffy chicks, babbling brooks, dappled sunlight, that sort of thing.'

I just know I'm going to laugh.

What if Boris turns up at the wrong moment? 'Rex let me in, hope you don't mind.'

Or Delphine: 'Can I borrow your lipstick? The rosy brown one?'

Or Lucia: 'Boo!' More hoots of laughter.

It all feels too grown-up, too earnest, too pre-Hoffman's.

We're going to have a proper wedding, in Brighton, after the flood season. I have a dress, adjusted by Moth. It was hanging in a wardrobe in a flat in Colorado House, zipped into a protective bag, unworn. Someone's future that never happened. Frivolous dreams wiped away with swift efficiency by a soaring fever and uncontrollable diarrhoea. There was a lace shawl too, and some silk flowers for my hair, preserved in a box, faded but still pretty.

You can't feel guilt about usurping someone else's fairy tale when there's nothing new left. If you don't take what's there, it will disintegrate and die. The philosophy of survival, a matter of common sense.

'It used to be so different,' says Moth. 'Nobody married the first person they met. They experimented, got to know all sorts of people. Lots of them didn't get married at all then.'

'This is post, not pre,' I say. 'We can't work like that. There aren't enough people.'

She sighs. She's good at sighing, letting out air instead of words, allowing herself time to think without giving the impression that she agrees with anything.

'Anyway, you and Popi got married.'

'Marriage was making a come-back then. Stability, loyalty, solid family units. And people wanted the ceremony. The rite of passage. Formal commitment.'

'Quite,' I say. 'The nutshell.'

'You're too young,' says Popi. 'You shouldn't have to settle for the first man who comes along. I've seen enough disastrous marriages in the past. Believe me, I know what I'm talking about.'

But does he? This has always worried me. The fact that everyone repeats the same wisdom in the same phrases shouldn't turn it into the only truth.

How much is my parents' knowledge, their advice, based on an accepted way of thinking, the result of something they were told when they were younger, when they lived in a different world? They're not necessarily right. How can other people's experiences stand in for your own? How can you learn anything if everyone else has done it before you?

People aren't all the same.

'It's beautiful,' says a voice at my side. I look down and Lucia is standing there. When did she come in? Seven years old, dressed in flowery trousers and a thick woolly jumper that doesn't match, clothes salvaged from an empty flat where neither Moth nor Popi can remember ever having seen children. She shouldn't be here. She has to be accompanied at all times when she travels through the building. Moth's law number two. She worries about freak accidents.

'You really should ring and wait for my permission to come in,' I say.

'I came with Boris,' says Lucia. 'Rex let us in.' She slips her hand into mine.

Boris has already disappeared into my computer room, where I can hear him setting up a game.

'Boris, leave the computers alone,' I call.

'It's all right,' he shouts. 'I'm not doing anything – well, not much, anyway.' He loves computers, constantly changing settings, looking for improvements.

'He'll make them work faster,' says Lucia. But he speeded them up last week. There has to be a limit.

I look down at Lucia's head of shining yellow hair – almost white, an unintentional reflection of the snow, quite unlike anyone else in the family – and experience a surge of affection for her. She's so trusting, so certain of her place with us.

'Hey!' shouts Boris. 'Hector's here.' They all like Hector, thrilled that the marriage has been granted government approval. It gives Boris and Delphine hope.

I put on my robe, tie the belt firmly round my waist and go through to the computer room, where Hector's head, four times larger than life, appears on three of the four walls. His green eyes beam out at us from three different angles, wide awake and cheerful. Every pore on his nose is magnified.

'Make him smaller,' I say to Boris.

He laughs. 'I like him big,' he says. 'Where do you think he got those little scars on his cheeks? Acne?'

'Hey! Drop the case,' says Hector. 'You're hurting my feelings.'

'Shrink him,' I say.

Boris presses a button on the computer console and Hector decreases gradually until he's a reasonable size. He has a mid-twentieth-century academic appearance: an immaculate white shirt, maroon bow-tie, cord jacket with elbow patches. Where does he get his gear? Presumably the drones ignored the Brighton supermarkets on higher ground – there can't be much left on lower ground, as the beach area floods regularly – but I'm not sure that is the source of his supplies. Out-of-town boutiques that were missed in the mistaken belief they were inhabited? Suitcases abandoned on high ground by eccentric men, who planned to escape and recreate a world of dusty archives, string quartets and book-lined studies?

His sandy hair, in need of a cut, is dishevelled, uncombed. His crooked nose – damaged in a skating accident when he was five – bends slightly to the right and is sprinkled with freckles, even in the dead of winter.

'Hi, Hector!' I say, now he's a recognisable shape. 'Up already?'

He's pleased with himself. 'There's a lot to do. I've been up since six.'

'Me too,' I say. I'm not really lying. He asks me to make things up, so that he can demonstrate his skills of perception.

He smiled. 'Nine o'clock, then.'

Clever chap. 'More or less. Has it started snowing in Brighton yet?'

'It certainly has. We're only just behind you, according to the forecast.'

'Are you going to work today?'

Hector, Boris and I work for TU, a research firm based in China, which analyses soil samples and designs pest-control. Boris hasn't finished his degree yet, but he enjoys numbers so much they've agreed to give him some occasional part-time work. He's too good to pass over. Hector's a theoretical scientist – he spends most of his time collating data – and I'm a translator. Chinese to English.

Tu means soil in Chinese. They're preparing artificial soil for a colony on Mars (bigger and more viable than the moon, they say, 'The Go-to World'), but their research is valuable for everyday use, too. For people who live in high-rise flats, for example, locked in by the weather, who would benefit from better indoor food production. We need to be prepared for the day when the last of the farming machines gives up.

'I never work on the first day of the snows,' says Hector. 'Matter of principle.'

'They won't like you in Shanghai.'

'Nothing unusual there, then. They're not impressed by jokes – they think they're frivolous. But my work's hot, so they don't complain too much.' Modesty is not his greatest quality.

'So do you have snow parties in Brighton?' asks Boris.

Hector's eyes swivel to examine Boris, who's positioned at the edge of his vision. 'Yup,' he says. 'Me and my mates.'

'Good to have mates.' Boris's voice is thick with envy.

He's perched on the edge of my office chair with his legs propped upwards on a desk. I knock them down and catch a half-full mug of coffee before it tips over. 'Please be more careful, Boris,' I say.

'I need to learn how to hang around,' says Boris. 'It's what young people used to do.'

'We're going to have a snow party too,' says Lucia.

'The expression is "hanging out", I think,' says Hector. 'And it's not meant to be literal.'

'I can't play all day,' I say, suddenly tired of the predictability of our existence. 'I have things to do.'

'You can't work on the first day of the snow,' says Lucia. 'Not for the Stair Game. Moth's already started cooking.'

'Well, I'll be Yankee Doodled!' says Boris. 'Last year she said she was giving up on the frivolous nosh.'

'I'm too old for this,' I say.

'No, you're not,' says Lucia. 'Come and have breakfast with us, Roza. That's what Moth said. Mushroom pancakes and baked apples.'

'OK,' I say. At least I won't have to endure the arctic conditions of the top floor, fetching eggs from the hen-house. 'Go and tell Moth I'll be down after my shower.'

'No,' says Lucia. 'I'll phone her and wait for you.' She smiles up at me, confident, trusting.

Lucia who isn't really Lucia at all.

3

We lost the original Lucia at the age of three during the flood season.

The rain could come at any time, but it was usually most persistent at the beginning of winter before the snowstorms, and again at the end, when it added to the volume of melting snow. Every now and again, it would pause for a few days, but we would still be trapped indoors, marooned between the rising waters of the stream and the torrents pouring down the hill from the ridge. That year, it started early, pounding relentlessly from clouds – *nimbostratus* – so low that the border between the sky and the land got lost, and for weeks we were hemmed in by walls of water. Rain filled the rivers, the lakes, the neglected drain systems, until they rose up, overflowed and became a torrential body of water that swept across the land. We had to trust in the skills of the old engineers, hope that the flats were well enough designed to withstand the battering. It would be impossible to do repairs. Nobody could negotiate the water at that stage.

The first Lucia had been blonde, too, but not the silver blonde of the present Lucia. Her hair would have darkened with age, like mine and Moth's, settling eventually into pale brown, the tarnished look of unpolished brass, not quite gold.

I was eighteen at the time. Boris, Delphine and I were all in the study, working on the computers, communicating on Highspeed with our online tutors – chosen by my parents from an approved list provided by Brighton – while Popi prowled round empty flats on the 14th, looking for spare parts and materials for his sculptures. Lucia, three years old, dressed in a yellow and maroon woollen dress and thick black tights, was playing with a stuffed penguin at the end of a piece of string and eating a stale hazelnut biscuit.

Moth was baking in the kitchen, grumpy and unapproachable. She's never enjoyed her domestic role. She's more interested in the online teaching, coaching clever children throughout the English-speaking world in genetic engineering, how to design computer models and compare research results. She bakes imperfectly, throwing everything together without attention to detail, unconcerned if the cakes are heavy or the potatoes lumpy. Quantity rather than quality. Cookery's a chore to her, a necessary evil, not an art form.

'There's nothing to stop you doing it yourself,' she says, if anyone complains. 'No problem. The kitchen is available to all.'

Lucia was restless and wanted some attention.

'*I have a little robot,*' she sang in a monotone, '*as smart as smart could be . . .*'

'What a nice song,' said Delphine, twelve years old, always calm. 'Shall I wipe the crumbs off your mouth?'

But Lucia wasn't interested in hygiene. '*He flies outside the windows . . .*'

I was struggling with a geometry problem. 'Why don't you cuddle down with the penguin?' I said to Lucia. 'You could make him a nice bed in here.' I rose from my desk and knelt down in the hollow where my feet had been, grabbing a blanket that was lying around and a towel so that I could shield myself from Lucia's half-chewed dribble.

But Lucia wasn't interested. '*And cleans them all for me!*' she sang.

'Oh, do shut up,' said Boris, leaning back in his chair and stretching. 'I can't concentrate.'

'No!' said Lucia. '*I have a little robot . . .*'

I sat down again, trying not to sigh. I needed to focus. The exams – international highers – were only six weeks away and I was worried about the mathematics. The languages would be fine, but I needed to pass the technical stuff or I would be unemployable. Moth, who has an instinctive feel for the subject, tried to help, but couldn't understand why I was finding it difficult; Popi, patient, unruffled, had been over the theorems with me endlessly; the online Australian tutor kept attempting new methods of explaining. I was still struggling.

'*As smart as smart could be . . .*'

'Ignore her,' said Delphine. 'Just pretend she's not there.'

'But I am here,' said Lucia.

'Why don't you go and find Moth?' I said. 'She might have another biscuit for you.'

'I don't want it. They've all got nuts. I don't like nuts.' Clumps of biscuit and saliva were bubbling away around her mouth.

'There might be different ones by now. Moth makes lots of lovely biscuits.'

Lucia wandered out of the room, trailing the penguin, like a dog on a lead, and we fell back into silence.

Most of the windows – algae windows – were sealed, constructed to respond to weather conditions and siphon off energy to help power the building. But there was a balcony, designed for the precious few weeks of sunshine in the spring before it became too hot. Moth used to make the most of the opportunity to be outside – she believed in fresh air, although Popi was concerned about the effects of too much ultraviolet on young, developing brains – and we often had meals on the balcony during the brief period of warmth. The double doors were electronically locked, accessible to Moth and Popi by fingerprint contact only. There were railings at the edge of the balcony, one and a half metres high, placed ten centimetres apart. The gaps were too small even for little heads to push through, and the railings too tall to lean over, designed by health and safety experts a long time ago. There was no possibility of an accident.

It was nobody's fault and everyone's fault, a set of circumstances that only became lethal in combination. Moth was distracted in the kitchen, baking more biscuits than anyone could eat because she preferred to get it all out of the way as quickly as possible, even if it meant everything became stale before she could summon the enthusiasm again. I shouldn't have allowed Lucia to wander off without checking where she was going. Delphine was the secondary child-minder, the one who should have questioned why I let her go, equally complicit in her neglect.

The previous autumn, Popi, the perpetual scavenger, had brought back some chairs from Montana House, two at a time, intending to sand and varnish them. 'Look!' he said. 'Antiques. Beautiful – they must be at least a hundred years old. A bit of work and they'll just glow.'

'A lot of work,' had been Moth's verdict. We already had a large selection of tables that needed restoration, stored on another floor. Dining-tables, coffee-tables, lamp-tables, all waiting for attention. 'They're not staying there,' she'd said, as the chairs gathered in the hall. 'I'm already falling over them.'

He'd put them out on the balcony, stacked them on top of each other so that they reached the top of the railings, two piles of three wheel-backed chairs with rungs between the legs that would make a perfect ladder for an adventurous three-year-old.

It was Boris's fault that nobody realised the locking mechanism wasn't functioning properly. He was good with his hands, good with technical problems, so he was responsible for the electronic devices. Later, we decided that the doors must have been malfunctioning for ages, possibly even when Popi put the chairs out on the balcony – so it was his fault twice, although he was sure they were working at the time – but nobody had been near them since then, so we couldn't be sure. But something had gone wrong. Lucia had been able to just push them open.

'Lucia!' called Moth from the kitchen, about half an hour after we'd sent her away.

'I thought she'd gone to help Moth,' said Delphine, looking up in surprise.

I pressed a button and sent off my maths work – I'd finally solved the problem. 'So did I,' I said.

Moth came into the room. 'Where's Lucia?' she asked.

A flutter of unease drifted through the room. 'Isn't she with you?'

'No,' said Moth. She turned to the door and called, 'Lucia!'

There was no response.

Nobody was too concerned at this stage. We all assumed she would be somewhere in the flat, playing with her penguin, chuntering away to herself and ignoring the calls in the background.

Boris got up. 'I'll check her bedroom,' he said.

He came back almost immediately. 'She's not there,' he said.

'You don't think she's gone downstairs to find Popi?' said Moth, and we could hear her starting to panic.

'No, of course not,' I said. 'She wouldn't be able to open the front door.'

'She could be anywhere,' said Boris. 'She likes hiding places.'

'She can't be far away,' said Delphine. 'The flat isn't big enough.'

I was the one who went into the dining room and discovered the door to the balcony slightly ajar. I could see Lucia outside, sitting on top of the pile of chairs and leaning over the edge of the balcony, fascinated by what she could see below. Rain was pouring over her, flattening her hair, soaking into her dress, dripping through her tights.

I stopped, realising I mustn't startle her. I crept back to the hall, pulled the door almost shut behind me and called the others. 'She's here, outside!' I tiptoed towards the balcony again, trying to appear unthreatening.

Then Moth was there, pushing past me, stepping on to the balcony, calm but urgent. Delphine and Boris were right behind her.

The unexpected flurry of activity confused Lucia. She glanced back towards us and then down over the balcony. 'Look!' she said, leaning over the balcony, pushing her head through the rain. 'Water!'

'Yes,' said Moth, trying to make her voice gentle, but having to shout to make herself heard. 'There's so much of it, isn't there?'

'Careful,' said Delphine, from behind me, her voice high and unnatural.

'Stay nice and still, Lucia,' I said, raising my voice so she could hear me.

Boris had been inching round the side of the balcony, and when Lucia turned to me, he lunged towards her. But she saw him coming and dodged out of his reach. With a curiously unhurried movement and a quick giggle, she tipped over the balcony.

There was a second of paralysed disbelief, then we all rushed to save her. But it was too late. We watched her tiny body falling twenty-four storeys, a flying toddler, plunging with a strange grace between the sheets of rain, like an arrow, straight and true. By the time she hit the foaming water, everyone was shrieking. Moth led the way into the hall, yanked open the front door and then we were running down the stairs on top of each other. We bumped into Popi on the 13th. With extraordinary instinct, he'd looked out of the window of the flat where he was working, seen Lucia hurtling through the air and understood what had happened.

When we reached the cycle floor, which was open at the sides, we raced to the edge and leant over the concrete wall. There were a few moments of silent concentration.

'There!' shouted Boris.

Lucia's body broke the surface, muddy yellow flowers on the maroon background of her dress, and slipped back under, reappearing a few metres further on, heading towards Idaho. She was being dragged by the current, tossed up and down as if she was an inanimate piece of wood, bashed against the pillars.

Boris threw off his shoes and pulled himself up the wall, digging his toes into small cavities in the concrete, until he was crouching on the top, preparing to launch himself into the flood below.

'No!' shouted Popi, who was also kicking off his shoes. He jumped up beside Boris. The water was only a couple of metres below them, slamming itself against the side of the building in a vicious, irregular rhythm. Rain was pelting down, blown over the wall by the blustering wind, hurling itself against us, and we could barely hear his voice.

Popi put his arms round Boris's waist before he could leap out. They struggled together briefly, and for a few moments it appeared that they would both topple into the water. Then Popi heaved Boris off the wall, away from the water and inwards, on to the cycle floor. Boris cried out with pain as he landed, but kept rolling in an attempt to break the fall. Popi was now poised, gathering the strength to throw himself out as far as possible towards the tiny disappearing body—

Moth grabbed one of his arms with both hands and pulled, her feet planted firmly apart, her arms braced, hanging on as he resisted her, refusing to let go. 'Help me!' she screamed at me and Delphine. Not sure if she was doing the right thing, but too shocked to reason, I reached out for his waist, while Delphine grasped the other arm and we all pulled.

An inhuman howl came from Popi as he tried to resist our combined strength, his voice joining the shriek of the wind and the clamour of the rain. We held him there, frozen into a sculpture of desperation. Then he stopped resisting and we lost our balance, falling on top of each other. Moth and Popi started to fight like children, their hands and feet scrabbling furiously. Popi was trying to break free, preparing to jump back up and leap over the wall to rescue Lucia, but every time he attempted it, Moth grabbed a leg, punched him, pulled him over again, refusing to allow him to get up.

Meanwhile, Boris was preparing to climb up for a second time, but Delphine and I raced over and held him back. Between us, we wrestled him to the floor and sat on him.

In the end, we all ran out of strength and collapsed in a heap next to the wall.

Popi was the first to speak. 'What have you done?' he said, his voice broken and cracked. 'I could have saved her.'

Moth was sobbing, great tears pouring down her cheeks. 'No, Nikolai, you couldn't. It wasn't possible.'

'I could have tried.'

'It wouldn't have done any good. Nobody could survive out there, not Lucia, not Boris, not you.'

'I stood a better chance than Boris.'

'Are you cracked? Do you think I want to lose my husband as well as my daughter?' She started to hit him again with her fists, weak but determined. He sank back and let her do it, exhausted, his face crumpled and sodden.

I stood up and leant over the wall, searching for Lucia again. It was increasingly difficult to tell in the driving rain, but I thought I could see the yellow and maroon dress, part of a pile of debris swirling around in ever-increasing circles, growing as it travelled, collecting everything in its path – a whole security door, which must have broken off a block of flats, a twisted bicycle wheel, an uprooted tree, an old street sign.

Moth was right. We couldn't have saved Lucia. She'd died the moment she left the balcony. Nobody, not Boris, not Popi, had the power to resist the water.

4

At first, no one cried, then everyone cried. For six months, while the rain kept coming, then froze, while the snow fell, we retreated into our separate worlds and stopped talking.

Moth gave up preparing meals and went to bed, occasionally emerging to mark enough work to give the impression that she was still functional, sending terse, irritated messages by Freight (usually used only for permitted admails, which no one opens anyway) to her pupils. I watched her set it up one day and asked why she wasn't using Highspeed.

She gazed into space for so long that I didn't think she was going to reply. I was about to give up when she spoke in a short, dull voice: 'Takes longer for them to find it and they can't accuse me of not responding.' So she wasn't entirely irrational.

Popi went out first thing every morning, maybe finding something to do in an empty flat, or maybe just sitting by a window and staring out all day at the inaccessible landscape. He came home late at night, eating whatever food Boris or Delphine or I had prepared and left to get cold.

I did my exams mechanically, without revision. I scraped through and was given permission to start the university course in October, although I couldn't decide if I had the energy to continue. Everything seemed pointless. Boris spent all day in front of his computer, playing games, refusing to speak, and Delphine went to her room where we could hear her improvising on her keyboard. The music was weird and muddled, full of discords and repetitive tunes, some familiar, some I couldn't recognise.

And Moth's voice, remembered from the past, floating above the dissonance: *Hush-a-bye, baby, on the tree top, When the wind blows, the cradle will rock.*

Disquietingly relevant: *When the bough breaks, the cradle will fall, Down will come baby, cradle and all.*

The men and women who had made up these songs, probably without knowing how to write them down, must have been familiar with tragedy. They wouldn't have known about babies from the future, the ones who didn't survive, the ones who had failed to be born, the ones who had never even been conceived. Their own world was already fraught with danger – impending disaster haunted everything they did. No point in worrying about future babies when you couldn't keep hold of your own. They expressed their fears with words, found solace in rhythm and rhyme. They couldn't have known that their songs would become nostalgia in a post-Hoffman's world, a sad reminder of the distant charm of childhood, or that nursery rhymes would become our way of salvaging something from the past to help us weather the storms of the future.

Winter started to lose its grip. The clouds thinned almost imperceptibly, allowing weak sunshine to filter through. The water started to drain away. This was usually the best time of the year, when the rain lost its power, before the temperature began to rise and bake the ground into clay and there was enough moisture in the soil to sustain new life, before the air became solid with heat. It was the time when everyone usually cheered up.

I went out on my bicycle, pretending I wanted exercise. It was good to feel the beginning of spring, I told myself, see new shoots emerging through the mud, breathe in fresh air.

But it wasn't about fresh air. It was about finding Lucia. I criss-crossed the network of roads that were still accessible, searching the empty expanses, shading my eyes against the glare of the sun with my hand as I peered into the distance.

I became aware that I wasn't the only one out there. I saw movement in the distance: Boris, I thought, pedalling at an inhuman speed, extending his search further than anyone else; Popi, not attempting to hide, calling into the distance as if he really thought Lucia would come running, in the vain hope that she had somehow been rescued by an unknown benefactor; Delphine, a glimpse of a pale purple dress, shadowing me on her own bike, not wanting to join forces, but determined not to lose sight of me.

Nobody found Lucia. Not a thread from her yellow and maroon dress, not a shoe, a lock of her hair, the stuffed penguin. No body. I imagined her being swept away, draining into the River Severn, pulled along towards the sea. I checked the maps and traced the river with a finger on the screen, heading west, south, broadening out past Bristol, into the Channel, heading for Ireland, perhaps, or America. I tried to think of her as part of the ocean, still looking like Lucia, small and perfect, swimming unconsciously backwards and forwards between the continents, maybe following a different river inland to an exotic place. But all the horror stories I'd heard crowded out the comforting image – sharks, whales, stingrays, piranhas.

I kept going back to the forbidden city centre, which I had discovered the previous summer, giving Delphine the slip, wanting to escape the tyranny of grief. I cycled down Broad Street – I'd accessed old maps, discovered the names of the roads – sometimes stopping and looking through shattered windows into deserted shops and cafés. They were still standing, but fragile. These were places that had been abandoned in a hurry, where belongings had been scattered, where lower floors were ravaged regularly by floods and higher floors destroyed by damp, where plants and trees had seeded themselves and established a home.

There was an old furniture store that seemed more stable than some of the surrounding buildings. It said 'Lee L' on the sign over the doorway. There had been more letters once, but they were now indecipherable, so LeeL was the name in my mind. Shortly after Lucia's accident, feeling more reckless than usual, no longer able to see danger in quite the same way, I decided to go in.

The ground floor was the same as all the older buildings that no one had ever expected to be flooded. Damp, black with mould. I found the stairs and started to ascend. With each step, I could hear the slurp of my boot pulling away from the mud on the previous stair. The second floor was high enough to have avoided the floods, and I realised for the first time that this dead part of the city, where no one ever came, was not dead at all, but alive with insects, animals and plants.

I tried to imagine how it had once been, when people came to choose furniture for their homes. The sofas were best avoided, rotting from inside and collapsing into piles of rusty springs and discoloured foam. But much of the wooden furniture, presumably constructed out of hardwood, was large and heavy, some with peeling veneers, but others carved and layered into elaborate patterns, still recognisable as cabinets, drawers, sideboards.

I walked across the floor, stepping carefully round the cavernous holes, avoiding collapsed pillars, into rooms that had presumably resembled people's homes. Had they lived like this once, surrounded by luxury, with monstrous tables and desks and wall units? How had they got the furniture up the steps to their flats when it was too big for a lift? How many people had they needed to transport each item?

Oh, Popi, how you would love it here.

But he wouldn't come. 'It's not safe,' he would say.

I was convinced he was wrong and Moth was right. I'd been coming here for over a year and I was still healthy and alive. Unlike Lucia. But Popi was comfortable with rumours, with unproven myths.

Besides, he would never come here now, even if he accepted it was safe. No one could motivate him to do anything. When he returned home late at night from wherever he went, he would take his plate of food to Lucia's bedroom and sit there on his own, unwilling to talk to anyone.

Nobody slept any more. When I woke during the night, I could hear them all moving in their rooms, tossing in their beds, or prowling through the flat, going to the loo or looking for something to eat, watching old films on their computers with the sound turned down but not low enough to be silent.

I wandered through the ghostly skeletons of past furniture, and marvelled at the skills of the craftsmen from the past, experts with the right tools and machines. Machines had smoothed the surfaces, slotted sections together, moulded the metal parts. The screws had sparkled then, new and shiny, when nails, hinges were all available in abundance.

I spotted a giant bedstead and went over to it, admiring the way the ends seemed to roll like a wave. It was in an alcove furnished with drawers, blackened mirrors, originally intended to resemble a bedroom. I walked round the side of the bed and froze with shock.

The bed was inhabited. Two people, locked together like links in a chain, rows of teeth grinning everlastingly at each other, bones dusted with fragments of cloth, wisps of hair still clinging to their shining skulls, paralysed in a twenty-year-old embrace. It was impossible to know if they were male or female, old or young.

I gradually became calmer. These people posed no danger to me. They had been there for so long that my presence was irrelevant. All I'd done was disturb the dust.

My pager beeped.

This was one of Popi's ideas because the phones didn't work any more. The masts had started to topple decades ago, going down like skittles as the winds grew stronger, but after Hoffman's there was no one left to put them back up, and the networks collapsed. I don't remember phones, but I've seen them in films, and we've watched the disaster movie *Don't Look Down* hundreds of times, so I know how all those phone-mast repairers lost their lives in storms.

Once we started going out on our own, Moth began to worry. She wanted a way to contact us and call us home if necessary. We couldn't use the PODs because there was no way of finding out the router passwords, so Popi placed a transmitter with a range of twenty-five miles on the roof of our block of flats, just above the goat's shed, next to the solar panels. He didn't invent the system – pagers have been around for ever – but he created a new set-up, and we all had a receiver attached to our PODs. This was the first time it had ever been used.

A steady pulse, a regular flash on my left wrist. No message because that wasn't possible, but I knew what it meant. Come home immediately.

Something had happened.

I ran carelessly down the unsafe stairs and out into the sunshine where my bike was still propped against the side of the building. I pushed it to the middle of the road and climbed on, setting off for the underpass, weaving my way through the course of cracks and potholes.

The entire family, except Moth, was assembled in the leisure room, and there was a child of two or three years old sitting in the middle of the floor.

Her hair was limp and wispy, clustered with knots, drooping well past her shoulders. She had very blue eyes, which stared out at us with an expression of challenging fear. The small patches of skin visible beneath a crust of mud were pale and white. She was so filthy that she'd been placed on a pile of towels, with some distance between her and the rest of the family. She was wearing very little except a disgusting nappy and a long-sleeved T-shirt, whose colour was impossible to identify. The remains of a sandwich lay on the floor beside her.

Everyone was staring at her. 'Hello,' I said, wondering why there was no discussion. 'What's your name?'

The child started to cry silently, tears cascading down her cheeks, tracing lines of pale flesh through the dirt.

'Well done,' said Boris. 'We'd just managed to stop her crying.'

'How was I supposed to know that?' I turned to Popi. 'Who is she? Where's she come from?'

'I found her.'

'What do you mean, you found her?'

'I was just cycling out towards the Lickeys, minding my own business, and there she was. Sitting on the side of the road in the mud.'

'On her own?'

'Yes, completely on her own.'

'But where were her family?'

'I don't know.'

I digested this information. 'But they must have been some-where nearby. Did you look for them? You can't just bring her home with you.'

Popi looked at me. 'Don't lecture me, Roza. I'm aware of my responsibilities to other people. But I could hardly leave the child. She wasn't safe. She had nothing to eat, no proper clothes. Completely neglected, as you can see. She'd have died without anyone to look after her. She's not old enough to scavenge.'

'Did you call, try to find her family?'

'Of course I did. I spent two hours cycling around, searching for someone, anyone, but the entire area was deserted.'

'How did she get there?'

He shrugged. 'I have no idea.'

'But they could be out there now, looking for her, desperate,' said Delphine.

I shivered, aware that it could have been us, searching for Lucia.

'Surely she's better off here, being looked after,' said Popi, 'than suffering from exposure, starving to death. Our priority has to be the welfare of the child rather than the parents' peace of mind. We can go out tomorrow and try to find them.'

Moth came into the room. 'I've run a bath,' she said. 'Come along, sweetheart.'

Sweetheart? She's never used those kinds of endearments for us.

She bent over and scooped up the child, wrapping her in a big towel. 'We'll soon have you sorted. I've found some lovely clothes for you. Just you wait till you're clean and smelling nice. And then it's time for bed.'

We stared at each other as Moth walked out of the door with the surprisingly docile child in her arms. This was Moth, who had barely left her bed for six months, who had not spoken to anyone properly in all that time.

'How did you get her to do that?' said Delphine.

Popi shrugged. 'I told her there was a child who needed her help and she just got up, dressed, and went to the kitchen to make her a sandwich.'

Later, as we all sat around the kitchen table, eating in the non-communicative way to which we had become accustomed, Moth came in with the child in her arms, wrapped in a blanket. The little girl looked almost contented, allowing her eyes to droop and losing the tight, watchful look that had been so noticeable when she'd first arrived. We could see now that her hair was silver-blonde, fine and floaty, almost luminescent.

'Now,' said Moth, brisk and more like her old self than she'd been in ages, 'why don't we have some soup with everyone else?'

The child didn't respond. Moth sat down with her on her lap and ladled some soup out into a bowl. But when she held up the spoon, the girl turned her head away. After a few attempts, Moth gave up trying and stood up. 'You're too tired, aren't you, Lucia?' she said gently. 'Come along, let's put you to bed.'

She walked out of the room and we stared after her.

'Popi,' said Delphine slowly. 'She thinks—'

'No,' he said. 'I don't think she does think that.'

'But she said—'

'I know what she said. But she knows what's going on, really. It just comforts her, that's all. Gives her a place.' He glared round. 'If anybody challenges her or tells her she's wrong, they'll have me to answer to.'

None of us spoke.

'Is that clear?'

We nodded and bent our heads to the soup. We weren't ready yet to go back to our old ways.

5

I go for whole days, sometimes even weeks, forgetting that Lucia is not Lucia. I suspect that Moth has allowed herself to forget completely. Popi used to remind her, but he's given up in the last couple of years, and I wonder if he thinks about it at all. Lucia is a golden child, quiet and obedient, clever and funny, an unexpected gift, and nobody wants to question her presence any more. She brings a clear-eyed simplicity to our view of life.

She chatters constantly and makes us sing together, the words and tunes of nursery rhymes hovering round us as a backdrop to our lives. Our voices rise and fall in a shared rhythm, a verbal dance:

Jack be nimble, Jack be quick,
Jack jump over the candlestick.

Meaning doesn't matter, because the simplicity of rhyme gives a shape to existence. It sketches the world of childhood, where things often don't make sense, but also the adult world, where so many other things will never make sense.

Every now and again, Moth brings out the precious book of nursery rhymes that used to belong to her grandmother, and we re-examine the pictures. Not too often, these days – it's growing old and beginning to come apart, the binding shredded and exposed, the pages loose. But the cover, in dark maroon leather, with the shape of a child embossed into it, remains intact. Even now, after all these years of handling, it's possible to trace the picture with a finger, feel the simplified contours of the curls in the girl's hair, her button nose.

The Stair Game involves a vast amount of running up and down, requiring strong muscles and boundless energy. It's partly a race (in which Popi always manages to reach the end first), partly a competition (which Boris usually wins after a bit of cheating, which we all tolerate because he's easier to deal with if he's happy), partly hide-and-seek and partly tag. Everyone wears hats – Moth had made them from felt and feathers when we were little – so that if we're running up or down a flight of stairs, we can spot someone below (you can see the hat before the person) and hide if possible.

The idea is to get to the top and down again without being caught, although the rules are applied fluidly, according to how much it matters to each of us. You prove you've been to the top and bottom with animal stickers (cute cartoon figures that Moth found in the corner of a child's bedroom many years ago, then hoarded until they were required), given out one at a time at the beginning and end of each round. They've lost their stickiness, but we line them up on the kitchen table, so they can be used again next time, a different image for each of us. Mine's a camel with curly eyelashes and a knowing expression on its face. Points are awarded for speed and the number of rounds, and deducted for physical contact with someone else.

We have to call into the family flat after each circuit to record our progress on a chart and to eat. Some of us like a break, but Popi and Boris are always anxious to carry on. For many years, Delphine and I operated together, but now we're allowed to run alone, as long as one of us takes Lucia. She flits between us, one at a time, sometimes determined to run, sometimes accepting a piggy-back, but always slowing us down.

It's a family ritual for the first day of snow. Moth usually stays at home and bakes – the lesser of two evils as far as she's concerned – producing enough apple and plum cakes to satisfy even Boris's appetite. She finds the racing up and down stairs boring, but she's prepared to do the occasional round, just to prove she should still be taken seriously.

'Taking part is more important than winning,' she says.

'Blather,' says Boris. 'The only people who say that are the ones who know they're never going to win.'

'Good point,' says Popi. 'If Moth wants to join in to support the rest of us, that's fine with me.' He grins. 'But I'm in it for the glory.'

Wyoming comes to life for a day, creating the impression that we've been invaded. Giggles, shrieks and footsteps echo through the building, booming up and down the stairwells, while at other times the noise is more subdued, depending on who's running and how much it matters to them. *Wee Willie Winkie runs through the town, Upstairs and downstairs, in his nightgown.* At first, the hens at the top, on the roof, above the 32nd, cluck raucously, bobbing their heads backwards and forwards as if they're encouraging the competition, as if they enjoy the spectacle of human beings behaving irrationally. After a while, they put their heads down again and carry on as normal, scrabbling around on the floor for grain, bored by the continual arrival of hot, sweaty, triumphant people.

Edward, the goat, ignores us assiduously, rolling her eyes briefly when we first emerge, then returning to her oats. During the summer, she spends most of her time outside on her hind legs, straining against her rope, contemplating the view across the countryside, or leaning against the three-foot barrier that separates her from the henhouse and studying the hens for hours and hours. Now the snow has come, she's retreated into her shed. She chews constantly and thoughtfully, as if she's making the point that she thinks our games are childish and irrelevant.

The lower point of the race is the bicycle floor on the 1st, where nearly two hundred elderly bicycles rust in orderly rows, fixed into racks but still leaning wearily to one side or the other as the bolts of their supports falter, in tune with the deterioration going on around them. It's usually too cold to linger here. The walls are open to the weather, so piles of melting snow or pools of water often accumulate after a storm.

What I like about these days is having a good reason to go into the empty flats. *Knocking on the window, calling through the lock, Are all the children safe in bed, it's past eight o'clock?*

Gradually, over the years, Popi has broken the locks and entered. For a long time, we'd hoped that the owners would turn up to pick up their old way of life where they'd left off. But it's been twenty years. No one's going to come now.

A conversation from many years ago between Popi and Moth has remained in my mind. 'They're all dead,' said Popi, apparently arguing, but probably trying to justify his intrusion into long-lost lives.

'Of course they are,' said Moth. 'There weren't any safe areas – you can't outrun a virus.'

'It would be crazy to waste a good supply of spare parts.'

'It still feels disrespectful,' said Moth. 'After all this time. As if we're plundering graves – like opening up the Pyramids.'

'They're not graves. There aren't any bodies.'

The flats are full of furniture, homes to be lived in. When their occupants died, there were no descendants to claim their inheritance, no one left with an interest in the generation that failed the country. Some people went out to work in the morning and never came back. Others departed in a hurry, throwing a few possessions into suitcases, heading for the hills, the countryside, remote parts, as far away from the centre of Birmingham as they could go without approaching another city. The elderly, the less mobile, remained, and my parents, with a toddler and a new baby due at any moment, stayed with them, deciding that if they were going to die, they might as well do it in familiar surroundings. They didn't know then that they were immune.

The only other tenants besides my parents who didn't succumb to Hoffman's – possibly because they had little contact with other people – died from old age fifteen years ago. To my seven-year-old eyes, Mr and Mrs Sung were ancient, survivors from the twentieth century, who somehow never quite grasped the extent of the disaster they would soon be leaving. Moth used to take me with her sometimes when she went up to help Mrs Sung for the few short weeks after Mr Sung died. I can remember watching her spoon watery soup down Mrs Sung's throat in a vain attempt to keep her alive: the papery texture of her skin disintegrating before our eyes; the snorts as she struggled to swallow; her determination to be loyal to her absent family. 'Thank you, Bess,' she would say to Moth, always appreciative, always grateful. 'My daughter will turn up one of these days, or one of her girls – I can't understand why they haven't come already – but they live so far away. They have so many other things to worry about . . .'

'I can't decide,' said Moth, to me, on our way down the stairs. 'Should I tell her that her children and grandchildren are almost certainly dead by now, or should I let her go on thinking it's lack of caring that keeps them away?' I can remember the way her voice faltered, the way she stroked her face as she talked. She must have been crying, I realise now, but I didn't recognise it then. 'I suppose it's better that she doesn't know.' She nodded, as if she was having a conversation with herself. 'It would be cruel to tell her.'

She propped Mrs Sung up on her pillows during the day, helped her with the commode, and left her in front of the television, which was playing news from five years ago on an endless repeat. 'She thinks she's watching a thriller,' she said to me. 'She doesn't understand it's all true.'

I don't think Mrs Sung was seeing anything.

After she died, my parents had to take her downstairs – the lifts were still working then – and place her in a specially designated place at the edge of the Woodgate Valley, outside the cultivated areas. There was no one left to run a crematorium. The official advice after the epidemic was to put everyone who died into marked areas and inform the authorities. Drones then disposed of the bodies. Deaths had to be registered, though. It's important to keep records.

My parents must really have struggled in those early years – Boris was born in the year of Hoffman's and I was just a toddler. Everything happened so fast. There was a thirty-day incubation period, which meant it was spreading without anyone being aware of it, but then most people died within the following four-week period. The barriers round Birmingham were constructed after six weeks (without any discernible effect, but at least it made everyone believe something was being done).

It still feels intrusive to go into other people's homes, but on the day of the Stair Game it's more of an adventure. There's a reason for being there – the need to avoid the others. Many of the cleaning machines, part of the original design, have seized up from lack of use so dust has accumulated and spiders have proliferated. Popi has told me how there were maintenance contracts when they first moved in, regular servicing, men on call. Things ran smoothly once.

'They were too old,' says Popi. 'They lost their will to live. You can't keep things going without spare parts.'

Is he talking about the dusting machines or the maintenance men? Or was he remembering Mr and Mrs Sung?

The only spare parts available are in flats with similar systems, so Popi, the scavenger, the make-do-and-mend expert, has been salvaging for years. 'It can't go on for ever,' he says, every now and again. 'They have a natural lifespan and we're at its furthest limits. We're living on borrowed time.'

Time borrowed from an old, tired world that had miscalculated. There's probably a mathematical formula to demonstrate how much time we've borrowed or stolen from those who didn't survive. Will it be enough to last us into future generations, to support our descendants, to help us survive the criminal loss of experience? We've borrowed time from all those grandparents whose genes will never be passed on; parents who aren't there with advice when you need it most; uncles and aunties who have failed to turn up with goodies, ready to whisk away stroppy children for fun days out; brothers and sisters who can't fulfil their duty to undermine, compete or support each other when the chips are down.

And the thousands of children. The hundreds of thousands of children, who fell like snowflakes, the first to go, the first to lose their right to time, followed by the children who were never born, those who were never conceived, who haven't been given the chance to exist. The missing children who are not waiting in the wings, ready to repopulate the country.

It's unlikely the chips will ever go up again.

Our family has been lucky. My parents have the gene of immunity, the unexpected privilege of undamaged reproduction.

But sometimes, in the face of the encroaching dust, in the endless, unpopulated space around us, it's hard to appreciate the luck.

I'm standing on the landing beside the fire door on the 21st, listening. I recognise Boris's footsteps, moving upwards, fast and urgent, driven by the desire to win, the need to be the best. I can hear Popi going down below me, his rapid breathing, his feet pounding on the tiled steps, skidding across each landing as he throws himself towards the next flight of stairs, pushing himself beyond his normal endurance, determined not to be beaten by his own son. Delphine and Lucia are together – they're whispering on the floor above, their voices tight and nervous.

'Come on, Delphine.' Lucia breaking out into normal speech. 'We've got to go up.'

'Ssh, ssh,' from Delphine.

Lucia's voice slipping into a whisper again: 'Boris has gone up. If we follow him, he won't know we're there.'

'Ssh.'

Delphine can flit from floor to floor silently on soft feet, creeping up on you when you're least expecting her, but she's restricted by Lucia.

I wait a few minutes, then decide to risk it. Downwards, following Popi, avoiding Delphine and Lucia. I'll hear Popi return and be able to hide before I meet him. I set off down the stairs, pausing at the end of each flight to listen.

It seems clear, so I take the next few flights more quickly, feeling the spring in my legs, the pleasure of testing my strength. Boris and Popi don't have to win every time. I can give them a run for their money.

A shriek from Lucia.

'Got you! Contact!' It's Boris.

I stop in alarm, thinking I've been discovered, only to realise that the voice is coming from the stairs above me.

Delphine's furious. 'You cheated! You hid!'

Laughter from Boris. 'That's the point, Sisto. That's what you do in this game. You're meant to hide.'

I look around. Boris hasn't had time to get to the top and back again. I must have miscalculated. He must have already reached the top and will now be heading straight down towards me.

He's moving, not pausing long with the girls. His footsteps are right behind me, heavy and purposeful. My breathing is deafening. Surely Boris can hear it too. There are sounds from below. Popi must be coming up. Which direction did Delphine and Lucia take?

I push open a fire door to the 17th, step on to the landing and examine the four doors behind the glass barriers. The footsteps are just behind me, getting closer.

In the distance, muffled by the fire door, Boris and Popi collide. They were both making too much noise, each assuming he was safe, so they didn't hear one another and met before they could avoid it.

'Got you!' roars Popi.

'No, you didn't!' shouts Boris. 'I got you.'

I push open one of the doors and slide into the flat. The layout inside is exactly the same as my own. The carpet is almost free of dust, as if the machines are still functional, switching themselves on when required, in the way they were always supposed to. One of the bedroom doors is open and I catch a glimpse of a wooden bedstead, a mattress, sheets and duvet covers piled up in a corner as if someone has only just thrown them aside, as if a real person has woken up this morning and climbed out of bed.

Whose flat was this? The numbers have fallen off many of the front doors, and there's nothing to distinguish one from another. Moth has told me about the Antonovs, the Comerfords, the Jhas, but I don't know the names of all the original occupants. I doubt she does either. Somehow, I must have missed this flat on my expeditions – it doesn't feel at all familiar. Maybe I've confused it with its neighbour, passed by in ignorance.

When my parents first moved into the block, about two years pre-Hoffman's, just before I was born, the flats were new, built to cope with the floods. There was a residents' association and my parents joined immediately, keen to contribute to the community. They helped with the produce from the Woodgate Valley. They filled the containers in the large storage room on the ground floor from which everyone could help themselves, then shifted them to the shelves on the 1st, at the opposite end from the bicycles, when the rain started. But there were plenty of residents they never met, who remained unknown and unknowable.

I walk into the leisure room and stare. Bookshelves line the walls. It's like the library scene from *Breakfast at Tiffany's* – the New York Public Library, where Paul declares his love – or the frozen rooms of the same library in *The Day After Tomorrow* without the ice, or the death scene in *The Lingering End*, in the British Library, where Leo dies under an avalanche of cascading bookshelves. The person who lived here must have decided to salvage the books when they were first thrown out, before they were burnt to make room for online screens in the libraries, before they were swept away in the floods. There are books everywhere, hundreds of them, all sizes and colours, filling the shelves and overflowing into piles on the floor, not in any obvious order, too many to read, not enough space. Their presence creates an unexpected tranquillity, as if they are breathing collectively, whispering a message of calm contemplation that's a century away from the present hysteria of the Stair Game.

It's extraordinary to see so many books in one place. Popi has told me how, pre-Hoffman's, when everything went onscreen and everyone else threw books out, his family kept theirs. He still regrets that he didn't take any with him when he married Moth – he assumed that the books would remain there, ready to be picked up and handled whenever he went back for them. But they were destroyed in the drone strikes. His parents, who were presumably at least partially responsible for our immunity, didn't succumb to Hoffman's. They were murdered in their beds by looters instead.

I study the spines of the books, overwhelmed by the variety, and pick out one or two: *A Photographic History of London*; *A Small Book of Large Drones*; *Tom, Bertha and the Android*. I leaf through the pages, fascinated, but eventually I realise I can't stay there for ever. If someone notices that I'm not running, Moth will panic. They'll be sending out a search party any minute now.

It would be nice to come back here later, with Hector, when there's more time. We could use it as it's meant to be used: as a real library, a place of peace and silence.

I grab a handful of books to take with me and return to the hall, glancing through the half-open door into the kitchen on my way out.

I stop.

There's a small picture of a black and white cat drawn on the door, no more than ten centimetres tall, its eyes round and surprised as if it's not expecting to see me here.

Identical to the cat outside the art gallery.

I place the books carefully on the hall table, so my hands are free, and push the door slowly, carefully.

It opens easily and I walk in, nervous, afraid of what I will find.

It's a light, airy room, the same size as my own kitchen, brightened by the snow falling outside the huge window. My walls are cluttered with pictures: Popi's sculpture sketches that I've rescued from the wastepaper bin; Lucia's portraits of us all, flat against a white background with a strip of blue at the top for the sky and a strip of brown at the bottom for mud. This kitchen is pristine, unadorned. There are no plants on the windowsill, no tendrils creeping over the edges and up the sides of the walls.

On the table – a worktop (laminated over black and white pictures from ancient films) built out into the centre of the room with tall stools tucked under the overlap – there's a mug that must have been sitting there for years, and a notebook with a telephone number scrawled on the top page, followed by a message: *Gone to Wales. Ring me.* A lost family member, a friend, a contact. I don't suppose anyone ever rang or even found the message. There probably wouldn't have been anyone to answer the phone if they had.

In the dryness of the air, there's a barely noticeable hint of something – sweat, stale food, washing powder? The smell of a recent presence.

Is this all a joke? Delphine, perhaps, on a search for clothes? Has she already been here, sat in the kitchen with a pile of books, then followed me to the city centre on her bike, slipped beneath Five Ways when I wasn't looking and left her mark outside the art gallery? Could it be Popi, telling me that he knows what I'm up to, that he's discovered my secret? Or Boris, enjoying the idea of a conspiracy? But Popi has his sculpture. He wouldn't waste time sketching cats. Delphine can't draw. Boris can't keep secrets.

Is there someone else in the building? Someone who's been here very recently, who's also been to the art gallery? Someone we don't know.

How could they possibly predict I would come here and see the cat? Are there lots of cats, all over the building, waiting to be discovered? Drawn by someone who's observed me in the city centre and wants me to know I've been seen?

Is there someone in the flat now, hiding, waiting for one of us to discover the cat? I turn in a panic, imagining an unknown person creeping up behind me. But the kitchen and the hallway are empty.

If he, or she, isn't here, where are they? Nearby? Silent, invisible, close?

We're all running up and down the stairs while there's a stranger loose among us.

I back out into the hall and wrench open the front door. The air on the landing shimmers with emptiness.

I pull open the fire door to the stairs and bump straight into Delphine and Lucia.

'Roza!' Lucia hurls herself at me and nearly knocks me over.

'Where have you been? We've been looking everywhere for you,' says Delphine.

'What's the matter?'

'Downstairs!' says Delphine, urgently. 'On the bicycle floor.'

'What?'

'There's a cat, no, no, a picture of a cat. None of us knows who did it. It wasn't Boris, it wasn't me or Lucia. Was it you?'

I shake my head slowly. 'Where's Popi?' I ask.

'I don't know. He might have gone back to the flat for something to eat.' Delphine hesitates, her long floaty hair trembling with her agitation. 'Is there someone else in the building?' she asks quietly.

I look over Lucia's head, where she can't see me, and nod. 'It's possible. Go and fetch Moth and Popi,' I say urgently.

'Where are you going?'

'I want to see the picture of the cat.' I know what it will look like, but I have to be sure.

'On your own?'

'Isn't Boris there?'

'Yes, he sent me to find you.'

'OK, I'll meet him there. But we need Moth and Popi to see it too.'

'Shall I take Lucia?' says Delphine.

'No,' says Lucia. 'I'm going with Roza.'

Delphine raises her eyebrows in a silent question. 'It should be OK,' I say. 'As long as Boris is still there.' Lucia and I set off down the stairs, while Delphine heads back up to the family flat.

Moth's voice echoes down through the stairwell. 'Lucia! Where are you?'

'It's all right!' I call up. 'She's with me.'

Lucia waves her stickers in front of my face – a dancing polar bear with a top hat and a bow-tie. 'I'm going to leave one here,' she says. 'So I can beat Boris.'

6

We step on to the bicycle floor, letting the door close behind us. There's no sign of Boris.

A guy steps out from behind a pillar.

Lucia gives a little shriek, and I instinctively push her behind me for safety.

He must be about thirty. His thick black hair, bouncy with an elastic energy, is pulled back into a loose ponytail, with stray strands creeping out and curling around the side of his face. His skin, a vibrant hazelnut brown, is gleaming richly, as if it's just been polished. His eyes, under unruly eyebrows, glitter with eager pleasure as he studies us, as if he's been looking forward to this moment. He leans nonchalantly against a pillar with his arms folded and one leg crossed over the other, a carefully orchestrated pose. There's a bicycle next to him, propped up against a stand, as if he's just arrived.

But, of course, he's been here for some time. *The man in the moon came down too soon, And asked the way to Norwich—*

'Hi,' he says, uncrossing his legs. The intensity fades from his eyes and he's suddenly boyish. Friendly, good-natured. *He went by the south and burnt his mouth, By eating cold plum porridge.*

He's not particularly tall, but his shoulders strain the fabric of his leather jacket at the seams, too wide for confinement, too strong to conceal. His khaki combat trousers cling to his legs, revealing highly developed calf muscles, and his feet, in solid-soled work shoes, are planted on the floor with absolute certainty, the toes pointing slightly outwards. Everything about him is confident and in control.

Trying to ignore the warning beacon that is beating urgently inside my head, I clear my throat and force myself to think. 'Who are you?' I say, relieved that my voice comes out coherently. 'Where have you come from?' Immediately I worry that I sound too hostile and try to rephrase it. He might react aggressively if he thinks he's being challenged. 'I mean – what do you want?' I give up. There doesn't seem to be a polite way of dealing with the situation.

But he doesn't take offence. He holds out his hand. 'Aashay Kent,' he says, with a curious accent that I've heard before, but can't place. 'You must be Roza and . . .' he hesitates for a second '. . . Lucia.'

A fresh wave of panic breaks through me. He hasn't just arrived.

'How do you know our names?' demands Lucia, coming out from behind me.

He turns his attention to her. 'I've been watching you,' he says.

She stares at him, her eyes wide and very blue. 'But what are you doing here?'

'Why shouldn't I be here?'

Lucia thinks about this before answering. 'Because this is *our* home.'

Well done, Lucia, I think. That's exactly what I wanted to say.

Aashay pretends to be amazed. It's overdone. 'Now, let's see,' he says. 'Thirty-two floors, minus the wheels floor and the hens and goat on the roof.' He's been up to the top then. 'Four flats per floor. That makes a hundred and twenty-four empty flats. And six of you. Room for one more person, don't you think?' He turns for a few seconds and contemplates the rows of abandoned bicycles. 'Approximately two hundred bikes here, I'd say. Thirty-five each?'

'Hmm,' says Lucia, becoming interested. 'I suppose we don't really need that many, do we? But we have to have spares for when they break. Popi mends them,' she says proudly. 'And we're sort of in charge of them all.'

'Shake hands with me, Lucia,' he says, his voice light with amusement. 'That's the polite thing to do.'

Lucia looks briefly at me, then reaches out and takes his hand. They pump up and down solemnly for a few seconds until she lets go. A smile transforms her face. 'I've never done that before,' she says.

'It's how you get chums,' he says. 'Come on, Roza, your turn. I'm offering friendship.'

I can't decide if we should be accepting contact with a stranger.

Shaking hands is an out-of-date practice, from a time when people felt safe touching strangers, getting close to each other, but we've never done it. We only know a handful of people outside our family – elderly men and women Popi encountered in the early days when he went out on his bicycle, searching for other survivors. He didn't find many. Most of the few families with children, and the small number of younger people who still had hope, departed for Brighton soon afterwards, encouraged by the government.

Moth and Popi chose to stay. They've never been inclined to follow instructions.

'I refuse to be at the beck and call of any government,' says Moth.

'We're perfectly capable of managing on our own,' says Popi.

There might be other families around with children, like us, but we've never found them, however hard we've tried. The ones who stayed lost their children to Hoffman's, and want to remain close to their memories. They like to think of themselves as our uncles and aunties, and when we visit them, they grab us and kiss us. They can't be bothered with the formality of hand-shaking.

'It's all right, Roza,' says Lucia. 'He seems OK.'

It feels rude to go on rejecting him, so I force myself to put out my hand. He immediately wraps his round it, as warm and all-embracing as a sheepskin glove. I almost gasp as a surge of energy flows from him to me. There's heat in his touch, but also latent strength, a tautness that suggests absolute competence and safety. I don't want to let go. Does he have the same desire to keep hold? I look up, and his eyes are fixed on mine, black, deep, compelling. The electricity that charges through us both is sparking in his eyes, dangerous but exhilarating.

'You have to move your hands up and down,' says Lucia from a distance. 'Like I did.'

'Pleased to meet you, Roza,' he says.

I manage to pull my hand away. It's like turning off a switch, cutting the electricity. 'I don't understand,' I say. 'Who – where–?'

'My name is Aashay Kent,' he says, rolling his eyes. 'Remember?'

'That's not what I meant. Your name doesn't tell us anything. Who are you?'

He puts his head back and roars with laughter. The sound echoes through the floor, bounces off the ceiling and jumps around between the bicycles. It's a rich laugh, infectious, as if he somehow understands everything, and Lucia starts to laugh with him, surprised and delighted. I don't join in, puzzled by his reaction. How does laughter answer my question?

When he stops, Lucia stops, too, and the three of us stand and regard each other in silence.

'So what exactly is funny?' I ask.

The fire door behind us bangs open. Moth's shout tumbles through. 'Lucia!' It's followed by Moth in person, her voice still resonating in the stairwell. Delphine is just behind her.

I experience a jolt of guilt, as if I've somehow been breaking the rules, behaving inappropriately. I grab Lucia's arm, worried that I'll be accused of not protecting her properly.

'Ouch!' she yells. 'You're hurting me.'

'Oh!' says Delphine, immediately alert to Aashay's presence. Her cheeks are flushed and damp with sweat. Her long, straight hair, normally immaculate, is damp and ruffled. She goes very still and stares with disbelief.

Moth sees him. Her chest rises and falls with the effort of running, and either the shock of seeing him or the effort of breathing prevents her speaking. Popi and Boris emerge behind her, but she's blocking their view.

'Let go!' whimpers Lucia. She pulls my hand, trying to release her arm. Should I pick her up to keep her safe? But she's heavy. I'm not sure how long I could hold her.

'What happened to you?' I ask Boris. 'You were supposed to be here.'

'I went for reinforcements, Popi, the cavalry.' He sees Aashay and swivels instantly into a position of defence, his hands up in front of him, his legs flexed and ready for action. 'Who are you?'

'What are you doing here – in our home? Where have you come from?' asks Moth, finally able to speak. Her eyes are fixed on Aashay. 'Who are you?' She grabs Lucia violently and pulls her away from my protection, attempting to envelop her in her arms.

'Moth!' gasps Lucia, wriggling furiously. 'I can't breathe.' Moth loosens her grip a little.

'I was under the impression we were looking for a cat,' says Popi, with a slight tremor in his voice. He places himself between Aashay and the rest of us. 'You don't look like a cat.'

'What's going on, Roza?' asks Moth, her face pale. 'Do you know something about this?'

'No,' I say. Why should this be my fault?

'Aashay,' says Lucia. 'That's his name. I've shaken hands with him.'

'You shook hands with a stranger?' says Popi.

'It's all right,' says Lucia. 'Roza did too.'

They all turn to face me. I stare back at them, not sure how to explain. I can feel a flush creeping across my face. 'He just appeared,' I say. 'With a bike.'

Boris lowers his hands, but remains tight and alert. 'You're trespassing,' he says, his voice deeper, more gravelly than usual. To me, he's always appeared solid, capable of looking after us, but next to Aashay he seems to shrink, no longer substantial enough to be our only line of defence.

Aashay doesn't flinch. He stands very still, but somehow poised and prepared, balancing easily on his feet, his hands hanging loosely at his sides. 'Not strictly speaking,' he says. 'There are only six of you, but a hundred and twenty-four flats.' The words are the same as when he spoke to me and Lucia, but they sound different, more challenging. 'There's no law to say I can't use one, if I want to.'

'We don't need laws,' says Boris. 'If we live here, it's ours.'

'So if I move in, it's mine too.'

Boris takes a step forward. 'Sorry, mate, it's not.' He should sound threatening, but he doesn't. Not enough practice.

'Stop it,' I say, embarrassed for him. 'Since when have you been in charge?' He wants to be an action hero, that's what it is. He really believes he can be Superman.

Popi comes up behind him and lays a hand on his shoulder. 'Easy,' he says. 'There's no need for violence at this stage.'

Boris doesn't show any sign of relaxing. 'He can't just walk in here and act as if he owns the place. It's not right.' He's leaning forward, his muscles tense, almost as if he's straining against a leash. He's still wearing the hat for the Stair Game, a jaunty green trilby with a purple feather sticking out on the right.

'For goodness' sake,' says Delphine, irritably. 'Can't we be civilised and welcome strangers? It's not as if we're overrun with visitors, is it?'

'We don't need visitors,' growls Boris. 'We're all right as we are.'

'No, we're not,' I say. 'You've always wanted to meet more people. Stop being so hostile.'

Boris actually snarls. I snort with incredulous laughter and Delphine giggles, going on for too long, apparently unable to stop herself.

Popi rubs Boris's back soothingly. 'Come on, son,' he says. 'Let's at least find out why he's here and where he comes from.'

I stare at Aashay. 'You've been inside some of the flats, haven't you?' I say.

Aashay smiles slightly, without giving the impression that he's relaxed. 'Ah, you've been exploring.'

'We don't call it exploring,' says Boris. 'We live here. We've always lived here. You haven't.'

'Come on, Boris,' says Aashay. 'Let's talk a little first, before deciding whether to fight or not.'

There's a moment of silence, then a snap of tension, as if someone has flicked a stretch of elastic. Popi and Moth seem to come to attention at the same time, as if they've worked out a puzzle. Delphine's face loses the laughter and closes.

Popi steps aside from Boris and fixes Aashay with a steely look. 'I hope you have a proper explanation for yourself, young man,' he says.

'What?' Aashay asks.

'You know my name,' says Boris. 'How?'

Aashay gives a short laugh. 'Oh, come on, Boris,' he says. 'You've all been shouting up and down the stairs all day. I'd be a dodo if I couldn't snap up your names. I reckon you're in the lead, by the way. You're a round ahead of your pop.'

The elastic relaxes a little. He's so casual, like an old friend, comfortable with us, understanding the way we work. He's dropped his bravado and decided to come clean. As if he's one of us, an ordinary chap, a man who just wants to pass the time of day with us.

For a brief second, I see how clever he is, how easily he makes us like him.

'Can he come for tea?' says Lucia, who hasn't understood the tension.

Moth watches Popi out of the corner of her eyes, while still facing Aashay. 'Maybe,' she says, her voice still tense. 'Does he like tea?'

7

Popi stands at the edge of the kitchen, tucking one of his long legs under the other as neatly as possible so that no one can fall over him, his hand resting on the worktop, as close to the knife block as he can reasonably manage without giving the impression that he's thinking about it. He's watching Aashay, presumably prepared to leap into action if necessary, but pretending he's not. Or maybe he's thinks he can prevent Aashay grabbing one of the knives if he turns out to be dangerous. I'm not sure Popi's up to the kind of heroics he has in mind – but we've got Boris to back him if things don't go according to plan.

Lucia and Delphine are sitting at the table on either side of Aashay. They're both leaning forward, examining him with open curiosity. Lucia's hair is tousled and fluffy, a shining, startled frame to her face and questioning blue eyes. Delphine's hair has settled back to the straight, pale perfection she usually cultivates and her face is oddly glowing, her mouth shiny with lipstick. She's been back to her room to smarten up. She's trying to impress Aashay. How interesting.

I help Moth take the biscuits and cakes out of the cupboards, nearly dropping one of the cake containers, clumsy with embarrassment, fearful that Aashay is watching me. I've never had the opportunity to learn how to move easily in the presence of young men, learn the art of nonchalance.

'Aren't you bored with all the same stuff?' asks Moth every year, hopefully. Our diet rarely changes, not even for the Stair Game. But Delphine and Lucia still see it as an exciting treat, and Popi and Boris will eat anything she puts on the table.

'What I'd like,' she says occasionally, 'is a big fat juicy steak.'

I've never had one, so I wouldn't know, but Hector says they have them in Brighton. There are small farms just outside the city, where they keep sheep and cows, the offspring of survivors from the mass culling when it was thought that domestic animals were carriers of Hoffman's. So a future treat for us, perhaps. Other than the produce grown on the Woodgate Valley, our supplies come from the drone drops, twice a year, at Junction 3 on the M5. Essentials, plus a few luxuries – I think that was the original premise. Flour, tins of meat and beans, tea and coffee, which run out after three months, soap, the occasional bag of sugar (if they're feeling generous) and toilet rolls. It's charity. It makes the Americans feel better.

Boris hovers in the opposite corner to Popi, arms folded, watchful and suspicious, close to the saucepans – his preferred choice of weapon, presumably.

'Come on, Nikolai,' says Moth to Popi. 'Don't just stand there. Make the tea.' She's twitchy, excited by the presence of a visitor.

Still keeping his eye on the knives, Popi reaches up and takes the teapot out of the cupboard. Moth snatches it from him, too impatient to wait, and drops in three teabags. This is wasteful. She could get away with two if she leaves it standing longer. She holds the teapot under the hot-water decanter, touches the pad and watches the pot fill.

Is Aashay a scavenger, one of the people we've always imagined exist, even if we've never seen them, who roam up and down the country, taking whatever they find, including other people's drops? The uncles and aunties have warned us about them, but no amount of watching has ever revealed them. Boris, longing for contact with someone new, used to make up stories about them, portraying them as adventurers, benevolent warriors in the spirit of Robin Hood. An army of Merrie Men, spelt that way in my mind because all our stories are myths and a link with the romance of the past.

'I'm going to be a scavenger,' he used to say, when he was little.

'You already are,' I said. 'That's why you go out on your bike, like the rest of us, and bring home interesting things.'

Should we be squandering our resources on a stranger? Especially one as strong and fit as Aashay?

But he's real, a manifestation of our myths. We've never encountered anyone so young before, not in the flesh. There were only ever those ghost children at Five Ways, and we've never been able to find them again. Aashay is here, in our kitchen, talking to us. A messenger from the outside world with things to tell, experience of other people, a whole new knowledge.

'Polly, put the kettle on,' sings Delphine softly. 'Polly, put the kettle on.' She's feeling it, too, this sense that we're standing on the edge of our old familiar world and glimpsing adventure.

Moth takes over, her voice low and tentative: 'Sukey, take it off again, Sukey, take it off again, Sukey, take it off again . . .' She and Popi are having a silent conversation, communicating, with looks, glances, messages that are invisible to the rest of us. She's more nervous about Aashay's presence than thrilled.

'They've all gone away,' Lucia shouts, childish and strident.

'But nobody's gone away,' says Delphine. 'Certainly not Aashay.' She lowers her eyelids and glances at him out of the corner of her eye. She's flirting! How did she work that out? She's cleverer than I thought. And Aashay is responding. He's half grinning at her, sliding his eyes away almost immediately, giving the impression that there's a conspiracy between them.

'I'll bet you've never had tea,' says Boris to Aashay, from his position in the corner of the kitchen.

Aashay stares at him for a few seconds. 'Mocking, Boris?' he asks softly. 'Just because I haven't had your privileged upbringing . . .'

'It's nothing to do with privilege,' I say. 'Tea's a national drink.'

'No,' says Popi. 'Lots of people gave it up after the Asian blight. Too expensive.'

'So why do they put it in the drops, then,' I say, 'if it's so scarce?'

'The situation is improving,' says Moth. 'Disease-resistant varieties. You should know this. Geography lessons.'

'You'll like it,' says Delphine to Aashay. 'Everyone else does.'

'Not me,' says Lucia. 'Yitch.'

'Well,' says Moth, 'you're in for a treat. It's grown in India – the part of the world where your ancestors must have come from, Aashay.'

He's suddenly alert, not exactly vibrating but thrumming with a hidden agitation, his fingers tapping on the table. He's become dangerous again, an unstable combination of chemicals that might explode any minute. 'My ancestors? What do you mean? Do you know more about me than you're letting on?'

'Oh,' says Moth. 'I didn't really . . . Of course, you wouldn't know about all that . . . although your parents must have . . . No, I suppose that was before . . . But perhaps you don't remember . . .' Her awkwardness, her desire to avoid confrontation, makes her vulnerable. Aashay's presence has somehow caused her to mislay her composure, her ability to explain clearly and succinctly.

'She means your origins are Asian,' says Popi. 'In the same way that mine are Polish and Moth's are English. She's not suggesting that she knows your parents.'

'Actually,' says Delphine, 'it's Earl Grey.'

'Oh, OK. Chinese, then. Sorry to confuse you, Aashay.' Moth pours the tea into mugs and passes them round before sitting at the table.

Aashay seems to relax, but there's still a tension below the surface.

Popi refills the pot. Boris remains silent and watchful.

Aashay contemplates the mug in front of him, sniffs, then takes a small sip from the side. He screws up his face. 'Are you trying to poison me?' he asks. 'Why would I want to drink perfume?'

'No,' says Delphine. 'It's just tea.'

He slams it down roughly and it tips over. Moth and I leap up and Popi throws us a cloth each to stop the wave of liquid spreading across the table and on to the floor. Delphine and Lucia remain sitting, trying not to stare, politely studying the laminated picture on the table (an image of a giant shark suspended inside a glass case, which Popi admires but the rest of us think is rather silly), pretending nothing has happened. Popi finds a glass and fills it with cold water. 'Maybe you'd prefer this,' he says calmly, handing it to Aashay.

'Sorry,' I say, squeezing out the cloth in the sink, expecting him to apologise in return. 'It didn't occur to us you might not like it.'

Boris is grinning for the first time since Aashay has arrived.

Aashay downs the entire glass of water in one go, then stares round at us with a challenging glint in his black eyes. 'Sheep's urine,' he says.

Lucia giggles loudly, then places a hand guiltily over her mouth.

'That's going a bit far,' I say, offended.

'You're a connoisseur of sheep's urine, then?' says Boris.

Aashay ignores him. 'What have you got to eat?' he asks.

'Oh,' says Moth. 'I forgot. There's plenty.' She hands round plates and takes the tops off the plastic containers. 'Tuck in.'

We dive at the food, even though most of us have been eating on and off all day. Aashay doesn't hesitate. He grabs the nearest cake, stuffs it into his mouth and starts to chew, his face softening and relaxing.

Popi leans over Moth's shoulder and helps himself to a blueberry cake, brushing his arm against her neck, offering reassurance. She's watching Aashay, enjoying his enjoyment. 'So where do you come from, Aashay?' he asks, his voice deliberately unthreatening.

Aashay doesn't hear him. He's operating a production line, a cake in each hand, ready to replenish his mouth as soon as there's room and lifting the next cake out of a container as soon as he has a free hand. He chews fast, glancing around all the time as if he's afraid it'll be snatched away from him before he's finished. But, no, that's not right. He's not a starving man, not someone who's struggled to find food. It's more that he believes everything belongs to him, that he expects to be given whatever is available. But he won't accept anything from anyone unless he wants it. Everything's on his terms.

'Looks like I've won the Stair Game, then,' says Boris, after a few cakes. 'Since we seem to have given up early.' He shaves every morning; he's strong enough to close the shutters on the top floor during the storms; we have interesting, analytical conversations about films and people and the future, leaning against each other on the sagging leather sofa in my leisure room, watching the weather. How can a game be so important to him?

'You weren't winning,' says Popi. 'I was in the lead.'

'Fantasy farm,' says Boris. 'Dream on.'

'It's only a game,' says Moth. 'It doesn't matter.'

'It's unproven,' says Popi. He's an artist, not a muscle man, but even though he talks about the life of the mind being more important than practical ability, I know he only half believes it. He's proud of Boris, who is becoming steadily stronger than him, developing more physical endurance, growing into his exact opposite. Popi would never acknowledge Boris's superiority in the Stair Game, because he refuses to indulge in any kind of sentimentality. We live in an uncertain world. Letting any of us believe that we're the best, that we can succeed without effort, would be bad for us.

'What's that supposed to mean?' says Boris. 'How can it be unproven when everyone knows I've done one more round than you?'

'Everyone doesn't know that,' says Moth. 'We'll check the stickers later.'

'You just don't want me to win.'

'Oh, stand down, Boris,' I say.

'So what else am I supposed to get excited about? There's not much going on.'

'I'll give you a ski race,' says Aashay, unexpectedly. 'Once it's stopped snowing.'

'You can ski?' asks Boris, cautiously. None of us is skilled at skiing. We've accumulated all the necessary equipment from other flats, reminders that people used to fly to Norway, Switzerland, Finland every winter, but we rarely get the chance to use it. The consistency of the snow is unpredictable and it quickly turns into flood water.

'Can I ski?' Aashay's tone is contemptuous. 'Can you eat apples? Ski, skate, cycle, run. You name it, I'm there.'

Boris studies him thoughtfully. Someone to pit his strength against. Even with the odds clearly against him, he can't resist the challenge. 'Yeah,' he says. 'Why not?'

How likely is this? I find myself rocking with uncertainty, half excited, half afraid. 'I'll race you,' I say.

Aashay turns and studies me with narrowed eyes, as if he's assessing me. 'You reckon you're up to it?'

Who does he think he is? 'Of course.'

'Then it'll be every man for himself.'

'Or woman,' I say.

'Can I race too?' asks Lucia.

'No,' says Moth. 'You're too little.'

'I'm seven.'

'Seven is too young for ski races.'

'I'll slaughter the lot of you,' says Boris, with satisfaction, gazing directly at Aashay.

It won't happen. This present snow will melt before we can sort out the skis, and Aashay will be gone long before the winter months, leaving us with a hint, a smell, of new worlds, but no actual taste.

A shaft of sunshine reaches the kitchen window and stretches out towards the kitchen table. It's stopped snowing and the clouds are thinning. The artificial light should have gone off by now, but it hasn't. I glance up at the sensor in the ceiling and wonder why it's not reacting.

Aashay looks up. 'I can fix that for you,' he says to Popi.

Popi smiles, but his eyes remain still. 'It's no problem. I can do it.'

'Fine,' says Aashay. 'Just let me know if you need help. I can fix anything.'

'Me, too,' says Popi. He won't be undermined by a younger man, a stranger. 'And Boris.'

We can now see right across the Woodgate Valley to the horizon. Great banks of snowclouds are still stacked in layers high into the atmosphere, as if they're planning a new offensive, but they're no longer moving in our direction, and patches of blue are appearing between them and Quinton. It's a long way to the horizon and, as far as I know, nobody lives between there and here.

'So where do you come from, Aashay?' asks Popi again. 'Where are your people?'

For a brief moment, Aashay locks eyes with him. Then Popi turns away and a shiver of unease runs down my back, like a gulp of cold water. He should have held Aashay's gaze. He shouldn't have backed down.

'I don't have any people,' says Aashay. 'Never did.'

'But someone looked after you when you were younger,' says Moth.

He shrugs. 'Noze. Dragged myself up. Didn't need anyone.'

'But you must have a home somewhere,' says Delphine.

He grins. 'I come from everywhere. You name it, I've been there.'

Delphine frowns slightly. 'What do you mean? You're a traveller?'

Could he be a messenger of some sort, sent by Brighton to check us out? An explorer, a mapper of boundaries, working for the government? Is he the forerunner of a new initiative, the herald of an expansion northwards? Will he be followed by families, industries, civilisation?

Or is he a dangerous man, a fugitive, who feeds off vulnerable, unprotected bystanders?

Either way, he's not telling us.

A long time ago, before my memories, large numbers of people passed this way, fleeing for the Welsh mountains where they imagined the air was clean. They were escaping from the city centre while the barriers were going up. They defied government decrees and sneaked past. They were probably infected, a danger to anyone who came into contact with them – except Popi and Moth – but they didn't stop. They carried right on past us and never came back. The last of the inhabitants of the flats

66

died and the world sank into emptiness. Now that someone else has finally arrived, we should be celebrating.

'We mustn't detain Aashay much longer,' says Popi. 'I'm sure he has plenty of other places to go and things to do.'

He's ignoring the fact that there's a lot of snow outside. Nobody will be leaving for a while.

Aashay pauses before putting a biscuit in his mouth. 'No,' he says. 'I'm fine.' He rolls the crumbs round in his mouth. 'This beats otter stew any day.'

Delphine gasps. 'You kill otters?'

'Of course not. All animals die from natural causes. I just find them on the riverbank. They drown in the floods, same as anyone else, or they get stuck in the mud and starve to death. No point in wasting good meat.'

'But otters—'

'It's meat. You can't be sentimental if you want to survive.'

Boris looks interested. 'Do you skin them?'

'Of course. I'll show you one day, if you like.'

'Yes, OK.'

Aashay's chipping away at Boris. He's looked him squarely in the eye and challenged him, made him suspicious, then refused to back down. But now he's unexpectedly softened the ground between them, relaxed and held out a peace-offering. I can't work out how much is instinctive and how much is calculated. How clever is he?

'Presumably you're married,' says Popi. 'In view of your age. What's happened to your wife? And children? Do you have any?'

'No,' says Aashay, after a pause. 'I'm an exception.'

'So how did you get out of that?' asks Popi.

Aashay grins. 'I don't give away all my secrets,' he says.

Lucia slips out from the table. She wants some attention. 'Can I show Aashay the book, Moth?' she says.

Moth looks startled. 'Well, I don't know . . .' she says. She's unsure about him too, half convinced, half sceptical.

'He might like it,' says Lucia. She leaves the room without waiting for permission.

She's searching for something familiar, a resumption of normality. She must be as aware as I am of the change in temperature that has come with the snow, the fresh, sharp wind that has blown Aashay towards us, and she wants to hang on to it, create a diversion, keep everything the same as long as she can.

Nothing works properly any more. We're running out of spare parts. Moth seems perpetually irritable, dissatisfied with so many aspects of our life. Popi's sculpture has become the culmination of everything he's ever created, and it's devouring more and more of his time, so while it grows and heads up towards the sky, he shrinks, sinks downwards. When it's finished there'll be nothing left of him, nothing left for him to do. Boris and Delphine are restless, dissatisfied. Brighton is beckoning. And in a few months' time I'll be married – exciting, terrifying. Lucia doesn't know any of this, but somehow, without understanding, she knows it all.

She returns with the book and places it on the table in front of Aashay. 'Look,' she says, pointing to a picture of a man with a large head and a big grin as he drifts down to the earth in the basket of a balloon. He's close to the ground, about to land on the night-darkened, snow-covered street of a village. The scene is lit by an enormous crescent of silvery moon. 'That's you. The man in the moon.'

How can she and I not be related? It's as if we really have inherited identical blood, genes, our way of thinking. She's picked out exactly the same nursery rhyme that came into my head when we first met Aashay.

He stares at the picture.

Lucia beams at us, delighted with her discovery. 'I'm right, aren't I? You came down too soon. Are you going to Norwich?' She looks at Moth. 'What is cold plum porridge?'

There's definitely something about the man in the picture that reminds me of Aashay. His black hair; the way he gazes out confidently, as if he knows exactly what he's doing; the set of his shoulders as he braces himself for the landing; his certainty that he'll be welcomed, despite the lack of explanation about his sudden arrival. And there's the curious coincidence of the snow in the picture. But none of us acknowledges this because we're nervous, conscious that our familiarity with the nursery rhymes is childish. We're all too polite to agree with Lucia.

Aashay examines the picture, his face puzzled. 'No,' he says. 'That's not me. Never been in a balloon.'

'*The man in the moon came down too soon, And asked the way to Norwich,*' says Lucia. 'Come on, join in.'

'I don't know the words,' he says.

Lucia's voice fades and stops. Something's wrong. I look at Popi, who's watching Aashay, like everyone else. He's seen what I've seen.

'Oh, come on,' says Boris. 'Everyone knows nursery rhymes.'

'Actually,' says Moth, slowly, her voice low and careful, 'that may not be true . . .'

'It's all right,' says Lucia. 'You don't need to know the words. You can read them.'

Aashay shuts the book with a thump.

There's a dangerous pause.

'He can't read!' shouts Boris.

Aashay sweeps the book on to the floor and stands up, sending his chair clattering to the floor behind him.

'My book!' cries Moth, in distress.

'I'll get it,' says Lucia, jumping down from her chair.

'He's an illiterate yonk!' yells Boris.

Aashay leans across the table and grabs him by his shirt collar. 'Do you want to repeat that?' he says, in a dark, menacing voice.

Boris really should know when to stop, especially with someone he doesn't know. 'You're an illiterate yonk,' he says obligingly. Why's he behaving so badly? Is it because he's never encountered another man, because he's surrounded by girls and should have done this kind of thing years ago, when he was a child, and got it out of his system?

Aashay stands up and grabs Boris round the neck, heaving him over the top of the table towards him. 'Shut up!' he says, through tight lips.

Plates skid off the table and fall to the floor, breaking with a series of loud crashes. The plastic containers follow, spilling their contents among the broken china.

We all jump up and move away from the table, astonished but fascinated.

'Nikolai!' screams Moth. 'Do something!'

Boris is rocking from side to side, trying to release himself from Aashay's iron grip, but laughing. He's enjoying himself. 'Aashay can't read!' he shouts. His voice is hoarse and faint, but still audible.

Moth tries to pull Lucia away. 'Roza, Delphine,' she shouts. 'Get Lucia out of here!'

Neither of us moves. Popi steps forward with some trepidation. He puts his hands on Aashay's arms in an attempt to break his grip, but even though he's clearly pulling with his full strength, he can't make a difference. After a few seconds, he loses his balance and falls uncomfortably to the floor, where he sits for a while, shaking his head from side to side.

'Boris! Aashay!' shouts Moth, her voice less shrill than before, as if she's trying to inject some authority into it. 'Stop it, the pair of you! You're behaving like toddlers!'

Which is exactly what they are. They probably see themselves as potential leaders of a pack fighting for supremacy.

Moth is doing something at the sink. I can hear the roar of water, but I'm trying to help Popi to his feet. He stands for a few seconds, trying to clear his head. I begin to suspect that he's preparing himself to tackle them again, summoning the energy.

'No, Popi!' I say loudly. 'You can't do anything.'

'Roza!' shouts Moth. 'Help me!' I go over to the sink and together we lift up a huge bowl of water. We stagger over to the table, carrying it between us, and throw it at Boris and Aashay.

There's a moment of inactivity and the sound of water whooshing across the floor. Aashay lets go of Boris and slips back into his chair. Boris pulls himself off the table and back into a chair on the opposite side.

There's a silence. They're both breathing heavily.

'I liked that china,' says Moth. 'Who's going to replace it?'

Another noise starts, softly at first, then expanding to fill the room. A keening, like the sound of pain. It increases, separates from the background noise and becomes clearer.

It's Lucia. She's holding the book of nursery rhymes in her arms, rocking backwards and forwards, clutching the fragment of a page that's been ripped away.

8

'I'm in go mode,' says Hector, leaning forward, grinning and winking at me. He's wearing a brown suit and a tie with an orange zigzag pattern on a navy background. Retro – 1980s maybe. 'All set. Well, I will be when panniers are packed, bike's serviced, maps loaded into POD, yummies and scrummies tucked safely into survival bag. On my way first thing tomorrow.'

The snow kept us indoors for a week, but it's melted away over the last fortnight and the air has warmed up again. It was a freak blizzard that never intended to stay, not a warning of an early autumn, after all. We're predicted sunshine and higher temperatures for the next few days but not a return to oppressive heat.

I'm still concerned. 'The meteos don't always get it right. What if there's another freak storm?'

'That's always a risk. We'll just have to trust them, won't we?'

'I've heard the computers are full of fluff and getting worse all the time. What if they've miscalculated?'

'Roza,' he says, 'if you want to worry about something, worry about Aashay. He's still there, I suppose?' I can hear the tension in his voice. He's extremely sensitive about the presence of Aashay.

'Not your problem,' I say. 'Concentrate on your journey. I'm expecting to see you here on Friday, on your bicycle, on time.'

'It'll be good,' he says, willing to be reassured. 'Weather forecasts are reliable. Gravity continues to function. Nobody's going to fall off the planet. If I'd set off three weeks ago, it would have been a disaster, but I didn't. The storm's rolled on, brought down a few more wind turbines and toppled the odd remaining steel spider while I slept soundly in my bed and missed the whole caboodle.'

I sometimes wish he didn't talk in riddles all the time. 'What's a steel spider?'

'Pylon.'

Obviously, his tone implies. Not so obvious to me. 'It's nearly September. If you'd come last month, when you originally said, there wouldn't have been anything to worry about.' It's not the first time we've argued about this, but we still haven't had any physical contact and I need something more substantial to hold on to. I want him here, in front of me, warm, living, breathing. Clever words are not enough. His presence in my dreams is too fragile, too fleeting.

He's as frustrated as I am. 'I know, Roza, I know. Write a letter of complaint to TU and threaten to withdraw labour if they do it again. But think sunshine. I'm on my way. I'm still your hand-some slade, your very own dragon-slaying Hollywood throw-back, your killer fiancé.' He leans forward, but his face is too close to the cam so his eyes bulge, his nose swells and the rest of his head shrinks out of focus. 'It will all be worth it,' he says. 'Start polishing your glass slipper.'

He still makes me laugh, even when I'm annoyed with him. I first encountered him at TU – a blast of fun in an earnest world. So why am I suddenly irritated? 'Don't get so close,' I say. 'It makes you outlandish.'

He retreats immediately, slightly hurt by the change in my tone, but sufficiently poised to make a rapid recovery. 'Look,' he says, 'it's going to work out. Everything will be solid. It's only a hundred and seventy miles max. I'll be there in no time, you'll see, and then the sun will shine all day.'

I feel guilty. 'You still think four days?'

'Depends a bit on wind and gradients. Not sure about all of that, never been your way before. Of course, on the map I'm going up, but that doesn't mean it's hills all the way. The motor-ways should be reasonably level – let's hope I won't have to make any diversions. My panniers are definitely on the heavy side, and the survival bag on my back will create some drag, so I'll be slower than if I'm travelling skin-light, but it shouldn't be too much of a problem. I reckon three days prox, four at the outside. There are oodles of waystations, so I'll be fine, even if the weather takes a turn for the worse. I'll be with you in the crunch of a biscuit. You'll see.'

There's a romance about waystations. We've all studied the ads on Freight. Beds in cubbyholes, piled on top of each other like honeycomb; sealed parcels containing toothbrush, razor and soap; packets of dried meals that can be prepared in two minutes on one of the rows of mini cookers in the eating room. But we've never travelled far enough from Birmingham to investigate them in reality.

'Don't believe everything you see on the net,' said Popi, when I asked if we could go and try one out. 'I've heard they're not as good as they sound.'

'Why not?'

'Well, for a start, who replenishes the supplies?'

'They have an army of travelling maintainers. That's what it says.'

'Think about it, Roza. Does anyone outside Brighton have any sort of army? Or a workforce, or even a handful of employees? Where would they get the people? Do they stand on street corners and enlist suitable candidates from the hordes wandering past, searching for work?'

'Well, they wouldn't need to replenish supplies very often. They probably last for years.'

'Now that seems more likely. But eventually even those supplies will come to end – or rot – and you know as well as I do that cleaning machines don't go on working for ever. The waystations are unlikely to be sparkling with polish and tempting menus.'

OK, so the ads have probably been there since pre-Hoffman's. What if there's nothing left for Hector? I try not to let him see my concern. 'And TU are still OK with you having the time off?'

He looks uncomfortable. 'Ah, well, they know I'll need travelling time, of course, but they're expecting me to get back to work as soon as possible. I wouldn't be amazed if they monitor my progress, check I'm not wasting time. You can't fool these

Chinese. They pretend their satellites have stopped working, but in my experience they have ways of finding things out. It's no hassle. We can slave away together, at your pad, and I'll admire your delicately turned ankles while I roll my numbers.'

This is a surprise to me. I was under the impression that TU were willing to allow us a holiday for at least a couple of weeks. I've been picturing us on the sofa together, watching the familiar films and discussing them together, exploring each other's minds; playing chess; ski races (it's unlikely, but it's a nice image), wrapped in bright woollies, snatching victory from Aashay. No – Aashay will be long gone.

'I didn't know TU could change their mind,' I say.

'Market forces,' he says. 'They claim to be as flexible as a steel spider in a tornado, able to absorb the onslaught, let it go right through and out the other side. According to their recruitment guff, they're ready for all eventualities. But, in my experience, they lose their flexibility when it really matters. Appeals to their good nature have the same effect as the wind – in, out – while they just stand there rigidly without reacting.'

'Well, let's hope TU stick around a bit longer than the pylons.' I half smile at him. 'You're going to find us boring here. It's not like Brighton.'

'You think this worries me? My pulse is already speeding up at the thought of those ankles.'

When I first told Hector about Aashay, it took him a while to grasp the situation. 'A guy in Wyoming? What do you mean? Who is he? How can he just appear out of thin air? Don't you have locks?'

'Of course we do—'

'But? You don't use them?'

'No, we do.' I paused, aware of how strange it sounded. 'We found him during the Stair Game – he's been living here in one of the flats, and we didn't know.'

Hector's voice started to rise with panic. 'You mean this guy got into the building without your knowledge? How could you allow that to happen? You can't let complete strangers into your home – it's not safe.'

I'm irritated by the implication that we're all too naïve to work this out for ourselves. 'We're not stupid, Hector. We didn't exactly welcome him with open arms.'

But we invited him for tea.

'So has he gone now?'

I hesitated. 'Well . . . no, not really.'

'"Not really?" What's that's supposed to mean? You can't just—' I'd never seen him look so agitated. His face had lost all its colour and he was struggling to form words.

'Look,' I said, 'he can't leave. It's snowing. But it's OK, honestly. You can meet him if he's still around when you get here.'

'That's ages away. You can't trust him, you know that, don't you? He mustn't be left alone with anyone. Anyone at all – do you understand?'

He's overreacting. 'We're capable of looking after ourselves,' I said stiffly.

Everything is in Brighton. It's Shangri-La; Mount Olympus (the government has to consume the ambrosia in the absence of kings and queens whose bloodline was annihilated by Hoffman's); the dreaming spires (the domes and minarets of Brighton Pavilion rise up through the flood waters like a half-submerged Atlantis – I've read on Freight that you can take boat trips through the ground floor in the summer); and the streets are paved with gold (although they've probably got the same potholes as elsewhere). It's where the remnants of the old government went – *There was an old woman tossed up in a basket, Seventeen times as high as the moon* – and set up a new administration. *Where she was going I couldn't but ask her, For in her hand, she carried a broom.* Starting again, sweeping clean.

I'd have ended up in Brighton eventually anyway, Hector or no Hector, to comply with the marriage law. 'They call themselves blue sky thinkers,' said Popi, when we were first told about this, raising his eyebrows, struggling to disguise his annoyance. '*Old woman, old woman, old woman,'* quoth I, *'Where are you going to up so high?'* *'To brush the cobwebs off the sky.'* Once, politicians were higher than the moon. Then Hoffman's just brushed them away.

The directive on marriage reached us when I was sixteen, Boris was fourteen and Delphine was ten. The message was tagged on to the end of the response to our latest requests for the drop.

'They've sneaked it in,' said Moth, incandescent with rage, 'hoping we wouldn't notice its significance. The bare-faced, hare-brained, two-whiskered nerve. Have they forgotten the conversation we had with them all those years ago?'

'What conversation?' I asked.

I watched her exchange glances with Popi, who shrugged lightly. 'Tell them if you want to,' he said. 'They're old enough.'

'Tell us what?' demanded Boris.

Moth hesitated. 'Well' – she said – 'after Hoffman's, once it all settled down and they'd set up their directorate in Brighton, they went to a great deal of effort to persuade us to move there. At first, they dropped leaflets, littered the entire countryside – absolute eyesore, took months to rot – demanding to know how many of us were still alive, asking all survivors to get in touch. They wanted us to make our way to Brighton. So they could protect us, they said, keep the children safe. They sent representatives in helicopters, applied pressure, told us we had no choice.'

'A red rag, as far as your mother was concerned,' said Popi.

'What do you mean?' asked Boris. 'Why would it matter to them where we were?'

Popi sighed. 'Isn't it obvious?' he said. 'Children are like heirlooms, incredibly precious. You represent the future. They don't want to let you run loose, in case anything happens to you.'

'Like what?'

He shrugged. 'That's what I said. We're your parents, we're capable of looking after you – probably more capable than they are. We like it here. This is our home.'

'So how did you persuade them to let you stay?' I asked.

'We simply refused to go,' said Moth. 'I told them they'd have to handcuff us, lead us in chains, nail us down when we got there. They weren't pleased, but even they could see there wasn't much point in taking us against our will. These things don't work without co-operation.'

Popi smiled. 'You know as well as I do, it's not worth arguing with your mother. They're not evil people. They believe in laws, same as before, free choice, that kind of thing – except for the restrictions on the internet, of course, which isn't really their fault. There are enough different opinions among Committee members to prevent a dictatorship, and they're reasonable most of the time. We just prefer to live here, make our own decisions.'

These people have always been anonymous to me, but after this conversation, Boris and I thought we should investigate further. We found the Committee – four men, four women – all old. Just aunties and uncles. Anyone can contact them if they want to, but none of us has ever found a reason to do so. They're there, we're here.

'They keep an eye,' said Popi. 'We don't like it, but you can't really prevent these things. Satellites, drones, directives on Highspeed, which we sometimes listen to – if we think they're sensible – and ignore if we don't. We do our best.'

'You don't have to co-operate with this marriage law,' said Moth. 'Nobody can force you.'

'It doesn't seem entirely unreasonable,' I said.

None of us wants to remain single for the rest of our lives and there's no coercion involved. They'll put our details into a database, appoint a matchmaker, arrange introductions. We're allowed to refuse as many times as we like, providing we accept someone in the end. Love is encouraged.

Boris, Delphine and I have been itching to go to Brighton for years. Now I've met Hector, I'll be heading there anyway, and Boris and Delphine have every intention of staying after the wedding. They're desperate to meet real people, eye to eye, to brush the cobwebs off the sky. 'It's where the machines are turning,' says Boris. 'Why wouldn't we want to chase the action?'

'Nobody has the right to tell you what to do,' says Moth.

'They need you more than you need them,' says Popi.

They're incapable of understanding that we don't mind. For them, freedom – the right to refuse – is the guiding principle in their lives, but their unwillingness to co-operate seems unnecessary and outdated. We've moved on. We don't have the same sensitivities as they do. I've studied the re-emergence of totalitarian governments that happened when they were younger, and I can appreciate their fears, but our history starts with Hoffman's, and we see things differently.

It's hard to live here, in the centre of nowhere. We're not exactly fighting off potential partners. The nearest aunties and uncles are a two-hour cycle trip away and they're old, like our parents. When we go to visit them in the short spring months, everyone just sits around and talks, going backwards, backwards, further and further into a past that has slipped out of their grasp and already taken on a mythical quality. I usually like to hear Moth and Popi talking about the way things used to be, but prolonging these conversations just seems indulgent.

'They're pedalling in the wrong direction,' says Boris.

'They need to think about the now,' says Delphine. 'Why can't they just get on with things and forget the world they grew up in? It's never going to come back.'

As soon as we return home after the visits, these people, these pretend uncles and aunties, invite us back.

'We could go on a holiday together,' they message on Highspeed. 'We need to make plans.'

'I have a new recipe for Scotch broth.'

'I've found some glorious curtain material you simply must see.'

None of this is true. They just want to be around children, have the chance of stroking smooth, unblemished skin, experience second-hand energy as they realise their own strength is starting to seep away. They want treats – snatched hugs, stolen kisses – but we're no longer willing. We've grown up, left our childhood world behind. We should be losing our attraction, but we're all they've got.

They're expecting invitations to my wedding, hungry for the pleasure of being part of something that reminds them of their youth, but they'll have to view it from the official online vid. They'd never make it all the way to Brighton. It's a daunting journey, even for us.

'I'm just finishing off a translation for TU,' I say to Hector. 'I'll have to go.'

'No probs,' he says. His eyes, green and amiable, crinkle into a smile. I would like to put my hand out and touch his cheek, lean into his chest, lay my face against the cool whiteness of his shirt. 'Eye to eye in three days' time,' he says.

'Or four, depending on hills. Bye for now, then.'

'Cherry-oh,' he says.

We blow kisses and he disconnects.

I walk over to the window and look out over the landscape. I can see a long way to the west. As a family, we usually go south to the uncles and aunties, on roads round the edges of Birmingham. The ring road, Moth calls it, although it's not a single road but a network of crumbling highways, mostly wide, always deserted. The roads I can see from my window stretch towards the horizon, an open invitation to new worlds, new people, new experiences. I've cycled them on my own, as fast as possible and as far as possible, always imagining I can escape before turning round and heading home in time for supper. I have the local area mapped in my head, but I've only ever gone about twenty miles.

I watch the clouds clearing, threads of red and gold, dashed across the pale blue of the darkening sky, the signature of a world that intends to continue, with or without human inhabitants. *Red sky in the morning, shepherd's warning, Red sky at night, shepherd's delight.*

Is it true? Can you read the weather accurately by observing the natural rhythms of the world? Do the rhythms exist any more, or have they become random, adrift from their old predict-ability? I would like to believe in them. One day, perhaps, we'll all have to live without machines. Nobody will have the expertise to repair or redesign them when they break down. It's all very well standing on the shoulders of giants, but what happens when the giants are long gone, and nobody can remember where they placed their feet? There must be experts somewhere in the world, but they're not much use to us if they're elsewhere. Here we are, in need of technical assistance, and nobody from abroad will ever come.

I've recently joined Free Thinkers, an online organisation I discovered by chance, on Freight, disguised as an ad for online courses in Chinese culture. I've kept it secret. Boris would mock, and my parents would worry. Free Thinkers believe we need a new approach. Forget the technology, stop trying to repair failing systems. If they can do it in Europe, abandon much of the Netherlands, let the land disappear under water, back to where it came from, no longer wasting resources on impossible solutions, why can't we be_equally resourceful? Water temperature in Iceland is still rising, after fifty years of warming. People are moving north, growing wheat and barley in places that were once impossible. We need to develop our ability to work with the weather here too, find land that's too high to flood, learn skills that don't depend on failing technology.

I work for another hour, snug in my office, before deciding to call it a day. I enjoy my work, but I'm not interested in overtime. Hector works for longer – a sense of duty, I suppose – but he'll have other considerations once we're married. I'm not sure he's grasped this yet. There's no danger of losing our jobs. TU need us as much as we need them. Population numbers are falling dramatically around the world – the very mild form of Hoffman's that affects fertility was much more widespread than everyone initially realised – and there won't be enough young people to replace the ageing experts. Unlike the rest of the world, which still uses currency, we're paid with knowledge – education, ongoing training – medical supplies and expertise. The Americans send everyday essentials in the drops, but China takes responsibility for our health. Medicines by drone. Emergency doctors in helicopters.

We've rarely had to test it out, but it will matter one day, when Moth and Popi grow old. Meanwhile, I like working. I enjoy my association with the research team at TU, the glimpse of camaraderie behind the technical language (even if most of them are a little too solemn by our standards). I can identify each scientist from the style of their messages, even before I read the sign-off.

Lianda (female): very dry, fact-based, even refusing to offer good wishes when she departs, but mellowing very slightly after communicating with me for a year. Last week she appeared briefly onscreen to check something and almost smiled. She refuses to do a holo interaction.

Fang (female, although I thought I was communicating with a man until we met as holos): warmer, with an occasional comment that doesn't make sense until it occurs to me she's attempting a joke. A heavy kind of irony that isn't funny.

Weishan (male): friendly, treating me as an equal. I worry that he thinks I know more than I do, that I can understand the implications of his work.

Fenji (male): a little flirtatious, as if he's known me for ever, wanting to speak in person rather more frequently than is necessary. I resist his requests for holo contact.

The one thing I've never managed to establish is how old my correspondents are. It must be a Chinese convention that age is not discussed, and even when we talk directly onscreen, there seems to be an unspoken conspiracy, in which everyone colludes, to disguise their age. It's impossible to know if they're twenty, forty or sixty. The women wear make-up, the men have thick black hair. There are no grey hairs, no wrinkles, no hollowing cheeks, no sagging skin round the eyes. They all exude health and well-being.

'They have surgery, take drugs,' says Hector, when I ask him. 'Eternal youth.'

'But they can't go on looking like that indefinitely.'

'Oh yes they can. I don't know how they look in real life, but they can go on enhancing their computer images for ever, if they want to.'

'How do you know if they're ill or near retirement or about to die?'

'You don't. Unless it's family or a close friend, you only find out when someone else tells you. Otherwise it probably doesn't matter very much.'

I find this oppressive. I would like to identify the young ones, the people of my own age who could possibly be friends. But even though some of my conversations with them seem to reflect a cheerful youth and optimism, I have a sense of uncertainty, a fear that I might be confiding in someone who's old enough to be my mother or father – even a grandfather – who's retained the skill of chatting like a young person. It's not right. There's a shortage of young people all round the world. We belong to an exclusive club. We should be able to identify each other immediately.

It's six thirty when I finish, two thirty in Beijing. I don't have to be available personally for the whole of TU's working day. They send a message on Highspeed when I'm not there, knowing I'll deal with it in the morning, unfailingly courteous, even when they're in a hurry. There's never a sense of real emergency, although they politely expect efficiency and dedication.

Moth has invited me and Boris for supper – she prefers us to do our own cooking, but she's occasionally generous – so I turn off the computers, and prepare to go down. When I enter the stairwell, I can hear voices from several floors below.

'No, hang on a minute, pull that one.' That's Popi.

It sounds good-natured. There's laughter. A series of thumps, silence, a yelp from Boris.

What's going on? I run down the stairs lightly and find Popi, Boris and Aashay on the stairs between the 2nd and 3rd, wrestling with a very large piece of driftwood. I recognise a tree-trunk that Popi salvaged from last year's flood. It had drifted to the bottom of the ramp and we all helped to roll it out of the water and up to the 1st where it could dry out.

Aashay, who seems to be insinuating himself more and more into our everyday life, is standing between the other two, issuing instructions. The wood is tied to a trolley and they're manoeuvring it slowly up the stairs with a complex system of ropes and brute strength. For some reason I can't work out, Boris and Popi are co-operating, letting Aashay take charge.

'Grab the rope on the right, Boris,' says Aashay. 'OK, are we all ready? One, two, three, heave-ho. No, stop. Nikolai, you'll need to get under it, I think. Give your muscles something to write home about. Now try again.' He takes the left rope above the trolley. 'One, two, three, heave-ho again. And again. *Heeeave.* Another encore – let's go, let's do it, people! And . . . rest.'

The trolley has moved up six steps and they set it down carefully so that it hovers alarmingly, swaying slightly, but held in place by the ropes in their hands.

'Where are you taking it?' I ask.

They look up, but keep hold of their ropes.

'Roza!' says Popi. 'Where did you come from?'

'Upstairs,' I say. 'Obviously.'

'It's Popi's piece of wood,' says Boris. 'You know, the one that's been drying out all year. He's going to use it for the sculpture.'

'It's for the head,' says Popi. 'I can take advantage of the winter months to get on with it.'

'Nice piece of hardwood,' says Aashay. 'Just the ticket.'

What does he know about art, wood-carving, aesthetics?

'Come on,' says Boris. 'Just a few more steps and we'll be there.'

'Good thing your workshop isn't on the 31st,' I say.

'Can't think why you didn't just stop on the 2nd,' says Boris.

'No space,' says Popi. 'Cluttered leisure rooms, too many computers.'

'It'll be easier taking it down,' says Boris. 'We can roll it.'

'I don't think so,' says Popi. 'I'm hardly going to spend all winter carving just so you lot can play ball games with it.'

'Let's get on,' says Aashay. 'Move over, Roza. Brace yourself, lads.'

Lads? Is he serious?

Popi's at the bottom, more wiry than strong, clever, artistic, apparently helping, but probably not making much difference, unable to summon the kind of brute strength required for this kind of operation. How had he intended to do it before Aashay showed up? Boris is on one side at the top, pulling the handle of the trolley, steadying it with ropes, strong and capable, his muscles taut as he prepares to take the weight, eager to demonstrate his strength, ready to push himself to the limit. And Aashay's on the other side, barely straining, as if he does this kind of thing all the time. His legs provide solid, rocklike support; his arms, thickly robust, hoist and carry. I can see the muscles of his back as they expand and contract beneath his T-shirt. There's something startling and unfamiliar about his strength, the way he does everything so easily, so smoothly, almost gracefully.

I step back when they reach the landing where I'm standing. Popi lets go too soon, but Aashay takes the extra weight, balancing it and keeping it steady until he's ready to set it down gently, as controlled as if it's an empty box. He could have done it single-handedly, but he's co-operated with Popi and Boris, given them the privilege of working with him, shown them the way, dignified them with the opportunity of helping.

Popi stands back and blows on his hands, clearly pleased.

Boris looks round at me, grinning. 'Are we the greatest or are we the greatest?'

'Not sure,' I say. 'Difficult to decide.'

'The correct answer is yes.'

I haven't seen him so cheerful in ages. For the last three weeks, in the presence of Aashay, he's been hovering on the edge and glowering. Now he's become childlike again. It reminds me of the first time he won a family race. We had a circuit of paths laid out on the Woodgate Valley, compressed over the years by our pounding feet, and we used to have picnics in spring and autumn, during those precious snatched periods when it wasn't too hot or too cold. To start with, Popi won most of the races, although Moth could give him a run for his money, sometimes beating him on a good day. She was a tidy runner, light and nippy, better in the long races than the short, sharp sprints, but she didn't always take part, so she didn't get enough training. My parents have never made concessions for us. If they can beat us, they do. They believe in challenging, making us competitive. It's probably to do with equipping us for survival, although they've never actually said so.

I started to win a few races as I grew older. Then Boris won for the first time, when he was about fourteen. He made a feast of it, of course, being Boris. He clasped his hands over his head and cheered loudly, as if he was surrounded by crowds of admiring onlookers. He insisted on running a victory lap.

There's no one left for him to test his strength against now. Before he was fully grown, Delphine and I could challenge him, hover at his elbows, sometimes overtake, but he's much too big and strong now for either of us to challenge. There's nobody left except Popi, and Boris knows he can beat him any time he wants. Everything has become too easy and he's fallen into a kind of bored stagnation, no longer interested in making an effort. But the arrival of Aashay has woken him up. Suddenly there's an edge to him, an eagerness that creates energy.

Aashay stands solidly, admiring the wood on the trolley, aware that he's the cause of Boris's satisfaction. He knows exactly what he's doing. He rocks easily on his feet, demonstrating that the activity hasn't really tested him, that he has endless reserves of strength, that he was nowhere near his limit. He grins at me good-naturedly, his face softening.

I catch my breath. Receiving his undivided attention is like being fed an empowering surge of electricity. I find myself smiling back foolishly, my cheeks starting to burn, a tight, fluttering sensation that destabilises my thoughts.

'Well done, everyone,' says Popi, as if he's been in charge. 'Good thing Aashay was here to help.'

'We'd have managed it on our own,' says Boris. He makes a loose fist, and for one moment it seems he's going to give Aashay a playful punch. He withdraws it just before he makes contact.

Aashay dances away from him, light and cheerful. 'Have you ever learnt to box?' he asks.

Boris shakes his head. 'You need two people for that,' he says.

'Haven't you tried it at the fair?'

There's a silence.

'What fair?' says Boris.

'What are you talking about?' I ask.

Aashay's eyes open wide with amazement.

'You've never been to a fair?'

Is he genuine, or is this a clever act?

9

'The fairs take place twice a year,' says Aashay, who's been invited to supper as a reward for his assistance. He's still living in the flat on the 17th, preparing his own meals, making himself comfortable, not showing any signs of wanting to move on. 'Two in autumn and two in spring. Four venues, ancient football stadiums – outside Norwich, Southampton, Coventry and Cardiff.'

'Coventry?' says Popi. 'That's only about forty miles away.'

'It's the best,' says Aashay. 'At the Ricoh stadium.'

'So you've been to all of them?' asks Moth.

Aashay nods quickly, still unwilling to give away too much about himself or his previous activities. But he's enjoying the attention. Of course he is. He has information that we don't, that we might never discover without his help. Or he might have. How do we know if he's making it up?

'I don't understand,' says Delphine. 'Who runs them? Who goes?'

'Everyone.'

But who's everyone?

'There are more people around than you think,' he says. 'You'd be surprised.'

'We've met them,' says Boris. 'And they're not very surprising at all, just old. Uncles and aunties.'

'There are others,' says Aashay. 'Young ones. You don't know as much as you think you do.'

But does *he* know as much as he thinks he does, or is he just trying to impress us?

'If that's true,' says Popi, 'why haven't we met them?'

'Because you don't go to the fairs,' says Aashay.

Could he be talking about those children we saw at Five Ways so long ago? Did they stay in Birmingham like us, or did they eventually find their way to Brighton like everyone else? Boris and I made many attempts to find them. We followed the path of the barriers, searched for landmarks we vaguely remembered, heading for Balsall Heath, Sparkbrook, Moseley, but most of the streets had become impassable and we never found any evidence that anyone lived there. Surely everyone must leave traces. Like us. They must imprint some whisper of their presence on our world as they move through it, some proof of their existence, which could be spotted by someone who's looking.

'Come with me to the next one,' says Aashay. 'In Coventry. You're just in time – it's on Thursday.'

'This Thursday?' asks Delphine, incredulously. 'The day after tomorrow?'

'Yup.'

We exchange glances, all of us suspicious. 'You've been here three weeks,' I say slowly, 'and you've only just decided to tell us?' He must have been planning this ever since he arrived. My stomach starts to quiver, divided between anger that he could be so casual about it and fear that he's only come for the fair, that he'll move on afterwards and we'll never see him again.

Aashay shrugs. 'Thought you knew. It's the same dates, same deal, every year. Everyone else knows them.'

'Why isn't there anything on the net?' asks Boris.

'Maybe they advertise on Freight and we didn't look because we didn't know it was there,' says Lucia, surprisingly. She's been playing Martian Olympics on the table with a beam from her POD and I thought she wasn't listening, but she's clearly been following the conversation.

'No,' says Aashay. 'No public ads. We keep it all sub.'

'So it's exclusive, then,' I say. 'Seems a bit unfair. Aashay Kent's Secret Society.'

He chuckles. 'No,' he says. 'Not mine. I'm just part of the organisation.'

'Oh,' I say. 'Now it's an organisation. Made up of who exactly? Are they all from Brighton?'

'I've told you,' he says. 'You don't know who's out there.'

'If you'd put it up on Freight,' says Boris, 'we'd at least have had a chance of finding out.'

Aashay's face darkens. 'Can't,' he says. 'It gets taken down faster than it goes up.'

Censorship. The tool of authoritarian governments. I'd have expected Moth and Popi to battle against it to their last breath, but they don't. We've had endless conversations with them about this. 'Who fixes the boundaries?' asked Boris one evening, several years ago. He'd been hitting buffers all day and he was angry and frustrated. 'Apart from Popi.'

All of us, at one time or another, have searched for hidden sites. We know they existed once – there are traces of the original tracks – but as soon as you make an attempt to sneak along them, the screen diverts. Popi's controls were easy enough to break. Boris managed it when he was about twelve. He worked out how to bend rules, sneak round corners, but even he reached the end of a line, a platform with no more stations ahead. There were deeper, more fundamental restrictions that none of us could penetrate.

'Well,' said Moth, 'there are complex laws now – they're worldwide, agreed long before Hoffman's. When I was a child, access was a human-rights issue, and I went on the marches with your grandmother, demonstrating to keep the lines open. But in the end there was no choice. The internet was so powerful it became like – like a dictator, an out-of-control monster, a megalomaniac, wreaking havoc at the touch of the button. Sometimes even before you touched the button. It was pouring out stuff – how to build bombs, how to kill other people, how to kill yourself. You couldn't separate truth from lies. It was a recruiting ground for terrorists, whipping up unstable children into suicide bombers, enabling psychopaths to buy guns, print out false passports and visas, giving them a free pass into whatever war took their fancy.'

Boris wasn't convinced. 'But most people aren't that stupid. They can separate good from bad.'

'That's why we tolerated it for decades,' said Popi, quietly. 'But when it escalated . . .' He lapsed briefly into silence.

'You don't want to know,' said Moth. 'Really.'

'I do,' said Delphine, surprisingly. At eight years old, she was already developing a strong sense of right. Especially if it concerned her personally.

'Well, I'm afraid we're not going to tell you,' said Popi.

'I was a trainee teacher,' said Moth. 'I had to organise the practices at school. Where to hide when the gunmen came, how to keep still and not make a sound, how to send for help.' She stopped for a moment. 'It was just to make everyone feel they were doing something. Nothing stops suicide bombers.'

'Britain was one of the first to sign up to the global agreement,' said Popi. 'It gave us back our lives.'

'But no one has the right to deprive us of information,' I said. 'We're capable of deciding for ourselves what we should see.'

'Why should anyone tell me where I can or cannot go?' asked Boris.

Moth smiled at us with weary pleasure, as if she'd just recognised a familiar friend. 'I've used those exact words in the past,' she said. 'Many times. But there comes a point – so many destructive people, so little control over our own lives . . . No one's stopping you communicating or finding out information, but everything on Freight has to pass through a filter – it doesn't take that long.'

'It takes for ever,' I said. 'That's why it's called Freight. It's slower than slow.'

'And it does stop us finding things out,' said Boris. 'I'm always being blocked.'

'Then you're trespassing,' said Popi. 'Going where you have no business.'

'It's better not knowing some things,' said Moth.

'I want to decide for myself.'

'You might think that now,' said Moth, 'but you wouldn't have then. You've been protected.'

'We're not babies,' I said. 'We don't need that much protection.'

'Unrestricted access simply doesn't work,' said Popi. 'The net had become unusable and most of us had given up on it. At least it's manageable now.'

'You had social networks,' I said. Moth had told us about surfing. 'We can't even get close to the beach. There's no chance of us catching the waves, let alone surfing.' Highspeed works better, but if you haven't met someone in person and exchanged addresses – and the only people we've ever met are uncles and aunties – you have to go through complicated, time-consuming security procedures to use it.

'It's a tricky balance,' said Popi. 'But, actually, I rather liked discovering time again. We used to have so many trivial conversations, so many exhausting choices.'

He would say that. Social networks wouldn't have suited him. He likes slow, thoughtful, one-to-one conversations with plenty of space to think, the opportunity to read the other person's expression.

'If everyone had been instantly in touch,' I said, 'Hoffman's might have been contained.'

'We can set off early on Thursday morning,' says Aashay, addressing Moth and Popi. 'Get to the fair in reasonable time. It's not far.'

He's probably quite keen on censorship, bearing in mind that he can't read. It puts him on an equal footing with everyone else.

'So can we go?' asks Boris, looking hopefully at Moth.

'No,' she says.

'You can't stop us,' says Delphine. 'If you even try, I'll never speak to you again.'

'Peace in our time, then,' says Popi, with a half-smile. 'Don't make promises you can't keep.'

'Come on, Moth,' says Boris. 'You can't deprive us of our chance to meet other people. You just can't.'

I watch Popi and Moth exchange uneasy glances. I think they're afraid, but they don't want to say so. 'We don't know how safe it is to travel out of our area,' says Moth.

We've been contained by familiarity, by physical limitations, by the younger children who can't cycle too far and a vague fear that the world beyond our immediate vicinity is dangerous and unpredictable. We've created natural boundaries, the M42, the M5 and the M6, the circle that contains Birmingham.

'You don't seem bothered about heading to Brighton for the wedding,' says Delphine. 'That's a lot further.'

'Of course we're bothered,' says Moth. 'But some things are worth the risk. Other aren't.'

'It's safer than you think,' I say. 'There's hardly anyone out there.' I wonder how far Boris and Delphine have travelled. I've gone inwards – towards the city centre. Maybe they've explored outwards, expanded their radius.

'How do you know?' asks Moth. She's more uncertain than I've ever seen her, her eyes dark and unfocused. Furrows of worry are burrowing into her forehead as if they've been waiting there, lurking under the skin, ready to reveal themselves at the right moment.

'You'd be surprised,' says Boris, mysteriously, looking at me. Does he know where I go?

'Whatever are you talking about, Boris?' asks Moth.

He's twenty years old, a man, not a child. They can't seriously expect him to abide by limits they set years ago. 'I've searched for people,' he says. 'And I've never found anyone. But we won't be staying here for ever anyway. We'll all end up in Brighton, sure as hens lay eggs, so if there's a chance of meeting other people now, we should be allowed the chance to get in some practice.'

He grins at me, exhilarated by it all. He knows we're on the same side.

'And the weather?' says Popi. 'What if it doesn't co-operate?' He's just searching for excuses.

'If we're stormed off, we don't go,' says Aashay. 'Obviously. Then everyone wheels up for the next one instead. That's why the dates are fixed.'

'I'm going anyway,' says Delphine. 'No discussion.'

'We have to go,' I say. 'We can look after ourselves.'

'Not Lucia,' says Moth.

'She'll be perfectly safe,' I say. 'We'll all be watching her.'

Popi looks at Moth, then Aashay, then all of us, one at a time. 'Let me think about it,' he says.

'Popi . . .' says Delphine.

'No,' he says. 'No hassles. I'm serious. I'll let you know my decision tomorrow.'

I join my parents to watch *The English Patient*. We prefer the older films – late twentieth century, early twenty-first – and find the small number of modern ones from Australia or India tedious. They're too concerned with style, cryptic and unfathomable, unconnected with everyday life. We want stories, a clear distinction between good and bad. There are only about a hundred films on Freight so they're all as familiar as nursery rhymes to us and represent comfort: *Star Wars*; the James Bond movies; *Doctor Zhivago*; *The Good, the Bad and the Ugly*; *The Great Turbine Disaster*. Most of our favourites are historical or science fiction, set in a different period from the time they were made.

'Why do you think,' says Moth, 'we know so few films that would teach you all about the life we lost? It wasn't a bad world. Not really, especially after the net controls were sorted. There were plenty of interesting things to do, loads of culture. Reliving the World Wars or whizzing around the universe in a spaceship wasn't exactly what we had our minds on.'

'Some of it's relevant, though,' says Popi. 'The Chinese want volunteers for their research centre on Mars.'

'Don't tell Boris,' I say. 'He'd be at the front of the queue.'

'They wouldn't have him. They still think we're contaminated.'

'It's high time someone challenged them over the quarantine,' says Moth.

'Go on, then,' says Popi. 'If someone's got to do it, it might as well be you.'

'Nobody's going to listen to me,' she says sadly.

'Hector's working on hydroponics right now,' I say. 'The Martian biodome.'

'They're hallucinating,' says Moth. 'One rogue virus and everyone's dead.'

'Not quite everyone,' says Popi. 'There are always survivors.'

I wonder if they're happy. Is this the only activity they have left to connect with each other? Nostalgia, old films depicting worlds they will never see again (or never actually saw in the first place), stories that have nothing to do with their present life. Is it enough? I'm expecting more from Hector. I want adventure. I'm not sure where it's going to come from, I don't even know if Hector is up to it, but we will not just be settling down for the next sixty years without a plan. If there are fairs, there must be other activities waiting to be discovered.

I'm starting to get excited.

I watch Popi settling back on the sofa. When I was younger, he had endless reserves of energy, the ability to tackle anything. Now he often has to spend all day sorting out electronic malfunctions, hunting out instruction manuals on Freight. He manages to keep everything connected, the electricity coming, the water flowing, but I don't think he enjoys it. He would be happier working on his sculpture, not having to worry about technical details. His lean, stringy body is losing its bounce. He's less bendy, less elastic than he used to be. I've recently noticed a hesitation before he moves, an awkwardness when he gets up from a seated or lying position, as if his knees are hurting. His eyes seem more prominent, the sockets looser and darker, and Moth has had to cut his hair less rigorously, so that the grey collecting at the roots won't be so exposed. He's slowly being transformed into a man who thinks rather than a man who acts. It may be a truer mirror of his nature, but it's not how he wishes to be seen. He's running out of power just as Boris is building up a great supply of surplus energy, flexing his muscles, preparing to come storming along on the outside, ready to overtake at the speed of light. They're still trying to outdo each other, but Popi can't always keep up any more.

Moth sighs a lot nowadays. Her brain is still sharp, but she seems tired for much of the time. Sometimes she disappears all day, without telling us where she's going. I suspect she's still searching for the old Lucia, hoping we can have two models one day, part one and part two. 'These youngsters,' she says every now and again, after conducting a tutoring session with her online pupils, 'they don't follow procedures. We'd never have got away with it in our day.'

'Our day brought Hoffman's,' says Popi.

'That was politics,' she says. 'Not enough funding. A willingness to cut corners.'

'So you reckon it could happen again?'

'Of course it could. Sloppiness breeds accidents.'

I understand her sighs. It would be hard not to experience disappointment as you watch your familiar world disintegrate and your whole life shrink into a flat in a high-rise block, surrounded by empty homes and empty buildings and empty land as far as you can see.

But we've survived. She had Boris in the year of Hoffman's, at a time when there was little hope of support, but there were no complications. The government was more involved when Delphine and Lucia were born. There was a midwife online, watching every stage of the proceedings, offering advice that infuriated Moth, and a doctor standing by with a helicopter, poised for action. But it wasn't necessary. Both babies were strong and healthy.

I asked Hector about the fairs when I talked to him earlier, just after supper. He looked at me blankly, raking a hand through his hair, messing up the parting and making himself into a small boy.

'Hasn't anyone in Brighton ever mentioned them?'

'They're probably illegal.'

'Why would they be?'

'Laws are a bit like that. Pointless unless you know the point. Look, I have to get on. Lots of last-minute preparations – mainly nosh, of course. I'm setting off at first light.'

'Not that early, then,' I say.

He raises an eyebrow. 'Cynic. Don't forget I'm not like you. I like mornings. I'm sorry, Roza, but there's so much to do.'

'OK,' I say. 'Make sure you get enough sleep.'

If the people who go to the fairs come from Brighton, why doesn't Hector know them? How does anyone penetrate their networks to find out about them? Could Aashay be right after all? Do they come from elsewhere, travelling between waystations, taking what they want and leaving, drifting in and out of the last remaining empty buildings, like shadows, their footsteps so shallow that we're not expert enough to see them?

In *The English Patient*, Hana is playing hopscotch in the grounds of the ruined villa – I like this bit, a reversion to childhood while the war rages on – when Popi sits up abruptly, as if he's been disturbed by a stab of indigestion. 'So, do we believe Aashay or not?' he says.

'Why would he make it up?' asks Moth, irritated that we're interrupting the film. 'What would be the point?'

'Not sure. But it's hard to know with him. When's Hector due?' he asks me.

'Friday,' I say. 'Could we get there and back in time?'

'It's quite possible,' he says. 'It's not that far.' He moves restlessly and glances around, as if he's afraid that Aashay's hiding somewhere in the room, eavesdropping. He lowers his voice. 'I just don't know if I entirely trust Aashay.'

'Stop being paranoid,' says Moth. 'He's integrating nicely. Even Boris is starting to enjoy having him around.'

Well, this is unexpected. Give her another few days and she'll be wanting to adopt him.

'We know nothing about him,' says Popi. 'He's a grown man, born pre-Hoffman's. He must have lived a normal life once. Why isn't he in Brighton now, married like everyone else of his age?' He pauses. 'You don't think he's after Roza or Delphine?'

Why does this idea make me so uncomfortable? Have I already thought it without putting it into words?

'Don't be absurd,' says Moth. 'Delphine's far too young and Roza has Hector.'

'I can't imagine either reason would deter him if he has his mind set on it.'

'Maybe you should ask him.'

'But you can't pin him down. Just when you think he's going to tell you about himself, he finds something else to do.'

'He needs our support,' says Moth.

'Does he?' says Popi. 'I don't think he needs anything from anyone.'

'He enjoys our company.'

'Is that really the only reason he's here?'

'Why not? He likes what we have and wants to be part of it.'

'Yes, yes. You're quite right.' Popi leans over and puts an arm round her shoulders. 'I'm thinking in the old way.' He grins. 'Still suspicious after all this time.'

She wriggles out of his embrace and moves herself along the sofa. This is why none of us is comfortable with physical contact: we've learnt it from our mother. She'll grab us in emergencies, but never just for comfort. What will Hector think of this? Will he find that we lack warmth? 'You didn't worry like this when Lucia came to live with us,' she says.

'That's ridiculous,' says Popi, giving up and withdrawing his arm. 'Lucia was just a baby. She'd have died without our help.'

'Aashay needs our help too,' she says. 'He's older, but he's vulnerable.'

'Bess, he's a powerful, healthy young man, perfectly capable of looking after himself. Whatever happened to him in the past, he's survived admirably. He does not strike me as deprived in any way.'

'I'm talking about emotional support, not physical. You can see how eager he is to be friends with all of us. Including you.'

'He could just be worming his way in, deliberately earning our trust so that he can take advantage later.'

'And what advantage will he take, exactly? What do we have of value that we can't replace? Our furniture? Is he going to load it all up on a cart and remove it one day? Personally, I'd help him carry it out. We have far too much junk. Or perhaps you think he'll ransack our winter supplies.'

Popi frowns. 'Well, maybe he's got friends, a gang waiting nearby, desperate for food.'

'Then he can bring them in and we'll feed them. Why would they be desperate? They can pick fruit and vegetables, same as us, while the weather stays safe. There's plenty there. We don't possess a single thing that we couldn't manage without.'

'Actually, that's not true. What about the spare parts?'

'We'd manage. We'll have to in the end, anyway.'

She's talking like a Free Thinker. Maybe I should show her the website.

'OK, then, the computers,' says Popi, determined to continue the argument. 'Losing them would be a disaster. We depend on them for Lucia's education – and Delphine's. How would you do your teaching?'

'Oh, for gum's sake, Nikolai. Aashay's not interested in computers. He can't read. He's a practical man. He can make anything or fix anything he wants.'

Popi crosses his arms and sighs. He's always been the one with the skills, the producer of magic, the one who makes things work again. Perhaps he's feeling usurped.

In the film, the Tiger Moth is taking off, its wings wobbling dangerously, the heat shimmering over the desert. It's hard to imagine a time when one person could climb into a plane and control it. Hard to believe there wasn't someone sitting in front of a read-out somewhere, telling it where to go, how high, how fast, how far.

'I just worry, that's all.' Popi's tone has changed. He sounds less petulant, more thoughtful. 'I can't help thinking there's another agenda, something we don't know about that he's not telling us. He seems particularly keen to get us to go to the fair.'

I do not like thee, Doctor Fell, The reason why – I cannot tell.

Moth softens. She puts out a hand and pats his arm reassuringly. 'I don't believe he means us any harm,' she says. 'What do you think, Roza? Can we trust him?'

'I don't know . . .' I say. 'How can you ever be sure?' Sometimes I like him, sometimes he makes me nervous. He's a human magnet, attracting everyone in his vicinity, gathering followers without apparently trying. Delphine, Lucia, even Boris – though he wouldn't admit it – would obey him without question. He can whip up enthusiasm, whirl it around, motivate everyone in a way that I've never encountered before. I don't want to be influenced by him, but he's not easy to resist. When he switches on the current, the world around us wakes up, shimmers, throbs with colour and promise. I feel more significant, more important, more able to contribute.

At other times, usually when he's not present, I wonder if he's just extremely clever, insinuating himself into our lives, making himself indispensable. But if that's the case, I don't know what he's after. Is he just intending to drink up our goodness, suck us dry and then move on?

Outside, darkness has settled and a powerful wind is scattering drops of rain against the windows – but, according to the meteos, this weather is only fleeting. If it's fine tomorrow, Hector will set off and be here in three or four days. And the fair will go ahead.

Perhaps Aashay's presence is nothing to do with us. Is he just killing time, making the most of our company while he waits for the fair to take place? In which case, when it's finished we might never see him again.

I want to go to the fair. But if it means that Aashay will leave us, I'm suddenly not so sure. A dullness creeps into the room, a cold draught that tugs at my ankles.

I shouldn't be thinking like this. I'm waiting for Hector.

'Maybe we should take a chance,' says Popi. 'Everything will change soon, anyway. You know that Boris and Delphine are planning to stay in Brighton after the wedding?'

'Of course they are,' says Moth. 'That doesn't mean we should let them.'

'They'll find Boris a wife,' I say, 'and then you won't have a say in the matter.'

'We won't be able to contain him,' says Popi, quietly. 'He has too much curiosity.' He sighs. 'Let's not predict the future. We can deal with the problems when they land at the airport, not worry about the ones that take off elsewhere and never arrive.'

'So that's the answer, then,' says Moth. 'Best to bury our heads. Delphine will have to come home with us from Brighton. She's only sixteen and needs to get a degree. Then she can decide if she wants to move.'

'Do you really think we can hold on to her once Roza and Boris have gone?'

'So now you're willing to abandon her to strangers?' says Moth. 'You don't think we should insist that she finishes her education?'

'She might find something else she wants to do,' I say.

Moth turns on me with anger. 'You and Boris have benefited from the learning, why shouldn't Delphine have the same advantages? She can make her choices when she's got the qualifications.'

The truth is, I want all of us to stay in Brighton, but Moth won't contemplate the possibility. She has an inbuilt resistance to authority, a fierce independence that hasn't faded with time. But she and Popi would be left alone with Lucia, surrounded by space and encroaching silence. She wouldn't find it easy. 'Delphine could still study in Brighton,' I say. 'And if you were there, you could keep an eye.'

'I like living here,' she says. 'It's where we've always been.'

It must be Lucia that ties her here. The old Lucia.

'So are we going to the fair or not?' I ask. They need to make a decision.

'The thing is' – Moth hesitates – 'we really can't let anyone know where we live. We've managed all this time on our own. I know Lucia . . .' She stops for a second, then starts again. 'But we've never asked for help . . . It's just that Lucia – we know nothing about her background. Suppose someone there . . .' She's afraid Lucia's relatives are nearby, waiting to reclaim her.

'We have to risk it,' I say. 'We've spent our entire lives

searching for people, and now we've finally got the chance, we can't possibly give it up.'

'If you'd mentioned you were looking,' says Popi, 'we could have compared notes, saved each other some time.'

'It's not as if we're invisible,' I say. 'Anyone cycling past in the dark would only have to glance up and see the lights. Anyway, Brighton knows we're here.'

'The authorities in Brighton are never going to be a real threat,' sayd Popi, 'whatever you think of their petty desire to make rules.'

'It's just Lucia I'm worried about,' says Moth. 'We'll be out in the open, exposing ourselves to random people, making a public announcement.'

'I think you're probably making it sound worse than it is,' says Popi.

I want a decision. 'Do you really have a choice? You could lock us in, I suppose, put us chains, but it's not exactly your style, is it? Or we go together. United we stand—'

There's a silence. They know I'm right.

'OK,' says Popi. 'We'll go – as long as everyone understands how careful they have to be.'

'I'm sure Aashay will look after us,' says Moth.

'Maybe,' says Popi. He won't commit himself wholeheartedly.

But this I know, and know full well, I do not like thee, Doctor Fell.

10

If I don't go inside the art gallery now, I might never have another chance. We're off to Coventry tomorrow, and Hector's due the day after or Saturday, so this is the only possible day. I don't know how easy it will be to get in, or even if there's anything worth finding but I'm determined to give it a try. If the art's still there, somebody needs to see it.

The skies are clear, with no indication of freak snowstorms when I arrive. Thomas Attwood is still sitting on the steps of Chamberlain Square, perpetually motionless. Life is more complicated for the rest of us. I'm contemplating the reality that parents and children eventually change places. Popi and Moth used to worry about me – they probably still do – but now I'm worrying about them. Did Thomas Attwood consider his parents when he jumped down from his plinth and went off to be a Member of Parliament? Was it the same then as it is now? Has anything changed at all?

Hector's planning to reach Thorpe Park today. We had a quick chat this morning just before he left. 'I'm intending to do sixty miles. I may be a desk-bound science fogey, but I can do it. Pull out the stops, push to the limit and all that sort of thing.'

'Stop being a martyr,' I said. 'You just need to be careful not to get too stiff.'

'Me? Stiff? I swim the Channel every day.'

'No, you don't. They'd arrest you if you went past the quarantine zone.'

'So I go half a mile, what's wrong with that? A mile there and back. You really must stop picking holes in my stories.'

'If you tell me they're only stories, I won't need to. It's when you tell them as facts that I have a problem. Don't forget to take notes on the waystation. A cam would be useful.'

'No jumble. The weather's going to be good.'

'Blue skies. Light breezes.'

'It was all arranged. I'm off now. See you soon. Cherry-oh.'

I push the double doors, not sure if they'll be locked. They're beautiful doors, big and heavy, divided into carved squares, with glass in the top half. There's a bit of resistance, so I stand back and kick. A sharp crack. Another well-aimed kick, and I'm in. I was expecting to step straight into the art gallery, but it's an entrance hall, coated with thick mud, which must have seeped through the doors, driven by the wind and the weight of water. There's a staircase on the right, with stone steps. No rotten wood, like in LeeL, the furniture store. The Victorians made buildings to last.

I wade through the mud, which is drying out after the snow, to the bottom of the stairs. I put my hand on the banister rail – hard and smooth – marble, perhaps. I've never encountered marble, so I can only guess. There's something disorienting about heading up the past rather than down. Am I the first person to come here in twenty years? There are landings on the way up, pauses in case you run out of breath. As I scrape the surface with my boots, I discover pictures set into the floor, mosaics, patterns of flowers, and I stop in admiration. I've drifted through these spaces online, seen the artwork as it was once displayed, the ancient pottery, the Saxon artefacts. I know the Romans liked to walk on mosaics, but it hasn't occurred to me that the Victorians also took an interest in floors, so I've never looked down. Yet it seems that when they designed buildings, they didn't just pay attention to the practical elements – the way they filled the skyline, the size of the rooms, the height of the ceilings – but they spent time on details, creating patterns where they might not even be noticed.

I turn the corner and continue up. The handrail changes, becomes metal, and I reach the first floor, which smells powerfully of damp and mould. The floor is also tiled, but coated with a layer of fine dust, hard to see through in the half-light. As I move across it, the dirt shifts easily and snowflake shapes emerge, brown and blue against a pale background, one on each tile. How wonderful that you can walk on art, have pictures beneath your feet, that you could create a floor like this for thousands of people to walk on and it could still be there nearly two hundred years later.

I walk through an archway in front of me and enter the round room. I've already seen pictures online, but it's even more impressive in reality, bright and open, illuminated by light coming in through the astonishing glass dome high above. Several panels are cracked and broken, but most of the plaster decorations at the base, circles, rectangles, crosses, have remained, more or less complete, although damp and stained, covered with grime. There's a cavity above the glass, so it's not possible to see the sky, but light is filtering through, hazy and tinged with green.

I stand for ages, just looking. Once upon a time, craftsmen put up scaffolding here, climbed up on to the wooden planks and created this wonder for the benefit of the people of Birmingham. Such ambition on the part of the Victorian architects, who wanted their city to be admired for centuries. How disappointed they would have been to know that it would be abandoned in less than two hundred years.

I asked Popi once why he'd decided to put his sculpture outside despite the problems with the weather.

'Art needs to be shared,' he said.

'But it takes so much time and effort,' I said. 'Is it worth it when it's just going to disintegrate in the end?'

'If life is hard, what would you prefer to see when you go out? Something that reinforces your misery or something that lifts your spirits? Isn't it always better to see something beautiful, something that makes you think?'

'So you're not going to put it on the roof, then.'

He smiled. 'I haven't decided.'

The tiles, with more dramatic, angular patterns, are looser here, unstable. In the centre of the circular floor, there's a statue, glistening in the dim light. It looks black, but when I touch it, dirt comes off on my fingers and there's gold underneath. It's a man with wings, an angel. Sculpted material is draped round the back of his legs, a skirt but not a skirt, that doesn't attempt to conceal. It's fluid and shimmering, almost too ethereal to be solid. His upper body is taut and muscled, very masculine, and yet his face could almost be a woman's. His hands are bent upwards in a curiously awkward position, with splayed fingers, the tips curled. I'm innocent, he is saying. It wasn't me. There's a plaque in front of it and I wipe it so I can read it. *Lucifer*, by Jacob Epstein.

Lucifer. Beautiful but evil.

There's a movement and I jump round in panic. I shouldn't be here. No one should be here. Have I been followed? Is there a security system that alerts someone somewhere? Is everything about to collapse now that I've stirred the atmosphere, created air currents?

But a bird flutters over my head. Looking up, I see nests high in the dome, in the cavity above the glass, and the floor is littered with droppings. The birds must have come through the broken panels. Perhaps hailstones penetrated the outer shell of the dome, or the intensity of the summer sun corrupted it. Maybe the branch of a tree was hurled by a tornado, or tons of snow, too heavy for nineteenth-century roofs, have caused its collapse. So the birds are not all afraid of the city centre. Some land and make their homes in the silence. They must appreciate empty places, where they can rear their young without disturbance.

I try to identify the bird, but it moves too fast and disappears before I can examine it properly. I'm disappointed. I have a book at home, a small home-produced volume I found in the flat of a man who lived alone, who was clearly more interested in knowledge than hygiene. *Birds of the British Isles*, leather-bound, soft and pleasing to hold, full of beautifully crafted pictures, all hand-painted. Many of the birds have disappeared, but I try to to memorise each one anyway, so that I'll know them if we ever meet.

The once red walls of the art gallery are dark with mould. Most pictures have broken away from their fixings, slipped down the walls and collapsed on to the floor, face down in heaps of broken wood and canvas. A few have landed the right way up, their original images still clear.

I go over to examine one. It's a painting of the past, of a time when England was barely industrialised. I've seen it onscreen. *February Fill Dyke.* The sky is stormy, the land puddled and wet, and two children are going home, past a low-lying house with a thatched roof, which is built into the landscape. Is this nostalgia? Is it intended to depict a happier, simpler life, when there were no machines, when everyone lived off the land? Or is it meant to imply deprivation, hardship, the misery of cold, wet winters?

The irony is that we have returned to that simpler world, where we're at the mercy of the weather again, where the elements win. Should we go back into the countryside, like these people, forget the complications of technology and build ourselves a real house at the top of a hill where it won't flood, huddle into the landscape, learn to work the soil? *Oh, the grand old Duke of York, he had ten thousand men; He marched them up to the top of the hill And he marched them down again . . .*

Backwards to a time before technology, forwards into comfort and progress, backwards into a different kind of comfort, a different kind of progress? Which would be the right direction?

Other rooms lead off this one, but they're inaccessible. I can see fallen ceilings, spaces stuffed with rubble, as if a bomb's gone off, fragments of china, sculptures, pictures. The curators must have hauled everything up here from the basements where they were stored, believing they were protecting their artefacts, trying to rescue them from the floods, save them before they themselves succumbed to Hoffman's. Perhaps they wanted to catalogue them, move them somewhere where they could watch over them: *And when they were up, they were up, And when they were down, they were down . . .* Too low down, the floods would penetrate; too high up, they might be plundered and stolen by knowledgeable thieves who could somehow get them through the barriers and away, abroad, where they could be sold. Perhaps that would have been the best option, saving the works of art by theft. But the curators were too late, and everything was trapped between staircases, abandoned when Hoffman's took its toll. *And when they were only halfway up, They were neither up nor down.* By the time the roofs fell in, the art was not high on people's list of priorities.

I would like to share this with Popi and Moth, and with Hector. I want to bring them all here, show them what remains, but I can't. How do I admit that I've broken the rules?

There's a sound behind me, louder than the fluttering of a bird. An oddly controlled sound, like the pressure of a foot on the tiles. There's the sensation of a presence. I freeze, unable to turn immediately, my breathing suspended.

Someone is watching me.

It must be a dog or a cat, or a wild animal that's managed to survive for so long that it will be fast and expert.

I turn round very slowly, preparing to defend myself against an attack.

Aashay is standing in front of me, his eyes round, his face open and friendly. The man in the moon. A cat.

As my fear subsides abruptly, I take deep breaths, fighting an unexpected weakness in my legs. 'What in the world are you doing here?' Relief turns to anger. 'Did you have to creep up on me like that?'

He holds his hands up in front of him, like Lucifer. Not my fault. Don't blame me. 'I didn't know there were rules,' he says.

I realise I'm not surprised to see him. 'What are you doing here?'

'I followed you.'

Of course. He goes whatever he wants. He can move without being seen. 'So you know about the underpass?'

'Everyone knows about the underpass.'

I stare at him, confused, unsure whether to believe him or not. 'What do you mean, everyone? Are you talking about my family?'

'Well – maybe not everyone exactly. Me, Delphine, Boris. Not sure about Boris, actually. He might have been here, but he's probably got more exciting things to do than follow you. It's possible your parents . . .' He waves his hands from side to side, rippling his fingers.

I don't know what to say, not sure which bit to address. That some members of my family know where I am and they've never said anything, that they, too, come here to explore; his implication that Boris is not interested in what I'm doing. 'So you're twitching your whiskers,' I say. 'Watching for prey.'

He frowns, not sure what I'm talking about.

'The cat – it's a self-portrait. You should have explained.'

He smiles. 'You know I've been here before, then.'

'Obviously.' The cats are his calling card, but this is the first time I've acknowledged his earlier presence in Chamberlain Square. I don't want to think that he's been watching me for ages.

Or that he found my family by following me home.

'He reminds me of you,' I say.

'Who?'

I gesture towards the statue. 'Lucifer.'

Aashay walks round him, clearing a pathway through the debris with his feet, peering forward to examine the way the wings appear to be tied with a strap across the angel's chest at the front but not the back. 'Well, I'll take it as a compliment,' he says. 'But he's too much like a girl.' He imitates the pose for a second, bending his hands upwards and curling his fingers. He's more sinister than Lucifer. His fingers are like talons. 'Nice wings, though.'

'It wasn't meant to be a compliment.' There's something cleverly confusing about Lucifer, as he presents the image he wants us to see without letting on what he's really like. 'He's beautiful, but at the same time you get this sense of mischief – no, something much stronger. Wickedness, that's what it is. Evil. He's not as he seems.'

'So you think I'm an imposter?'

'You might be. Prove that you're not.'

'I don't have to prove anything to anyone.' There's an edge to his voice, almost a teenage resentment, incongruous in a man of his age. In the greenish light that's filtering down from the glass dome, shadows gather round his cheekbones and his eye sockets, creating new hollows, lines I've not seen before.

I thought I'd begun to know him reasonably well in the last few days, but now he's a stranger again, a powerful man, definitely not a teenager, a potential threat. 'We don't know anything about you. You've had the opportunity to observe us on our home ground, work out how we all interact, but we don't get the chance to see you in the same way. You could still be a thief or a conman or a gangster, for all we know.'

He steps towards me, balancing comfortably on his legs, almost rocking, easy in the knowledge of his superior strength. His breathing is steady and even. It's as if he's sculpting a benign image, moderating his irritation by slowing down his pulse. He radiates effortless power, almost perfect self-control, confidence that he can manipulate me into exactly the position he wants. A position that he has calculated in advance.

I try to take a step backwards. I will not allow him to lead me anywhere I don't want to go.

But he leans forward and takes both of my hands, pulling me towards him. The same surge of electricity that I felt when we first shook hands flows from him to me. I resist, attempting to stand my ground, refusing to let him make decisions for me. But he won't allow it. I'm acutely aware of my physical weakness in comparison to him, my inability to prevent him doing whatever he wants. He's too strong. I can smell him, see the pinpricks of sweat on his forehead, above his lips, feel the heat of his body. I almost believe I can hear his heart beating. His cheeks are curiously smooth, as if he never has to shave, but there's a long, thin scar across one side of his face, almost black against the brown of his skin.

He grins, clearly enjoying himself. 'You can ask me whatever you want, Roza,' he says, in a normal voice, loud in its proximity to my ear. 'And I'll answer you if I can.'

He makes it sound as if I'm special, as if he'll talk only to me, not to anyone else.

I swallow hard, conscious that if he suddenly lets go I'll lose my balance. I don't want him to know about the internal vibration that's threatening to paralyse me. 'OK,' I say, forcing myself to be calm. 'Let's start with your background.' I'm pleased with my intonation. I sound composed, not intimidated. 'Did your family all die with Hoffman's? Where did you grow up? Why can't you read?'

He laughs, not the loud laugh that he produced when I first met him, but gently as if he's nice, kind, human. For a moment, he reminds me of Hector. But he's holding me too close.

'OK, in order. Yes. Oxford. Dyslexia. Next?'

It's all very well getting straight answers, but if they're not elaborated on, they don't tell me much. 'So why are you staying with us? Where do you normally live? What do you do?'

'Now you're taking advantage.'

'It's what I want to know. They're perfectly normal questions, and you said you would answer.' I test the strength of his grip, but there's no sign of any weakness. I worry that he's cutting off my circulation, that he can control the flow of my blood.

Why do I find the warmth of his touch exhilarating? Despite the discomfort, I feel as if some of his heat is draining into me, as if I can steal his strength, filter off his knowledge and experience and store it up for my own use.

'I have a question for you,' he says.

'Well, that's a sneaky way to avoid giving information.'

'Why are you marrying Hector?'

'Why shouldn't I?' My voice rises with indignation. I can hear my defensiveness and it infuriates me. He will read insecurity in it. I sound as if I'm making an excuse.

'Well,' he says. 'That's convincing.' He's quiet for a moment, as if he's considering his options. 'Is that it? You're marrying him because you might as well, because you can't be bothered to look elsewhere, because it's convenient?'

He has no right to question my motives. It's none of his business. How can he criticise Hector when he's never met him and knows nothing about him? 'No, that's not the reason at all.

He's good, kind, patient, clever, funny. How much more do you want?'

His grip finally loosens. 'Roza, Roza,' he says gently. 'Listen to yourself.'

What's he talking about? They're all good reasons for marrying someone. 'You probably haven't noticed,' I say coldly, 'but there's a shortage of good men. Finding Hector was like finding a bottle of champagne at the back of a kitchen cupboard in a flat where no one's set foot for twenty years.'

'Don't imagine that the world you see on Freight is the whole world, Roza,' he says. 'The best stuff is eye to eye.'

What's that supposed to mean? I flex my wrists tentatively, wondering if it's worth trying to make a break for it. Unexpectedly, he lets go, but grabs me again, pulling my shoulders towards him, crushing my body against his own. It's all a bit Old Romance. Am I supposed to sink into his arms willingly and surrender? He can think again.

'Let me go!' I say sharply, my voice too shrill. 'What do you think you're doing?' I'm conscious of a loss of power, a blurring of vision. My face is squashed against his jacket. I can see the stitching at the edge where it's beginning to loosen and fray, the thin shine of wear, the splashes of food and drink grown hard and dark with neglect. No one looks after him. No one checks his clothes, makes sure he's clean. I can hear his heartbeat. It's not as slow as I thought it would be. I could surrender, I suddenly think, sensing my resolve slipping away in an unexpected surge of excitement.

He slides his hands round my waist and lifts me up. My feet leave the ground, hover in mid-air. I'm staggered by the ease with which he does this, as if I'm not heavy at all, as if I have no substance. I'm flying, completely in his control. He could do whatever he wants – swing me round, lift me above his head, throw me away . . .

He places me carefully on the floor, lets go and steps back. 'There,' he says. 'I'm not going to molest you.'

I force myself not to sway, breathing deeply but not audibly, so he doesn't know that he's interfered with my body's functions. I clear my throat to make sure my voice will work properly. 'That was unacceptable,' I say, as levelly as possible.

'It was, wasn't it?' he says. 'Sorry. I must have got carried away. It's what men do every now and again, you see. We sometimes find it difficult to control our instincts.'

'Actually,' I say, 'most men don't treat me as if I'm an object to be picked up and put down again whenever they please.'

'And how many men do you actually know? Except Popi and Boris, of course.' For some reason he finds this highly amusing and chuckles.

'The trouble with you,' I say, 'is that you always think you're right.'

'That's because I am,' he says.

'You're also arrogant,' I say. I've had enough. I'm exhausted.

I can hear him smiling. 'But you can't help liking me,' he says.

I need to think of something normal, so I go over and examine the picture of the cottage, the countryside from the past. The sky fills half of the canvas, the last light of day filtering through streaks of cloud on the horizon and lighting up the heavier clouds in the foreground, creating a sea of glowing waves. '*Altocumulus stratiformis duplicatus*,' I say, hoping to impress him. Bare trees are silhouetted against the sky. The flooding in the picture is not the same as our flooding. It's watery and muddy, but the children can still walk home. In our world when it rains we're stranded for weeks.

I can hear him coming over, standing by my side. I know exactly where he is without looking. 'Perhaps we should live like that now,' I say.

'What do you mean?'

'Abandon our high-rise flats and go back to live on the land. Work with the weather, rather than hide from it.'

He thinks about it for a while. 'No,' he says eventually. 'One winter and that house would be washed away.'

'There must be ways of living with the weather,' I say. 'We shouldn't just accept that it dominates everything we do.'

'The people in the picture are poor,' he says. 'Their lives were hard and they died young. We can do better than that. We've worked out ways of surviving.'

'But we're still dependent on machines. What if they pack up?'

'They're not going to. The rest of the world is still producing, still developing and finding ways of improving.'

'What about the lack of children? What if there's no one left to maintain everything? Supposing the next generation isn't up to it? What then?'

'No point in worrying. None of us can do anything to change it. Why don't we think about what we *can* do?'

'You don't really come from Oxford, do you? You come from the north.'

He tenses. 'Why do you say that?'

'You have an accent.'

'No, I don't.'

'Yes, you do.'

'How would you know how people from the north sound?'

'One of our aunties. She came from Newcastle, I think. You sound like her.'

He pauses. 'There's nobody there any more.'

'There's hardly anyone here, either.'

'It's not the same. There's you, Popi and Moth, your brother and sisters, and apparently there are aunties. The further north you go, the emptier it gets. You can travel for miles and miles and never see a soul.' For a moment, there's a bleakness in him, a coldness. He seems to be revealing something about himself. The trouble is, I don't know what it is. 'If you want a cottage, Roza,' he says suddenly, brightly, 'I'll build you one. Boris can help. But it won't last, mark my words.'

'Let's go home,' I say.

We cycle along the main road out of the city, the old Broad Street, past LeeL, back towards Five Ways. Aashay lets me go in front, so that he doesn't get carried away, I suppose, and leave me miles behind. I'm not comfortable with him behind me, but I'm exhausted and just want to go home. I thought I wanted to share the experience of being in the forbidden places, but I've changed my mind. I've always come here on my own, and if others have followed me, I never knew, so it remains a place of solitude, a private world that should belong only to me.

Sun filters through the crumbling buildings to the right of us, and I'm aware of all those people who once filled the streets, who worked here, who ate here, who believed they would go on following their routines until they decided not to. The people for whom everything terminated so abruptly.

Are there other ways of sneaking through – pathways, under-passes, along the canals? I've been arrogant in assuming that no one else is interested or brave enough. I can hardly be the only person with curiosity. Are there more people like Aashay, who flit between the empty spaces? Are they out here now, hiding in the shadows, watching us pass?

We stop to admire the library. It's shining brightly, an exotic wedding cake. The sunshine glows and dances through the outer layer of circles within circles, creating patterns of dark and light, while the secret cavities beneath the surface remain unillumi-nated, evidence of a heavier, less enchanted reality. Most of the metal circles are blocked, clogged with decades of debris depos-ited by the wind and rain, trapped there for ever. It's a fort with a lookout post – although maybe not, since there don't seem to be any windows – the bridge of a ship with a golden turret, round and perfect from this distance, housing the archives for which it was designed.

'Have you been inside?' asks Aashay.

I shake my head.

'Don't.'

Immediately, I want to go in. 'Why not?'

'It's a mausoleum.'

'What do you mean?'

'It's where they all went to die. The ones who were trapped in the city when they put up the barriers. It's a gigantic cemetery, full of skeletons that no one ever buried.'

'You've been in, then?'

He nods.

'What happened to the ones who didn't die? If they had immunity like us and were trapped inside the city, what did they do?'

'They'll have found a way out. You can't seal up a place as big as this without leaks. It's impossible. Don't forget the canals. There are secret exits that you wouldn't even dream of.'

'They had guards by the canals. Popi told me. Soldiers in big white suits with helmets – and guns. He says it was disgraceful. They had no right to shoot people just because they wanted to live. And it didn't work. Almost everyone died in the end, whether they were in the city or not.'

'Who needs a library, anyway?' says Aashay, turning away. 'If there aren't any books.'

'You don't know that,' I say. 'Just because you don't read books doesn't mean they've all been wiped off the face of the earth.' I get back on my bike and pedal away furiously.

He overtakes me in about thirty seconds.

11

At six o'clock the next morning, Thursday, I meet Boris on our landing. He's blurry-eyed, still half asleep, but he's found time to shave and dress carefully, anticipating people, determined to make an impression. He's stuffing a small neat box into his rucksack, pushing it well in and testing the vel to make sure it's secure.

'You're taking your electronic tools, then?' I ask him.

He blinks, slightly embarrassed, struggling to articulate his need for familiarity, then shrugs. 'They're valuable,' he says. 'You never know when they'll come in useful.'

I've been through the same crisis – I couldn't bring myself to leave my *Birds of the British Isles* behind. I need to take something that's valuable to me, something that will tie me to home. I've spent so much time with this book, sitting quietly on the edge of the Woodgate Valley, trying to identify birds. It's a way of touching the past. I've never seen a thrush or a woodpecker, but there are plenty of sparrows and tits of all shapes and colours, and they seem to be multiplying now that there's no one left to appreciate them. If anything happens to us, I'd like to have the book with me, hold it in my hands, draw comfort from its familiarity. The feel of it is as valuable as the contents.

Boris meets my eyes and smiles nervously. We recognise in each other the same feverish excitement, but also the fear. Will we meet dragons on the way? How big will they be?

'Come on,' he says, touching my arm. 'Let's do it.'

We stumble down together, triggering the lights in the stair-wells, and meet the others at the bottom of the ramp that leads down from the cycle floor. We're the last to arrive. Aashay, dressed entirely in black, is testing his gears, adjusting the electronic readouts, checking cables, making last-minute adjustments. The rest of us are confident. Boris and Popi spent yesterday servicing the bikes. We know the risks. A breakdown away from home would be a disaster. Never travel without a repair kit.

Lucia is dancing around among us all, wrapped tightly in a jacket that's too small for her, hair stuffed into a woolly hat and a scarf wound round her neck twice, tied at the back so that she can't get it off. Her cheeks are red and shiny. 'I helped Moth pack the food last night,' she says to me. 'We've got boiled eggs, raspberry biscuits out of the freezer, potato cakes – I love potato cakes – watercress . . .'

We're dressed for the early-morning chill, our waterproofs packed into our panniers and rucksacks on our backs. I climb on to my bike, muffled and hunched, and grasp the handlebars with gloved hands. The sun hasn't yet emerged above the horizon, but the early rays of pre-dawn are already climbing the sky, spreading out silently, and the darkness is losing its intensity. We can see enough in the half-light to know where we're going. Popi balances on the tandem with his feet on the ground, while Moth helps Lucia to climb on to the rear saddle. The pedals have been adapted for her, but there are foot rests for when she's too tired. There was much discussion yesterday about how to transport her. She wanted to cycle independently.

'It's too far,' said Popi. 'Remember Clent?'

It would be hard to forget the expedition to the Clent hills. Lucia's refusal to go any further. Our efforts to persuade her.

'I'm bigger now. I can do it.'

'Coventry is a whole lot further,' said Boris.

'Please,' said Lucia.

Popi dithered. 'What happens if you get too tired? We'd be too far from home to just go back.'

'No,' said Moth. 'You can't go on your own bike. We'll take the tandem.'

'Oh,' said Lucia. She started to whine, then stopped abruptly, taking a big gulp, as she always did if things didn't go her way, as if she was swallowing whatever didn't agree with her. She started to sing, yet another nursery rhyme, to hide her annoyance: '*Mary, Mary, quite contrary, how does your garden grow?*'

I suspect this is her way of not thinking, so that she can still appear sunny and sweet even when she doesn't feel like it. Does she ever recall anything of her previous life? I wonder sometimes if she has memories she doesn't completely understand, that make her think we might reject her, that she has to convince us she's worth having around.

With silver bells and cockle shells, And pretty maids all in a row. Lucia, wearing our discarded clothes, trying on our shoes, keen to be part of a band of sisters, pretty maids. Why would she want to be anywhere else?

Aashay studies the tandem for a few seconds, his lack of faith in Popi's strength evident. 'Do you want me to take the big rig?' he says to Popi. 'You can use my wheels if you want.'

'I can handle it,' says Popi, clearly offended.

'Cracking,' says Aashay, turning away.

We line up, each of us with one foot on a raised pedal, the other on the ground, poised for action.

'Let's go,' says Popi, and lurches out on to the road, wobbling slightly, but gaining confidence and stability as he continues.

'We're off!' calls Lucia, into the cold, empty air.

We cycle along the A456 to the Five Ways roundabout, circle round the edge of the barriers, taking the northern route – Ladywood Middleway, Icknield Street, New John Street West – with the barriers on our right, until we meet the old Aston Expressway at Dartmouth Circus. We're about to head into the unknown.

Hector went straight past Thorpe Park yesterday, making better progress than he'd expected, and ended up in Uxbridge. As soon as I went online last night, he was there, waiting for me, grinning with triumph, his face flushed, his hair considerably less immaculate than usual.

'You've caught the sun,' I said.

'No,' he said. 'It wasn't sunny.'

'It was here,' I said.

'Overcast most of the way – cloudy but warm.'

'It'll be the fresh air, then. You're not used to it.'

'I don't spend my entire life indoors, you know,' he said.

'Of course you don't.' He's not exactly an outdoor type, though.

'Birmingham tomorrow, I reckon.'

'Steady on,' I said. 'Stick to your original plan – Bicester, or maybe a bit further tomorrow, and Birmingham on Friday.' He's not normally competitive. It's one of the things I like about him – his ease with his own abilities, or lack of them, and his refusal to make unreasonable demands on himself. 'What's the waystation like?'

He considered the question, then nodded thoughtfully. 'Yes – nearly whishy, I'd say, but missing the mark in places. A bit dusty. And not all the equipment is working properly, although I've managed to get a decent meal from the microwave. Spag bol. The bed seems bearable, a smidge claustrophobic, perhaps – I'm not the man for small spaces. The notices tell you to shake everything out to check for scorpions—'

'Scorpions? Are you serious?'

He laughed, pleased with himself. 'No, of course not. I wanted to make you feel sorry for me. The wifi works, though, as you can see. I had to hunt for the password. I expected it to be hidden away discreetly, so I wasted hours opening cupboards, checking behind doors, only to discover there was a huge sign just inside the entrance.'

'I'm really glad it's OK.' I put a hand up to the place where his cheek should have been and stroked the air. 'Don't overdo it tomorrow, will you? There's no point in turning up early. We won't be back till late, so you won't be able to get in.'

'You're really going to the fair, then?'

'You know we are. We've already discussed this.'

'Yes, of course. I just . . .'

'What?' Why was he sounding so uncertain? Is the waystation more unsavoury than he's letting on? 'Hector, don't worry. I'll let you know all about it when we're eye to eye.'

'Roza – you won't talk to strangers, will you?'

'Don't be daft. Everyone will be a stranger except Aashay.'

'Are you sure he hasn't got an ulterior motive? He could be trying to lure you away.'

I laughed. 'No one's going to attempt to have their evil way with me, not in front of the entire family. Who'd want to take on Boris?'

'Fair point.'

'I bet we'll meet people from Brighton. We might even come across someone you know. Visitors from the great metropolis—'

'Or reasonably large village, depending on how you look at it.'

'—and Aashay seems to think people come from all over the country.'

'He's almost certainly exaggerating.'

'Even so . . .'

'You will be there on Friday, won't you?' He sounded subdued, uncertain.

I was too excited to respond to his change of mood. 'Never fear. The bunting will be out, the feast on the tables, the band playing. We'll be home by tomorrow evening, preparing the fatted calf.'

When I contacted him again this morning, ten minutes before I left the flat, I wasn't really expecting to find him awake. But he was there, bleary-eyed, his face pale and exhausted. 'You were right,' he said.

'I'm always right. What are we talking about?'

'I'm stiff.'

I resisted the urge to laugh. 'How bad?'

'Let's just say sitting down is not an option.'

I'd wondered why he was standing at such an odd angle. 'Tricky,' I said. 'Do you think you should rest today? Give yourself a chance to recover?'

'No way,' he said quietly. 'It's deadly nightshade here, without even the dull murmur of wind or rain to confirm that my ears aren't blocked. A guy could turn to concrete in a place like this and not be discovered for another hundred years.'

'How will you cycle if you're in pain?'

'No worries. I can pedal from a standing position.'

'Not for sixty-odd miles,' I said. 'You'll have to make today's journey shorter.'

'I was aiming for Banbury, but I'll see how it goes. It might be wiser to settle for Bicester.' He half smiled. '*Roza, Roza, give me your answer do, I'm half crazy, all for the love of you.* Thank goodness you're going to marry me. I'll be transformed by the acquisition of common sense.' He was searching for his good humour, but lacked conviction.

I was suddenly embarrassed by his misery and my excitement. 'I wish you were here now, Hector. We could go to the fair together.'

'*You'll look sweet upon the seat, Of a bicycle made for two.*' His voice was uneven, his mouth too dry.

'You've left out a bit,' I said. 'Something about marriage, but I can't quite remember.'

'Not appropriate,' he said. '*It won't be a stylish marriage, I can't afford a carriage* – I thought you wouldn't be too keen on the idea of a budget wedding.'

I laughed. He knew I didn't really care. My POD pinged. Time to go. 'Hector, we're leaving now,' I said. 'Please be sensible and stop if you're too tired.'

'Cherry-oh,' he said.

At Dartmouth Circus, we dismount and study the road labelled 'Aston Expressway, A38(M)' on Popi's map.

'How can it be both?' asks Boris. 'Either it's the A38 or it's a motorway.'

'It's blue, so it must be motorway,' I say.

'It's the A38 really,' says Moth. 'But they wanted people to behave as if it was a motorway.' She points over the bridge at the road ahead. 'Can you see how it changes colour in the middle? Well, it's not obvious, but it used to be red. They changed the direction of the lane according to the time of day. Open for incoming traffic in the morning and outgoing traffic in the evening.'

'What if the cars got it wrong?' asks Delphine.

'Well, I think most people just got it right, although there were probably mistakes and accidents in the early days. They had overhead signs, crosses and things. Before my time, so I don't really know much about it.'

'Let's face it,' I say. 'Normal people aren't going to go charging towards cars coming in the opposite direction. Even a half-functioning imbecile can see that it wouldn't be a good idea.'

Boris is intrigued by the idea of people driving themselves. 'But what if you weren't expecting the direction to change? Say you needed to switch on your music, or you were unwrapping a jam sandwich, or you had an itch in your foot and you glanced down at the wrong moment—'

'That's why everyone switched,' says Popi. 'Computer-driven cars were a lot safer.'

'I bet there were loads of people who wanted to keep control, though,' says Boris.

'There were just as many who shouldn't have been allowed to be in control in the first place,' says Moth.

We stand for a while, inspecting the road below. The surface is mostly soft and green, coated with moss and scattered with weeds. Huge potholes reach out to each other and join up, forming deep trenches. There are seven of us, quite a crowd, but we shrink into insignificance in the centre of this vast system of once-thriving highways. The A38 emerges from under the bridge of the roundabout and stretches out ahead, five lanes then six, surrounded by towering concrete walls. A warm breeze passes over us, ruffling our hair, a welcome promise that the weather will be fine for a while, and I can hear the silence at its core. An unbroken silence that goes on for miles and miles. Maybe people are out there somewhere, but we have no connection with them. It feels as if we're alone.

I'm keeping an eye on Aashay, worried that he'll take off without us. He's still sitting on his bike, ready to go, bored with our discussion, keen to ride the motorway. He's probably been up and down these roads hundreds of times, maybe alone, maybe with other people. His eyes are far away. Is he remembering previous occasions? Does he have any interest at all in nostalgia, or is everything based in the present and the past is just a point of reference that helps him work out how to proceed? I suspect he's looking to the distance, to the fair, the end of the journey.

He lifts his feet and adjusts his gears. 'Let's roll!' he calls over his shoulder as he heads for the slip-road.

Boris leaps back on to his bike, galvanised into action. 'We have lift-off!' he yells, as he races down the slope, slicing through the air.

Delphine and I look at each other. We're not going to let them get away with that. 'Onwards!' she shouts, as we skid away.

I can hear Popi in the background. 'Careful!' he shouts. 'Mind the loose gravel!'

His voice fades as the air surges past my ears, and I put all my energy into pedalling. I'm drawing slightly ahead of Delphine, but she's not giving up. I can see her front wheel out of the corner of my eye. Boris and Aashay are in front, almost level with each other, but far apart in the wide space of the road. We're enclosed by the high concrete walls. The road stretches ahead, straight and empty. All I can hear is the swish of my tyres and the bluster of the wind as it sends my plait streaming behind me. I'm gripped by excitement. I can do this. I can challenge Aashay and win.

Delphine can do it too. She's parallel with me. It's an open road and it's here for us. Just us. No cars, ever again. Ahead, the walls slope downwards and disappear. At the edges of the road, huge damaged electronic billboards stare blankly in our direction as we sweep past them. They're dead but we're alive.

Our order of arrival at the point where the roads divide was inevitable. Aashay first, closely followed by Boris, then me, then Delphine. Aashay was always going to win. He's stronger and fitter than all of us, and could outrun even Boris without seriously trying. But he understands Boris's need to challenge him and he allows it, letting him believe he's in with a chance.

I skid to a halt next to them. They're both grinning with excitement. Delphine is right behind me, gasping for breath.

'Not bad,' says Aashay.

I glow with a sense of achievement.

'Thanks,' says Delphine.

'I nearly won,' says Boris.

'Nearly's no good,' says Aashay. 'You win or you don't.'

'Sometimes,' I say, 'it's easy to forget you're an adult.'

He stares at me, his eyes round and ingenuous. 'Don't push me,' he says.

I look back along the motorway and see Moth, Popi and Lucia miles behind, tiny figures in the distance, pedalling slowly and doggedly.

'I think the weight of Lucia and the extra bags are slowing Popi down,' I say, carefully, not wanting to acknowledge any weakness in him.

Unexpectedly, Aashay turns and heads back up the road towards them. Delphine looks at me. 'Do you think we should go back too?' she asks.

'No point,' says Boris. 'The tandem's only got room for Lucia and one other person.'

We stand in the middle of the road and look around. There are several routes and it's not clear which one we should take. Most of the signs are unreadable, battered by storms. Ahead of us, I can see something like a forest rising up, growing out of the roads, a complex system of pillars and bridges, with concrete branches and tendrils that seem to be tied into knots.

'Which way?' I ask.

'Ask Aashay,' says Delphine, watching him cycle away, her eyes narrowed.

'Aashay doesn't know everything,' says Boris.

'He knows most things,' she says, with unexpected authority.

I study her. She seems older. Her skin is almost flawless, silvery pale in the light of the morning sun. Her long hair is tied in a ponytail at the nape of her neck, but there are wisps escaping at the front, gently wavy, soft against her cheeks. Has she been using the curling tongs? Her blue eyes are watery after the battle against the wind, but wide and sparkling.

Only a few weeks ago, she was my slightly awkward younger sister, but now she's become more confident in her movements, more graceful. I don't see as much of her as I used to, now that I have my own flat – but Boris and Lucia still hang around. Why not Delphine? Do I know her world any more? I experience a moment of panic. What else is changing without my knowledge? 'You can't believe everything Aashay tells you,' I say.

'I don't,' she says, with a slight frown that implies she does, but would prefer me not to point it out. 'But if he doesn't know the way, how do we get there?'

'We have maps,' I say.

Boris is circling us on his bike, a huge grin on his face. 'Well done, you two,' he says. 'You nearly kept up with me and Aashay.'

'You're being patronising,' I say. 'Stop it.'

'I was trying to be nice.'

'Don't bother,' says Delphine. 'You only got here first because you started without warning us.'

'Here they come,' I say.

Aashay has taken over the tandem. Lucia is grasping her handlebars firmly, as if she's contributing to the momentum, but her feet are up on the footrest, motionless. She's laughing uproariously.

'Yay!' she shouts. 'We're the greatest! Faster, Aashay, faster!'

And he obliges, grinning hugely, sweeping past us without pausing. 'Follow me,' he shouts, over his shoulder.

Delphine and Boris leap on to their bikes and go straight after them. I wait for Moth and Popi to arrive. Popi is struggling with the unfamiliar gears on Aashay's bike and Moth is holding back for his sake. They pull up beside me, breathing heavily.

'Watch which way they go,' says Popi. 'We don't want to lose them.'

'We can manage,' says Moth. 'The maps are reliable.'

'That's not the point,' says Popi. 'We should keep Lucia in sight.'

I look at him in surprise, but he won't meet my eye. 'She's all right,' I say. 'She's with the others.'

'I want to be able to see her,' says Popi.

We follow them, taking the left fork, then the right lane. It narrows and goes round an enormous bend. According to one of the signs, just decipherable, we're on the M6. Ahead of us, bridges rise up, balanced on concrete stilts, roads over roads, huge and wide and empty. They circle in all directions, curving above us, like a giant puzzle, waiting patiently for someone to come along and reorganise them. Some have collapsed, lying where they fell, vast chunks of rubble. Trees are growing alongside, between the pillars, and lakes have accumulated in the hollows at their base, between the motorways, spilling over on to the roads, sheltered by the branches of the overhanging trees.

We carry on round the bend, unable to see the others ahead, but trusting them to be there. It's cold under the bridge, dark, silted with mud, and we're silent, conscious of the paths we're following, the people who used to come here in vast crowds every day, but who will never come this way again. We keep going and start climbing, puffing with the exertion until we reach the top, where Aashay and the others are waiting for us. We pull up next to them and stare down at the complexity of the systems below us.

'What is this place?' asks Delphine. She's less composed now, and her face, hot and sweating, has lost its serenity.

'Spaghetti Junction,' says Popi.

'It's beautiful,' she says.

And she's right. How can something so concrete, so manmade and industrial, have such soft lines, such pleasing curves? Spaghetti Junction. I whisper the name to myself. It's perfect. A tangle of roads, carefully designed, winding and twisting in every direction, apparently aimless but each one with a purpose. It's a meeting of motorways. They have all made their way here from different parts of the country and converged, consulting with each other, then threading their way past to where they need to go. You can join any of them, but you have to know what you're doing or you'll end up going in the wrong direction. A writhing nest of snakes, a sculpture with purpose.

'Once,' says Moth, 'these roads were crawling with cars, lorries, buses, coaches. Lorries so big you could be at one end and not see the other.'

'It's difficult to believe it all worked,' says Boris, shading his eyes against the sun with a hand as he studies the patterns of bridges. 'It's so complicated.'

'Actually,' says Moth, 'it didn't work when the satellites went down and everything came to a halt. But it wasn't dangerous. The automatic stop mechanisms were very efficient.'

'An appalling waste of everyone's time, though,' says Popi. 'I got caught in one of those jams once, and had to wait eight hours while it sorted itself out.'

'Don't exaggerate,' says Moth. 'It was seven hours last time you told that story and six hours the time before.'

'I ended up on the M6 heading for London, when all I really wanted to do was go home.'

Moth laughs – I don't know if it's because we're talking about the old days, or because we're going somewhere different and expecting to meet new people, but she's more relaxed than usual. 'I was so furious with you.'

'And it wasn't even my fault.'

'Of course it was. Most people knew how to reset their carpods. They didn't just blindly follow instructions. They used the override.'

Lucia gets down from the tandem and runs to the side, leaning over the barrier. 'You can see for miles,' she says.

We're high up, on a raised section of what must have been the M6, and we can see a very long way, over a flat landscape spreading out to the horizon. Trees are flourishing, seeding themselves, forming a nascent forest across the land. They're thriving on the melted snow, revitalised after the brown exhaustion of the summer. A few isolated walls and crumbling buildings are still standing, small sections that were missed by the drone demolition or simply failed to collapse. These remains stand, like half-dreamt ghosts, fragile and uncertain, eroded by wind and rain and snow, but somehow still managing to survive, clothed with the green uniformity of their surroundings. Weeds creep and spread, embracing everything in their path. And every-where, as far as the eye can see, there are lakes, great bodies of water that no longer dry up at the height of summer, that contain enough water to spread and swallow every low-lying area, mining permanent beds for themselves, ready to be expanded by the next winter's torrents.

From the opposite side of the motorway, we can see the city centre, still intact, much of it coated with the same mossy green as the roads: the post-office tower rising up through a confusion of buildings; several very high blocks of flats, one a delicate blue, tinged with green, oddly artificial, dotted with darker patches where the decorative panels have come loose and fallen down; the rotunda; the few remaining silver discs on the sides of the old Bullring.

'You wonder why they didn't flatten the cities, don't you?' says Moth. 'They're not much use to anyone in that condition.'

'They're trying to keep a record,' says Popi, thoughtfully. 'And, to be fair, they wouldn't have known then how long we'd have to stay away. But it's becoming more like Stonehenge every day. All a bit mystifying to future generations.'

Should I tell them I've been into the city centre? Should I confess so that everyone else can feel free to confess too? I let the silence settle.

'I'm hungry,' says Lucia.

'Me too,' says Boris. 'Let's have the picnic here.'

'Good idea,' says Moth. She unfastens the basket on the back of her bike and starts to unwrap the food.

'Once, we didn't need maps,' says Popi. 'Satellites showed us the way. On a small screen. They'd pinpoint our exact position and tell us how to get where we wanted to go.'

'What happened to them? Did they fall out of the sky?'

Popi shrugs. 'I don't know. Maybe they just stopped working.'

'Or somebody decided to deny us access,' says Moth. 'Because, apparently, we don't count any more.' She's always annoyed about this sort of thing. The passwords, the drops. 'They're willing enough to use our brains, though.'

We stand by our bikes and eat, all of us ravenous after our exertion, gazing out over the exhausted city that once held millions of people. It's beyond imagination. How did they all fit in? I sometimes doubt Moth and Popi's information. It's as if they have to exaggerate to get our attention, always more interested in a good story than the truth.

'It'll all be forest one day,' says Popi, and he sounds satisfied.

Aashay stuffs the food down, but clearly doesn't want to linger any longer than necessary. 'Come on,' he says. 'There'll be plenty of time to eat when we get there. Tromping stuff. Things you don't normally get. Steak, ice-cream, fresh cakes.'

'Steak?' says Popi.

'Ice-cream?' says Moth.

The rest of us roll our eyes at each other. 'You two spend far too much time thinking about food,' says Delphine. 'It's not healthy.'

12

We pass a fallen wind turbine at the edge of the motorway, a monster felled by the forces of nature it was meant to harness. It was originally part of an arc that should have swept out to the horizon in an elegant, unbroken wave, but is now little more than a line of broken teeth, an uneven parade, full of gaps. Some have been severed at the top, just below the blades, others at the base, all victims of an orgy of winter destruction. Only a handful remain intact, vast follies that watch over the land, like sentinels, waiting patiently for the men with repair kits who will never come.

'Jack's been past here!' I call to Lucia.

'Jack and the Beanstalk?'

'No, Jack the Giant Killer.'

'Do you think Jack met Jack?' says Delphine.

Lucia giggles. 'I wish I'd seen them.'

I haven't been so close to one before. Our wind turbines on top of Wyoming House are tiny in comparison. They close down during the bad weather, shutting up their blades and sliding neatly into individual storage capsules. They store enough electricity for our use until the worst of the winds calm down and then rumble back out again. How could any force – wind, rain, snow – defeat something as big as the one in front of us? It lies on its side, two blades buckled by the impact with the ground when it tumbled down, while the third blade points upwards to the sky, distorted and humiliated, a signpost to nowhere. *Humpty Dumpty sat on the wall, Humpty Dumpty had a great fall . . .* The innards have burst out and spilt across the ground, a generator that no longer generates, a bloodless mechanism that failed in the final battle. *All the king's horses and all the king's men, Couldn't put Humpty together again.*

As we get closer to Coventry, Aashay becomes more protective, cycling backwards and forwards between us, like a sheepdog – on his own bike again – corralling us into a closer unit, slowing Boris down, encouraging Moth and Popi to keep up. Every now and again, he offers to take over the tandem, but Popi refuses to accept any more help.

'You obviously think I'm ancient,' he says, after Aashay's third enquiry, 'but I consider myself to be still in one piece and functioning reasonably well.'

'I want the man in the moon!' shouts Lucia.

Popi turns round and fixes her with a severe look. 'You'll get what you're given,' he says.

'*Cross Patch, draw the latch, sit by the fire and spin. Take a cup, drink it up, then call your neighbours in.*'

'I hope that's not aimed at me,' says Popi.

'Of course not,' she says. Two little dimples appear in the centre of her cheeks when she smiles in that secretive way, without opening her mouth. You only see them occasionally, but it's worth the wait.

I suspect she's brought the nursery-rhyme book with her, hidden in her rucksack. Since the fight between Boris and Aashay, it's disappeared from its normal position in the bookcase and Moth wouldn't move it, so it must be in Lucia's possession. She shouldn't take risks with something so valuable, but persuading her to hand it over would be difficult. If Moth knows, she's probably decided to say nothing and wait for the right moment to retrieve it.

It belongs to all of us. It's our heritage, even though the past it portrays goes a lot further back than our collective memories, or even those of my parents. But the pictures are embedded in my mind – brightly coloured characters with rosy cheeks and shining button eyes, dressed in unrealistic clothes, full of sweeping fabrics that represent an artist's idea of the Middle Ages. The landscape is saturated with a benign light, an optimism, a cheerful world where all is well. These illustrations represent everything in my childhood, my family, my home.

Two cyclists whizz past us, almost silently. An elderly man and woman, brown-skinned, dressed smartly but sensibly in loose trousers and quilted jackets. Without consultation, we slam on our brakes, taken by surprise with this evidence that there really are other people around, people we haven't met before. After going a few more metres, the couple look at each other, slow down and stop. They turn and stare. Then, without a word, they wheel their bikes around and walk back towards us.

'Hi, Aashay!' says the man, as if they're old friends. I experience an instant flash of relief. If Aashay is known to this couple, he must be who he says he is and the fairs must exist.

Aashay smiles briefly and nods, but seems reluctant to engage in conversation. He remains on his bike and starts to circle us, almost impatiently, as if we're short of time.

'Hello,' says the woman.

'Hello,' says Moth. The rest of us smile politely.

'Are you heading for the fair?' she asks. She's short and plump, and wearing large round glasses. Her cropped hair, more grey than black, is plastered to her scalp as if it's wet.

'We are,' says Moth. She climbs off her bike, places it carefully on the side of the road and goes over to them. 'We're the Polanskis. I'm Bess, this is my husband, Nikolai, and our four children, Roza, Boris, Delphine and Lucia. Aashay is our guide.'

Clever. She's separated Aashay from the rest of us but given him a role.

The couple study us, perfectly still, but with agitation working below the surface, betrayed by the quick movements of their eyes. They keep glancing at each other, backwards and forwards with an excitement they can't disguise, considering each one of us almost surreptitiously, until their gaze comes to rest on Lucia. 'How splendid,' says the woman eventually, her voice dry. 'Are they really yours?'

'What kind of a question is that?' says Moth. 'Are you suggesting we've kidnapped them?'

'No, of course not,' says the man, who is managing to contain his reactions more successfully than his wife. He's much taller, skinny and angular, with a stoop in his back. 'I'm Tariq. This is Farzana. Please excuse my wife. It's so long since we last saw children that we don't know how to react any more. Where are you from?'

Popi hesitates, then gestures vaguely behind us. 'Over there,' he says. 'How about you?'

The couple look at each other, as if trying to decide what to say. 'North,' says the woman, eventually.

I know why Popi is secretive. But what do this couple have to hide? A mansion stocked with luxury goods? Secret underground cages where they keep all the spare children in the world locked up, available to pet when they feel like it?

'I thought the north was deserted,' I say. 'That's what Aashay says.'

'He's probably right,' says Tariq, his face softening with a smile as he turns to me. One of his front teeth is discoloured and slightly crooked, as if he's bumped it on something and damaged the root. 'We're not really that far north. Just beyond Birmingham.'

Farzana clears her throat. 'I wonder why we haven't met before,' she says.

'We've only just found out about the fairs,' says Moth.

'We were like that at first,' says Tariq. 'Living in isolation, thinking we were the only ones left. We have a cottage in the country, you see, miles away from anywhere, on the mountain. There was something wrong with our online connection, and it was impossible to find out anything. But we came across another couple while we were on our travels a few years ago, and they introduced us to our first fair. Never regretted it. A whole new world, new friends, new activities.'

Aashay seems reluctant to engage with Tariq and Farzana. He continues to circle irritatingly, tailed by Boris. 'We should get going,' he says. 'It's not much further now.'

'Stop it!' says Moth to Boris.

'What do you mean?' he says, stopping.

'It's bad manners to continue cycling when we're talking.'

'Oh,' he says. 'Sorry. Can't we ride while we're talking? So we can get to the fair.'

But Tariq and Farzana aren't in a hurry. Tariq smiles at me again. 'Not in Brighton yet, then?' he says.

'Soon,' I say, blushing a little, embarrassed by his close attention. 'I'm getting married in the spring.'

'Ah,' he says. 'Don't you resent being manipulated by the government?'

'It's not like that,' I say indignantly. 'Hector and I met on online. We know what we're doing.'

'Of course,' says Tariq.

I want to defend myself but can't without descending into the kind of language they use in films: we're soul-mates; it was love at first sight; we were meant for each other; we're marrying for love. I don't have a vocabulary that can express emotion without resorting to clichés. I've been watching the wrong films.

'We're not being manipulated,' says Delphine, slightly too loudly. 'Nobody pushes us around. It's just a matter of common sense.' She doesn't add that she can't wait to go to Brighton, but I know she's thinking it.

'I'm sure I've asked you this before, Aashay,' says Tariq, following him round with his eyes, 'but shouldn't you be in Brighton, too? I'd have thought they'd be sending enforcers after you by now.'

Really? Nobody's ever mentioned enforcers.

Aashay stops, puts his feet down and considers the question. 'I've been and gone,' he says. 'I'm more use to them travelling around.'

Permission to travel? An assignment from Brighton? He's making it all up, I'm sure, wanting us to think he's special, that he can find a way round the rules. I know exactly what he'd say if I challenged him about why he hasn't already supplied us with this information. 'If you want the right answers, you have to ask the right questions.'

Farzana approaches Lucia on the back of the tandem. 'Hello,' she says, in an artificially high-pitched voice that's presumably meant to be suitable for children. A tenderness creeps over her face, softening the cheekbones, a touch of motherly warmth, an expression that is self-consciously awkward after years without practice.

Lucia stares at her. 'Hello,' she says, her voice clear. But there's no smile hovering on her lips. She's tense, suspicious.

'What's your name?'

'Lucia.'

Farzana puts out her hand, an elderly hand, the skin wrinkled and thin, to touch Lucia's cheek. Lucia leans backwards in alarm, almost tipping herself out of the saddle. I understand this feeling, this fear of being touched. It's an automatic reaction, distaste at the proximity of an unfamiliar adult, an unformulated fear, a protest against fuss. I wheel my bicycle over and stand beside her. 'She's not used to strangers,' I say.

'Oh, I'm sorry.' Farzana withdraws her hand immediately, almost with terror. 'I didn't realise. Of course, it must be difficult for you all, being children in a world of adults.'

Has she lost all ability to interpret age? 'Some of us are not children any more,' I say.

'Of course not.' She smiles awkwardly, instantly aware that she's said the wrong thing.

I feel sorry for her. 'But we're hoping to meet others of our own age,' I say. 'That's why we're going to the fair.'

'Naturally,' she says, and smiles again.

Tariq is studying Aashay intently. 'Where do you go between the fairs?' he asks.

'Here and there,' says Aashay.

Tariq nods thoughtfully. 'And in what way are you useful to the government when you travel around? Are you a spy?'

Aashay smiles, warm and friendly. He sets off on his bike again without replying.

He's so careful with his information, always sifting it through before telling us anything, never tricked into saying more than he intends. Does the absence of an answer mean he really is a spy? But whom would he be spying on, and why? Us? But there's nothing to discover. As Popi explained, Brighton keeps an eye. What information could Aashay possibly give them that would be any use?

'Well,' says Popi. 'We'd better carry on. Since we're all heading for the same place.'

'Can we cycle with you?' asks Farzana, diffidently. 'It'll give us some kudos, turning up with a family.' Her tone is light, gently mocking, as if she's laughing at herself.

I decide that it might be possible to like her.

As we approach Coventry, we encounter a few more people. We don't stop for them, but they join us anyway, cycling alongside or just behind, watching us across the motorway carriageway, clearly delighted to see us, full of questions.

'Who are you?'

'Where have you sprung from?'

'Why haven't we seen you before?'

'How old is the little girl?'

We throw back similar questions, thirsty for information. But, like us, they're evasive, unwilling to give too much away.

Boris and Delphine race around madly, thrilled by it all, trying to talk to everyone, but too excited to maintain a proper conversation. It's exhilarating, being in the centre of a group, surrounded by people. Lucia shouts a greeting to everyone who approaches, singing nursery rhymes at every available opportunity, trying to find out if other people know the same ones we do. But they maintain a respectful distance from her, watching Moth and Popi, somehow aware of the need for care. Moth and Popi smile and greet each new cyclist, projecting a polite reserve, a formality that carries a warning: please be careful; remember, we don't know you and you don't know us. I alternate between bursts of exuberant activity with Boris and Delphine and a compulsion to stay by my parents, silently endorsing their caution.

Tariq and Farzana remain close. Look at us, they're saying. We saw them first. Aashay continues just ahead, not allowing anyone to approach him, checking regularly that we're still following. He gives the impression that he's in charge and we're his responsibility.

Most of the people are closer to my parents' ages than ours, although a few are probably in their thirties or forties. There are no children, none who could have been born post-Hoffman's. Then a couple in their early twenties sweep up beside us, both towing trailers. They must be survivors, hardly older than me.

'Hello!' calls the woman, in a cheery voice. She's mousy-haired, wearing tight-fitting trousers and big boots.

'Hello,' I call back, staring at them with eager curiosity. I want to know everything about them. Where do I start? The man's face, smiling cheerfully, is weather-battered and scarred, but his cheeks are plump, almost childlike.

'Paula,' says the woman. 'And Joe.'

'Have you come all the way from—'

A yell from Aashay interrupts. He's stopped abruptly, pointing to the right. 'Look! There! We've arrived!'

Through the trees, a large building looms up, its empty, black windows gaping outwards. A handful of metal rods rises up from the top, bent and twisted, markers of what was once a structured design, a sign, perhaps, or a symbol that might have been significant to the supporters, welcoming them to their football matches.

We sweep into the car park in a convoy, negotiating our way through enormous empty spaces, over crumbled tarmac, every surface penetrated and ravaged by weeds. This is where the fans would have left their carpods. They're divided into sections by low barriers, row after row after row, disappearing round the corner as far as the eye can see. It's hard to believe there were ever enough cars to fill them all. Aashay leads us towards a kind of tunnel. A large number of bicycles has been parked neatly in racks on either side of the entrance, all secured with padlocks. With a flutter of excitement, I try to count them. There are almost as many as on our bicycle floor, each one ridden here by an individual, someone who's placed the bike neatly in a docking station, locked it and then walked into the stadium.

'Welcome!' says a voice, as we enter the tunnel – male, tinny, high-pitched. 'The match will be starting shortly, so please find your—' It rises to a babbling whine, and fades to nothing.

'Someone should have told him it's over,' says Moth. 'I wonder what they use for a power source.'

We cycle through the open doors, down a dark corridor, burst out into the sunshine of the stadium and skid to a halt in astonishment. It's like stepping into a film. There are more people here than I've ever seen in my life, every shape, size and colour imaginable, all talking, laughing, arguing. They merge, like a flock of starlings, into a solid mass of bodies, with individuals separating out, branching off, then rejoining and becoming part of the whole again. It's a crowd, a real crowd!

'Zowee!' says Boris.

'Where are the children?' says Lucia.

'Look at her dress,' says Delphine, pointing out a skinny black woman, with a halo of curls, who hovers briefly in front of us. 'I've never seen anything like that before.' The material shimmers and reflects the colours of everyone else's clothes. The woman spots someone she knows, waves with a flutter of her fingers, swirls, and disappears into the crowd.

'How about them?' says Boris, staring at three tiny elderly women, almost identical, who drift past arm in arm, as if they're part of some private club. They're wearing black trousers, black jackets, wide-brimmed black hats. He grins. 'Might suit you.'

'The day I listen to your advice on style,' says Delphine, barely looking, her eyes jumping from person to person, 'is the day I—' Another woman has caught her attention: straight red hair, white skin, tall, plump. 'I want her shoes.'

'But how does she keep her balance?' I ask. I've seen plenty of heels on films, but none quite as tall as these.

'I reckon there's a hundred people here,' says Boris.

'Easily,' says Moth. 'More, maybe.'

I make rapid calculations, counting in blocks of ten, but it's impossible. Everyone's moving around and it's hard to focus on them as individuals. I want to see their faces, but I'm dazzled by the clothes, the colours, the patterns, the way everyone seems to move around with such confidence.

'Let me down,' says Lucia. 'Quick.'

'Stay where you are,' says Moth.

'But I have to find the children. You said there would be children to play with.'

'Give us a few breaths,' I say. 'We need to know what's going on first.'

It's like an amphitheatre, although rectangular, and much, much bigger than the one outside Birmingham Art Gallery. The area in the middle, where they presumably played football once, is covered with compressed grass, weeds and a few trees. It's surrounded by rows of wrecked seats – grey plastic, with lethal splintered edges. They rise upwards, a layer at a time, higher and higher under what must have once been a glass roof but is now just a twisted structure of metal girders.

Moth follows my gaze and frowns at the sight of the damaged roof. 'Is it safe, do you think?' she asks.

'It must be,' says Popi. 'Nobody looks worried.'

On three sides, the seats go up, like a gigantic staircase, to a point high above us where they meet a wall just below the roof. On the fourth side, there's a building behind the seats, rooms where people would presumably have sat behind full-length windows and watched the football in comfort. The glass all broke long ago, leaving jagged edges and dark, empty, sinister rooms, which are no longer protected from the weather.

Everyone is gathered on the grassy central area, although there are some smaller groups along the edges, sitting in folding chairs they must have brought with them, huddled close, as if they're conducting meetings, or discussing important business transactions. Grass that would have grown high in the spring and turned to hay in the summer drought is now trampled and flattened. Green shoots, brought back to life by the melting snow from the blizzard three weeks ago, peep through the hay, pushing their way to the light wherever they're safe from shuffling feet, urgently seeking the nourishment of the sun.

Tables have been set up in rows, with pathways between them. It's like the German market in Chamberlain Square that Moth has described to me. Most are piled with food: cheeses, cakes, fresh fruit, meat grilled over an open fire, the source of a comforting, restful smell. There are clothes as well: intricate hand embroidery, freshly knitted sweaters, boots and shoes that look as if they've never been worn. There's an empty area marked out with ropes. Games? Races? Boxing? There's even a little train wending its way through the stalls, with plastic benches and chains to stop the passengers falling out. BENDY WENDY, it says on the side, in big red letters.

Everyone is talking. There are heated debates coming from one group, a spontaneous cheer from another, a shout of laughter from further away. It's the sound of pleasure, of well-being. People enjoying themselves. How could all this delight possibly be frowned upon by the government?

As they gradually become aware of our presence, their laughter fizzles out, their voices fade and negotiations cease. A curious quiet settles over the area closest to us, broken only by the sizzle of meat cooking and the creak of the train as it glides clumsily to a halt. Men and women stop what they're doing and stare at us, their eyes gravitating towards Lucia.

We stare back nervously, not knowing what to do. Even the cyclists who've arrived with us seem uncertain about how to restart the hustle and bustle.

'Hello, everyone,' says Moth, after a few moments, her voice strong and authoritative in the surrounding stillness. 'We're the Polanskis. How lovely to meet you all.'

One or two people laugh, others start to talk again, unnaturally strident, and most of them return to their business, all the time keeping an eye on us, as if we're invaders and they're not sure if they're safe. They seem on edge, expecting something to happen. They glance at each other, trying to give the impression they're not observing us, while people further away are moving towards us.

I look round for Tariq and Farzana, Paula and Joe, hoping they'll introduce us to their friends, show us around, but they've melted away, following their own agendas, drifted into the crowd and become part of the background activities.

'Come on, Popi,' says Boris, urgently. 'We've got to have some of that meat. I'm starving.'

'How unusual,' says Delphine.

But Popi holds back, clutching the tandem, trying to decide where to leave it safely.

'How do we pay for the meat?' asks Boris. 'We don't have any money.'

We stop in our tracks. 'Oh dear,' says Moth. 'Why didn't we think about that?'

'Actually,' says Popi, 'I did consider the problem, but since we don't possess any money – and, as far I know, neither does anyone else – I couldn't come up with an answer.'

'Ask Aashay,' says Delphine. 'He must know what to do.'

Aashay hasn't abandoned us, but he's working his way round a group of nearby men, shaking hands with each one. 'Hal,' he says. 'How's it going? Lewis! Long time no see. Jonnie, what you doing here? Crossing boundaries?'

Are they real friends, or just acquaintances? Are they people he's known all his life, or is some kind of trading going on? You come and mend my roof, I'll find you a new bike. What is Aashay's role in all this? Men see him from afar, interrupt their activities and come over as if he's a long-lost friend. They slap him on the back, mutter in his ear, playfully scuff him with their fists. Then, gradually, made secure by his presence, they lose their inhibitions and come over to us.

We stand together with our bikes, keeping a careful grip on them. 'Why didn't we bring padlocks?' says Popi. 'We could have found some if we'd thought about it.'

'We didn't think about much, really, did we?' says Moth, grimly.

The longer we stand there, the more people seem drawn towards us, as curiosity overrides their uncertainty. We find ourselves in the centre of a circle, and we huddle together, not knowing what to do. An elderly woman reaches out and touches my plait, stroking it gently. 'I'm Amanpreet,' she says.

'Hello,' I say, trying to move my head away, but smiling at the same time, not wishing to appear unfriendly. 'I'm Roza.'

'Such pretty hair,' she says.

Another woman, only slightly older than me, with pink cheeks and feverish eyes outlined in black make-up, leans forward and grabs Lucia's hand. 'Hello, darling,' she says. 'You're a pretty one, aren't you?'

Lucia stares at her, her eyes round and confused. Moth pulls her away roughly. 'Don't touch her,' she says loudly.

The woman steps back. 'All right, all right!' she says, her hands up in front of her.

Popi suddenly loses patience. 'Aashay!' he shouts.

'Goodness,' murmurs Moth. 'The lion roars.'

Aashay appears through the crowd. 'Come on, folks,' he says, pushing people out of the way. 'Let's have a bit of space here. Give our guests room to breathe. You'll have time to talk later.'

They're surprisingly obedient, as if they've always let someone tell them what to do, as if Aashay has an authority they respect; they fall back easily, allowing him to come through.

'We just need to get used to everything first,' says Popi, apologetically, to anyone who will listen.

'It's sorted,' says Aashay. And he's right. Everyone goes back to where they came from, unsatisfied, but prepared to wait, eyeing Lucia greedily.

'What shall we do with our bikes?' asks Popi. 'Should we leave them outside with the others?'

'No need.' Aashay waves to a quieter corner of the stadium near the entrance. 'Just leave them there.'

'But might someone steal them? Everyone else has locked theirs.'

Aashay shrugs. 'Everyone's got their own transport. Why would they take yours?'

'Ours might be better than theirs,' says Moth.

'Really?' He raises his eyebrows.

'Depends if they're short of spare parts,' says Boris. 'I'd take one of theirs if I was desperate.'

Moth is scandalised. 'Boris! Have we brought you up to steal?'

'No,' he says. 'You've brought us up to survive. To make the most of every available opportunity.' He grins at her and I can see her struggling to find a reasonable response. He's too honest, too amiable. He's been studying Aashay and learning the technique of charm.

'Survival should be possible without resorting to criminal behaviour,' says Popi. 'Nobody else seems to have a tandem.'

'Stop rattling,' says Aashay. He doesn't understand our anxiety because he's resourceful, accustomed to finding his way around with whatever's available. If his bike disappeared, he'd improvise, find another one. I doubt he believes in the concept of ownership. He sees me watching him and softens. 'Actually,' he says, 'no one's going to take the tandem. They're far too interested in Lucia to threaten her existence.'

Moth finds this unsettling. She puts an arm round Lucia's shoulders. 'OK,' she says. 'We'll leave the bikes there, but everyone must keep an eye on them. Just be aware, that's all.'

'Nice one,' says Aashay.

'How do we buy things?' Boris asks him. *Simple Simon met a pieman, Going to the fair. Says Simple Simon to the pieman, Let me taste your ware . . .*

'It won't be a problem.'

'But they're not just giving everything away.' *Says the pieman to Simple Simon, Show me first your penny. Says Simple Simon to the pieman, Indeed I have not any.*

'They barter. But nobody will refuse you. They all adore anyone under the age of twenty-five. Everyone here will want to feed you, give you things. They'll fight over the privilege.'

'If you'd warned us,' says Moth, 'we could have brought goods to barter with.'

Aashay stares at her, amusement in his face. 'What did you have in mind?'

She's offended. 'We're not entirely without resources,' she says. 'I can bake cakes, make jam, that kind of thing.'

'We have access to all sorts of useful equipment,' says Popi. 'We're surrounded by other people's abandoned possessions.'

Aashay smiles. 'That may not be quite what these folks want.'

'Nonsense,' says Moth. 'They can't produce anything better.'

'Trust me,' says Aashay. 'Everyone will want to supply you, not the other way round. Enjoy yourselves. Make the most of it. That's why you've come.'

I think of Hector soldiering on, pedalling his way towards me, and feel guilty that we're having this opportunity in his absence. If only he'd come earlier, he could have shared the experience, seen that there's nothing to worry about. 'Can we get online?' I ask.

Aashay points to a large screen just above the entrance. 'The password,' he says.

'So, what about the meat?' says Boris.

'No probs,' says Aashay. 'Follow me.'

13

The smell is coming from a spit turning slowly over an open fire. The joint of meat, the remains of a large animal, crackles and hisses as it cooks, making a wordless protest about its treatment. Several slow-burning logs are glowing in the fire below, not producing flames, but giving off a heat so intense I can feel it from several metres away. A young guy with dazzlingly blond hair is standing at the side, turning the handle smoothly and methodically. The same age as me, I decide, born pre-Hoffman's, like Paula and Joe. I glance round, wondering if I can see them, but there's no sign. I need to talk to them – there's so much to ask. The guy is gazing into a vacuum with an expression of utter boredom, but when his eyes drift towards us, he snaps awake. He ignores Popi, Moth and Lucia, studies me with open curiosity and half grins at Boris. Then he turns his attention to Delphine, lengthens his neck, flexes his shoulders and seems to stretch. There's a brief interruption to the movement of the spit. He winks at her.

Delphine stares at him with surprise and uncertainty. She glances at me and widens her eyes in a silent question, but I don't have any advice. I'm as taken aback as she is. Why's he more interested in her than me? Does this mean she's attractive, special in some way that none of us has recognised?

'Hi,' he calls. 'I'm Lancelot.'

'Hi,' I say. Boris takes no notice of him. Delphine doesn't respond. 'Are you from Brighton?'

'What are your names?'

'Roza, Boris, Delphine.' I indicate each of us in turn. 'My parents, and Lucia.'

'I'd come and talk,' he says, 'but I'm busy.'

'We've noticed,' I say.

He grins, almost shyly, wanting Delphine to speak, but she's studying her shoes with unusual interest. 'What do you do when you're not here?' I ask.

The owner of the meat stall steps out towards us, clearly delighted that we've come to him. He opens his arms generously, and I back away, worried that he's intending to enfold us in a welcoming hug. He's tall and thin, almost bald, with a grey, sunken face, as if he's harbouring some hidden disease. 'Hello!' he says. 'I'm Pete. I hope you're starving because you're standing in front of the best food at the fair.'

Popi peers at him suspiciously. 'You're a butcher? Do you do this between the fairs as well? Where?'

Pete ignores him. He picks up a long knife with a blade so thin it's almost transparent and goes over to the meat on the spit. He cuts through the outer surface as easily as if he's slicing tomatoes, catching each piece, thick and curled, oozing with juices, on a metal dish in his hand. He divides the meat into equal portions and hands us each a small plate. He stands uncomfortably close to me.

'Get that down you,' he says. 'It'll put colour in your cheeks.'

He ought to take his own advice. Shouldn't he be plump and healthy if he has regular access to this kind of food? I lift the plate and sniff. My toes tingle, my mouth waters and my head spins. I glance at the others. Delphine is nibbling at the edges cautiously, while Moth concentrates on helping Lucia to cool hers. Popi is reacting in the same way as me, testing first, slightly suspicious of the ease with which we were given the meat, but Boris doesn't waste time. He takes a large bite immediately. It's too hot. He opens his mouth to let out the steam and flaps his hand up and down wildly.

'Patience has some advantages,' I say to him.

'Patience isn't my type,' he says, continuing to stuff the meat in, chewing rapidly and swallowing. 'She can sort out her own problems.' Grease coats his chin and he wipes it away on the back of his hand, grinning at us. 'Whizzario!' he says. 'Best thing I've ever eaten.'

'What is it?' asks Delphine.

'Haven't you had meat before?' asks the man.

'Of course we have,' I say, wanting to take a bite, but determined not to be patronised. 'All the time.' Actually, that's not true. We have the hens and Edward the goat, but it would be counterproductive to kill them for meat, since they provide our eggs and milk. One or two of the aunties and uncles catch wild animals and offer us cold leftovers, but we've never been very good at finding our own meat. Popi is not a hunter. 'It's not goat meat, is it?' I don't want to eat one of Edward's relatives.

He considers before answering, as if he can't decide how much information to give us. 'Wild pig,' he says eventually.

'I thought all the pigs died with Hoffman's,' I say.

'Not the domestic ones,' he says.

There's something about the way he says this. As if he's hiding something. I study the meat on the chipped china plate in my hand, trying to work out why he would lie. Was the animal diseased? Has it mutated so that no one knows whether it's safe or not? Or has he acquired it in some illegitimate way? *Tom, Tom the piper's son, stole a pig and away did run . . .*

No one else is suspicious. Even Moth and Popi are tucking in, biting, chewing, beaming at each other. Boris is on his second slice, eating more greedily as the temperature becomes more manageable. Delphine is still nibbling the edges, delicate as always, then taking larger bites as she begins to enjoy it. Neither of them looks as if they're being poisoned.

I take a bite. Juice drips into my mouth, thick and aromatic, and my tastebuds burst into unaccustomed action, straining with excitement at this new sensual experience. My whole body grows warm with pleasure. It's so delicious that I abandon my earlier caution and cram more and more into my mouth, unable to think of anything except the thick tenderness of the texture and the richness of the taste.

'Have some more.' I turn and the man is next to me again. I try to step back, but another slice is thrust on to my plate, and

I'm diverted by the intoxicating smell. I grasp it eagerly and bite again and again and again.

Suddenly, I'm over-full, an unfamiliar sensation.

I glance at Delphine who's wiping her mouth with her hand. 'Licious!' she says.

I nod at her and grin. 'Careful, Boris, you'll be sick,' I say, as he accepts another plateful.

'Find your own road to cycle,' he says, through a mouthful. 'I know where I'm going.'

'Boris!' says Moth. 'Manners!'

'Carry on,' says Popi. 'Enjoy it while you have the opportunity.'

Three young guys are heading in our direction, chucking a ball back and forth between them, fast and powerful, passing it on the moment it touches their hands, as if it's too hot to hold, but always preventing it flying into the crowds. They're talking loudly, their movements slightly exaggerated, conscious of the attention they're attracting. I wait for Boris to spot them.

'Can we explore?' asks Delphine.

Popi and Moth frown at each other.

'Please,' she whines. 'We can't hang around with you all day. It's humiliating.'

'Check in with me once an hour,' says Popi. 'On the dot, or I'll be coming for you.'

Moth is less willing. 'We don't know any of these people. We really should stick together . . .' She pauses, sees the sign over the entrance, exchanges a glance with Popi, and gives in. 'Code the password into your PODs – now, not later. At the first sign of trouble, anything that makes you uneasy, anything at all, you press the alarm.'

'Yes, Moth,' says Delphine, rolling her eyes.

Boris is poised to run off, but Popi grabs his arm. 'Agreed?'

He sighs. 'It's done. Did it the moment we arrived. That's what you do with passwords.' Boris, the expert. He's gone, almost before Popi has loosened his grip.

'Are you coming?' says Delphine to me.

'Hey!' A shout makes us turn back. It's Lancelot, waving frantically from his position by the spit, his bright hair flashing in the glow from the fire. 'Don't leave me! Are you coming back?'

Delphine smiles. The meat seems to have given her a new confidence. 'We're here all day,' she calls. 'See you later.' She flutters her hand briefly in the air, casual and in control.

I'm impressed.

We find a stall piled with clothes, most of them worn and faded, similar to our own. But there are a few interesting dresses hanging by the side, unusual colours, decorated with bright appliqué patterns of trees and leaves. Delphine grabs one, and holds it up. When she moves it from side to side, the colours shimmer and shift in the changing light, grey, then green, then blue. We've never seen anything like it before.

I've examined plenty of abandoned clothes, in wardrobes that will probably never be opened by anyone except me or Delphine. They might sway coquettishly in the stagnant air, attempt to be sleek and glamorous again, but in reality they're just rotting. Apart from the wedding dress, which was never worn, they don't excite me, and I've only ever taken the barest necessities. Their musty smell reminds me of old people. It undermines the concept of clothes having the power to transform you into someone better than you are.

'Try it on,' says a woman's voice.

We turn guiltily. She's about the same age as Moth, black-skinned, her short hair rolling vigorously over her head in coiled springs.

'Oh, I couldn't,' says Delphine. 'It's too beautiful. I'd be afraid of damaging it.'

'Try it anyway.' The woman indicates a small tent behind her and pulls open the flap. 'You can change in there.'

'No, thank you,' I say.

'It's all right,' says Delphine, looking inside. 'There's no other way in or out.'

The woman smiles at me. 'I'm Olisa,' she says, 'and I've got two girls of my own, so I wouldn't let anything happen to your sister.'

'You've got girls?' says Delphine, looking round. 'Where? How old?'

The woman laughs. 'Oh, they'll turn up, you'll see. Go in the tent with her, if you want to,' she says to me.

'Hurry up then,' I say to Delphine, not wanting to watch her change. 'I'll wait here.' I'm not entirely convinced about the existence of the girls.

She disappears inside the tent and emerges a few seconds later in the dress. She swirls in front of a large mirror on the side of the stall, lets the folds settle, then turns the other way so the material follows her in soft waves, as fluid and flexible as water.

'Oh!' I say, shocked by the way it transforms her.

'Beautiful,' says Olisa.

'But where does it come from?' I ask.

She frowns. 'We never ask about origins,' she says. 'It's here and that's all that matters. We have to trust each other.'

I'm immediately suspicious. She's implying there might be reasons why we shouldn't trust each other.

A couple of girls, their skin as rich and dark as Olisa's, one a little older than Delphine and one younger, appear round the corner of the tent. We stare at them. Teenagers! The first we've ever seen.

'Yay!' says Delphine, recovering first. 'Are you real?'

'I reckon,' says the older one, watching us curiously.

'Hi,' I say awkwardly. They're not connected to the children we saw at Five Ways all those years ago. Different colour.

'I wanted that dress, Ma,' says the younger one to Olisa, her voice slightly petulant, keeping her eyes fixed on Delphine.

'Too late,' says the other. 'She's wearing it.'

'I'm only trying it on,' says Delphine, eager to please. 'I'm not going to keep it.'

'These are your children?' I ask Olisa, still trying to process everything. 'Post-Hoffman's?'

She nods, pleased and proud. 'Both of them post.'

'Where's their father?'

'Oh, he's around, doing whatever he does. He becomes slippery whenever we come to the fairs. Can't keep hold of him.' She sighs. 'He's OK for the rest of the time, though.'

She seems so normal. 'Where do you live?' I ask.

'South. You came with Aashay, didn't you? Has he told you most of us are from Brighton?'

Interesting, I think. 'He only tells us what he wants to,' I say.

'Well it's not a secret,' she says. 'Can't see why he'd make it one.'

'But it's a long way. Why bother to come all the way up here?'

She laughs. 'Questions, questions. Are you considering a career as a private detective? Not much demand for that nowadays.'

I laugh obligingly, but I want to know the answer, so I wait.

'It's nice to get around,' she says. 'Travel, make new connections.'

So, lines of connection. This must be what Aashay does. Link people up, sit back and wait to see what happens. 'Are there more families?' I ask.

Olisa's animation fades a little. 'Not many – hardly any children, even in Brighton. And you're the only young people I've come across from round here. It's mostly the older ones who stayed put. They come to the fairs looking for friends, people to visit.' She turns to Delphine. 'The dress is yours, if you like it,' she says.

'That's not fair,' says the younger girl. 'If you're giving it away, why didn't you give it to me?'

'You can have a new dress any time you want, Ogechi.'

'It's OK,' says Delphine. 'I don't need it. You have it.'

Ogechi looks startled. 'No,' she says, after a pause. 'I don't really mind. Plenty more where that came from.'

But where did it come from? 'We can't pay,' I say.

'No one uses money,' says Olisa. 'Just tell me your names.'

'I'm Delphine, this is my sister Roza and our parents are around somewhere.'

'We don't have anything to exchange,' I say, needing to be absolutely clear.

Olisa puts a hand on my arm, firm and friendly. 'Roza, there's nothing to worry about. This is Onyeka, this is Ogechi, so now we all know each other. We'd like you to keep the dress, Delphine, and wear it as you go round the fair. It'll be an advertisement.'

Is this a trap? Is there something we're not seeing? *Curly-locks, Curly-locks, wilt thou be mine? Thou shalt not wash dishes, nor yet feed the swine . . .*

Delphine looks puzzled.

'When other people see it, they'll be so impressed they'll ask you where it came from. Then you can send them to my stall to see if they can find something nice too.'

Delphine laughs. 'What a good idea!'

'Come and have some cake,' says Onyeka to her.

But sit on a cushion and sew a fine seam, And feed upon strawberries, sugar and cream.

Delphine looks at me and raises her eyebrows, wanting my approval.

'Would you like to come too?' Onyeka asks me. But I can tell she doesn't want me there. I'm older than they are and they probably see me as an adult.

I look round and see Popi and Moth, not far away, wandering between the stalls with Lucia, stopping to talk to people as they go. It's not as crowded as I'd first thought, and it's possible to keep an eye on everyone from a distance. 'Check in with Popi,' I say to Delphine. 'Tell him what you're doing and where you intend to go.'

Olisa smiles at me. 'Don't worry,' she says. 'I won't let anything happen to your sister.'

Delphine has made up her mind, and she's already walking away, chatting to Onyeka and Ogechi as if she's known them for ever. I watch her approach Popi and exchange a few words. Moth glances at me and smiles, more relaxed than earlier. She puts a hand on Popi's arm and he looks in my direction, waves and nods.

'Necklaces?' says a man's voice. 'Earrings? We pierce ears.'

I turn to find a bald, fat man with large ears staring at me intently. He has white, pasty skin, crinkled and sagging, thick folds gathering in the gap where his neck should be. He's standing behind a table with a display of jewellery in front of him.

'No, thank you,' I say, intending to walk past. But my attention is drawn to the necklaces, hanging from the branches of miniature plastic trees, rotating gently in the sun, scattering their surroundings with little points of light.

I suddenly think of all the jewellery that must still be scattered across the country, lying around in collapsed homes or abandoned shops, under layers of mud, buried by the floods. Moth has told me how you used to be able to hear the wail of alarms through broken shop windows in the early days after Hoffman's, the sound echoing across the empty countryside from miles away, until the renewables malfunctioned and the grid failed and the electricity died. Grilles would have come down over the shop windows, but there were no police to come screeching up the road with their driverless cars set to emergency, sirens blazing – I've seen enough episodes of *Midland Cops* on the net to know how it worked; no security men; no insurance companies to investigate.

Jewellery would make a good bargaining tool with the rest of the world – if anyone ever bothers to give us the chance. Or it could substitute for money here at the fair. It's hard-wearing – no deterioration over time, no need for spare parts. I wonder if the government in Brighton has considered the potential.

'Try it on,' says the man, holding up a silver pendant – a flower of rubies and diamonds. He's grinning, but he makes me uncomfortable.

'Maybe later,' I say, backing away.

I wish I could find Paula and Joe. I can see Aashay close by, surrounded by a group of men. He's doing all the talking, gesturing earnestly. The men are listening to every word, respectful and solemn, nodding in agreement. I want to wander over and listen to what he's saying, but I suspect he'll change the subject if he sees me.

I can't shake off a suspicion that things aren't exactly as they seem. I'm probably being unreasonable – the people are all so nice. But everything seems too good to be true. Is something going on below the surface? Is that why Paula and Joe seem to have disappeared? I can't understand where the luxuries come from, and Olisa's unwillingness to tell me adds to my unease. Do some places have better drops than we do? If so, why? And not many of these people can be local — how could they have concealed evidence of their existence so completely for the last twenty years? If Olisa is telling the truth about most of them coming up from Brighton, then Hector can't have been entirely honest with me. How can he possibly know nothing?

I need to talk to him. I wander round to the back of the stalls in search of a quiet corner and press my POD, waiting for the screen to form on the back of my wrist, for an acknowledgement that he knows I'm trying to contact him. But he's not switched on. He'll be cycling northwards, upright on his bike, unable to sit down but determined to keep going. I hope he's not being foolish and trying to finish the entire journey today. I imagine gliding round the corner of Wyoming and finding him sitting by the entrance — well, maybe lounging on his side, since he can't sit — playing Raindrop Dodge on his POD, waiting for me. The image is comforting and I find myself smiling, going over the conversation we'll have when we meet properly for the first time.

'Hi, Apple Crumble,' he'll say. 'It's me. The man from beyond the M40.'

His voice is in my ear, undistorted by the POD, masculine, capable, the tone more vibrant than onscreen. Will he mind if I put my hands on his shoulders, touch his face with a finger? How soft is his skin, how salty his sweat?

But I need him here physically. Imagination is unsatisfactory.

Back at the fair, I find a stall of books, all pre-Hoffman's. The edges of the pages, smooth as china, cleanly sliced inside the shrink-wrap, gleam whitely, while the fluorescent covers pulsate with 3D images of characters who push themselves forward and withdraw again as you move. If I'd known they'd be interested in untouched books at the fair, I could have brought some with me. One of the flats in Colorado has shelves full of them. They line the walls, right up to the ceiling, intended only for decoration. They've never been opened, never read, unlike the well-thumbed ones in the flat where I first discovered Aashay.

A pile of small pamphlets with the sketch of an old house on the front catches my eye. I pick one up and examine it. The house has a very steep pitched roof and it's built on stilts. *All About the Weather Watchers*, it says on the cover. It reminds me of the picture in the art gallery. A cottage huddled into the landscape.

'Hello, Roza.' I turn to find Farzana, our companion from the motorway. 'Are you interested in this kind of thing – managing the country without technology?'

'I've heard of Weather Watchers,' I say. 'I've seen the name online.'

'In that case, you might like to meet some of my friends.' She holds out a hand, as if she's expecting to take me there. 'Come with me.'

I step towards her, but don't take her hand.

She lets it drop and leads me away from the bookstall. I follow, not because I believe she has something interesting to show me but because I don't know how not to do as she says. She's like Moth, with a natural authority that makes it hard to disobey.

I look round briefly. I can only see Popi. He's standing in front of a stall of small carvings of animals, picking up each one in turn, smoothing his hands over the sculpted wood, engaged in an enthusiastic discussion with the man behind the stall. The man, who has presumably done all the carving, is tall, stooped, with wispy grey hair that flops back whenever he lifts a hand to push it out of his eyes. Popi, who has never had a good enough reason or interest to find contacts online – 'The demise of social media liberated me. You cannot begin to imagine how many hours were lost' – seems to have found someone he wants to talk to.

I follow Farzana to the further edge of the grass, where there's a tight circle of six people, all grey-haired, seated on plastic chairs. They're leaning inwards, concentrating on a small compact man in baggy trousers, who's talking intently. His voice is rich and multi-coloured, slipping easily through a wide range of pitches, although I can't make out the words properly from this distance. As soon as we've reached the edge of the circle, he stops and looks up. Everyone turns.

'Sorry,' I mutter, backing away, embarrassed.

'No,' says the man, leaping to his feet. 'Come and join us. You're most welcome. I'm Graham. Here, have my seat.' Others jump up to offer me their chairs, until everyone is standing. If I sat down now, I'd be the only one sitting. But two more chairs are produced, the circle is widened slightly and everyone, including me, is accommodated.

'Have a piece of coconut ice,' says a woman with a sky-blue silky scarf round her neck. She passes round a small china bowl with pink and white cubes inside. 'I'm Daiva,' she says, smiling at me. 'I made it myself yesterday.'

'Oh, yes, please,' says Farzana, taking a piece and popping it into her mouth.

I examine the square in my hand, and bite off a small section. It's crunchy and full of sweetness, leaving hard, dry crumbs in the mouth after the flavour has gone. To quote Boris, Whizzario! I've heard about coconut, but never tasted it. I resist the urge to devour the rest in one mouthful, and keep my eye on the bowl as it gets passed around. I wonder about the etiquette of taking a second piece if it comes back my way.

'This is Roza,' says Farzana. 'I thought she might be interested in our project.'

'You're most welcome, Roza,' says a man in a purple sweater with an image of a tree on it. 'I'm Terence. Do you know much about our movement?'

'No, not really,' I say. 'I've just seen the name online – are you similar to the Free Thinkers?' I don't want to tell them I've joined the other organisation in case they're offended. 'Are you connected to them?'

There are a few frowns, as if I've said something wrong. Terence smiles kindly. 'No,' he says. 'They're much too militant for us. We're more interested in working with the weather and the land, co-operating with the government rather than standing against it. We don't always agree with Brighton, of course, but, unlike our more aggressive rivals, we don't harbour any desire to overthrow it.'

I'm shocked. I hadn't picked this up from the website. 'But I just found them on Freight. Surely they wouldn't be allowed to advertise if they wanted to bring down the government.'

'They're clever,' says a woman from the other side of the circle. 'They know how to look innocent. You can only get to their real agenda if you know how to penetrate deeper on the net.'

It's probably just as well I don't have the skills. Would they have led me down their more devious paths eventually, though? I swallow with sudden panic. Thank goodness I didn't say anything to Moth. 'Are you sure that's what they—?'

'Glossy enough on the surface,' says another man – black hair, wide teeth. 'But if you go far enough into their files, you'll see they're anarchists. Out to destroy, not preserve.' He smiles. 'Don't worry, some of us were fooled by them to start with. That's how we know. Got out smartish, I can tell you. I'm Angelo, by the way.'

I feel stupid. Moth and Popi are continually warning us about wandering around online without direction. But how do I know I can trust these people? I haven't even seen their website, let alone penetrated the deeper recesses of their more sensitive files. They look so benign. Smiling, open and friendly. There's no way of knowing if they're genuine.

Farzana pats me on the arm. 'Let me explain,' she says. 'We're a recently formed organisation who believe we should develop a new way of life before it's too late. The rest of the world isn't interested in our country any more.'

'They don't care. They're never going to lift the quarantine – they're too scared,' says a woman on my left. 'I'm Karina.'

'They must care a bit,' I say. 'They're still doing the drone drops.'

'Interesting point,' says Graham. 'How reliable are your drops?'

'Well,' I say, 'I suppose they've changed over time. When I was little, we used to go out once a month – except during the floods, of course – and find everything we needed – more than we needed, in fact. We couldn't use it all – there weren't enough people to share it.'

'I remember that,' says Daiva. 'It was, like, really exciting. You never knew what they were going to send us.'

I can remember Moth guiltily sorting through, reasoning out loud that we could only carry so much, only consume so much. 'If they see we don't use it all,' she said, 'they'll stop sending it. We shouldn't appear ungrateful.' To start with, we left everything we didn't need inside the capsules, closing the door to keep out wild animals, assuming that other people would come and help themselves, but when we returned, nothing had ever been removed or even disturbed. The smell of decay was so overwhelming that we had to find a way to dispose of the unwanted food. So we buried it. A line of artificial graves close by, full of rotting food, rejected toiletries, unnecessary tools, surrounded by the empty pods.

It's not so often now, just twice a year. The end of autumn and the beginning of spring. Can we be sure it won't become even less frequent? Once a year, perhaps? 'It's true they're not so good as they used to be,' I say slowly, thinking. 'We sometimes ask for specific things, but we rarely get them. Boris – my brother – thinks they throw in anything they've got too much of. Food that's nearly out of date, stuff that's been badly made, faulty equipment . . .'

Everyone laughs. They're trying too hard.

'We think they'll stop altogether in the end,' says Karina.

'We could manage without them,' says an earnest-looking woman in glasses. 'I'm Freda. We have clever people among us, people with expertise. We want to set up groups in the rurals, invent our own systems.'

Moth would be interested in this. She might be able to help them. 'My mother—' I stop. I shouldn't let them know that Moth has scientific expertise. They might want to use her, take her away from us. We don't yet know whom we can trust.

'You must remember that we are private,' said Popi before we left. 'We don't share our lives with other people.' We were all sitting around the kitchen table when he said this, and he kept glancing over his shoulder at the half-open door. I knew he was thinking of Aashay. We can never be sure that he isn't outside, listening, storing up information. He walks in wherever and whenever he wants to. He doesn't knock on doors or call out to announce his presence. He just appears and you suddenly find him in places where you don't expect to see him, standing silently, as if he's thinking – or listening.

'Everyone's drops are becoming more irregular, more eccentric,' says Farzana. 'They put in strange things we don't want . . .'

She's right. In the last few years, we've been sent ten electric whisks, twenty-three pairs of black stockings, several boxes of toothpicks ('Toothpicks?' said Boris, incredulously. 'Toothpicks? What century do they think we live in?'), small china dogs in garish colours that seemed to serve no useful purpose – as if somebody had pressed the wrong button somewhere, or the machine wouldn't turn off, and they'd made more than they needed. When they didn't know what to do with them, they parcelled them up and sent them to us. Why would we need – or want – thirty-six china dogs?

'We've become their rubbish dump,' says Terence.

'Some of it's useful,' I say. I'm thinking about sugar, the sweetness that makes so much of our cooking palatable. The treats, like apple crumble, plum cake, coconut ice. And what about spices, shampoos, soap, tea, coffee? 'Would we really be able to manage?'

'Of course we would. Mankind survived for centuries without technology.'

Not necessarily comfortably. 'They didn't always have a very high life expectancy, though, did they?' These people may not believe in technology as much as we do, but they benefit from its knowledge. If you want the information, you need the net. I touch my POD. I'd soon miss it if it no longer worked.

There's been no hint of vibration. Hector must be miles from an accessible router.

'You're right, Roza,' says Freda. How does she renew her glasses if they break or when her sight deteriorates? It must still be possible to get prescription glasses in the drops, after having your eyesight tested online. 'But those of us who live north of Brighton could enjoy a good lifestyle if we used the world around us more productively.'

'What Freda is saying,' says Farzana, 'what we're all saying, is that the time will come when we can no longer rely on outside sources. We need to be capable of managing our lives here independently and we believe that we should be pursuing this now, rather than waiting for the time when we're abandoned completely.'

I would like to point out the obvious problem with this. They're all old – at least as old as my parents. How can we depend on a generation that will soon die out? 'We'll always need contact with the rest of the world, though,' I say.

'Not necessarily,' says Graham. 'If the routers pack up.'

'They can't,' I say, with confidence. Boris has explained this to me. 'There's a huge international station in the middle of the Atlantic, built just before Hoffman's. It communicates with the central stations and onformation centres, which then connect with the routers and filter out to the branch lines. Wifi won't let us down. It rides the radio waves – it's much more reliable than the old phone system. If a router goes down, everything hops to the next one. In a couple of seconds, you're up and running again. Even if Atlantic International packs up, it'll all get redirected through Europe.'

'Not much use to us, wherever it comes from, if we don't know the passwords,' says Graham, clearly preferring the negative outlook.

Everyone nods solemnly.

'You can't crack the security,' says Terence. 'We've tried.'

'Obviously,' says Farzana. 'Otherwise it wouldn't be security.'

'My brother reckons it can be done,' I say. 'It'll just take time. Wifi is indestructible. Like electricity.'

'Electricity can fail.'

'No, not really. The renewables can go on indefinitely.' Except the huge wind turbines, of course, that we passed on our way here. And we need someone to maintain our smaller localised turbines and solar panels, someone with the knowledge and access to parts. I begin to feel uncomfortable. These people are undermining my confidence in the future.

'Computers,' says Graham. 'That's our real weakness. If we don't get replacements, our devices will let us down. We're already miles behind the rest of the world. They'll leave us so far in the background we won't be able to communicate with them at all in the end.'

A shiver of nervousness dances up my back. I've always assumed the drops will continue to keep us supplied. It hasn't occurred to me that they haven't been keeping us up to date. How would we manage if we couldn't go online? How could we be educated, work? Would we lose touch with knowledge? 'I work for the Chinese,' I say. 'They'll send us new equipment if we need it.'

Farzana smiles at me. 'Those of us who don't work for them are less confident, Roza. And they'll only supply what you need for work, nothing extra. But we're a long way from all that now. We just believe we should start to prepare. We have the skills to live independently, even if there aren't very many of us, so we should use them.'

But the problem is greater than lack of supplies. It's the lack of people. Boris, Delphine and Lucia were all born post-Hoffman's, so we know it's possible, and we now know Onyeka and Ogechi. But that's not enough to run a country. There are some younger survivors, like me, Paula and Joe, and a few guys who might be pre or post, but not many. Children below the age of twelve, the real hope for a successful future, are curiously absent.

'If we act now, we can set an example to the rest of the world,' says Terence. 'With fertility dropping so quickly and the possibility that Hoffman's, or another virus, will re-emerge, we'd be able to offer them help, hand on our expertise and experience.'

'If we're equipped for it,' says Graham. 'And if we care to.'

They're so serious, so earnest, but none of them has made any concrete practical suggestions. They're too eager to see disaster.

Boris suddenly runs past with the boys we saw earlier. They're laughing uproariously, throwing the ball around, catching it on the run, scuffling as they try to take it from each other. 'Hi, Roza!' he shouts.

'What are you doing here, Roza?' It's Aashay, his hand on my shoulder. 'Get rolling – you mustn't miss your chance. There won't be another fair until next spring.'

Even without his voice, I'd have known it was him. A burst of pleasure vibrates through me. I stand up unsteadily. 'Thank you for explaining all this,' I say to Farzana and her friends. 'I need time to think about it.'

'We're delighted that you came,' says Graham. He puts out his hand and we shake solemnly. His skin is shrivelled and thin, a further sign of his age. 'We're grateful for your attention.'

They're all nodding seriously. They're not annoyed or offended, just pleased that I sat with them for a while. Because I'm young. Like the aunties and uncles, they feel privileged to have contact with me. 'Thank you for bringing Roza to the fair, Aashay,' says Terence.

Aashay flashes them a grin and grabs my hand. 'Come on!' he says.

It's the electricity again, that dangerous spark of excitement. 'They were interesting,' I say.

'Take no notice,' he says. 'There are people like them all over the country, making plans, imagining they can save the world, without knowing what they're talking about. They're building trees out of paper, painting pictures of bananas when they can't remember what bananas look like. They're too old.'

I'm offended for them. 'They're trying to be practical,' I say.

'They're cobwebbies.'

'No, they're all right.'

But he doesn't want to listen to me. He whirls me about and snakes his arm round my waist briefly until I shake myself free. He's showing off. He wants everyone to think I belong to him.

His touch, the awareness of his arms, powerful and capable, weakens me. I can't stop imagining myself being wrapped up in those arms. Enclosed, held, protected.

But I don't belong to him.

14

'I'm surprised you're not playing football with Boris and the others,' I say to Aashay, as we head back to the centre of the pitch. There are voices all round us, layers of conversations that I'm tempted to listen to as each new strand, each interesting line of argument, reveals itself. The sound is overwhelming after the quiet of our normal existence. So much talking; shouts from the owners of stalls; cheering from a group engaged in a game with a racquet and ball; snatches of songs coming from a group of women who are sitting together, laughing uproariously. Has Moth heard them? She'd recognise some of the tunes. She should be there with them, but I can't see her.

I see Popi not far away and try to catch his eye. As soon as he looks in my direction, I wave. He waves back. Good for another hour, then.

'Football's for kids,' says Aashay.

'I'll remember that,' I say, 'next time I see you kicking a ball around with Boris at home.'

He glances at me with a half-smile.

I shouldn't have said that. It's our home, not his. I know from his brief silence that he's heard the word, registered it and stored it away. He's swaggering now, kicking his way through the flattened grass with nonchalant ease. But I don't want him to start believing we accept his presence, that he has a right to be there.

'What were you saying to all those men?' I ask.

'Which men?'

'I went past earlier. You were rabbiting and they were hanging on to every word. It looked really serious.'

'Everyone knows me here,' he says, with quiet pride. 'I've been coming for years. Have you tasted the ice-cream?'

'No. I haven't seen any yet.'

'Follow me.'

He stalks off, expecting me to run after him, which immediately makes me want to slow down. If he can't be bothered to walk with me, why should I bother to follow him? My POD buzzes. I glance down at my wrist and check. It's Hector.

'Hang on,' I call to Aashay. 'I have to do something first.'

He turns with raised eyebrows. 'Like what?'

I don't want to tell him. 'Work,' I say. 'I need to speak to someone online.'

He's irritated. 'So what about the ice-cream?'

'It'll still be there later, won't it?'

'Maybe. They might run out.'

'I don't even know if I like it. It's hardly going to change my destiny if I don't get it now.' I'm already turning away from him. 'I'll be back in no time.'

He hates having his intentions challenged. It undermines his sense of authority. 'Maybe I won't be here.'

'Why? Where are you going?'

He heads away into the crowd, where he immediately becomes the focus of attention. People stop to talk to him, whisper in his ear, pat him on the back, offer him a mouthful of food. He's famous here, a man who knows everything, a man they trust. I can't see that he needs any more disciples.

I watch him for a moment longer, wondering what he's failed to tell us, how he knows them all so well. What does he do when he's not with us? I can't decide if we're privileged to be in his circle of influence or if we're just the next in a long line of gullible hangers-on. Could everyone be laughing at us?

I head for the edge of the grass, behind the stalls, hoping to find some privacy for a conversation with Hector. There's a kind of tunnel between the seats that leads into the derelict building beyond. The grass has grown tall here and collapsed into a tangle of stems, dry and weary after the unforgiving rigour of the summer, untouched by the casual destruction of passing feet.

I slip into the dark, musty emptiness of the tunnel, pressing the button of my POD, setting it up for a holo. No reception. I go back out and stand in the entrance while I try again. A thin silver ray emerges from the device and forms itself into a shrunken version of Hector, his head only coming up to my shoulder. Why is my power so low? It should be charging automatically, feeding off the energy generated by my everyday movements. Hector blinks and relaxes with a smile when he sees me. I bend down and pretend to kiss him, my lips sliding through the air into empty space.

'Roza! You've grown.'

'No, you've shrunk. Something's wrong with my POD.'

'Are you at the fair?' he says sharply. 'Is everything all right?'

I'm surprised by his concern. 'Of course it is. Why wouldn't it be?'

A look of awkwardness creeps over his face. 'Sorry,' he says. 'I just worry about you, that's all. I've got to think about something on the journey to combat the repetitive rotation of the pedals, the open road, the ills of the hills.'

His concern feels slightly oppressive. I'm not incapable of looking after myself. 'Well, it's good to know I'm at the forefront of your mind.'

'Believe me, you are, Roza, you really are.' He's blinking rapidly, strangely uncomfortable. 'You're the beacon towards which I'm directing my entire energy output.'

'Is anything wrong, Hector?'

He grins instantly. 'Not a sausage. Everything's hunky.'

'How's the journey going today?'

He winces. 'Well – painful would probably be the best way to describe it. Lots of stops. Don't know how I'd have coped without my mum's nosh. Done about thirty miles so far – not so good as yesterday. I'm at a waystation near High Wycombe. Only a short break. I'm salmoning on, upstream, against the current, jumping the weirs. If the fish can do it, then so can I. Reckon I'll make Banbury tonight and your place tomorrow.'

'I'll be there, waiting for you. We're heading back this evening.'

'Make sure you allow plenty of time,' he says. 'Lucia might slow things down – children often do – and you don't want to get caught out after dark.'

Since when has he been an expert on children? 'You're living in the wrong age to criticise children. We're the centre of attention here. Everyone's queuing up just to give us things. They appreciate us.'

'I appreciate you too,' he says. 'But you're not a child. You've got more to offer.'

He sounds tired. The physical activity must be wearing him out. Aashay skids into my consciousness, powering along the M6 on his bike, with his vast reserves of energy, his incredible strength. But Hector wouldn't be Hector if he was like Aashay.

'I've never seen so many people,' I say. 'And they all seem to know each other. As if the entire country's been in on a great big secret and nobody thought to tell us. Loads of them have travelled up from Brighton. You must have heard something, even if it was only a whisper.'

He shifts uncomfortably, as if I've stepped on his toe, or knocked against his arm. 'Well,' he says, 'the truth is . . .'

I stare at him. 'I knew it,' I say. 'You've been lying to me.'

'Not lying,' he says, avoiding my gaze. 'Just trying to protect you. In fact, my younger brother, Horatio, and a group of his friends go to the fairs. Southampton, and sometimes Norwich, I think . . .' His voice fades.

'I don't understand. Why the secrecy?'

'I've never been to one,' he says urgently. 'I genuinely don't know anything about them.'

'You don't talk to your brother, then?'

'Well, no – not really. We don't have a lot to do with each other.'

'But when you knew we were going to Coventry, you could have said something.'

He doesn't reply. I stand in front of him in silence, my thoughts whirling. It wouldn't have occurred to me to question what he says. He gave the impression he knew nothing about the fairs.

Why wouldn't I believe him? It's not helping that he's shorter than me – it's hard to show respect to someone who only comes up to your chin.

He clears his throat. 'Roza, I'm really sorry – It was stupid of me—'

'Stupid? You think stupid is sufficiently descriptive? Mudlike, bog-brained, vacuum-minded might be more appropriate. You must have known I'd find out eventually. What did you expect to happen? Did you think we'd just forget about the fair and potter along in the same old way, not caring about our ignorance? Do you have any idea what it's like, thinking there are no other young people anywhere near us, believing we're alone, then suddenly to discover we're not? And my fiancé, who I would expect to be open and informative, knew all about this and never thought to tell me.'

Hector tries to defend himself. 'But that's why you're special, Roza. Your separation gives you a refreshing clarity of mind, a unique outlook on life. I didn't want to risk contaminating it.'

'Now you're just spouting garbage. What gives you the idea that you can make decisions about me and my life without asking? What else don't I know? How much other useful information have you kept from me?'

'There isn't anything else.' He sounds so sad, but I'm not yet prepared to be forgiving.

'I tried to discuss the fairs with you on the night before you set off,' I say. 'Remember? I specifically asked you and you acted as if you'd never heard of them. How could you do that, Hector?'

He shakes his head slowly, as if he's sorting through the contents of his mind, trying to bring some order to them. 'I don't know. I suppose I didn't really think you'd go. I assumed your parents wouldn't give their permission, and by the time I realised they had, it was too late to say anything.' He sighs. 'I haven't handled it right, have I? I'm sorry.'

'And this business about them being against the law?'

'Not strictly true, but most people in Brighton disapprove of the fairs. They consider them to be frivolous.'

'Hector,' I say, 'you like frivolous.'

He tries to smile. 'Yes,' he says. 'I do – sometimes. But it's more than that. Everything's arranged by word of mouth, not on Freight, so there aren't any checks – it doesn't go through filters – and the whole set-up feels somehow not right. As if there's something fishy going on. Cod and halibut—'

I will not be drawn into his joke. 'But your parents allow your brother to go.'

'No, you don't understand. It's a huge cause of contention. They have rows every time, serious shouting matches. It's hard to know what to believe, but they think the fairs are anti-government in some way, dangerous. They accuse Horatio of putting friends before family, threatening their reputation. They forbid him to go, every time, but he laughs at them and goes anyway.'

Anti-government? Dangerous? 'But what are they afraid of? Everyone's perfectly respectable.' If he'd told me this earlier and I'd passed on the information to my parents, they would never have agreed we could go. Then we'd have been the ones having the rows. But Hector should have trusted me to make the decision. An uncomfortable thought occurs to me. 'Has this got anything to do with the Free Thinkers?'

'Roza,' he says, suddenly urgent, 'what do you know about the Free Thinkers? They're a dodgy lot.'

So he knows more about this too. 'Dodgy in what way?'

'They use violence.'

'What do you mean? They fight people?'

'I've heard they blew up an internet station. Somewhere in the north. An old man died, the caretaker. And they destroy wind turbines.'

'That isn't strictly necessary. The weather does that without their help.'

'Well, they want to hurry things along, speed up the pace of destruction so we're forced to go back to a more basic way of living. There are posters up in Brighton asking us to report any information we might have about them. They're genuinely dangerous.'

'How do you know the posters are true? It could just be government propaganda.'

'Roza, stop it.'

I'll probably unsubscribe as soon as we get home, but I'm not going to be pushed into it. 'Maybe they've got a point. We might not be able to depend on technology indefinitely.'

'That doesn't mean we should destroy it prematurely. Like you say, the weather does it anyway. They're a bunch of loonies in search of a cause. If it's not the weather, it's the drone drops, or foreign aid, or contaminated water supplies. They want to be destructive.'

'What about the Weather Watchers? Have you heard of them?'

He shrugs. 'I don't think so, but I've met the type. Usually about thirty years older than us, similar in age to our parents, survivors. They want to do something worthwhile, leave a legacy for the next generation, compensate for Hoffman's. There are so many of these groups. Earnest people, with names like Gordon or Patience or Margaret. I hope you haven't got involved with any of them. It's really not a good idea.'

I flush. He's so much more experienced than I am. 'Maybe . . .' I say, not wanting to admit he's dead on. 'But there's some truth in what they say. What if all our equipment becomes obsolete? What do we do then?'

'It won't,' he says. 'Computers self-repair. New software can be downloaded. Trust me, they'll go on working.'

'Trust you?' I say. 'I assume that's a joke.' Nothing is as straightforward as he makes it sound. What's his explanation for the problem with my POD? And what about the heating, the dust machines, the lifts, all the equipment that's stopped working? 'Aashay's been to Brighton,' I say. 'Did I tell you that? I bet you've met him, haven't you? Another little secret you've been keeping to yourself.'

'It's a big place,' he says. 'I don't know everyone.'

'A large village, you said. The government knows about him.'

'I work for TU, not the government.'

'He's over twenty-five. Why haven't they arranged a marriage for him?'

Hector frowns. 'That's a good question.'

'Ah! Found you, Roza.'

I swing round. 'Aashay! Where did you come from?' How long has he been standing there? Has he heard any of our conversation?

'Who's the little guy?'

'This is Hector. Haven't you met before?'

'I'm not really this small,' says Hector. 'Roza's power is low.'

They stare at each other, but there's no flicker of recognition between them.

'Not met,' says Aashay, 'but you've mentioned him.'

'Good afternoon, Aashay,' says Hector. 'We meet at last.'

Aashay examines Hector's reduced form, half smiles, then turns back to me. 'So how about the ice-cream, Roza?'

'Oh,' I say, confused. 'Give me a few more minutes. I'll be there shortly.'

Aashay places an arm round my shoulders and draws me towards him, out of Hector's line of vision. 'I'll be waiting,' he says.

I flush and try to pull away. Hector's only a holo: he doesn't have enough flexibility to see anything not immediately in front of him. I struggle to free myself, but Aashay resists, determined to keep the contact. It's like trying to move an iron girder. 'Aashay,' I say. 'Please let go.'

'Well,' he says slowly, 'I'll be off, then. You're both far too clever for me – I couldn't possibly keep up with your intellectual discussions. I'm just a muscle man. I hope Roza's told you that, Hector. She's completely safe under my protection, though. While we wait for you to get here.'

'Take your hands off my fiancée,' says Hector, in a strangely high-pitched voice. 'Show her some respect.'

Aashay starts to laugh. 'Woo-hoo! A man of action.' He withdraws his arm slowly, but remains close for a few more seconds. I can hear his breathing, light and controlled. I'm aware that he's bouncing lightly on his feet, testing his balance, as if he can take on a holo and win. 'I'm not sure you're in a position to get mouthy with me,' he says cheerfully. 'After all, you're not really here, are you?'

'Don't tempt me,' says Hector, with surprising spirit, but Aashay doesn't wait to hear his reply. By the time I've turned, he's gone. I glimpse the back of his black-clad leg as he disappears round the side of a stall.

'Keep away from him, Roza,' says Hector. 'If there's anyone dangerous at the fairs, it's him. Don't trust him.'

It was a mistake to mention trust again. 'It's not necessary to tell me what to do, Hector. I'm capable of working things out for myself.'

'Of course you are, Roza,' he says. 'I know that.' But he sounds nervous. Who's he afraid of? Aashay or me?

'Look,' I say, 'none of us is at our best right now. I've never been anywhere like this before, never seen so many people. It's all new. Let's not get too worked up.'

'You're right,' he says, breathing out slowly. 'We have yet to meet in person, but our prospects are good. I will proceed with extreme haste. Onward, ever onward.' He's back to the Hector I know. 'The day is young, the road is straight – I hope – and with any luck the hills are behind me, or at least the up ones.'

'Don't overdo it. You don't want to be even stiffer tomorrow.'

'No, but I do want to reach you in the shortest time possible.'

'Not too early,' I say. 'Or we might not be up.'

'Roza, Roza, I can never be too early to see your beauty, to gaze into your blue, blue eyes—'

'Brown actually,' I say. 'I'm just here, in front of you. You've only got to look.'

'—lose myself in your brown, brown eyes and balance the weight of your glossy golden plait in my hand.'

'The hair's brown too – light brown.'

'Just to be corrected by you is a privilege,' he says.

'That's enough, Hector,' I say. 'Let's just concentrate on reality.'

'OK, I'm off,' he says. 'Roads to travel, distances to cover, destinations to reach. Take care, Roza, until I'm there to protect you.'

'Bye, Hector.'

'Cherry-oh.'

I terminate our connection and he fades rapidly, condenses into a silver streak and vanishes.

I can hear someone playing a snatch of melody on a clarinet and a run of notes on a keyboard, so I wander over to have a look. A group of musicians have gathered together in one corner of the stadium and are preparing to play. There are two women, one with a clarinet, the other with a trumpet, a man on the keyboard and a bass player, who keeps spinning his instrument, like a toy, letting it go and catching it again, as if he's more interested in the spectacle than the music. Fragile, yellowed pages, the edges ragged as lace after years of handling, balance precariously on stands, ready to dip into old creases at any moment, fold into the past. Some of the manuscript is newer, handwritten in dark ink, with whole sections crossed out and rewritten underneath. Is there a composer among them? In the absence of radio stations, who'll remember their work? How will anyone ever know if a genius has been roaming the country, another Bach or Mozart? Maybe their tunes will be handed down to future generations until they become part of the landscape like the nursery rhymes, dances for fairs, another musical tradition. Known and sung by everyone without knowledge of their origins.

The musicians eye each other, nodding as they debate the speed, tapping their feet, setting a beat. They play a chord, a bright, strong combination of notes that shimmer and hang in the air, sending out a message. People are gathering, calling to each other to come and listen. I see Olisa, the woman who gave Delphine the dress.

She smiles and waves me over. 'I'm so glad you're here for this, Roza. It's always the highlight of the day. You're going to enjoy it so much.'

How can she possibly know what I would enjoy? 'Where's Delphine?'

'Oh, she's off somewhere with the girls. There they are, over the other side.' She lifts her arm and they wave back without interrupting their conversation. Their mouths are opening and shutting non-stop, as if there are too many words to exchange in too short a time. Delphine is pink and flushed, clearly delighted with her new friends.

She's doing so much better than I am. I need to find some people of my age, but I seem to have got stuck in some kind of fault line between Hector and Aashay, and even when I manage to escape for a short time, I just end up with more potential aunties and uncles.

I wonder why Popi isn't anywhere to be seen – he likes music. I wander around for a while, looking for him, but the stall with the carved animals is closed. The wooden top has been folded down and the bottom folded up so they meet in the middle in an ingenious locking system. It now resembles a wheelbarrow.

I find Aashay and Boris at the centre of a group of men. Aashay's busy strapping enormous, padded gloves on to Boris's wrists. So much for the ice-cream.

'Boris!' I call. 'What in the world are you doing?'

He looks up briefly and grins, waving his free arm. 'Hi, Roza. Look at me!'

'I am looking. Should you be doing this? You don't know how to box.'

'Aashay says he's going to teach me.'

But the other men don't give the impression they're there to watch a training session. They're jostling each other, laughing, making jokes. It's obvious that they're expecting a match and they don't rate his chances highly. 'Is this really a good idea?' I call anxiously.

'No probs,' he says. 'I'm good.'

'Have you checked in with Popi?'

'Roza, stop flurrying. Popi and I have communicated. We're in tune.'

I wander back to the musicians as they lurch precariously into a cheerful jazzy rhythm. They're not very good. I can hear mistakes, a slight dragging of the beat when the trumpet part gets difficult, a few false chords on the keyboard, a missed high note from the clarinet, but nobody seems to mind. I stand and watch for a while, wondering if I could go and join in. I'd like to, but I'm nervous about making a fool of myself. I make my way round the edge of the watching crowd towards Delphine, and people part easily to let me through. Some hold my plait briefly, letting it run through their fingers, as if they've never seen one before, offer me snippets of advice – 'Careful now, mind you don't slip'; 'You've got the thickest hair I've ever seen'; 'Watch out for Hank over there, he's a bit loose in the head' – and they give me chunks of meat, as I pass, cakes, biscuits, sweets. They're competing with each other to make the best offer, but I'm not hungry enough. The earlier meat and the coconut ice were enough to sustain me all day.

'Roza!' Moth appears at my side. 'Where is everyone?'

'I'm here,' I say. 'And Delphine is over there with her new friends.' I point her out to Moth. 'I can't find Popi, but Boris is about to take part in a boxing match.'

She looks horrified. 'Boxing? Seriously?'

'Well, you try stopping him. He's not taking any notice of me. Where's Lucia?'

'She's right behind me.'

'No, she isn't.'

Moth swings round. 'Yes, she is.'

But she's not. 'She was just there,' says Moth, her voice rising in panic. 'I told her to hold on to my skirt. Where's she gone? She's not safe!'

'I'm sure she is. Nobody here wishes us any harm.'

'Don't be ridiculous! How can you trust people you don't know?' She starts pushing her way through groups of people. 'Lucia!' The music stops while the musicians sort out a new piece, and Moth's shout echoes unexpectedly loudly. Other people hear her distress, realise something might be wrong, and start to call as well, their voices mingling with hers. They form a kind of humane harmony, not too distraught, believing that

Lucia is just around the corner. As if calling for a child is still a natural concept, as if they remember doing it in a long-distant past, or it's something they've always wanted to do but never actually experienced. 'Lucia! Lucia!'

We can hear the cries in the distance, travelling through the arena. Where's Popi? Why hasn't he heard and come running? What about Delphine? Is she so distracted she can't hear, or has she gone too? Removed by the hands of a stranger? Are we all going to disappear, one by one?

I follow Moth through the crowd, running faster and more frantically as people direct us to different places.

'Over there!'

'I saw her going that way!'

'I think she was by the sweet store.'

And then suddenly, just as Moth starts to scream in earnest, Lucia's head pops out from the crowd, her head just above their waists, her hands crammed with trinkets – surely not a china dog? – and her mouth bulging with sweets. 'I'm here, Moth,' she says. She's wearing a pink bonnet with ribbons hanging down the side, and holding the hand of a middle-aged man in brown corduroy trousers and wellington boots.

The music starts up again, as if in celebration.

Moth grabs her too roughly, pulling her away from the man. 'What were you thinking? You can't go wandering off on your own. I need to know where you are at all times.'

The man leans forward and speaks to us quietly. 'You need to be very aware,' he says. 'I found her walking towards the gates, hand in hand with a large woman who was feeding her sweets.'

Moth glares at him. 'If I see you anywhere near her again . . .' she says.

'Moth,' I say, 'this is the man who saved her.'

She raises her hand and, for one frantic moment, I think she's going to slap my face.

'Moth!'

Her hand falls and she stands swaying slightly, almost puzzled by her actions.

The man smiles kindly at me, bending over to disguise his threatening height. 'It's good,' he says. 'As long as the little one's all right.'

'Thank you for helping us,' I say. 'My mother's just wound up.'

He touches my arm gently and nods. 'Be careful,' he says. 'Don't trust anyone.'

Lucia starts to whine. 'I just—'

'I know,' I say. 'Someone showed you nice things.'

She nods. 'Lots and lots. Have one of these, Roza. They're licious.'

Another elderly man pats Lucia on the shoulder and smiles benignly at Moth. 'Don't fret,' he says. 'She's safe now. Most of us are watching. We're all thrilled to have her here.' He shuffles away, suddenly shy about his own confidence, still smiling to himself, as if referencing some memory that he's still replaying after years of isolation.

'Nice hat,' I say to Lucia.

She nods. 'I know,' she says.

'Come on, Moth,' I say, taking her by the arm while holding Lucia with my other hand. 'It's all OK. Let's go and listen to the music.'

They're starting to dance on a patch of grass in front of the musicians. Some older couples join hands in a line and move their feet together in an impressive display of learnt moves, while others jiggle around in a vaguely rhythmical way – as much as one can with the uncertainty of the beat – and wave their arms in the air. Some, mainly the younger ones, are more athletic, jumping up and down, swinging each other around with exuberance.

Delphine appears at my side, holding hands with Lancelot. 'Just watch and learn,' she says, alive with anticipation. 'My great talent is about to be revealed.'

'What happened to your friends?' I ask. 'The girls?'

She looks surprised. 'I don't know,' she says, looking round. 'I thought they were behind us.'

'Don't be fooled,' I say to Lancelot. 'She's never done dancing before.'

'No confusion,' he calls as he turns away. 'Everything rolls. There's no right way.'

'There you are,' says a voice behind me. I turn and it's Paula, with Joe beside her. 'We've been looking for you.'

'Hello,' I say, suddenly shy. 'Where did you disappear to?'

'We had to work,' says Joe. 'On our stall. We're specialists – swimwear. Our regular customers know where to find us, so we steer clear of the main action.'

'Swimwear? Seriously?' Fashion for the flood season, something attractive to put on when you go out to unblock the filters in the pouring rain?

'Don't you ever go to the coast?' says Paula. 'The seaside's a wonderful place in a drought.' She takes my right hand. 'Come on, let's join in.' Joe takes my left, and they lead me into the action.

'I don't know what to do,' I say.

'Copy us,' shouts Paula. 'You'll soon pick it up.'

We join the row of older ones, tag on to the end of a line, stepping forwards, backwards, half skipping, wriggling our hips, picking up the moves from everyone else. After a while, it becomes easier. The main thing is to move with the beat, although a lot of people don't seem to understand rhythm. I'm wearing far too many clothes – they're restricting my movements and I'm overheating.

Delphine swishes past me in her newly acquired dress, followed closely by Lancelot. 'Seems to me she does know what she's doing,' he yells, as he sways along in her wake, bouncing with the music, his face earnest with worship.

'Roza!' It's Aashay, at my shoulder, forcing me to let go of Joe and Paula.

I move out of the way of everyone and glare at him. 'Is Boris OK?'

'He's fine. Learning how to punch.'

'As if he needs to be taught,' I mutter. 'Is it safe to leave him?'

Aashay laughs. 'Who knows? I'm not going to tell him what to do. He can look after himself.' He grabs my hand and leaps into the dancing.

He's surprisingly good at it, jumping with unexpected grace, bending with double-jointed flexibility, leaping and twisting, his arms forming exotic shapes in the air over his head, winding himself up, like a coiled rope, then unwinding, grinning and serious at the same time, barely sweating with the exertion, every movement effortless and mesmerising.

I try to imitate him, but I can't keep up and I resent his expertise. How can he be good at everything? Where did he learn to do this? When he was in Brighton? How many girls has he danced with as he's wandered round the country, picking them up and discarding them, transferring his skills and moving on to the next, ever more successful as he goes?

Stop it! I say to myself. It's Hector I should be thinking of. He should be here now, dancing with me, not Aashay. I resent the fact that he's not, that he didn't set off earlier, that his holo is too small, that he's not the one teaching me how to do this. I pull away from Aashay and make my way to the edge of the crowd and stand for a while in the middle of the watchers, getting my breath back, watching Delphine and Lancelot, Paula and Joe.

Lancelot's hair swings as he moves, long and uncombed. It needs cutting. It's white-blond, glittering as it catches the light. For a moment, he seems to be performing for the benefit of a group of three women who look like him, who have the same hair. His mother, perhaps, and sisters? He waves at them and one of the younger ones waves back.

I stare at her. She has a way of moving, a bubbly confidence, that's familiar. Her fluffy hair shimmers in the afternoon light, a shining frame to her face. She has questioning eyes, too far away for me to see the colour, but they seem to reflect the sky, and as she starts to smile I can see two little dimples on either side of her mouth.

The sun loses its heat. Clouds threaten to engulf me. I forget to breathe.

Where's Moth? I need to find her, want to call out but hold my breath, terrified of drawing attention to myself. Why isn't Popi here?

I find Moth eventually, slightly back from the crowds. 'You need to come with me,' I say.

'Hello, Roza.' Lucia's face, sticky and grubby, appears from behind her. She's still munching sweets, grinning. Moth is holding her tightly by the hand.

'What's the urgency?' asks Moth.

I pull her to the front of the observers, where she can see. 'Look,' I say, indicating with my head.

'What am I looking at?'

I can't point. It would be too obvious. 'Over there, those three women standing on the edge, the ones with blonde hair.'

'Yes, I can see them. What am I looking for?'

'Who do they remind you of?'

She's puzzled. 'I don't know.'

'You do. Look again. Especially the youngest one.'

'Oh!' A sharp intake of breath.

She's seen it too. It's not just me. Lancelot's sister, presumably, slim and untidy, with white-blonde hair. She's staring at the dancing, laughing with everyone else, swaying with the music, childlike in her movements.

She looks exactly like Lucia.

15

'Find the others,' Moth says, trying to keep her voice down. We edge our way out of the crowd slowly, carefully. 'I'll wait for you outside the stadium. Quick as you can, but not too obvious. We mustn't look suspicious.'

'Make her keep the hat on,' I say.

'She's only been wearing it for the last hour. Her hair was in full view when we first arrived. Why hasn't anyone else noticed?'

'Maybe it was less obvious when we were all together.'

'Don't say anything to Boris or Delphine. We mustn't draw attention to ourselves.'

It's easy to say, but how am I going to persuade them to come? 'I'll need an explanation. What if anyone notices that something's going on?'

'Tell them I'm ill.'

'They've probably got medicines,' I say. 'They'll want to help.'

We pause for a moment. 'I'm infectious,' says Moth. 'That should do it. I can't imagine anyone wanting to risk coming near us. Our only solution is to go home.' She pulls Lucia's hand. 'Let's go outside for a bit,' she says.

Lucia is watching BENDY WENDY with intense curiosity. It's chuntering towards us, half empty, creaking, emanating a faintly unsavoury smell of rotting. It must be running on some kind of biofuel – beetroot, potatoes, turnips? The driver, a small, wiry man with luxuriant eyebrows, has spotted us and clearly believes that we are his next potential customers.

Lucia's eyes are fixed on the train. 'No,' she says. 'Let's stay here.'

'I'd prefer you to come with me.'

'Can't I stay with Roza?'

I smile at her. 'No, go with Moth for now. She's not feeling well and you'd be really good at looking after her.'

'But I want to go on the train.'

'Maybe later. There'll be plenty of time.'

Moth leads Lucia away, singing softly. They hold hands and swing their arms. It's all fun. No urgency. The train veers off to the side, clearly disappointed by our lack of interest. The driver yanks on a cord and releases a thin, reedy hoot.

I find Popi sitting in a fold-up chair next to the man who was selling the carved animals earlier, drinking coffee. Both are gazing outwards, as if they're intensely interested in what's going on around them, but it's an illusion. They're not seeing anything. They're engaged in a complicated conversation, gesturing freely as they talk. I've never seen Popi so animated.

'We travelled to Chicago to see the river sculptures when I was a child,' he's saying. 'It was like waking up after an operation, discovering that the world was constructed in a way that had previously been hidden. The fluidity of the shapes, the flow, the way every thread seemed to circle in on itself and merge with every other thread. Endlessly entwined.'

'I met Henry Walker – about thirty years ago. Fascinating guy. He carried a chisel in his pocket so he could work on any rocks or stones that caught his attention on his hikes. It really was sculpture in motion.'

'Popi!' I say, but he's too engrossed to hear. 'Popi!'

He finally allows himself to be interrupted, focuses his eyes and sees me. 'Roza! Come and join us. This is Phil. We have a lot in common, he and I.'

Phil chuckles. 'You're one of the daughters,' he says. 'Come and join us, my dear. You look like you could do with a nice drink.' He's an older model of Popi, maybe old enough to be his father, more shrivelled and gnome-like. His memories must go a long way back, before the beginning of the century, before the big floods, before the droughts, pre-Hoffman's.

I want to ask him why his coffee smells so much better than ours. 'We have to leave,' I say.

'Don't be absurd,' says Popi. 'We've only just arrived.'

'Really,' I say, looking into his eyes. 'We have to go.'

He starts to smile, then visibly deflates. 'Is something wrong?'

'Moth needs to talk to you,' I say.

He hesitates for one more second, then acknowledges the urgency. 'Right, then,' he says. 'We'd best get going.'

Phil stands up with him. 'It'll be the child,' he says.

I stare at him. Has it been obvious to him right from the beginning? Why didn't he say anything? 'No,' I say. 'It's just my mother. She's developed a nasty cough – we think she might be allergic to something here.'

'Moth?' says Popi, surprised. 'I've never—' Then he realises it must be more complicated and doesn't know how to continue. 'Oh, yes – of course. That time in – Wales . . .'

'People aren't rational with children around,' says Phil. 'I've seen it so many times. They can't keep their hands off them. It upsets the parents. You don't want strangers mauling your kids – it's not nice. Makes everyone cranky. You need to get off now. Wait till she's a bit older, or leave her at home with someone. That's what the others do.'

So there are other children. They just don't come to the fairs. Everyone feels safer with them out of the way, unseen, less of a temptation.

Popi gathers up his possessions. He takes bags of cakes and meat out of his rucksack, stuffs in some of Phil's carvings, then replaces the food, forcing the vel together at the top. 'We must meet up again,' he says. 'There's so much to talk about.'

'I've got to find the others,' I say, wishing he would speed up.

'Let's chat online,' says Phil. 'Here's my card – it's got my contact details on it.'

Popi studies it, clearly impressed. 'Your printer's still working, then.'

'I order the cards from Amazon,' says Phil, 'and they drop them off, little parachutes, straight to my door.' We stare at him, but then he winks. 'No,' he says sadly. 'I just go on mending the printer, same as everyone else. Spare parts, eh? Lifeblood of the age . . .'

Popi smiles and offers his hand. They shake, looking each other in the eye. 'I'm glad we met,' he says.

'Stay in touch,' says Phil.

Delphine is harder to persuade. I find her by the jewellery stall, standing closer than necessary to Lancelot. In the jaws of the lion, oblivious to the sharpness of his teeth. He's too smitten with Delphine to have noticed Lucia.

'Have you got all your things with you?' I ask Delphine.

She's examining a ring, trying it on different fingers and holding up her hand so she can admire it.

'All the gems are genuine.' says the man who owns the stall, watching Delphine's face almost hungrily.

'What do you think of this one?' Delphine wiggles the middle finger of her right hand where she's placed a ring with a large diamond and two fiercely blue sapphires. The stones drape over her finger diagonally.

I want to grab her and pull her away, straight out of the stadium, but I lean over to admire the ring. 'Lovely,' I say.

'Zowee,' says Lancelot, lacking the necessary enthusiasm. 'Do you want me to haggle for it?' He keeps raising his arm behind her, as if he's intending to ease her away, but I can see that all he really wants to do is to put it round her waist.

'You have beautiful hands,' says the stall owner, in a gravelly accent that's hard to place. 'Designed for jewellery.' He leans forward to peer at her, as if he's checking. Making sure she's the newcomer, the one with the little sister.

'Really?' says Delphine, flustered, not sure how to take this.

I touch her shoulder. 'I'm sorry,' I say, 'but we have to go.'

She looks round blankly. 'Don't be silly. It's far too early.'

'Moth and Popi need to speak to you.'

She frowns and studies my face. I can see she wants to argue, so I put on the gravest expression I can manage, hoping to convey the urgency of the situation. 'It's really important.'

'No,' she says. 'I'm busy right now.'

Lancelot gives in to temptation. His hand finally snakes round her waist and pulls her closer. He's offering her his support. She gazes up at him, her eyes slitted, her expression silky, apparently enjoying his proximity. She's learning fast.

The man behind the stall reaches out and encloses her hand within his own. 'If you want the ring,' he says, 'it's yours.' I can see the pleasure on his face as his battered, calloused fingers come into contact with the softness of her skin. His thumb twitches very slightly, as if he wants to stroke the back of her hand, but then he seems to decide that would be going too far and releases her.

She gives him a full smile this time, relaxed and friendly, her mouth widening, her teeth peeping through. The effect it has on him is extraordinary. His face seems to slip, to soften and melt.

She waves her hand in front of her and admires the ring again. 'Thank you,' she says.

He's an old man who must have spent many years alone. His fingernails are long and yellowed, his face scarred, his hair bushing out halfway down his back, wild and neglected. He gives the impression of extreme toughness, a man who would bow to no one, but I can see that he would give Delphine anything.

'Please come,' I say. 'Moth isn't well. She has a cough.'

She stares at me. 'Really?'

'It's good,' says Lancelot. 'We can go and find your parents, if you want.'

'I don't,' she says.

'You have to,' I say. How am I going to get rid of Lancelot? 'But I think it would be best if you come on your own. If Moth's ill, we have to be really careful. We've already been exposed to her germs, but you haven't, Lancelot. I'm sure your mother wouldn't be happy if you came into close contact with a new virus.'

He looks confused. 'I haven't got a mum,' he says.

I'm surprised. 'Oh, I thought I saw you waving to her – when you were dancing. She looked just like you.'

He thinks for a moment, frowning. 'No,' he says, 'that was my aunt. She's nothing like me.' He turns to Delphine. 'Best do what your sister says. Pick up the info. Hopefully, it'll just be an indoor thunderstorm. I'll meet you back by the meat stall.'

This isn't a good idea. When she doesn't turn up, he'll want to find her, possibly try to follow us. 'She may not manage that,' I say. 'If our parents decide to go home we'll have to go with them.'

Lancelot looks appalled. 'But I have to see you again,' he says to Delphine. 'Give me your address and I'll come for you. Doesn't matter if it's the other side of the country. I'll find you.'

I can see Delphine hesitating.

'Use Freight,' I say to her.

'Don't be gaga,' says Lancelot. 'Why wouldn't she use Highspeed?'

Delphine is staring at me in astonishment, but I look directly at Lancelot. 'Best to be careful,' I say. 'Freight's more secure and you don't need speed. You can stay in touch and work out where to meet again. It won't matter if it's slow to start with.'

'Oh,' he says. 'Yes, OK – but I'll have to remember to check. I hardly ever use Freight.' Would he really just give out his address to strangers? There are so many uncertainties.

I can see Delphine calculating, not certain what's going on, but finally aware of the need for caution. Lancelot is the first young guy she's ever met, and she's not going to give him up easily. In the end, she aligns her POD with his and keys in her Freight address. There's a short, low beep and she breaks contact. 'There,' she says. 'Friends for life.'

He smiles, sweetly shy, and leans towards her. 'We'll meet again,' he murmurs, loudly enough for me to hear. Then he whispers something I can't catch.

She smiles and gives him a kiss on the cheek. It's all very correct.

I pull her with me towards our bikes. 'What's going on?' she asks, glancing over her shoulder at the forlorn figure of Lancelot on the edge of the crowd.

'Wait until we've found Moth and Lucia. I don't want anyone else to hear.'

'They'd better not be asking us to leave. It would be so unfair.'

'He seems nice,' I say.

She shrugs. 'He's OK. Plenty more fish, though.'

I'm amazed at her composure. She's more poised, more in control than I would ever have expected.

Boris is the last to join us outside the stadium. He emerges through the exit with his bike, as instructed by Popi, accompanied by the three young guys who were playing ball earlier. Somehow, in the heightened atmosphere of the adventure, Boris has failed to pick up the shiver of tension in the air.

Moth, Delphine and I are huddling by the wall with Lucia, poised for flight, trying to make ourselves invisible among the rows of parked bicycles. There's nowhere to hide. The car parks open out into the distance, wide and desolate, thick with mud, green with moss. Pools of water have accumulated in the crumbling tarmac, their depth uncertain and threatening. When we arrived, the space had seemed gloriously open, an invitation to an exotic new world. Now it feels sinister.

Lucia is hopping between us, singing softly. '*Pussy cat, pussy cat, where have you been? I've been to London to visit the Queen.*'

Popi is propping up the tandem on its stand, watching Boris and his friends. He raises his eyebrows at Moth in exasperation.

Moth pushes Lucia behind me and walks towards Boris. He's leaning over his bike, fiddling with a cable on one of the wheels, while the other boys crowd around, not interested in any of us.

'Could be the drive-train,' says one.

'Neg,' says another. 'Wrong kind of vibes.'

'More like the bar-end shifters,' says the third.

'Boris!' says Moth, flashing a rare dazzling smile. 'There you are. Who are your friends?'

Boris stands up, runs his hand through his hair, and gestures to each in turn. 'Edgar, Krishan, Johnson.'

'How nice to meet you all,' says Moth, as if there's no urgency, as if we do this sort of thing all the time.

'She's good, isn't she?' mutters Popi. 'If theatres still existed, she'd be up there with the best of them.'

The three guys drop their heads and smile clumsily to themselves, murmuring their versions of hello. They haven't had the benefit of Popi and Moth's instructions on the etiquette of visiting uncles and aunties: look people in the eye; respond smartly; never mumble.

'*Pussy cat, pussy cat,*' sings Lucia. '*What did you there? I frightened a little mouse under her chair.*'

'Ssh,' says Delphine.

We hear the splash as Lucia jumps into a puddle and giggles. Water spatters the back of my legs, soaking through my trousers.

'Careful,' hisses Delphine. 'You nearly got my new dress.'

'Sing quietly,' I say to Lucia, turning round. I keep my voice low, wanting to radiate calmness and give the impression that everything's normal. If she picks up our anxiety, she'll become more uncooperative.

'What's going down?' asks Boris. 'There I was, all set for the boxing match, freshly trained, ready to slaughter Fantasmic Fred, when Popi comes along and pulls me out. It's ungood. We come here for merries and you go and spoil everything.'

'You didn't exactly rush, though, did you?' says Delphine, who's moved closer to me, trying to shield Lucia from the guys.

'Do you know how long it took to put the gloves on? Never mind take them off again. And the odds were improving as I stood there. They could judge my form just by looking at me.'

'Gambling?' says Moth.

'Nothing to do with me,' says Boris. 'If other people want to bet on my form, I can't stop them.' He's talking as if he hangs around with groups of betting people all the time, as if he has personal experience of human nature.

'It was still ten to one against,' mutters Krishan.

'Once they'd seen my technique, the whole thing would have rocketed into the stratosphere,' says Boris. 'They didn't know what was going to hit them – neither did Fantasmic Fred. And now they never will.'

'Did you see his biceps, though?' says Edgar. 'Like tree trunks, they were.'

'How can you have a technique,' says Delphine. 'when you've never done it before?'

'I really think you boys need to get back to your folks,' says Moth, her voice and manner too brisk for someone who's supposed to be ill. 'I don't know if Boris's father explained, but . . .' she glances round at us, suddenly aware that she's giving the wrong impression '. . . Roza, Boris's sister, is feeling unwell, and we don't want to pass on any infection. Of course, we don't know for certain, but it may be a virus and we can't take the risk. Thank you so much for accompanying Boris out here, but the time has come for you to part company. I'm sure we'll meet again at some later date, and then you can continue your fascinating discussions about bicycle parts and gambling.'

'What a loss to the country it was when the schools closed,' says Popi. 'Your mother would have made a superb headmistress.'

I experiment with a cough, dry and rasping, hoping nobody compares notes about who's ill. *Ring-a-ring of roses* – not bubonic plague, apparently, just a skipping rhyme. *Atishoo, atishoo* – still suitable for our age.

'Not bad,' says Popi, in my ear. 'Try to make it rougher.'

Moth flaps her hands at the boys, herding them back towards the entrance of the stadium. 'Come along now, boys. Your families wouldn't thank you for exposing yourselves to risk.'

'How old are they?' I ask Boris, as we watch them leave.

He stares at me as if I'm mad. 'How would I know?'

'You could have asked.'

'Why would I?'

'I'd like to know if they're pre-Hoffman or post. And where do they come from?'

'No idea,' he says. He pauses. 'Nowhere near us, though,' he adds, after a moment.

'Did you tell them where we live?' asks Popi, sharply.

Boris looks uncomfortable. 'No, of course not. I could just tell. They're not from round here. They don't know where anything is.'

Moth takes a deep breath. 'I thought they'd never go,' she says. 'Whatever are we going to do?'

Popi takes her hands. 'Don't fret,' he says. 'We'll sort it.'

'How exactly?' Her voice is tight and hard. 'Half the people here must have seen the resemblance. Once information is out, you can't just pull it back in and file it away. It'll seep into the air.'

'Could we talk to Lancelot's family?' I suggest. 'They might be reasonable.'

'Would we be reasonable if we found someone had adopted the real Lucia?' says Moth. 'Are we likely to say, "You've done a good job, you might as well keep her"?'

'The fact remains,' says Popi, 'that she's not the real Lucia. There's always been a possibility that her parents would turn up one day.'

'Oh, I see,' says Moth. 'You think we should give her back. We don't know anything about these people, but you want us to hand over Lucia – our Lucia – to them. How could we possibly trust anyone careless enough to lose their daughter in the first place?'

'That's not entirely fair,' says Popi. 'Things happen that are out of our control.'

'And we lost the real Lucia,' says Boris.

'She might not be the mother,' I say. 'She could just be a relative, which would make it easier.'

'They'd still have a claim over her,' says Delphine.

'We're never going to know unless we go back and talk to the family,' says Moth. 'And we can't do that.'

'Did the woman look nice?' asks Boris.

'What kind of question is that?' says Delphine. 'Some people are just good at pretending.'

'Let's face it,' I say, 'the nicest person in the world is not going to hand over her children to anyone. Any more than you would willingly give away the real Lucia.'

Lucia, who has been running backwards and forwards between two posts, timing herself with her POD, suddenly pushes herself between Moth and Popi.

'Stop it, Lucia!' says Moth. 'Go and play over there.'

'What do you mean, "the real Lucia"? Is that me?' she asks. 'Or am I just pretend?'

We stare at her. We really should have considered the possibility that she would listen.

'Of course you're the real Lucia,' says Moth, putting her arm round her shoulders and drawing her close. 'The one and only.'

'Delphine,' says Popi, 'can you play with Lucia? Preferably out of earshot.' He gestures vaguely to an area of weeds and puddles.

'Right,' says Delphine. 'Now I'm just the babysitter, not important enough to have a say in decisions.'

'We have to leave,' says Moth, suddenly decisive.

Popi thinks for a few seconds, then nods. 'There isn't much else we can do.'

Moth starts checking rucksacks, putting things into the panniers, making sure everything is secure.

'I want to go on the train,' says Lucia. 'You said we could, Roza.'

'Not now,' says Moth.

'Why not?'

Moth rubs Lucia's cheek. 'Sometimes,' she says, 'we can't always do what we want. I'll explain more to you when we're home, but right now, it's important that we leave as quickly as possible.'

Lucia searches her face. 'OK,' she says. 'Can we come back another time?'

'Of course. You'll be able to go on the train then.'

She's surprisingly convincing for someone who's avoiding the truth.

'The man in the moon,' says Lucia, suddenly. 'Does he know we're going?'

I'd forgotten about Aashay.

Popi looks up from his POD. 'No,' he says. 'We don't have time to go and find him.' He wants to leave him behind. It's a good opportunity to lose him.

'Poor Aashay,' says Moth, quietly.

'He can take care of himself,' says Popi. 'Our priority is Lucia and the rest of the family. He knows where to find us.'

Is he thinking what I'm thinking? Aashay knows Lucia and he must know Lancelot's family. Why didn't he see the resemblance? Or did he?

Did he lead us to the fair for a reason?

16

We pedal west in silence. The thickening *cirrus fibratus* unfurls upwards and outwards in long, misty streaks, spreading across the sky, like a half-open fan, converging on the horizon. Boris and Delphine are ahead of me, but I'm not trying to catch up. We're too disappointed to talk. I put my head down and watch my feet rotating while the road slips away beneath me.

Little Bo Peep has lost her sheep and doesn't know where to find them . . .

Everything has changed. Nothing can be the same again.

We're returning to our old, predictable world, our known, safe existence . . . *Leave them alone and they'll come home, bringing their tails behind them*. Behind us is a newly discovered paradise, a dangerous but glittering place where anything is possible, unexplored territory where the air itself shivers with hidden potential. Are we right to abandon it, to reject everything so readily? We were bursting with naïve exuberance when we set off this morning and now it's all gone. Now we're sneaking off, pulling our tails with us, heading back to stagnation. We want to stay, but no one can find a way to do it without jeopardising the entire family.

I messaged Hector just before we left. 'Heading home. Tell you eye to eye.'

His reply came through as we cycled out of the Ricoh car park, still in range of the router. I stopped to listen to it, letting the others overtake.

He's guessed something's wrong. 'Is all well? Have you been poisoned by the fare at the fair? Are you escaping the attention of unwanted suitors? Are they littering the ground as they fall at your feet, swearing undying love? Resist them, Roza, resist them.

I'm the slade for you.' He's bouncing back, determined to make amends for his lapse of communication, but still anxious about Aashay.

'Nothing to fear. Can't stop now. See you tomorrow.'

I concentrate on the movement of my pedals and the swish of the tyres, on keeping upright as I bump and sway through a particularly bad cluster of potholes. We're saving Lucia, I say to myself. We can't turn her over to strangers, even if she is related to them. It wouldn't be right. She belongs with us. She can make her own decisions when she's older, but she needs our protection now.

Boris will find a way back. And Delphine. They won't be able to stay away for long, now they know there's an alternative world. The possibilities are endless: fun, gossip, girlfriends, boyfriends. How many internet addresses have they collected? How many people already have their contact details?

They'll become different people. Once you know something, you can't unknow it. It's like standing in water. I've been out with Popi once or twice, after the first sweep of the floods, but before the water has completely cleared, to remove debris from the entrance to Wyoming. I know how it feels. You think you can keep your feet on the ground, but the power of the current sweeps you along and you move without realising. Popi always insists on a safety harness, fixing us to the side of the building. Now we've been unclipped, allowed to drift. Do Boris and Delphine know it's happening?

Our acquaintance with Hector brought a shift in our outlook, a change in our expectations, but the arrival of Aashay has speeded up the process. I heard Boris talking with Aashay the night before we left.

'Why would you want to go to Brighton?' asked Aashay.

'It's where the saw's cutting,' said Boris. 'Everyone knows that.'

'Who's everyone?'

'You know, everyone. And we have to go, don't we? It's the law. Find the girls, the señoritas, the *bakku-shan* – that's Japanese.'

'Yeah, yeah.' Aashay never reacts well to the suggestion that he might not know something. 'But it's not the Brighton women you're after.'

'Are there others?'

Aashay laughed. 'Wake up, Boris, and smell the snow on the wind. You're only hearing what they want you to hear. There's a whole world out there and it's not Brighton.'

'What do you mean?'

'Think about it. How far away is France? We're only separated by the Channel – a thin strip of water – and then there's Ireland, not much further, and you know the language.'

They moved out of earshot. I was shocked. France? Ireland? Crossing forbidden boundaries? Does Aashay go to these places? Why is he suggesting them to Boris? Then I was annoyed. He was just spinning outlandish tales, nursery rhymes in another guise, giving Boris the impression that the world is smaller and more attainable than we've been led to believe, pretending anything is possible. He needed to be challenged. But I could hardly say that to Boris without letting on that I'd been listening.

Aashay has made us doubt our place in the world. 'Follow the storms,' he was saying. 'Don't hibernate during the floods. Swim, float, go with the current.'

Is that possible?

I'm starting to think differently too, changing without intending to.

When I saw Popi talking to Phil, I caught a glimpse of the man he must have been, a man I've never known. How easy is it to bury a whole portion of your personality? Now he's opened the door a crack, will he ever be able to push everything back in again?

And Moth. Trapped by her devotion to Lucia. She can't realistically meet these people again for another eleven years, until Lucia is eighteen and can make her own decisions. It's a long time. Even visiting the aunties and uncles might have to stop, to be on the safe side, isolating Moth and Popi more and more. Moth's never trusted online relationships, finds chat boring. Did the excitement of the fair touch her, wake her up a little, cut through her cynicism?

An alarming thought occurs to me. Will it be safe for me to go to Brighton with Hector now? What if Lancelot's family live there or are known there?

A sudden blast of wind catches me and nearly knocks me off my bicycle. I look up at the sky with surprise. Despite the tranquillity of the weather where we've come from, clouds are congregating above us, racing in from the east. They're stacking up into towering layers of *cumulonimbus* – I'm not sure yet if it's *calvus* or *capillatus* – a sign of impending rain. This is unexpected and alarming. We won't be able to cycle through serious rain or hail. We'd be swept off the motorway.

Hearing a shout, I brake hurriedly and turn round.

Popi and Moth have stopped. They're both gesturing wildly, yelling something indistinguishable, clearly summoning us. I check ahead. Delphine's already coming back towards me, but Boris seems oblivious.

I cup my hands round my mouth. 'Boris!'

He glances at me over his shoulder, wobbles slightly, and carries on. I wave my arm, beckoning him with a large movement that he can't misinterpret. Delphine pulls up beside me, wipes the sweat off her forehead dramatically and rolls her eyes. 'He's not listening,' she says.

'Boris!' I shout again. 'Stop!'

He turns away, puts his head down and starts pedalling furiously away from us.

'No idea why he's being so bog-brained,' says Delphine.

'It's a protest,' I say. 'He's annoyed about having to leave the fair.'

'We're all annoyed,' she says. 'Doesn't mean we behave like delinquent sheep.'

After a few more seconds, he turns his bike in a tight curve and starts to cycle back towards us, very fast, as if he's racing an invisible rival.

'Woolski,' says Delphine with contempt, and sets off back to Moth and Popi without waiting.

Boris is heading directly for me, not slowing down, apparently planning a spectacular collision. I stand my ground, knowing he intends to miss. He slams on his brakes at the last minute and swings to the left, nearly overbalancing as he skids to a halt. He manages to recover without falling over and starts to circle me, laughing. 'Bet you thought I'd get you.'

'Feeling better now?' I say, in a tolerant voice that I know will infuriate him.

He wobbles, sticks out his knees and regains his balance. 'What's going on?'

'I imagine Popi wants us to leave the motorway. He'll be worrying about the weather.'

We return to where the others are waiting. The light is rapidly thinning as the clouds spread ominously above us, creating the uncertainty of a false dusk.

'Look!' says Popi, as we reach him. He's pointing at the over-grown landscape beyond the barriers.

At first I can't see anything. But then – a faint flicker. 'A light!' says Boris. A glimpse in the distance, between the trees.

'What do you think it is?' I peer through the gloom, straining my eyes, longing to see a building. It's possible to imagine all sorts of things in the semi-darkness.

'Not sure,' says Popi. 'It could just be a reflection from the sun.'

'There isn't any sun,' I say. 'It's all gone.'

'Could it be a waystation?' asks Delphine.

'Unlikely,' says Popi. 'There weren't any waystations this close to the city. People preferred hotels.'

'So what's there?' I say. 'A block of flats like ours? People?'

'Let's go and take a look,' says Boris.

I turn to Moth. She's unusually silent, not yet recovered from the shock of discovering that we could lose Lucia. She sees me observing her, wriggles her shoulders slightly, as if shifting an unnecessary weight, and nods. 'What choice do we have? We can't stay here.'

Boris is fiddling with his POD. No point. He's never going to get connection out here in the open. When the motorway maintenance men and breakdown services died, the passwords would have died with them.

'It's north, maybe north-west, according to the compass.' Popi slips a cloth map from the outer pocket of his rucksack, unfolds it, spreads it out over his handlebars and peers down. He stabs at the map with his forefinger on a place called Coleshill. 'That's where I reckon it's coming from. If we take that exit, just ahead, and turn right on the roundabout, we should see it. Somewhere off that road.' He bends down closer to read the number. 'The A446.'

I've never heard of Coleshill.

'It's low ground and there's a lake over there that isn't on the map,' says Moth, pointing over the barrier. 'What about flash floods?'

A low, sinister growl echoes through the air, rolling around as if it's specifically searching for us, tumbling across the sky like wooden toy bricks, thrown to the floor by a child in a prolonged display of petulance.

'Put your waterproofs on,' says Popi. 'We're in for a soaking.'

Lucia has gone to sleep and her head is lolling sideways against the headrest, her mouth slack and slightly open, a pinkish dribble from a half-sucked sweet snaking out of one corner. I help Moth put her into her waterproof, unfolding her arms, easing the coat over, sealing the vel so there aren't any gaps, and smoothing the hood as close to her head as possible. She moans a little, resists us, then settles back into sleep.

'How far away is the light?' I ask.

'Hard to say,' says Popi. 'Further than we think, though. These things are deceptive, especially through rain.'

'I'll scout ahead,' says Boris. 'When I've reconnoitred, I'll come back for you.'

'It's not a film,' I say. 'We're not an army.'

'I'll go with you,' says Delphine. 'In case you get lost.'

'No,' says Moth. 'We should stick—'

But they've already gone, shooting ahead and veering off to the left, up the slip-road and out of sight. A gust of wind, sharp and chilly, leaps over the barriers and throws itself against us, echoing along the motorway, booming in our ears.

We get back on our bikes. I can see the anxiety in Popi's face. The wind is trying to prevent us leaving the motorway, hurling powerful blasts from the side, tugging at our clothes, attempting to wrestle us from our bikes. The rain starts, thin, sharp needles, stinging my face.

Moth leads the way. Popi's struggling to keep the tandem upright, so I stay behind in case he overbalances. Like Moth, I'm nervous about leaving the motorway, getting caught on narrow roads, trapped if the water rises and sweeps down on us. The light has nearly gone and we might not be able to see anything at all on a lower level. But at least there's a possibility of safety. If there's a light, there's a generator, which must be on higher ground, protected from flooding. Otherwise the renewables would have given up years ago.

We have to go uphill on the slip-road, so we set off in low gear, shifting down, standing on our pedals to create momentum. There's a fierce ache in my back and the muscles in my legs are on fire, the skin hot and tender against my trousers. I fix my eyes on Moth's rear wheel just in front and keep going.

We level out as we approach the roundabout and cycling becomes easier. Wind whips through the surrounding trees, bois-terous and threatening, making it hard for us to talk. We take the right turn and follow the road away from the motorway. It's darker here, narrower and less open. I peer ahead through the half-light, worried about holes, about the angle of the road. 'Keep it slow, Nikolai,' calls Moth. 'It's hard to see.'

After some distance, Boris and Delphine suddenly appear ahead of us, bursting out of the shadows with an unexpected exuberance. 'We've found it!' calls Delphine, her voice muffled against the force of the rain. 'It's a kind of warehouse on stilts, enormous, goes on for ever. That's how we could see it from the motorway. It's mostly hidden by trees, so you'd only know it was there in the dark – when the lights come on.'

'Any sign of people?' asks Popi.

'Not that I could see,' says Boris, pulling up beside us. 'It looked deserted.'

But the solar panels wouldn't still be operating without people. Renewables work only with someone to look after them, to clean them, to repair wind damage and the kinks in the wires. Nothing will last for twenty years without attention.

'High land and a roof,' says Moth. 'That's all we need. We've got enough food and warm clothes to wait out the storm.'

'How much further?' asks Popi.

'Just round the corner. We're nearly there.'

'Then I think it would be safer to walk.'

We dismount and follow Boris and Delphine cautiously. The road is overhung by trees and thicker mud makes it harder to work out where to tread. 'Follow Boris's tracks,' I suggest. But it's a ridiculous suggestion. Water is running through the mud and erasing any footsteps as soon as they appear. A flash of lightning opens up the scene in front of us, illuminating our surroundings, giving us a moment of clarity.

We continue in single file. Boris at the front, then me, Delphine and Moth, with Popi at the rear, balancing the tandem so that Lucia can't fall out of her seat. The rain is dense and penetrating, pounding against my face with numbing force. My hands, inside the waterproof gloves, are trembling with cold. I can see the light ahead. 'Careful,' says Popi, in a low voice. 'Don't go charging in.'

We're all aware of the need for caution. Now that we've found the source of light, our anticipation has given way to uncertainty. We don't know who's there. Will they be friendly or hostile? We'd whisper if we could, but then it would be impossible to hear each other inside our hoods, where the roar of the rain is amplified. Are we trespassing or seeking sanctuary? We push our bikes cautiously forward and find ourselves in an open area, surrounded by overgrown grass. There's an enormous warehouse in front of us, resting on concrete pillars.

It hovers above us, a rectangular spaceship, so vast that we can't see the end of it in either direction. There's a platform running along the side of the building, halfway up, and lamps have been attached at regular intervals to the metal railings. They flicker through the rain, like landing lights.

Another flash of lightning, as if someone's pressed a switch, and the building takes on an ethereal appearance, becomes a castle in the air. The pillars spread out before us like a forest, curiously spindly, but clearly much stronger than they look. This was designed for chaotic weather patterns, expected to stand tall for a long time. Are the lamps there as beacons for passing drones? A message to the silent computers on satellites that no longer work or even watching eyes further out in the solar system? We're here. We're surviving. Come and support us, since the rest of the world has abandoned us.

We huddle together and stare up at it. The rain eases as we stand there, and a welcome hush settles over us, which we're reluctant to break.

'Crumbs,' says Moth, eventually.

I push back my hood and experience a rush of fresh air, soft rain on my head.

'Well,' says Popi, after a while. 'I wasn't exactly expecting this.'

'What do you think it's for?' asks Boris.

'It's Grand Central Station,' says a man's voice. 'An Internet Central.'

The voice comes as a shock and our heads swivel, as we try to locate its source.

'Over here,' he says. The voice must be coming from someone on the platform, but we're blinded by the lights. After a few seconds, a stretch of them goes out with a click. 'Is that better?' The voice is deep, old, woody.

We can just see his outline. Enough to identify a stooped man with hair standing out from his head in a burst of dishevelled curls, leaning forward over the railings. It's impossible to know if he's smiling or snarling at us.

There's a moment of silence, then Popi pushes the tandem towards me. 'Hold on to this,' he mutters. He steps forward. 'Hello! We're the Polanskis.' Was it only this morning that Moth said exactly the same thing when we arrived at the fair? It seems so long ago. 'I'm sorry to intrude, but we're looking for somewhere to shelter. There don't seem to be any waystations around these parts, and I'm anxious to protect my family from the weather.'

'How many of you are there?'

'There's me, Nikolai, my wife, Bess, and our four children.'

'Children?' There's a brief silence. 'You've got children?'

He sounds as if he doesn't believe Popi.

'My nose is wet.' Lucia's voice carries through the air with a sharp clarity, unmistakably childish. She's sitting up, gazing around with an expression of annoyance. 'Can we go on the train now?' She pushes the hood off her head.

The man peers out at us more intently, searching for Lucia. When he's located her, he stares for several seconds in silence. 'Of course you must come in,' he says more warmly. 'It's not often I get visitors. You can't stay out there in the rain. It floods, you know. Not safe at all. There's plenty of room for you to stay overnight or until the storm passes.' He produces a curious croaking sound that rises and falls in volume.

'I think he's laughing,' mutters Moth.

Popi looks around. 'I can't seem to see—'

'On your right,' says the man. 'There's a doorway.'

We see it. Four of the pillars are blocked in by thick plastic walls, which form a kind of entrance hall. At ground level, there's a reinforced door, so well sealed that it's almost invisible. As we watch, the door swings open, revealing stairs that head upwards into darkness. It's in good condition, clearly maintained, designed to withstand the weight of water.

'His remote controls still work, then,' says Boris. 'Wonder where he gets the parts.'

'He'll have supplies,' says Popi. 'A place like this would have been built for self-sufficiency, spare parts for at least a hundred years, I'd have thought.'

'What do we do with the bikes?' asks Moth, looking up at the man on the balcony.

'You'll have to bring them up,' says the man. 'Otherwise the floods'll take them. You don't want to wake up in the morning and find them gone.' He laughs again, more than seems necessary, as if something hilarious is going on that we don't know about. He doesn't seem quite normal.

'I'm getting down,' says Lucia, bouncing in her seat, clearly refreshed by her long sleep.

'Careful!' I say sharply, as the tandem sways dangerously. Boris grabs it and helps me hold it upright.

'Well, keep it still, then,' she says, unclipping her safety harness and climbing down. 'Where are we?'

'Where indeed?' says Moth.

Popi and Boris pick up the tandem, ready to lift it over the threshold, and pause in front of the dark entrance before going in. The stairs are just visible, wide and straight.

'Let's hope we don't have to make a quick getaway,' says Boris.

We should have thought about this. We're voluntarily entering an unfamiliar building at the invitation of an old man we know nothing about, maybe only because we have Lucia with us. *Come into my parlour, says the spider to the fly*. The whole world wants children and he's probably no exception.

I'm cold, wet and exhausted. I just want to crawl back to our old way of life. At least there was an order to everything in it, predictability. We knew where we were and what was going on.

'Come on, Boris, let's get on with it,' says Popi. 'Moth, if you and the girls can get the rest of the bikes inside, Boris and I'll start carrying them up. There must be a space at the top of the stairs where we can leave them. The sooner we can close the door, the better.' He steps into the entrance, lifting his end of the tandem. 'I never thought I'd miss Aashay,' he says.

A light comes on and we can now see up to a landing, with a second flight of stairs beyond. 'Welcome to Amazon,' says a friendly woman's voice. 'I hope you enjoy your visit.'

Popi and Boris nearly drop the bike. 'Who said that?' says Lucia, looking round in surprise.

'It's automated,' says Boris. 'Set up ages ago to welcome visitors.'

Moth laughs. 'Amazon,' she says. 'I don't believe it. What are they doing here?'

Popi pauses before climbing the stairs. 'It can't be one of their warehouses, can it? It's not big enough.'

'It's gigantic,' I say.

'We'd have seen it from Coventry if it was Amazon,' says Moth. 'You could buy cars from them, prefab houses, personal drones. Their warehouses were like cities. I went round one once – they did tours. On a train. They had restaurants where you could stop and rest. But most of them were destroyed post-Hoffman's, I think. Too low on the ground. No one left to manage the flood defences.'

'Where are my sweets?' asks Lucia. 'I've lost them.' Her voice rises, indignant and shrill.

Moth takes off her rucksack and rummages through it. 'Here,' she says, pulling out a lollipop and handing it to Lucia. Lucia takes it, but doesn't put it in her mouth. She leans against Moth and subsides into a series of deep yawns.

'We'll all have something to eat in a bit,' I say, lifting my bike up over the step. 'Can you give me a hand?' I say to Delphine.

'It's all that stimulation,' says Moth. 'We're not used to it.' She sounds exhausted. 'And I can't even begin to calculate how many miles we've cycled today.'

We manoeuvre all the bikes into the entrance and prop them against the walls, waiting for Popi and Boris to carry them upstairs.

'Please shut and seal the door behind you,' says the voice, pleasantly.

'Of course I will,' says Moth, equally politely.

The old man is waiting for us at the top. 'Good, good,' he says. 'Thank you for locking up. That'll save me time later.' Close up, he's even more peculiar, with a long beard and a back so badly hunched that he can't stand up straight. His natural position seems to be leaning forward with his face down, as if he finds the floor endlessly fascinating. *There was a crooked man, who walked a crooked mile, Who found a crooked sixpence upon a crooked stile . . .* To look at us, he has to force his head up at an awkward angle.

'Osteoporosis,' he says to Delphine, who's openly staring at him. 'They didn't send the preventive medicine until it was too late. Once the bones crumble, there's not much you can do about it. Those drops – they get worse and worse. They'll be the death of me.' He chuckles. 'Literally.'

We're in a kind of hallway at the top of the stairs, small and enclosed, with several doors leading off. *He bought a crooked cat, which caught a crooked mouse, And they all lived together in a little crooked house.* 'I'm Dan,' he says. 'As in Desperate, if you know what I mean.'

Delphine and I look at each other and raise our eyebrows. What is he talking about?

'In what way are you desperate?' asks Boris. 'Or is that your surname? Dan Desperate?'

The man starts to laugh, on and on, rising to a high-pitched cackle and ending with a a breathless cough. We watch while he pummels his chest, wondering whether or not we should help. Eventually he stops, sways on his feet and takes deep, heavy breaths.

'Are you all right?' asks Moth uncertainly.

'Oh, yes,' he says. 'No probs. I just love your boy's humour. Dan Desperate, indeed.' He almost laughs again, but stops himself. 'I was jesting. Everyone's heard of Desperate Dan. Haven't they? I mean, I know you're all babies, with not even the memory of a smell from the old world, but even so, I'd have thought you'd have heard of him. Comics, you see. On paper. Once upon a time, before even I was born, that was the only entertainment.'

'We don't often read on paper,' I say. 'There's a limited supply.'

He raises his head and stares at me. He seems to be looking beyond my face, trying to interpret my thoughts. 'Never mind,' he says. 'I'm too old to be desperate. I like the name, that's all. Just call me Dan.'

He opens one of the doors and we follow him through into a

dimly lit room. In front of us, visible in the half-light, are rows and rows of computers, set out like houses in streets. They're bristling with wires and connections, linked to each other, bonded with thick coils of wires. The cables sneak through the corridors between the machines, creeping around the vast space like giant multi-coloured snakes, slithering, silently hissing. At intervals, between the computers, on recessed walls, there are thousands of switches. I've never seen so many in my life.

'Zowee!' says Boris.

'I'd agree with that,' says Popi.

'What is this place?' I ask.

'If it's a Grand Central Station,' says Moth, 'what's it got to do with Amazon?'

He seems pleased that she's asked. 'Amazon sponsor Grand Central, so we allow them to put their onformation centre on the same premises – right up at the far end. Don't hardly go up there now, though. Too far to walk and the trolleys aren't functioning like they used to. Don't want to get stranded – I'd die of starvation before I could get back. We're the biggest of the three Grand Centrals, see. The Big Daddy.'

'When you say "we", does that mean you're not alone here?' asks Moth, looking round as if she is expecting to see people hiding in the shadows, hordes of unknown watchers, ready to race out and mug us, beat us up, murder us. Unlikely, I'd say. We'd have seen some evidence of their presence.

He ignores the question. 'Everything's stored here, linked, sent out again. We're the network that runs the networks that run the networks.' He beams, proud of his empire.

'But there are hardly any networks left now,' I say.

'Course there are, gorgeous,' he says.

I stare at him, momentarily diverted. Is he talking to me? I cringe with embarrassment. I might be able to cope with compliments if I'm given the chance, but it's impossible to know how to react if they come from a man called Desperate Dan – maybe – who can't stand up straight and therefore can't see me accurately anyway.

'Connection is life,' he says, as if he's quoting a slogan. 'You've got a Personal Online Device, I've got one, everyone's got one. Mine's in my arm – that's what they did then before they realised it could affect the nerves – but yours are on your wrists. Even your little sister's got a POD. As long as there are people in the country, we can connect.'

'You still need passwords,' says Delphine.

He stares at her. 'Everyone knows the passwords,' he says.

'We don't,' I say.

'Amazon,' says Moth, gently. 'I'd almost forgotten.'

'You used to worry they were taking over the world,' says Popi.

'Maybe I was wrong to worry.' She sighs. 'Let's face it, they could hardly have made things worse than they are now.'

'It's all a bit sad, isn't it?' says Popi. 'This would have been an international hub once. Now it's just a redundant shell, sitting here with nothing to do.'

'We connect,' says Dan.

'But who with?'

'Everyone. There are two other Grand Centrals – St Andrews in the north, High Wycombe near London – then the smaller stations, on the branch lines. Everything comes through here – we're in the middle, see. Charlie in St Andrews, Ben in High Wycombe, they're my mates. We were here right at the beginning, all three of us. Survived the plague – protected by the computers. They give off these waves, you know, keep us safe. Can you hear the hum? It gets in your ears, washes away the germs. They've kept me and Charlie and Ben together. Course we connect. We're not stupid.'

He seems to stretch as he tells us this, growing with importance, expanding outwards as well as upwards. He smiles at us, delighted with himself. Does he really believe that's why he didn't die of Hoffman's?

17

We wander up and down between the rows of computers, trying to find a large enough area to accommodate us all. We're tired and hungry and no longer interested in the novelty of our surroundings.

'This'll do,' says Popi, stopping at a crossroads, a meeting point where four separate pathways converge.

Moth looks around doubtfully. 'Do you really think it's big enough?'

'It's good,' says Boris. 'At least we can all lie down.'

'I'm having that path,' says Lucia, pointing to one corridor.

'Stay close,' says Moth, putting down her bags and stripping off her waterproofs.

We drop everything with gratitude and Popi finds a groundsheet in his rucksack, which he spreads out in the centre. We make ourselves as comfortable as possible, discarding our waterproofs on the surrounding floor, using our bags as cushions, while Delphine and Moth sort out the food. There's plenty of it, mostly the same as this morning, but there are a few interesting additions. Boris, rather unexpectedly, produces a large pile of meat, neatly sliced.

'Boris!' I say. 'This is so generous of you. Are you sure?'

'They gave me too much,' he said, 'so I put this aside for later.'

I stare at him. 'Breadcrumbs!' I say. 'I didn't know you had a "full" button.'

'And you're prepared to share it with us?' asks Delphine, with interest, watching him hand it around.

'Only to those among us who are nice to me,' he says mildly. 'Anyway, I don't know how long it lasts before it goes off.'

'Oh, it'll be all right for a day or two,' says Moth, 'providing it's well cooked.'

Dan appears along one of the corridors, carrying a pile of coloured blankets. His beard looks smaller and neater than before, as if he's trimmed it. 'Thought you'd like to be a bit more comfortable,' he says, dropping them in a pile.

'Oh,' says Moth. 'That's kind of you. Tartan. I haven't seen that since I was a child. It went out of fashion long before Hoffman's.'

'Provided right at the beginning,' says Dan, 'so we could have picnics under the stilts, I suppose. Had their heads in the clouds, those designers. There's even a barbecue at the end of the building. Only been there once. Too far, even on a trolley.'

'Can we use the internet?' I ask. I need to contact Hector.

He stares at me, genuine confusion clouding his eyes. 'That's what the computers are for.'

'But what about the password?'

He smiles kindly, as if he's talking to someone of limited intelligence. 'I've told you, it's accessible to all. You won't need a password here. We're Grand Central. We supply routers right across the country. We enable.' That must have been another slogan once. He's heard it so often, he believes it. He shuffles away, with a sense of bafflement rather than annoyance. He's used to being the authority. He can't understand why we would question him.

'It makes me feel young again,' says Popi. 'You didn't need passwords in public places then. Or not often, anyway.'

'So what changed?' asks Delphine.

'Privacy laws. Too much stuff being listened to by people who shouldn't have been listening. So they introduced passwords. And then they realised that actually they needed to overhear conversations. But that's government for you. One step behind, never out there, ready in advance.'

'Who'd want to listen to other people's conversations?' asks Boris.

'Oh, come on, Boris,' says Popi. 'Two words. James. Bond.'

'How do you think they fought terrorism?' says Moth. 'Remember the film *The Day of the Cut-off* – mutual destruction by disablement?' She shakes one of the blankets. Dead spiders fly out and scatter all over the floor, along with other unidentifiable black specks, and a damp musty smell fills the space. 'Hmm,' she says. 'I suspect Dan's not servicing the dust machines.'

'Grots,' says Delphine, wrinkling her nose.

'The blankets will come in handy, though,' says Moth, 'for sleeping. Shall we drape them over the computers?' she asks Popi. 'Give them a chance to air?'

'We might as well,' says Boris. 'It's not like the computers are loggable.'

'You don't know that for certain,' says Popi.

'Dan believes in them,' says Moth. 'And we mustn't destroy the purpose of his existence.'

Boris is not sympathetic. 'He'll have to get a grasp on the real some time soon.'

'Why? If he's happy, believing he's useful, what does it matter?'

'Don't jump to the wrong conclusion just because you don't find him personally credible,' says Popi. 'There's some connection going on. We just don't know how much.'

'So is it safe to cover them up?' says Moth.

'It can't make that much difference,' he says, picking up a blanket. 'There are plenty of computers to go round.'

Dan appears round a corner, carrying a tray with glasses of water. 'Here we are,' he says. 'I expect you're all thirsty after your ride.'

'Whizzo,' says Boris. 'Water! I haven't seen any of that for at least thirty minutes.'

'Boris!' says Moth. 'Manners.'

'Sorry,' he says, and winks at me.

'Actually, a drink would be good,' says Delphine. 'I'm really hot.'

The computers, quietly busy, are generating heat. The background hum creeps up on you, a low-level throbbing that might be there or might not, until it forces its attention on your ears, and then it's everywhere, a soft vibration, a song without words, booming gently in your head.

'Have one, Dan,' says Moth, offering a container of raspberry cakes. He stares at them greedily, then takes two. He studies them both for a few seconds, weighing them in his hand, as if he can't decide where to start, then bites into one. He eats with his mouth open, bits spilling out and landing in his beard. Before he starts on the second, he wipes the crumbs from his hands and scatters them everywhere, as if he's outside. It's at this point that I realise how dirty the floor is. I edge my legs on to the groundsheet carefully, conscious of all the germs that must have accumulated over many years. Who knows when the dusting machines packed up?

'Yes, good,' says Dan. 'Where do you get the sugar?'

'The drops,' says Moth. 'But not as often, these days, so I don't know how much longer we'll be able to make cakes.'

Dan crouches next to Lucia. 'What's your name, darling?' he asks.

She stares back at him with curiosity. I can see her examining the crumbs in his beard, politely trying to hide her distaste. 'Well, it's not "darling",' she says. 'It's Lucia.'

'Now that's a pretty name. I knew a girl called Lucy once. She was really good at jokes – used to keep me laughing for days. Not as pretty as you, though.'

Lucia smiles at him through her jam sandwich, still taking small bites, but careful not to talk with her mouth full. 'What happened to her? Did she go on telling jokes when she grew up?'

He freezes for a moment, paralysed by some distant thought, his body stalled and his mind absent. But he quickly recovers, able to push the memory neatly into the background, and carries on as if there hadn't been a break. 'Gone, pigeon,' he says. 'Long gone.'

I've seen that look before. From uncles and aunties. Moth and Popi. He's just another survivor, struggling with his own history.

'I'm not a pigeon,' says Lucia.

'No, you're not,' he says thoughtfully.

'Go on, then,' she says. 'Tell us some of Lucy's jokes.'

It's obvious he wasn't expecting her to ask this. He opens his mouth and closes it again, thinking. He takes a deep breath, as if he's going to start. We all stop eating, waiting to see if he has any good jokes. 'OK,' he says. 'Why did the chicken – um – have jam sandwiches for tea?'

'I don't know,' says Lucia. 'Why did the chicken have jam sandwiches for tea?'

'Because . . .' He stops and thinks for a few seconds. 'I don't know. I've forgotten.'

Boris sighs loudly. Another disappointment.

'Never mind,' says Lucia. 'It's difficult to remember jokes.'

'Especially if you have no one to tell them to for twenty-odd years.'

'Why are the years odd?'

'Because they're not even,' he says, and laughs loudly. This might be a joke, but we're not sure, so Moth and I give little half-hearted giggles to make him feel we're taking him seriously. Boris ignores him.

There's a violent explosion from overhead. Lucia screams and dives into Moth's lap. It's thunder, a giant car crash of sound as invisible vehicles collide, shatter, separate and drive headlong back towards each other, rolling recklessly along a phantom road in the sky, continuing to throw themselves around over and over again, even though the initial impact can't be replicated, rumbling on until they're forced to part and limp away, still aggressive, still growling, their undercarriages scraping on the non-existent road.

There's a long silence, followed by the rush of heavy rain. It's distant, insulated by the roof, but we can hear its power. It takes time to think properly after all that sound.

Popi recovers first. 'That was a bit close,' he says. 'Have you ever been hit?'

Dan shakes his head. 'Good lightning conductors. And a reliable caretaker. Me. I climb up once a month and test them all.'

'When was the last time you had visitors?' asks Moth.

He pauses before answering, as if he's calculating. 'Twenty years,' he says.

We stare at him. Has he really not spoken to anyone for twenty years?

'So how did you know if your voice still worked?' I ask.

He grins and reveals an almost toothless mouth. 'I talk to myself. Recite poetry. Listen.' He stands up and wriggles his shoulders, pushing himself up into a straighter position than he has managed up until now. He opens his mouth, takes one or two deep breaths through his nose, letting them out through his mouth. Then he starts to recite:

'The north wind doth blow and we shall have snow,
What will the robin do then, poor thing?
He'll sit in a barn, and keep himself warm,
By hiding his head under his wing, poor thing.'

There's a new resonance in his voice, as if he's reciting to a large crowd, and a curious dignity settles over him, making the words seem more significant than they really are. When he finishes, nobody speaks.

'It's not Shakespeare,' he says apologetically. His performance has changed him in some way. 'It's what I know. We learnt nursery rhymes when we were kids, see – my mum was taught them by her mum – so that's where my old mind goes most easily. I learnt other things at school, but it's mostly forgotten. All I remember is films – *Spiderman*, *Superman*, *The Silver Claw* – but I'm not super anything, so I do poems instead.' He's half defensive, half proud that he's entertained us.

'We know them too,' says Lucia. 'We have a book.'

He nods. 'Quite right,' he says.

It's a surprise to find that he knows the same rhymes as we do. As if he's sneaked into our childhood. But that's nonsense, of course. Nursery rhymes are a shared inheritance. That's the point of them. Everyone's supposed to know them, or half know them, so they can join in if someone else starts, access a distant memory, even if it's not entirely accurate. There's something satisfying about an idealised world that existed long before ours. I wonder if Dan remembers as well as he says he does, or if he's searched for them online and relearnt them, pretending he's got children to comfort with rhyme and rhythm. How else could a crooked man exist for twenty years without speaking?

'I make my own audience,' he says. 'Holos, artificial children, lots and lots of them, so I can perform in front of someone.'

I imagine him with a classroom of machine-created children, staring at him with open mouths, feeding his need for attention, making him believe he's real.

'I worked in a school once,' he says. 'A caretaker then, too. I'm good at fixing the little things, things that don't need much cleverness.'

'Popi's good at fixing things too,' says Lucia. 'And Boris.'

'You have to be good at it now,' says Popi. 'Otherwise you don't survive.'

'Why did you leave the school?' asks Boris.

Dan examines the floor sadly for a few seconds. 'It was a misunderstanding,' he says eventually. 'You don't want to know.'

'I do,' says Lucia.

He smiles at her, his face softening. 'No, sweetheart,' he says. 'You don't.' He puts out a hand to touch Lucia's cheek, very gently. But she stiffens and draws her head back slightly. A glimmer of annoyance drifts across Dan's face. He hides it almost immediately, brushes it away with a smile, but I catch it and he sees that I've seen.

Moth starts to clear up the food and pack everything away, attempting to bring an end to the conversation. We're all exhausted and need to sleep.

'So how long have you been here, Dan?' asks Popi.

'Twenty-eight years,' he says proudly. 'I've kept the trains running – all connections good. Have a look around if you want. Some of it's backed up into sidings, safe and sound, but the lines are all clear. Ready to go in an instant.'

He thinks the computers are connecting with millions of other computers all over the country, linking vast networks. He doesn't seem to realise how few people are left to log on. He must have known about passwords once, but he's lost in an earlier past, the one that Popi remembers. He seems unable to consider the possibility that the place he's protecting is too powerful, too efficient for the handful of people it serves.

'Did many people come here when you first took the job?' asks Moth.

'Well, the tech guys dropped in now and again, and we had one or two visitors, mainly for Amazon – not my department – but nice people. Not so much now, though. We caretakers are picked because we like isolation. We live on our own, but we like to connect, me and Ben and Charlie, send messages, play Scrabble online. I'm champion this year – have been for seventeen years. Not surprising, really. Ben's vocab's too basic and Charlie's bone lazy. He goes for easy options. Sometimes think they've both got bits missing.'

Is it wise to insult the only people in the world you communicate with?

'Do you have toilets here?' asks Boris.

Dan looks at him almost with pity. 'That's a daft question. I live civilised, you know. Come on, I'll show you.'

They disappear between the rows of humming machines, their voices fading into the distance.

'He's mad as Max,' says Moth. 'He really believes it all, doesn't he? Thinks he's the Fat Controller. As if Amazon is still functioning in this country, making a fortune, buying out all the other retailers.'

'I wonder why Amazon put the lady there to greet you,' I say, 'since hardly anyone came anyway.'

Popi chuckles. 'She's probably there for Dan's benefit. To make him feel better about living alone. That's why she's female.'

Delphine yawns and stretches. 'Well, I'm grateful to her and Dan,' she says. 'If they weren't here, we'd still be on our bikes, ploughing through the rain.'

Lucia cuddles up next to her and they drift into a doze together. I curl up, too, keeping my legs on the groundsheet. I should contact Hector, but I'm tired, and the artificial lights are making my eyes ache. I'll give myself fifteen minutes, then go and find a private corner where I can speak to him.

'Poor Dan,' says Moth. 'One minute he's the centre of the entire country, the next he's redundant without even knowing it.'

'I didn't realise Amazon had such a huge role in our infra-structure,' says Popi thoughtfully. 'They were even more power-ful than we thought. I wonder if they sponsored the other two Grand Central Stations.'

'You have to admire them,' says Moth. 'They knew how to run a business. Probably still do, elsewhere in the world.'

'Dan's like a lighthouse keeper,' I say.

Popi smiles. 'Something like that.'

'It's hard to believe Ben and Charlie are still there,' says Moth. 'A bit of a coincidence that all three of them survived Hoffman's.'

'That'll be the computers,' says Delphine, solemnly. I'd thought she was asleep. The even breathing must be coming from Lucia. 'The vibrations.'

I remember what Hector told me about the Free Thinkers. Could it have been Ben or Charlie who was killed?

'Presumably it all runs on solar power,' says Moth. 'Impressive.'

'It wouldn't need a lot, though, would it?' says Popi. 'I bet the computers on the outer edges are powered down, never needed. He just doesn't realise it.'

'He's a border guard,' says Moth. 'In the nineteenth century, they had guardian angels posted at the entrances to Salt Lake City, the Mormon capital. Old men, ex-gunslingers, half mad, guarding the city against marauders, ready to shoot anyone they thought was dodgy.'

'I've read that,' I say. Online, about three years ago. 'Mark Twain. Roughing It.'

'He's not going to shoot us,' says Popi. 'At least, I don't think he is. He'd probably miss if he tried.'

'It's a different situation,' says Moth. 'There aren't any baddies left.'

'I'm not so sure about that,' says Popi.

'Whatever do you mean? Who are the outlaws?'

'What about Aashay?'

They look at each other. 'Rubbish,' says Moth. 'Aashay's just a young man with no one to look after him.' She wants to cling to her belief that he's a lost child, but she sounds less convinced than she did yesterday.

I'm struggling too. *Yankee Doodle came to town* – Why did he come? What does he want from us, from me? There's something so compelling about his strength – *riding on a pony* . . . Even now, when I think of him, an uncontrollable tremor stirs deep inside. *He stuck a feather in his cap and called it macaroni.*

Macaroni puts him in his place. He's not a mythical creature with a mission to lead us to a better world, triumphant, all-conquering. I don't have to take him too seriously. With a feather in his cap? Without a feather? I don't know how to read him. I can feel his hands round my waist again, hear his heart beat, smell his sweat—

I sit up abruptly, feeling foolish and guilty. It would be a mistake not to take him seriously. He took us to the fair. He knows everyone, so he must know Lancelot and his family.

We mustn't underestimate him.

'I know what Aashay does,' says Delphine, sitting up, her eyes blurry, but her voice clear.

Why would Aashay tell Delphine something he hasn't told me? 'He does lots of things,' I say. 'Do you have something specific in mind?'

'He's a smuggler.'

There's a silence. Suddenly we're all very alert.

'What do you mean?' asks Popi. 'What does he smuggle? Where from?'

'He crosses the Channel to Europe or goes to Ireland. He brings all sorts of things back.'

'Don't be silly,' says Moth. 'That's not possible.'

'Yes, it is. That's where all the stuff at the fair comes from. The meat – it wasn't wild pig at all, it was the kind of pig they used to breed here before they died out. They brought it in from abroad. And my dress. I knew straight away it wasn't old – the smell wasn't right. Aashay's got a whole business going. A lot of the men we saw at the fair work for him. That's why he doesn't go to Brighton. He doesn't need the government. He can do everything he wants on his own.'

'How can you possibly know all that?' asks Moth.

She's making it up. Aashay wouldn't have told her.

'Onyeka and Ogechi, the girls at the fair. They told me.'

I'm irritated by the sense of relief that floods through me. Why should I care if Aashay confides in her or not? 'Can you believe them?' I ask. 'They might have got it wrong.'

Delphine looks at me with contempt. 'They're not kids. They all know Aashay – everyone does. He's famous. They see him as a kind of Robin Hood, out to help them without profiting himself.'

They've got that wrong. Aashay would never do anything if he didn't benefit from it.

'What an incredibly dangerous thing to do,' says Moth. 'They shoot people who break the quarantine.'

'That was what you were told twenty years ago,' I say. 'It might not be true any more.'

'If it wasn't,' says Delphine, 'everyone except us would be whizzing off to France and they wouldn't be calling it smuggling.'

'If you think about it,' says Popi, 'the Channel would be an impossible border to patrol. Anyone with local knowledge of tides and weather conditions could get round a blockade – look how they managed it in the Second World War. Even if the satellites see them, the government can hardly launch missiles. You can't zap people for civil disobedience, especially when you're short of people anyway, and it would take time to launch a boat to intercept them. That's probably how he gets away with it.'

'But what about Hoffman's?' says Moth. 'He'd be taking the risk of transferring it to the continent.'

'You've always said it's died out,' I say. 'You told us the quarantine was unnecessary after all this time.'

She goes silent for a few seconds. 'Even so,' she says, 'it seems foolhardy . . .'

And then I see why we'll never be able to break the quarantine.

Nobody, not even the experts, can ever be absolutely certain. If Moth, who has scientific knowledge, has her doubts, there's no chance of anyone else exercising common sense. It's too much of a gamble. Better not to risk it. Just keep us supplied with enough to keep us happy and hope we die out in the end. Avoid contact for several centuries: as long as everyone believes the land is contaminated, the rest of the world is safe. A good plan.

I stand up. 'I'm off to explore,' I say. I don't want them to see how shaken I am by all this. A whole new side to Aashay that none of us could have guessed – something he didn't think he should mention. Once again, it turns out that he's more than he seems. I shouldn't be surprised, but I am.

I head in the opposite direction to the one taken by Dan and Boris, anxious to avoid being overheard if I talk to Hector. I won't get lost if I keep going in a straight line, but I still need to pay attention and keep some kind of map in my head. The machines go on and on, regimented, ten thousand men marching in formation up to the top of the hill and back again, all exactly the same, with only Dan, the grand old duke of York, to keep track of them. They stretch out ahead, maybe for miles, without a break. There must be a readout somewhere, a computer screen, lights blinking to highlight problems, so the engineers can locate the source of a malfunction.

Maybe there are clues on the ground to tell you where you are. I look for indicators, signposts, and eventually realise that the machines themselves are changing colour. They start off white, sparkling, shining, then they're cream, then yellow, orange. From where I'm standing, I can see red in the far distance and a hint of maroon beyond that. So, further away, beyond my ability to see, they'll be blue, navy, getting darker and darker until they're black. There are probably even shades of black. I've seen potholers on film, and deep-sea divers. The lower you go under-ground or below the surface of the sea, the further away from light, the less distinct the colours become, until you reach a place of perpetual darkness, beyond the reach of power supplies. A world where people never go, so far from the surface it's almost impossible to find your way back.

So the engineers would know their position from the colour of the computers. They'd probably use a handheld device to lead them to the faulty machine. It would be easy. Just keep on walking until you get there. Although they might need help to cover the distance. Dan mentioned trolleys, but I wonder why nobody thought of installing moving pavements, like the ones they used to have in stations and airports.

Moth remembers them with fondness: 'An invention that genuinely improved your life,' she says. 'You just had to step on with your luggage, stand still and wait until you got there. You could glide across huge distances without breaking your back.'

I stop in a moment of panic. There's something about the uniformity of the computers that's stops you thinking clearly. Can I be absolutely certain that I haven't turned a corner? I slip off a shoe and place it in the corridor, so that it points back the way I've come. Now I can't get lost.

I go a little further, then press the button on my POD and a stream of silver light comes out immediately, forming itself into Hector, even smaller than last time. The Weather Watchers were right. It's the hardware that will fail us. What am I going to do if it packs up completely?

'Halloollilo!' he says, with relief. 'Back from the land of the disappeared! I thought I'd lost you for ever. Been planning the memorial service. Roses, of course. White, perfumed, petals falling and carpeting the floor, violins, mournful tunes. I thought I'd wear a white suit to match the roses—'

I'm beginning to realise that he's not very good at tone. He misreads atmosphere or doesn't read it at all. 'A little premature, don't you think?'

He grins quickly, mischievously. 'I was just missing you, worrying, that's all. It's more manageable if you face up to things, consider your options, create an alternative.'

'I'd hardly describe my funeral as an alternative solution.'

'Not funeral, merely a memorial service,' he says. 'You could have made a comeback at any time without altering the sincerity of my tribute. I was feeling insecure, that's all. No probs.'

I want to reassure him that I've forgiven his failure to be honest about his knowledge of the fairs, that he shouldn't feel threatened by Aashay, but it's more important that I tell him about Lucia and Lancelot's family.

'Can you be sure you haven't been followed?' he asks, when I've finished.

This hasn't occurred to me, but now that he's made the suggestion, I realise I don't know. 'Do you think that's likely?'

He hesitates. 'People are irrational when it comes to children. We've had problems in Brighton, you know. There have been kidnappings.'

'Are you serious?'

'Deadly.'

'You really should have mentioned this before. It might have influenced our decision to go to the fair.'

'I'm sorry,' he says meekly, and pauses for a few seconds. 'What about this caretaker guy? Is he safe?'

'How would I know? We've only just met him. He's an old man, completely deluded about his own significance. He's unlikely to be a kidnapper. He doesn't seem the type.'

'Roza,' says Hector sadly, 'no one acts rationally when they see children. For all you know, he could be part of a nationwide organisation, placed there as their eyes and ears. They exist, you know, these people. That might be the reason for his lights, to attract passing travellers.'

The witch's gingerbread house in *Hansel and Gretel*. The Pied Piper leading the children out of Hamelin with his music.

Can I be certain that this whole expedition wasn't some complicated plot to bring us out of the shadows of anonymity and into the light of everyone's attention? 'Dan doesn't seem to have contact with anyone, except two other caretakers. I wondered if one of them could be the man you told me about, who was killed.'

'Ah, yes – the Free Thinkers. That's quite possible. But he

might not be telling you the whole truth about his associations.'

How could we possibly know? When people, the uncles and aunties, give us information about themselves, I believe what they say. Why wouldn't I? You have to have a basic trust in people. How could I know if they were lying? Is it possible to work it out from their faces, their eyes, their gestures? But the best liars must be experts in sincerity – that's presumably why they're good at it. They know how to come across as nice people.

I'm going round in circles. 'I don't know . . . I just don't . . .' I need time to think about this, to discuss it with Popi and Moth. 'Did you make it to Bicester before the storm?'

'No, straight past and on to Banbury. I'm safely holed up at the waystation, getting personally acquainted with the rain. Hoping to be at yours about mid-afternoon. As long as it stops raining.'

'We should be there before you, then. How's the waystation?'

He hesitates. 'OK.'

'You don't sound enthusiastic.'

'Well, it leaks. I'm standing in the middle of the restroom, listening to a symphony of falling rain, a concerto of splashes, a sonata of drips. They're good. There's harmony, rhythm, melody. Listen.' He stops talking so the POD can pick up the sound. I can hear water trickling, the ping as it hits the floor. 'I was searching for a dry spot when you rang. This must have been a busy waystation once, well used over the years – not many untouched cubicles left. I can't imagine why it's so popular.'

'You're not that far from Oxford, are you? Maybe that's the attraction.'

'Why? What's Oxford got that Brighton hasn't?'

'It was a big academic centre once, a famous university. It might have avoided drone destruction – maybe it's one of the few cities that wasn't given barriers.' Aashay would know – he's probably been there – but I can't be sure that he'd tell me the truth. 'It could have been preserved for history. There was a big library – that would be a reason for going there. What was it called? The Bodleian.'

Hector looks uncomfortable.

'You don't know about Oxford, do you?'

He shakes his head slowly. 'Well . . . not much. There are lots of these old places. We have to work with now, not then.' So books are not relevant to him. Slightly worrying.

'I imagine everything in the library is out of date anyway,' I say, wanting to reassure him that it doesn't matter. 'Books couldn't save us from Hoffman's.'

'What's it like where you are?' he asks. 'Are you dry?'

I move my POD in a slow, wide sweep, so he can see. 'Dry,' I say, 'but monotonous.'

'Those computers look dead,' he says.

He's right. They're not humming here. If they're receiving power, they're not using it. They're sentinels of a redundant world, unconscious until the day in the distant future when the call to duty wakes them up. Empty receptacles, awaiting the resurrection. 'I think they're asleep,' I say, 'rather than dead. Popi said there probably wouldn't be enough power to keep them all going.'

He yawns. 'I'm going to crash in a minute. It'll be log-sleep, even in my cold, damp cell, where the cockroaches roam and the woodlice vie for supremacy with the centipedes, and they all see my sleeping body as their personal playground.'

'You're exaggerating.'

'Yup. I'm after your sympathy. Early start, as soon as it's light.' His voice changes, becomes more serious. 'Roza, we're nearly there. We're going to meet properly tomorrow. Eye to eye.'

It's hard to believe it will finally happen. We've known each other for so long, but we can't really know each other until we experience each other's physical presence. It's exciting, but frightening. 'Everything's going to be fine,' I say.

'Course it is,' he says. 'The world will be our octopus.'

'I think that's meant to be oyster.'

'No reason why we have to follow the trend. Originality, that's what we've got, Roza. Porpoises, shrimps, sea bass—'

'Hump-backed whales—'

'Jellyfish—'

'I've never seen the sea,' I say sadly.

'You will. We'll do the seaside together. We'll ride the waves, taste the spray, build sandcastles in the sky . . .'

I smile at him. 'I've missed our conversations today, Hector,' I say. 'Safe journey.'

'Never fear. All will be well. Cherry-oh.'

We disconnect. I stare round at the computers fading into the distance. It feels as if they're listening, judging, planning. I hurry back, picking up my discarded shoe on the way. I need to settle down for the night as soon as possible if we're to be ready to set off in the morning.

Just before I reach the others, something catches my attention. A tiny drawing on the front of a computer. A cartoon. A cat, grinning cheekily, eager for my attention.

I stare at it. We're out of our depth.

18

I wake with a jump and know immediately that all is not well. Something . . . a noise – the collision against the window of a stray branch that has become lethal in the wind, a crash as someone unknown drops a heavy object on the floor (a knife, a chisel, a bicycle?), the bang of my front door as Boris leaves? Where am I?

Against the background of the pounding beat of my pulse, I lie still and listen, forcing myself to breathe evenly. Once I've remembered that I'm in Grand Central Station, among the computers, I can reject each theory – there aren't any windows here; everyone else would be awake if something large fell on the floor; I'm not in my flat so there's no front door – until I arrive at the reality. It must have been a small sound, magnified by the silence.

Every part of me aches: my head, my bones, my muscles. I suppose that's what happens if you spend so much time cycling, then end up lying on a concrete floor. I have one of Dan's blankets underneath me, my rucksack as a pillow and two spare cardigans draped on top to keep me warm, but none of it has produced any real comfort. My left leg, bent awkwardly underneath me, is numb from the knee down. I roll on to my back and wriggle my toes for a few seconds until pins and needles dance under the surface of my skin with restless, irritating intensity. The miracle is not that I've woken up but that I went to sleep in the first place.

It's pitch dark and this suddenly strikes me as odd. When we settled down, the overhead lights were on. Economy measures that were set in place over twenty years ago ensured that the output was low but we could recognise where we were, see the expressions on each other's faces when we talked. There was just enough light to guide a pre-Hoffman's tech guy through the rows of computers.

The computers – they've stopped humming. Why aren't they emitting their gentle background of soft glowing light, which was there when I settled into sleep? Have they been shut down? Who's switched off the power?

Could it be Aashay?

I've seen the cat. I know Dan has not been entirely honest.

Another sound. I freeze. Not as loud as I first thought, not a crash or a crack or a click, but a shuffle, a movement. It's only small, but it echoes through the black space. Where's it coming from? Why is it frightening?

Wee Willie Winkie runs through the town, Upstairs and down-stairs, in his nightgown.

I can hear breathing. Of course. Everyone except me is asleep. Popi's snoring, his breath entering and exiting his mouth with a strong, regular beat; Moth is whistling softly through her nose. Boris mutters to himself incoherently, Delphine whispers and Lucia sighs. There's a harmony in the breathing, a comfort, the gentle rise and fall of a collective experience, a family sleeping together, dreaming of rhymes, of familiarity, of rhythm: *Knocking on the window, calling through the lock, Are all the children fast asleep? It's past eight o'clock.*

But I've heard something alien, something that shouldn't be here. It's a deliberate movement, the sound of someone awake and alert, someone with purpose. There's a sense of stealth, secrecy. An interloper who knows the layout so well that he can move through the dark.

I wriggle around, raise my left arm to press the button on my POD. The light is dim, but it's enough to illuminate my surroundings. Everyone's in the right place, where I expect them to be, motionless, huddled under sweaters, mounds of sleeping bodies.

But someone's standing over Lucia—

I sit up.

It's Dan. He looks into my eyes and straightens up as far as he can with his bent back. For a second, an expression of guilt drifts across his face. Then he puts a finger to his lips.

'What are you doing?' I whisper.

He smiles, a curiously unconvincing smile that doesn't seem to express anything. As if he's been practising how to do it. 'Just checking,' he says.

'Checking what?'

'Making sure you're all right.'

'We're fine,' I say fiercely, because I'm convinced he's lying but I can't find the words to accuse him. He's not just checking. He shouldn't be here at all. 'Why aren't the lights on?'

'Turned them off so you'd sleep better. You've got a long journey home tomorrow.'

How does he know how long our journey is? 'Shouldn't you have told us you were going to do that?'

'Didn't need to. The request came from your ma and pa. Reckoned it would be best for the little one. Said you could use your PODs if you wanted the loo.'

I can't prove him wrong, but I can't persuade myself to believe him. I think back to when I returned from talking to Hector. Everyone was sorting out sleeping spaces, trying to create as much softness and comfort as possible, so I'd missed the last conversation with Dan. 'What are you doing here now? Why were you bending over Lucia? Why didn't you have a light on?'

He lifts his hands, spreading the fingers, and I've seen that gesture before. The statue in the art gallery. Aashay. Not my fault. Nothing to do with me. But he doesn't reply to my questions. He reminds me of Boris when I've caught him pinching biscuits from the kitchen cupboard, pretending he's suffering from an upset stomach and needs a little something to settle it, or sneaking out with his skis during a snowstorm when Popi has forbidden it. He can't think of an excuse, so it's easier to remain silent.

We stare at each other.

I want to wake Moth and Popi for support, but I'm afraid he'll try to stop me. There's something about him, an edginess that wasn't so noticeable earlier, a desperation that is only just contained.

But, after what seems for ever, he sighs, unlocks himself from my gaze and shuffles away along the corridor between the machines towards the entrance, presumably back to his own territory, his living quarters, wherever they are. I stare after him for some time, trying to convince myself that I've imagined the whole thing, that it was just a dream.

I lean over to see if Lucia's all right. She's on her side, tightly curled like a cat, her knees drawn up to her stomach, her left hand cradling her cheek. Her mouth is moving in and out, sucking on the distant memory of a thumb or a bottle. Her back rises and falls regularly with her untroubled breathing.

I lie back down and turn off my POD. It's instantly black again. I remain motionless for a while, listening, checking everyone's breathing, wondering if he'll come back. The lights weren't bright enough to disturb us. We've always had lamps by our beds, glow lights in hallways and landings to make it easier to find our way around if we wake. I don't believe that Popi and Moth would suggest he turn off the power.

Why was he here? What did he want?

I sit up again and turn on my POD. 'Popi,' I say urgently, leaning over and shaking his shoulder.

He stirs, snorts violently and sits up. 'What – what?' I can hear the dryness in his mouth, his difficulty in producing enough saliva to speak. I wait while he struggles to gain consciousness. 'Roza? What's the matter?' His voice is blurred.

'Was it your idea to switch off the lights?'

He rubs his eyes. 'What are you talking about?'

'Dan was here – in the dark. I couldn't see a thing until I put on my POD. Did you tell him to switch off the lights?'

I can hear a choking sound, a hard cough. Moth is waking up. 'When?'

'I don't know. He said you both spoke to him.'

'But there's a light on now.'

'That's my POD.'

Popi looks puzzled. 'We didn't discuss the lights. I didn't know they could be turned off. When did you speak to Dan? What were you doing wandering around?'

'I wasn't. But he was.'

229

Moth is sitting up now. 'Has something happened?'

'I heard a noise – it woke me – and it was pitch dark, so I switched on my POD. Dan was here.'

'What do you mean, here?'

'He was standing here, between you and Popi, bending over Lucia.'

Moth gasps. She leans over and puts her hand on Lucia's forehead, her eyes blank as she waits for the heat to transfer to her palm. She smooths a stray hair from her face, tucking it behind her left ear. 'She's fine,' she says, after a long pause. 'What exactly was he doing?'

'I don't know. I asked him, but he said he was checking. As far as I could tell, he hadn't actually touched her.' Perhaps he just wanted to see her, to experience the close proximity of a child.

But it was dark. He couldn't see her. Was he simply listening to her breathing? Or did he have a torch that he switched off when he heard me move?

'Hector says children in Brighton have been kidnapped,' I say.

There's a sudden stillness from Moth and Popi.

'We'll have to leave,' says Moth, struggling to her feet. 'Is it still raining?'

We listen. Earlier we'd heard the rush of rain as it swept in after the thunder, a distant drumming on the roof high above us, but I can't hear it now. It could still be pouring, just not so heavily.

'We can't leave in the middle of the night, whether it's stopped raining or not,' says Popi. 'It's too dangerous in the dark.'

Boris sits up, instantly awake, his eyes wide. 'What's going on?'

'It's OK,' says Moth. 'We're just discussing when to leave. We need to get going at first light.'

'But how will we know without any windows?' I ask.

'It's two fifteen,' says Popi, consulting his POD. 'The sun comes up round about six at this time of year. We'll leave then. Unless there's local flooding.'

'We go anyway,' says Moth. 'Even if we have to build a raft.'

Popi smiles at her. 'Don't worry. We'll be fine once we can see where we're going.'

'What's the hurry?' asks Boris, too loudly, not gauging his volume accurately enough.

'Ssh,' says Moth. 'You'll wake the girls.'

'We're worrying about Dan,' says Popi. 'He's turned the power off. We're not sure if we can trust him.'

Boris nods, but doesn't comment. He's grasped the situation unexpectedly quickly, as if he, too, has had doubts. 'I thought someone should stay on guard,' he says. 'I meant to keep awake.'

'If you were worried about him,' I say, 'why didn't you tell us?'

He shrugs. 'It wasn't as if there was anything obviously suspish. I just thought he was fishy – you know, kind of slithery. I wanted to keep an eye on things.' He grins sheepishly. 'But then I went to sleep.'

When did Boris, my amiable but not always perceptive brother, acquire the skill to read beyond the obvious? 'Well,' I say, 'Boris the great protector.'

'I did my best,' he says, 'but all that meat from the fair must have had a relaxing effect. I couldn't keep awake.'

'Actually,' I say, 'I'm impressed that you picked up something we all missed.'

He searches my face to see if I'm mocking, then nods. 'Thanks,' he says.

'I think Aashay's been here,' I say. 'There's a cartoon cat on the front of a computer.'

There's a silence. 'Really?' says Boris.

I nod.

'How do you know it was Aashay?' asks Moth.

'Well, if it wasn't,' I say, 'Dan has produced a remarkably accurate copy, which would be odd if he's never met Aashay.'

'So,' says Popi, sounding almost pleased, now that his suspicions are confirmed, 'there's more going on than either Aashay or Dan are prepared to tell us.'

But none of us knows what. Could this be a place Aashay passes regularly, where he drops in to maintain his network of supporters? Or buyers, perhaps, for his smuggled goods?

We divide up the rest of the night between us. An hour each. I offer to take the first shift, since I'm already wide awake. Popi will do the last hour and wake everyone at five thirty. With any luck, we'll be gone long before Dan wakes up.

'It's best to stand up every now and again,' says Popi. 'Walk around a bit. We don't want you to do a Boris and doze off when you don't mean to.'

He and Boris settle down again, dropping almost immediately into a deep sleep. I'm not so sure about Moth. I can hear quick, conscious movements coming from her that indicate she's awake.

She sits up and stares at me as if I'm not there. Is she awake or having unpleasant dreams? 'Moth?' I whisper.

Her eyes focus on me and she smiles. 'Sorry,' she whispers. 'I can't concentrate on sleeping. I keep worrying that someone has followed us here.'

'That's odd,' I say. 'Hector thought the same thing. But you know Hector. He likes a bit of drama.' We're suddenly seeing danger everywhere. One small step out of our normal, predictable life and we've crossed from light to shadow, tumbled into a sinister world of spying and stalking and kidnapping.

'Well,' says Moth, 'in general, I believe in keeping my feet on the ground. But the ground isn't looking all that solid right now.'

'I can't believe we've been followed. Surely we'd have seen them.' But did we look? Did anyone think to turn round, or were we too intent on where we were going? Could someone have been behind us, just far enough away to keep out of sight? Although the motorway's empty, it's not always straight. It would have been possible to hide in the bends, blend into the murky greyness once it clouded over.

'Do you really think Aashay's involved in all this?' says Moth, after a long pause.

'Nothing about Aashay would surprise me,' I say. He's a catalyst, a chemical that either neutralises or blows everything up.

232

Why is it so hard to work out what side he's on? None of us really knows him, but he's fooled us into thinking we do.

'I've always liked him,' she says. 'And you have, haven't you?'

I catch my breath. What has she seen? 'He divides us,' I say slowly. 'He has the effect of putting us on opposite sides.'

He's selected his team: Moth, Lucia and Boris – although you can't really count Lucia, since she's short on experience and she'll go wherever there's fun. I'm not sure about Delphine. She's less forthcoming. She's interested in him, but it's impossible to know how much she believes in him.

Popi's on the opposing side, worrying.

'So which side are you on, Roza?'

'I don't know.' I fluctuate. He draws me to him with an irresistible magnetism, but I'm suspicious of the way he just appeared, out of nowhere. The way he left his cat sketches for me to see makes me think it was all calculated, a way of nudging his way in, making it easier for me to accept him. Does he have a plan? I've asked him – so many times – to explain himself. Where he comes from, why he turned up in our block of flats, why he followed me to the art gallery.

But he never gives proper answers.

'You don't want to know about my childhood,' he said once.

'I do,' I said.

'No child should have to live the kind of life I did, scavenging, living like a wild animal. . .'

'Now you're being melodramatic.'

'I had to hide from the kind of people you don't even know exist, live in ditches, shelter in trees.'

Who were these people? 'What happened to your parents?'

His eyes were wide, his expression open and honest (I thought). 'Dead,' he said, and his face crumpled very slightly, almost imperceptibly, before rebuilding itself.

I was moved by that small glimpse of vulnerability, embarrassed by my previous flippancy. Now I wonder if it was all calculated.

'Water under the bridge,' he said then, with a huge grin, as if he was wiping away his past suffering.

He's confided in me, I thought at the time. I'm privileged that he's revealed something about his past, let me share something personal. He's learnt to survive and become strong. And on the way he's acquired the greatest skill of all, making people like him.

Is he even cleverer than I realised, moving around secretly, then announcing his presence with the cartoon cat? He can produce charm whenever he needs to, give the impression that he trusts you. He's worked out that he can make people believe they're special if he confides in them, and that gives him power. But the smuggling changes everything. It makes him more sinister, more alarming.

Is the cat a threat, a reminder that he knows where I am?

'Hector's a good man,' says Moth, unexpectedly, 'but I'm not convinced he's entirely right for you.'

'And Aashay is?'

'Goodness, no! He's far too dangerous.'

Why has she brought Hector into the discussion? 'But you like Aashay.'

She doesn't comment for a while. 'I suppose I see something in him. Excitement, a spark, perhaps. He's an adventurer.' She sighs. 'He's not like your father.'

I smile. 'No, Popi's far too law-abiding. Hector's more like him.'

'Aashay likes being in charge. That's what the smuggling's all about. He enjoys controlling people. You should never get involved with a man who wants control, Roza. You'd never be happy.'

'Hector isn't controlling.'

'No, he's not. You're right. Ineffectual is probably a better option. At least you'll have a say in the progress of your life.'

'That's not fair!' I feel protective towards Hector. First Aashay attacks him and now Moth. Can't they trust me to see for myself?

'Mind you,' she says, 'all men like to be in charge. Even Popi, in his own way.'

'I just can't work out what Aashay wants from us,' I say.

'I think he was drawn to our family life,' says Moth. 'He's never experienced anything like it before.'

I'm beginning to wonder if he came for Lucia.

'Do you believe that people are kidnapping children?' she asks, as if she can read my thoughts.

I've been thinking about everyone we met at the fair and their reaction to Lucia. They've been starved of the charm of a child's perspective, and the reminders of the nursery-rhyme world. They are losing their memories of teddy bears, big bad wolves, ginger-bread houses, and they're not happy about it. 'Well, I suppose Hector could be exaggerating. Maybe it's only happened once.' But it only takes one person. How could any of us guess which one?

'I don't think Aashay is a kidnapper.' Her voice is fading, as if she's struggling to form the words. 'How would he benefit? It can't be for a ransom – nobody's got any money. And you can tell he doesn't care much about children. He craves attention for himself.'

She's right. He wants to be the child in his own story. If he's involved, it's for some other reason – admiration, perhaps, ever-lasting gratitude from appreciative customers. People naturally look up to him. Everyone at the fair was delighted to see him, slapping him on the back, jostling to get close to him, queuing up to speak to him. He was expanding before our eyes, nourished by the attention, the respect. That's what makes him powerful. The hardest thing for him is when we're distracted and don't have time for him – when Hector has my attention instead of him.

'We shouldn't encourage him,' I say to Moth.

But she's slipped down on her blanket and has fallen asleep. On her back, with her mouth open.

Why did he decide to tell us about the fairs? Was it a desire to help us meet other people or part of a more complicated plan? Could he be a spy, as Tariq suggested, here to find out more about us before luring us into a trap? My eyelids are starting to droop. I jump to my feet, remembering Popi's advice, and start to patrol up and down until my POD finally pings and my hour is up. It's Boris's turn.

'Go away,' he mutters, when I try to wake him, waving his hand in front of his face as if he's brushing away a fly.

'Come on, Boris,' I say softly. 'Guard duty.'

He sits up and groans. 'I can't sleep properly anyway. The floor's too hard.'

'Don't talk flannel. You were utterly zonked. Come on, stand up. It'll help you wake up.'

Boris switches on his POD. It's much brighter than mine. 'Whizzo!' he says with pleasure. 'That's a bit more like it.'

I lie down, conscious of the unyielding concrete, but too exhausted to care. I'll never sleep, I think, as Boris's voice fades away.

I've hardly closed my eyes when I'm being shaken. 'Roza, wake up,' says Moth's voice, low and close to my ear. I sit up. Everyone's awake – I'm the last, except for Lucia – rubbing eyes, gazing blearily at each other, only half conscious. Popi's POD has been placed in the centre so we can see to gather up our belongings. Moth is rolling up blankets, tucking food neatly into boxes and then into her bag. Her hair is sticking up oddly, but her mind is on organisation, escape, not on the state of her hair.

'Has it stopped raining?' I ask, my voice dry.

She nods. 'Popi has found the door to the balcony – for some reason it wasn't locked – and been outside. It's getting light and there's no sign of flooding in the immediate vicinity. It's all quite settled. He thinks we'll make it home without any problems.'

Boris is explaining to Delphine about my encounter with Dan during the night.

'You mean he was wandering around here while we were asleep?' She shudders. 'Creeps.'

Eventually, Moth kneels down beside Lucia. 'Time to wake up, sweetheart,' she calls gently.

Lucia stirs, flings her arms out and moans. 'No.' She pulls her knees up and wraps her arms round them, refusing to unbend.

'Come on, Lucia,' says Moth, more firmly. 'It's time to leave. Up you get.'

She sits up reluctantly, staring round in the half-light, glaring at us all.

'What shall we do with the blankets?' asks Delphine.

'Just leave them here,' says Popi, throwing them into a corner. But Moth picks them up, one at a time, folding them carefully and creating a tidy pile.

'What's the point of that?' asks Boris.

'He was kind enough to offer them,' she says. 'We can at least show him the courtesy of looking after them properly.'

'But he's not kind,' whispers Delphine. 'He wants to steal Lucia.'

'We don't know anything for certain,' says Moth. 'We can only guess. And even if it were true, at least he has the good taste to appreciate something beautiful.' She smiles across at Lucia, who doesn't smile back. Moth wants us to remain civilised, maintain our ability to behave well in difficult circumstances, put reason over instinct. She's right, I think. If our family is the best place for Lucia to live, then we should prove it to ourselves by demonstrating humanity, kindness, compassion.

The lights come on.

Moth gasps. 'Oh, no. He's awake. He must know we're leaving.'

'They could be automatic,' says Boris.

'That'll be it,' says Popi, deliberately calm.

Lucia stares at Moth in surprise. 'Aren't we saying goodbye to Dan?' she asks.

'No,' says Moth, in a cheerful voice – keeping it soft. 'We don't want to disturb him. Come with me.' She grabs the last bag from the floor with one hand and picks up Lucia's sweets with the other. 'There, I think we've got everything.'

'Why are we whispering?'

'We don't want to disturb Dan,' I say, taking her hand. 'It's still quite early and he's probably asleep.'

'He needs his beauty sleep,' she whispers.

'Absolutely,' says Delphine. 'Just like the rest of us.'

'No,' says Lucia. 'He needs it more than the rest of us.'

We find our way back to the entrance, pausing at the top of the steps to shut the door to the computers behind us. The bicycles are all there, leaning against the walls, waiting for us. I wonder where Dan's bedroom is – there must be a caretaker's flat somewhere.

'I want to go to the toilet,' says Lucia.

We stop and stare at each other. Now what?

'Right,' says Moth. 'We'll use the bushes once we get outside.'

'No' says Lucia, starting to moan. 'I don't like it in the bushes. It prickles.'

'The toilet's just round the corner,' says Boris. 'Through that other door.'

Everyone hesitates, unsure what to do. 'I'll take her,' I say. 'But you'll have to show us the way, Boris.'

'OK,' says Popi, after exchanging glances with Moth, who nods almost imperceptibly. 'It'll take a minute or two to get the bikes downstairs anyway.'

Boris puts down his bag by the computer-room door and leads the way to a small toilet. I watch while Lucia goes in. Boris stands next to me like a bodyguard, his legs apart and his arms folded. Expecting trouble, capable of dealing with it, curiously comforting.

'Should you go and help Popi and Moth?' I say.

He sighs, but doesn't relax his position. 'They'll manage,' he says. 'Best to be safe.'

'I won't feel safe until we get home,' I say.

'But Aashay knows where we are.'

'Do you think he'll tell other people?'

He looks at me uncertainly. 'What do you think? You probably know him best.'

Do they all think I have some kind of relationship with Aashay? 'You know him as well as I do,' I say.

'I wish he'd told me about the smuggling,' says Boris. 'I wouldn't have betrayed him.' He's annoyed. He likes the idea of it – camouflaged boats zipping through the high seas, dodging drones. He wants to step on to foreign soil, maybe even speak to some Europeans, bring back goodies. The lawlessness excites him. The thought of it releases him from everyday life. He hasn't considered the danger.

'Never mind,' I say. 'No doubt there'll be plenty of opportunities in the future.' He's strong, fearless, foolhardy, prepared to break the law. Who's going to stop him? Not Moth or Popi.

Lucia comes out. 'It's all right,' she says. 'A bit dusty, but quite nice, really.'

I take her hand. 'Come on, we need to hurry.'

'Why?' she asks.

'Well, it's a long way, and—'

She's looking behind me. I turn round and confront Dan.

'You're leaving,' he says. 'Why such a hurry?'

Doesn't he realise that his presence in the middle of the night would have been frightening? I stare into his eyes and try to work out what he's really thinking. His face is a mask. I can't read anything.

'Quick,' says Boris, grabbing Lucia and pulling her down the stairs.

'Stop!' she says. She turns back to Dan. 'Goodbye, Desperate Dan,' she says, with a little smile, her dimples flashing in her cheeks.

'Goodbye, princess,' he says.

She clatters down the stairs, aware that there's no need to keep quiet any more. I look at Dan and try to smile. Maybe he never meant us any harm. 'Thank you for your help,' I say. 'We appreciated the shelter.'

He doesn't smile back. His eyes seem to expand, glitter in the half-light, and I see what I'm not expecting. An enormous sadness, which seems to soak through him, bleeding out of him as if he's unable to contain it. It's like peering into a deep, dark hole, an abyss that goes on and on, never ending. If I dropped in a pebble, we would never hear it reach the bottom.

He doesn't move, doesn't say anything. He just watches us.

Perhaps we shouldn't have panicked. He's an old man who likes children, no danger to us because he's as weak as a child himself. Even I could probably overcome him if it came to a contest of strength.

I turn away and head down the stairs.

'Thank you for visiting Amazon,' says the nice lady. 'I hope you enjoyed your visit. Please come again.'

Probably not, I think, swinging open the door at the bottom to let Boris and Lucia through. Moth and Popi and Delphine have managed to get all the bicycles outside, and they're loaded up, ready to go. Standing next to them, just visible in the early dawn, leaning on his handlebars, is Aashay. He's grinning, as if he's just discovered the cure for infertility. Popi and Moth are silent and uncomfortable in his presence.

'How did you find us?' I ask, staring at him with astonishment, refusing to smile, ignoring the leap of pleasure in my stomach.

'Thought you'd be here,' he says. 'Lights to guide you through the dark.'

'Hoi! You!' We look up and Dan is on the balcony, peering down at us, his face dark with fury, pointing with a trembling finger. 'Get away from here! You hear me?' He's been feeding on all that sadness, nurturing it, and now it's translated into anger. 'Taking advantage, treating my station like a hotel, abusing my hospitality.'

But is he talking to us or to Aashay?

'Quick,' says Popi. 'On your bikes.'

19

We cycle together, tight and close, back towards the intersection with the M6. The rain is draining away to the sides of the road, running into ditches that are already full and overflowing into the undergrowth beyond.

Popi sets the pace. He's struggling with the double weight of Lucia and the tandem, still tired from the previous day and lack of sleep, but he won't consider letting anyone else take over. The rest of us hover nearby, keeping our speed down, ready to help if necessary. This Popi seems weaker than usual, as if he's wearing out. Not that he would admit it. He's our Popi. He's in charge, same as always.

'I can take the tandem for a while, if you want,' calls Aashay, coming up alongside the rest of us.

He's behaving as if everything's normal, but he must be annoyed with us for leaving the fair without explanation. So why doesn't he say something? Why are we all cycling with him as if nothing's changed? I imagine him watching everyone pack up after the fair, preparing to leave, suddenly realising that we've gone. But why would he care? All those followers and hangers-on, they were much more respectful than we've ever been.

Popi doesn't appreciate the offer of help. He slows down, almost to a standstill, and glares at Aashay. 'I am perfectly capable,' he says quietly, before picking up speed again.

Aashay slips back behind him. 'No hassles,' he says, balancing with his legs and holding his hands up in the air. Innocence personified. As always. 'You go ahead. I'll cover your back.'

What's he expecting? An ambush? An army of fair-haired families, hiding in the surrounding trees, waiting to spring out and grab Lucia? No, he'd need to be in front if he was going to thwart that kind of plan. Robocops behind us, then, whizzing up the A446, clutching WANTED posters in their hands, in case they don't recognise us?

Well, if they're after us, he's the one who would know.

Everything is damp and heavy. A fine drizzle floats in the air, and it feels as if we're cycling through a muslin curtain, a panel of lace. The moisture attaches itself to everything, soaks into our clothes and bags and adds to the weight. It makes pedalling harder, demands more effort, greater strength in the legs. The rising sun seems reluctant to emerge, dragging itself up through the grey mist as if it's preparing for a major battle and expects to be defeated before it gets going. Why make an effort to get out of bed when there's nothing to do?

I have a strong sense that we've mislaid something, left something vital behind at Grand Central Station. Our sense of fun has deserted us, but it's more than that. It's to do with the way we carve our way through the world, our justification for existing, the waves we leave behind us. A loss of security and an absence of certainty.

'Fancy a race?' I call to Boris, hoping that his natural competitiveness will rise to the surface and he'll shoot off ahead of us, lifting our spirits with a desire to prove his superiority. But he ignores me.

'Forget it,' says Delphine, gliding up beside me. 'He's learning to be responsible. We shouldn't discourage it.'

At least she's still thinking normally.

Anyway, it would be unwise to go too fast. The roads are still wet, partly submerged in places where the surface has crumbled. If we hit any unexpected potholes, we'll buckle a wheel. There were houses here once, lining the sides of the road. I hadn't noticed this last night when we came along so tentatively in the gloom, aiming for the light in the distance. They're just ruins, piles of broken concrete and exposed foundations, but you can still see where they once were, the plots marked by ghostly traces of fences. Their contents would have been vaporised by drone blasts, the last traces spilling out over old pavements and on to the road, pulverised by rain and snow until they were all gone.

I wish the government hadn't destroyed everything so comprehensively. But then I remember there was no choice. They had to dispose of the dead and halt the spread of Hoffman's – even if there was hardly anyone left to catch it. At least they were efficient. Blast away death, wait for the floods to sweep the last remnants into the rivers, into the sea. As far away as possible. Battered into submission. Neutralised.

We pass through an area of Japanese knotweed. It stands tall in the water on both sides of the road, creating a barrier between us and the rest of the world, the branches above reaching out and touching, temporarily darkening our progress. It's flattened slightly by the rain, but unbowed, claiming the land for itself, preparing for ultimate victory, unaware of the containers of beetles standing by in warehouses. When the satellite pictures are eventually noticed, someone in Brighton will give an order, someone else will press a button, and the drones will take off, airlifting the beetles to the site and dropping them down to a beetle banquet. We've seen it happen once before, several years ago, at the far end of the Woodgate Valley. It's very effective.

'We're coming to the meeting of the M42 and the M6,' says Moth. It sounds poetic, like the sky blurring into the horizon, or the connection of intellects when two strangers understand each other and find points of agreement.

We stop on the approach to the roundabout and lean over the railings to examine the roads below. Now we're higher, we can see further, and it's evident that we made the right decision to find shelter last night. Much of the area has flooded. Streams have become fast-moving rivers, overflowing and spreading. How easily it all fills, transforming the landscape into a watery wilderness.

The roads loop round in so many different directions, overlapping, doubling back under and over each other. How do we work out which one we need? A large sign towers above us, impossible to read. It was green once, with traces of blue – you can just see tiny flecks of paint clinging on, defying the corrosive blast of wind and rain. It's twisted into an outlandish shape, rusty and unreadable, no help to us.

'How are we supposed to work out which road to go on?' asks Delphine.

'Intersections are always complicated,' says Popi. 'You needed roads on and roads off and more roads where the motorways merged with each other and even more roads that just happened to be running alongside. There was no time for anyone to stop – they were all going too fast – so the approaches had to be long, and if there were bends, they needed to be gradual.'

Looking at all the emptiness, I find it hard to imagine.

'Can't see why they bothered,' says Delphine. 'The cars were all remote-controlled in the end. The computers could have slowed them down.'

'The roads were built before the carpods.'

How did we manage to negotiate this road system last night? In the dark, in the rain. It seemed straightforward at the time, but now it seems extraordinary that we ever found the warehouse. I'm relieved we're all here together and I'm not the one who has to work it out. An enormous weariness is threatening to overtake me. 'Is that where we're going?' I ask, pointing. 'The M6?'

'Not sure,' says Popi. He pulls out the map from his rucksack and opens it, smoothing out the wrinkles. 'Here we are,' he says. It's hard to follow the different-coloured lines meandering across the page. 'We should be able to work it out once we're on the roundabout. Some of the motorways go underneath, and some go over – you can't tell by looking which is which.'

The roads on the map enclose blank spaces. No man's land. Emptiness, where nobody lives.

'Just make sure you get it right first time,' says Moth. 'We don't want to end up on the wrong motorway or find ourselves going down the wrong lane of the right one.'

'We can go in either direction,' I say. 'It doesn't matter which side we're on.'

'Of course it does. You might be prepared to lift the bikes over the central reservation, but I'm not.'

'Moth,' I say. 'We can go whichever side we want. We don't have to go in the direction it tells us. There's no one to bump into.'

She stares at me for a few seconds, then cottons. 'Oh,' she says, sighing. 'You don't always think in a straight line when you're tired.'

'Where's Aashay?' says Delphine.

I whirl round in surprise. He's not there. The road behind us is deserted.

'It's not like him to disappear without a word.' I look at Boris. 'Did you see where he went?'

He's as surprised as I am, but he grunts dismissively, deliberately not interested. 'No idea. Don't know why he turned up anyway. We don't need him. We can take care of ourselves.' I suspect he'd had the same reaction as I did when Aashay appeared outside Grand Central Station. Delighted to see him, thrilled that he'd come to our rescue, then suspicious about why he was there, how he'd found us. He feels betrayed, like the rest of us.

I peer back along the road towards Grand Central Station. It's impossible to see now. Trees fill the uninhabited places, growing out of deserted gardens and spreading, sending their seeds out on the wind, rising up and connecting with each other, constructing a canopy over the landscape. It's only at night, when the lights are on, that the station becomes visible. Is that how Aashay found us? Lights flickering in the sky, high up in a darkened landscape, an unknowing beacon announcing our presence. Was he diverted during one of his journeys across the country, beckoned by the promise of human presence?

'Let's have some breakfast,' says Popi. 'There's still a long way to go.'

It's a relief to realise we don't have to hurry. We dismount and prop our bikes against the railings. I crouch, easing the muscles in my legs. Moth sorts through some of the bags on the tandem and brings out various containers. 'Look,' she says. 'Cheese. They had loads of different sorts at the fair, so I took a good selection.' She unwraps the packages and passes them round. We breathe in the smells. 'I thought I'd keep them for this morning. A surprise.'

'Yitch,' says Lucia. 'Slug slime.'

'It's an acquired taste,' says Popi.

I nibble a bit. 'Actually,' I say, 'it's quite nice.'

There's a pause as everyone roots through the containers to see what's available. We eat silently, washing down the crumbs with water, too exhausted to make conversation.

Boris goes back to his bike and climbs on. He balances for a while in one place, waiting for the bicycle to tip before putting his feet down. It's not like him to reject food.

'Stop it, Boris,' says Moth, after he's lurched towards us for the third time. 'It's irritating.'

'The thing is . . .' says Boris, teetering precariously again before grabbing the railings. 'Um . . .'

'What?' asks Popi.

'I've left my rucksack there. By the door in Grand Central. It was when Dan appeared out of the blue. I grabbed Lucia and ran. I forgot the bag.'

'Are you sure?' But as soon as I've asked I can see it there, black with orange zigzags down the sides, propped against the wall when we took Lucia to the loo.

'Check all the bikes,' says Popi. 'It might have been picked up and put on the wrong one.'

But it's not here.

'How important is it?' asks Moth. 'Could you just leave it?'

'No!' says Boris. 'It's all the things from the fair.'

'What things?' asks Delphine.

'You know, stuff.'

'If it's just stuff,' says Popi, 'you could live without it.'

Boris stares ahead, dangerously sullen, and it's clear that he can't live without it. 'There are other things,' he says. 'My electronic tools – the ones I use all the time. They're personal, I've had them for years. I'd never be able to replace them. It was a stroke of luck I found them in the first place, remember? We couldn't believe it. That flat in Montana House – an old man lived there, obviously an engineer, never came home.'

'Why ever did you bring them?' says Moth.

'Why shouldn't I?' asks Boris, in a burst of angry justification. 'They're mine. I can do what I want with them – you never know when they'll come in useful. And, anyway, it's not safe to leave valuable things at home. If anyone came, a traveller, they might think we'd all gone or died and take whatever they wanted. I bet I'm not the only one who brought things with them.'

He's right. Lucia has the book of nursery rhymes. Delphine has changed her shoes more than once. And I have the book of birds.

'I should have my tools with me at all times,' says Boris.

'Except when you leave them in Grand Central Station,' says Delphine.

He rounds on her. 'Haven't you ever made a mistake? I was worrying about Lucia. Don't you want me to look after her?'

'That's enough,' says Popi. 'It's too late to start blaming each other. I suppose you'll have to go back.'

'Not on his own,' says Moth. 'We'll all have to go.'

'You don't need to,' says Boris. 'It's not that far.'

'We shouldn't separate,' says Moth. 'What if something happens to you? How would we know?'

'I'll be fine,' says Boris. 'I can take care of myself.'

'How will you get in?' asks Delphine.

'I'll ask Dan. If that doesn't work, I'll find another way. Over the balcony, maybe.'

I make a decision. 'I'll go with you.'

'No,' says Boris. 'That's dodo. I can cope on my own.'

'I'm sure you can. But if you didn't come back, we'd all be in Wonderland, only able to guess what happened. If we stick together, at least I can tell everyone how you fought the dragons.'

There's a silence. 'Roza's right,' says Moth, after a while. 'It's safer if there are two of you. Two brains make better decisions.'

I nod. 'Keep an eye open for Hector – he could turn up at any time and he might find the flats confusing. You've got to be nice

247

to him.' I didn't speak to him this morning – there wasn't time – so he'll probably be worrying, but there's nothing I can do. It's his turn to trust me.

'No problem,' says Delphine. 'We're OK with welcomes.'

I eye her suspiciously, wondering what she has in mind. 'We'll probably be back in plenty of time, but just in case . . .'

'I'll look after Hector,' says Lucia. 'I'll watch out for him from your leisure-room window so I can see when he's nearly there.'

'You'll catch us up before then,' says Moth. 'It's not far and your cycling's better than ours.'

'Now, listen, you two,' says Popi. 'It's in and out. No hanging around. I'm expecting you back as quickly as you can manage. Don't stop for anything. And keep an eye open for strangers. If you see anyone, avoid them if at all possible.'

Boris nods seriously. He doesn't want me with him, I can tell, but he knows he doesn't have a choice. 'You'd better keep up, Roza,' he says. 'I'm not going to dawdle.'

It's hard leaving the rest of the family. They stand on the roundabout and watch us as we take the slip-road on to the A446, going the wrong way, back to where we've just been. I keep alert, automatically scanning the roads in all directions, checking for lone cyclists, for anyone who might be following. There's no sign of Aashay in the distance, no sign of anyone. We're safe, I think. We made a clean getaway from Grand Central Station. It's bad luck we have to return.

I turn and wave. Moth and Popi are still there, curiously small, somehow vulnerable next to Delphine and Lucia. Four hands rise into the air as they wave back, fading into the drizzle as the gap between us grows larger. I have to resist the fear that I'll never see them again. This is nonsense, I say to myself. We'll get the rucksack, race back and be home in time for Hector's arrival.

The approach to Grand Central Station feels different in daylight. Boris and I haven't said a word since we left the others, both of us too weary to talk. I find myself thinking about Aashay again. He must have left us shortly after Popi rejected his offer to help with the tandem. Where did he go? Why didn't he tell us he was going? I imagine him zooming along the road towards us, clutching Boris's rucksack in triumph, expecting to accompany us home now that he's done his good deed and proved himself loyal.

'You didn't tell me you were leaving the fair,' he'll say, 'so why should I tell you when I'm leaving you?'

'Good point,' I'll say.

I'm relieved he's not with us. But why does everything seem so flat without him?

We try to avoid the puddles, but there's plenty of surface water, so we inevitably splash each other, scowling, but still not talking. It's only as we approach Grand Central that I start to watch Boris more carefully, waiting for him to give the signal to slow down.

'OK,' he says at last. 'We're nearly there. Just try to be as quiet as you can. We don't want to attract Dan's attention.'

No, I think, I'm going to sing: *Ding, dong bell, Pussy's in the well . . . Hark, hark, the dogs do bark, The beggars are coming to town.*

Or I'll shout: 'We've returned, Desperate Dan! Are you ready for it? The shoot-out at Grand Central Station.'

We dismount and stare at the building. It's dull and ugly in daylight, a gigantic concrete box, built for convenience, not beauty. The forest of pillars below is black with mould and plastered with debris, tidemarks left by the floods. The greyness of the day seeps into the building and somehow merges with it so that the edges seem blurred and unsteady. When we arrived last night, it had seemed romantic, a safe haven, a promise of rescue. Now I can't see anything attractive about it. Even the balcony, edged with lights, is a symbol of functionality, like the tenements where criminals used to hide, where drugs changed hands and secret people lived chaotic lives. I've seen those places in films. I know enough to experience a shiver of fear at the association.

'Do you think he's gone back to bed?' I ask, in a low voice, half expecting Dan to appear on the balcony and start shouting at us.

Boris shrugs.

'Don't blame me for this,' I say, annoyed by his refusal to engage. 'You're the one who left the bag.'

We stand for a while longer, listening intently. But we're surrounded by silence. Wind whistles between the pillars. Water drips off the sides of the balcony, plopping miserably to the ground.

'Come on,' says Boris at last. 'We can't stand here all day.'

We prop our bikes against a pillar, close to the entrance. The door is ajar. Why? Last night, Dan asked us to lock it. Is he expecting us? As we approach, we hear the charming female voice inviting us in, repeating herself every few seconds, triggered by the open door, unable to stop until it closes.

'Welcome to Amazon.'

When they named Amazon, they were thinking of the river, not the army of female warriors. They didn't know I would be coming. But I'm here now. I'm not afraid.

We step over the threshold and creep cautiously up the stairs. It doesn't feel the same as it did last night. There's something different, something not right. I can see the tension in Boris – the inflexibility of his head on his neck, the way he keeps trying to ease the tightness in his arms – and I know he's worrying too.

'Welcome to Amazon!'

Does Dan know we're here? Is he watching us on a computer as we climb the stairs, chuckling quietly, waiting for exactly the right moment to appear? Can he seal the doors so we can't get back out?

We stop on the halfway landing and listen. I can hear the computers, murmuring away to themselves, chuntering on quietly as they send out the messages no one receives. We didn't hear them when we came up the stairs last night. They should be hidden behind the door at the top, invisible and silent.

Boris looks at me, frowning slightly. He's heard it too. I open my mouth to speak, but he puts a finger on his lips. I nod. We don't want to make it easier for Dan than it needs to be.

We start to climb the second flight of stairs. After a few steps, I can see Boris's rucksack leaning against the wall, near the door. I put my hand on his back and he stops. I point. There. He nods.

We only need to grab it and run. We don't have to know what's going on, why the door is open, why we can hear the computers.

Boris leaps up, taking the stairs two at a time. I stay where I am and wait, ready for flight. It doesn't need two of us to get the bag.

'Welcome to Amazon.'

The door to the computer room has an automatic device that pulls it shut whenever anyone passes through. When we left this morning, it closed, silently and efficiently, a reminder that the computers were the important entities here, that the whole building was constructed for their protection.

'What?'

Boris's voice is unnaturally loud, apparently no longer concerned with stealth, frightening in the space of the stairwell.

'Ssh,' I say nervously, convinced that Dan is going to appear behind us with a carving knife, yelling like a madman.

But Boris is ignoring his rucksack. He's stopped with his back to me, his whole body rigid as he peers into the computer room.

I climb the last of the steps to the landing to see what he's looking at.

Something – a shoe, a boot? – is jamming the door open. Inside, where the computers continue to murmur as if there's no problem, a large object is blocking the entrance.

It's a person, someone lying on the floor.

Boris leans against the door and pushes, straining to shift the weight behind it. As it inches open, I can see inside.

It's Dan. He's lying in a bizarre position, with one leg bent sideways into an impossible angle and his arms flung out in a gesture of outrage.

I hear myself cry out, a thin sound in the immensity of the space, insignificant against the background of busy computers. I grab Boris and he doesn't push me away.

'Is he . . .?'

'I don't know,' he says. He bends over him and I hear him catch his breath.

'Do you think he's had a heart attack?' I say at last, my voice hoarse. 'Did we do that, by running away, by making him angry?'

But Boris is running his hands over Dan's face. 'No,' he says, his voice just above a whisper. 'Look.'

He strokes Dan's hair away from his forehead, the long, wild hair that was alive such a short time ago, the hair that made him so distinctive. His eyes are wide open, staring intently into nowhere, blank and glazed. There's a huge hole in his forehead, a deep cavern, and black liquid has oozed out of it, down his face, now dry and crusted.

You don't need previous experience to recognise death.

With a grunt, Boris puts his arms round the body and heaves him over. There's another hole in his back and much more leakage. The floor underneath him is dark and sticky and the colour of the liquid is not black. It's red.

I step back, terrified. I open my mouth to shriek again, but nothing comes out. Cold creeps through me, a hard frost that gathers in my stomach and sends out icy, paralysing tendrils along my arms, tight and painful in my hands.

I can't think. Words burst into my head and disappear again. Dead – shot – no! – how? – bullet – impossible—

A gun. Someone somewhere has a gun.

'Boris,' I say at last, and the syllables stretch out slowly and awkwardly. I try again, slightly more coherently. 'Boris.' I manage to look across at him. He's fixed into his position by the body, no more in control than I am. I don't know how much time has passed. 'Boris!' My voice is louder, sharper, more demanding.

He pulls himself to his feet slowly, like an old man, his face white and stiff, his breathing ragged.

'I think we should get out of here,' I say.

He clears his throat, as if he's going to speak, then nods. He puts out his hand and grabs my arm, pulling me away from the body towards the door. 'Hurry,' he says, in a thin voice. 'We need to go.'

We have to step over the body and it's difficult to avoid the drying blood. I can't take my eyes off Dan. Only a few minutes ago we were afraid of him, but now he's just a broken old man, collapsed and discarded like a toy, his face still transfixed by the surprise of his death. I wish we had been kinder to him. I see the pile of blankets, flung to one side in the moment of shock when he met his killer, recognised what was going to happen and tried to run, turning his back on the gun. I go to pick one up, trying not to think about his fear, shake it out and lay it gently over his body. I want him to look more peaceful, to hide his final humiliation.

The humming of the computers is hurting my ears. They seem so loud, almost deafening, as if they understand and are singing in sympathy, a death-song for Dan, a desire to give some purpose to his life.

'Come on,' says Boris, impatiently, stepping out on to the landing.

'Welcome to Amazon.'

He jumps, whirling round with fright.

'It's all right,' I say. 'It's only the computer.'

He takes a few deep breaths and heads for the stairs.

At the last minute, I see his rucksack, still standing in the corner, propped against the wall. I grab it, then leap after him. *Jack and Jill went up the hill to fetch a pail of water.* We throw ourselves down the stairwell, taking the steps in twos and threes, half sliding on the banister, falling over our feet. *Jack fell down and broke his crown and Jill came tumbling after.*

We burst through the door, seize our bikes, run alongside them for a few seconds, too panicked to stop and get on. Once the building has sunk back between the trees, we scramble on and pedal very fast.

We sweep along the road side by side, grim and determined. After about five minutes, we stop, as if we've both run out of energy at the same time. We realise we have to talk before we catch up with the others. We halt by the side of the road, glancing round continuously, up and down the road for clues that someone might be following us. We stay on our bikes with our feet down, ready to flee if necessary, gasping for breath and waiting until we're capable of speaking. But neither of us knows what to say.

'What do you think happened?' I say at last.

'Someone shot him.'

'But who? And why?'

'We're not likely to find an answer to that, are we? We didn't know him. He could have had all sorts of enemies. It's not something you tell passing strangers.'

I think again of him lying there. He was just a man who had been left behind, a survivor of Hoffman's with no family to keep him balanced, whose only friends were probably computers. He might have been a threat to Lucia, but we can never be sure. I was reluctant to come back because I thought he was unpredictable and possibly dangerous, but I didn't want to hurt him. That's a different matter altogether. Why would anyone want to kill him? There's enough space in the country for us all. It would be easy enough to avoid someone you didn't like. 'Where did the gun come from? I didn't know there were any left.'

Boris sighs. 'Just because you've never seen one, Roza, doesn't mean they don't exist. We can't be certain of anything.'

'But even pre-Hoffman's they weren't used by the general population. It's not America. We don't live inside a film.'

'Apparently we do.'

I remember something. 'What about the Free Thinkers?' I say. 'They've done it before, according to Hector, killed a caretaker in an onformation centre.'

'Who?' says Boris. He's studying the road while we talk, his eyes never still.

'Do you think we're in danger?' I ask. 'Whoever did this can't be far away. It's all happened very recently, between the time we left and the time we returned. He could be out there now, possibly just round the corner, listening to our conversation . . .'

'He won't be interested in us. Why would he be? We don't know him. And who are we going to tell? He'll be heading off, carrying out some kind of plan that we know nothing about.'

'You're probably right,' I say uncertainly. A terrible thought strikes me. 'Boris . . .'

He looks at me. Is he thinking the same as me? 'What?'

'You don't think . . .'

He shakes his head. 'No,' he says. 'No. It's not his style.'

Why is Aashay the first person we think of? 'But how can you be so sure? He could have come back here after he left us.'

'We don't know when he left. Nobody noticed.'

'Exactly.'

'He didn't have a gun.'

'How do you know? He'd hardly have told you, would he? And even if he didn't have one when he was with us, even if you'd been through his things to check, which I don't believe, even if he hadn't hidden it in a secret place that you had no chance of finding, even after all that and he really didn't have a gun, what was to stop him getting one from someone at the fair?'

A loud rustle from the trees makes us jump round, but a crow flies out, flapping its wings slowly and mournfully, black against the grey drizzle.

'Let's go,' I say, my voice shaking. 'I'm scared. I want to catch up with the others.'

He manoeuvres his bicycle on to the road again. 'Look,' he says, 'let's not say anything to anyone else yet. Wait till we get home. There's no point in scaring them.'

'OK,' I say. 'It's a good thing I picked up your bag.' It's been hanging from my handlebars, so I hand it to him and he has the grace to look abashed as he slips his arms through the straps. 'Please let's go. I don't want to be here any more.'

We set off, accelerating recklessly, our eyes fixed in front of us, determined to put as much distance between us and Grand Central Station in as short a time as possible.

20

When we reach the motorway intersection where we left the others, we realise that we should have paid more attention to Popi's map. It's not clear which way to go. We circle the roundabout slowly, checking all the roads that lead on or off.

'The slip-road will be going down a hill,' I say, remembering that we'd been looking at the motorway from a bridge above it.

'But which one?' asks Boris. 'We don't want to end up going to London.'

I'm losing my bearings. 'Where's the road we came in on? They all look the same.' It would be impossible to know if someone was following us. We can no longer identify forwards or backwards. We're just as likely to meet them eye to eye as have them creep up behind us.

Suddenly Boris skids to a halt. 'There they are!' he shouts. He waits for me to join him, then points into the distance.

They're tiny, so far away that they don't seem to be moving. I have to blink a few times, concentrate, peer intently, before I can make them out in the mist.

'It's not that far. They must have waited before setting off. Come on, we'll eat those kilometres before they have time to sing a song of sixpence.' He has an impressive ability to bounce. Within a period of only a few seconds, the pleasure of seeing the rest of the family has created enough energy for him to leap, catlike, on to a previously unscalable wall.

'Boris!' I call, as he shoots ahead of me. 'Stop!'

'Now what's the matter?'

'Your jacket,' I say.

He slows down. 'What are you rabbiting— Oh!' He's just seen the bloodstains on the sleeves.

'Did you bring any other clothes?' Unlikely. The rest of us brought spares. Boris's mind would have been on food and drink and, of course, his tools.

'Why would I need two jackets?'

'Turn it inside out.'

'I can't do that. It's ungroovy.'

'When have you ever worried about groove? Nobody'll notice, and if they do, just pretend it's a mistake and you can't be bothered to change it until we get home. Nobody's going to care that much. They're all too tired.'

We tear along the motorway, desperate for the comfort of belonging, greedy for safety in numbers. They don't turn round, intent on their own progress, and we line ourselves up alongside them before they notice we've been chasing them.

When Moth sees us, she nearly falls off her bike with surprise. 'Well,' she says, pulling up abruptly. 'A warning might have been helpful. A shout, a POD beep.' She's grinning, relieved and delighted to see us.

'Roza!' cries Lucia. 'You've been gone for ages.'

'No,' I say, doubled over my handlebars, struggling to get my breath back. I lean over and give her a quick hug. 'We're back before you've had time to say *Hey, diddle diddle*.'

'*Hey, diddle diddle*,' she says, '*the cat and the fiddle*—'

'See?' I say. 'You've only just said it and I'm back.'

'We weren't expecting you quite so soon,' says Delphine. 'Have you been using solar to increase your speed?'

'Sun?' says Boris, pointing at the heavy cloud cover. 'Are you serious?'

'Did you go all the way there?' asks Popi, suspiciously. 'I wouldn't have thought you'd had time.'

'We raced,' I say. 'Boris goes faster if there's a chance of winning. He thinks I can't keep up, but I can.'

'Did you find your bag, Boris?' asks Lucia.

Boris nods, jerking his thumb behind him to indicate the rucksack on his back.

'Any problems?' asks Popi, watching us closely. Can he pick up our unease, read beyond the words?

I look at Boris, but he's swigging water from his bottle. 'All good,' I say. 'In and out in the flick of a switch. Didn't speak to Dan.' I'm not lying. You can't speak to someone who's dead.

'Were there any problems getting through the door?' asks Moth.

'No, it was open.'

'How strange. Do you think he was expecting you?'

'No,' I say. 'The rucksack was exactly where we left it. Did you notice all that Japanese knotweed further back? How big an area will it need to cover before they drone in the beetles?'

'Enormous, if it's anything like that patch on the Woodgate Valley,' says Popi. 'I think they like to wait and see what happens before they do anything. Some weeds have a natural limit – rather like viruses – and die out on their own. Otherwise we'd have been overrun by bindweed centuries ago.' He's watching me and Boris, his eyes thoughtful. He's worked out that something's not right. He won't ask now because he's concerned about getting us all home, but he'll want to know more later.

We have to stop more frequently than on the outward journey, exhausted, heavy with damp, our eyes aching with the effort of peering through the drizzle. I'm longing to get home, hoping – unreasonably – that Hector will be there already. It's hard to believe, but very reassuring, that by the end of today we'll be eye to eye and it won't matter so much if my POD packs up altogether.

A great weariness seeps through us as we leave the motorway and cycle round the outskirts of the city centre. We're moving more and more slowly, cycling mechanically, barely awake, as if every revolution of the pedals is almost too much to bear.

Then at last, with a great burst of joy and renewed vigour, Boris, Delphine and I ride on to the Five Ways roundabout and familiarity. The white of the barriers shines through the drizzle with a comforting welcome, so soaked by summer sun that it can afford to release its brilliance slowly and kindly, creating a dazzling display for the entire winter.

'Yahshee-banshee!' yells Boris. He puts his head down and starts to accelerate, his energy restored, whizzing past me and Delphine. He sways from side to side, pumping the pedals furiously, as he sets off on a circuit of the roundabout. While we stand and wait for Moth and Popi to join us, he completes his first lap and carries on. Just before he reaches us for the second time, he raises his hands over his head in a clasp of victory and howls with delight before coming to an abrupt halt and nearly falling off.

'Feeling better?' I say.

Moth and Popi are pedalling laboriously up the approach road. Moth is a few metres in front, hanging back for support, while Popi, weighed down by the extra weight of the tandem, strains to keep up. Lucia is trying to help, her short legs whirling earnestly, but her adjusted pedals don't have much effect on their overall speed.

'Go, Popi, go!' calls Delphine.

Boris gets off his bike, props it against the side, and runs back down the slope. He positions himself behind the tandem and starts to push. This produces a bit more momentum and Popi summons a last burst of energy for the final stretch. We all cheer as they reach the top and level out on the roundabout.

I help Lucia climb down from her seat for a short break.

'Bravo!' says Delphine. 'Just the home run now.'

Lucia manages a small victory dance before collapsing on the ground.

'Stand up, Lucia,' says Moth. 'It's wet.' She swallows some water and hands the bottle to Popi.

He drinks deeply. 'Am I good or am I good?' he says, when he's finished.

'You're good,' says Moth, and unexpectedly kisses his cheek.

'Boris,' says Delphine. 'Your jacket's inside out.'

He looks down. 'Oh, yes,' he says. 'So it is.'

She rolls her eyes at me. 'He's just not going to measure up to Hector, is he?'

We take the A456, speeding up a little, revived by the

proximity of home. As we round the corner and freewheel down the hill to our group of flats, I examine the grey, silent entrance to Wyoming with a mixture of excitement and anxiety.

No sign of Hector or his bicycle. It's too early. He's got fifty miles to cover, much further than us. I'm being unreasonable.

'You should have left the sculpture out,' I call to Popi. 'It would have been nice to be welcomed home by a giant girl, headless or otherwise.'

'I made the right decision,' he says. 'It won't be safe until it's got a lightning conductor and I've weather-proofed it – paint, sealant. It'll be indestructible.'

It's going to be a beacon, a monument to the first post-Hoffman's generation. Good for the next hundred years or so.'

Now that I'm in touch with our router, I check my POD. Come on, Hector, you can't be far away.

He's tried to get through to me several times this morning, but left a message only on his last attempt. 'Either you're asleep, dreaming dreams, or you've left even earlier than me. Don't overdo it, Roza. I'm really . . .' His voice weakens and fades. I've never heard him sound so tentative before. Could he be experiencing the same nervousness as me, now that we're so close? He clears his throat. 'I'm so looking forward to meeting you.' The formality is touching, a reminder that most of what he says is just waffle, words for show, the outward display of a carefully constructed personality. Every now and again he lets me glimpse his vulnerability and it moves me. I enjoy his public performance, but he's somehow nicer without it. 'I'm setting off. Today's the day—'

We sweep up the ramp to the cycle floor. We only left yesterday morning, but it feels as if we've been round the world and back. Everything looks the same, but it's not.

I head straight for my flat. I want my own space, my own bedroom, and my own company. 'Can someone come and tell me when Hector arrives?' I say.

'What makes you think any of us will be awake?' asks Moth.

I stop outside the family flat as Popi unlocks the door 'Lucia will be,' I say, watching her push past us, wriggling out of her rucksack.

Popi yawns. 'She'll probably be the only one.' He follows me to the base of the stairs where I'm standing, about to go on up. 'Do we need to talk first?' he asks quietly.

I see Dan on the floor, the black-edged hole in his forehead, his blood sticky under my shoes. I switch off the image abruptly. 'I can't . . .' I breathe. 'Can I tell you later? When I've had some sleep. It's too—'

'So something did happen?'

I nod, unable to reply, ambushed by the threat of tears. I angle my head slightly backwards so they don't reveal themselves.

He touches my arm gently. 'Don't worry, Roza. Get some sleep. We'll talk later.'

He stands and watches me head up to my own flat. I intend to turn back and smile, but can't summon the energy. I know he would like me to, but I'm afraid of just dissolving.

When I reach my landing, I can hear Boris behind me, leaping up the stairs as if he still has energy to spare. I wonder if I should call out to him, ask him if he wants to tell Popi, but decide not to. We will discuss it, but not yet.

I step inside my flat and close the door behind me.

'Good afternoon, Roza,' says Rex the computer, in his soothing voice. 'The weather forecast for the rest of the day is promising.'

'Rex!' I say, with genuine pleasure. 'How lovely to hear you. Have you missed me?'

There's a pause while he decides how to react to this unscheduled enthusiasm. He's not programmed for casual conversation. 'Would you like a temperature adjustment, Roza?'

'Oh, never mind,' I say, waving my hand in the air to cut him off. His voice has cheered me, but his responses are too limited.

I stand in the hall and let the silence and the space seep into me, as if I'm sinking into a hot bath. Everything is in its usual place, familiar and safe, untainted by anyone else's presence. I can hear the slow, restful tick of the clock I found a few years ago in Colorado House, a self-perpetuating device that doesn't need batteries. It has to be wound once a week with a small neat key attached to the back. I do it every Saturday morning, a soothing ritual: I convince myself that I'm reconstructing time, building up hours for the future. When I wind it, I can feel the spring tightening inside, the tension increasing until it reaches full capacity. It's an everlasting clock, a miracle of invention from history.

I slip off my waterproof, hang it on a hook by the front door and place my rucksack on the hall table, running my hand over the pine surface, tracing the familiar scratches with my fingertips. It was rejected by Moth and Popi – too imperfect, too dented from earlier collisions. 'It's soft wood', says Popi, 'not much use as long-term furniture.' But that's what I like about it, the way it absorbs damage as it travels through time. It hasn't needed to retain its original perfection. It's adapted, bent a little with the imprints of past owners, kept going.

I catch sight of myself in the large circular mirror with bevelled edges that always greets me on my entrance. It's a reminder that I exist, that I'm not a whisper from the past but a reality, someone with a home of her own. My plait curls down over my shoulder, heavy with damp, matted with neglect. Wisps of stray hair stand out around my head. My face is grey and weary, and there are dark patches under my eyes. I look slightly mad, not ideal for the arrival of my future husband. But everything will seem easier to deal with once I've had some sleep.

I touch my POD and listen to Hector's last message again. 'Leaving now, eight o'clock on the dot.' There's a pause while he tries to think of something significant to say. 'This is it – the meeting, crunch time, hold-your-breath time, the-purpose-of-our-existence time—' He stops, either because he thinks he's overdoing it or because he can't think of anything else to say. 'Cherry-oh, Roza,' he says, and switches off.

I take a deep breath, hold it for a few seconds, then let it out slowly while I walk into the leisure room.

The blinds are open, controlled by Rex, who continues to

follow routines in my absence. I stand at the window for some time, peering into the weak, watery light, trying to spot a lone figure on its way, cycling over the empty land, heading in my direction.

But there's no one. Just the same empty world of trees and deserted roads as always. The small number of weeding machines on the Woodgate Valley that still function are huddled on their platforms, waiting for heat and warmth before returning to their duties. It's only a matter of time before they surrender, cease to function, join the mass suicide of their contemporaries and allow themselves to be swept away in the floods.

My eyes ache. I'm going to fall over if I stand any longer, so I stumble towards the bedroom, not convinced I'll be able to sleep. My mind is full of images of Dan: alive, playing Scrabble, talking online to an easily defeated opponent without taking any notice of the replies; reciting nursery rhymes to a class of imaginary children; blocking the doorway with his feet, dead. I picture Hector pedalling towards me, propelled by nervous energy, composing lunatic eulogies. But when I see my bed, I'm filled with a nostalgia out of all proportion to the time I've been away. I kick my shoes off, keel over and crash instantly into a deep sleep.

'Roza, Roza!' A voice penetrates my dreams.

It's Hector, leaning over me, about to give me the kiss that will wake me from my hundred-year sleep.

It's Lucia, wanting me to come and play with the toy fair she's set up in her bedroom.

It's Farzana, wanting me to help draw up a new constitution for the Weather Watchers.

It's Aashay, leaning over me, polishing the surface of his gun, blowing across the hole at the end, smoothing the barrel down my cheek, leaning over to give me the kiss that will wake me from my hundred-year sleep.

My eyes open and I stare blindly upwards, confused by the daylight, my heart pounding.

Popi, sitting on the side of the bed, is gently shaking my

shoulder. 'Roza, you need to wake up. You've been asleep for ages. Best not to sleep too long. Save it for tonight.' Disguising his concern with practical details.

I pull myself up into a sitting position. 'Has Hector arrived? What's the time?'

'About four o'clock. He's not here yet.'

I stare at him, calculating. Hector reckoned it was about fifty miles from Banbury to here. If he averages ten miles an hour – depending on the gradient, of course, and I have no idea if most hills would be going up or down – it should take him about five hours. Stops and rests and meal breaks might make it seven, although he'd probably move faster on flat, straight stretches. It was unreasonably optimistic to expect him to be waiting outside Wyoming when we got back, but if he left at eight o'clock this morning, he really should be here by now.

'What's wrong?' I ask Popi, who's studying me gravely.

He sighs and leans back against the foot of my bed. 'I've spoken to Boris.'

'Oh.' I would prefer not to have to remember.

'Oh, indeed. That sums it up, really, doesn't it?'

There's a long silence.

'I was wondering . . .' He hesitates.

'What?'

'Well, it's not easy to know if someone's dead,' he says. 'Are you quite sure?'

I think of all that blood, the way it had spread across the floor and congealed. 'I didn't get close enough to him,' I say, 'but Boris did. He bent over him, checked his face. I'm sure he was dead, Popi. There was so much blood, and the way his eyes were staring – they were so . . . empty.'

Popi nods. 'OK,' he says. 'A nasty business.'

'Yes.' I don't know what he's expecting me to say. It was shocking at the time and it's shocking now. 'I thought all that stuff in the films was just pretend.'

'Well, it wasn't exactly pretend, but I hoped it had all faded into the past. Now we seem to have stumbled into a kind of recreated underworld – and the rules have changed.'

'Or we've been led into it.'

He studies me for a while before replying. 'I was under the impression you liked Aashay.'

I'm furious to discover I'm flushing. Stop it! I say to myself. Don't give him further reason for thinking something that isn't true. 'Well, I've talked to him quite a lot.'

'Everyone's talked to him. That's what he's good at. Gaining people's confidence.'

I'm startled by this. He seems to be suggesting that Aashay has had private conversations with each one of us, separating us out and giving us individual attention, making us all feel special. Even Popi? 'It's hard to believe – even if he's a bit – he's always helped us.'

'It's too much of a coincidence. I suspect Dan contacted Aashay last night, told him we were there. How else could he have found us so easily? Then, when he left us on the A446, he must have headed back towards Grand Central. The time available to enter the building, shoot Dan, then get away before you and Boris arrived was quite short, so it's hard to believe anyone else could have managed it. OK, it's circumstantial – but convincing.'

'Why would he kill Dan?'

He sighs deeply. 'I don't know. A genuine accident, perhaps. Or Dan had something he wanted. Or it's part of a struggle for control between rival groups. Who knows what deals are being struck, promises broken? Once this kind of thing starts, it always escalates and violence becomes a way of life. It's about power – as ever.'

I don't know what to say. I've rarely seen him so despondent.

He puts his head down, running his hands through his hair. 'I've never understood why people can't just talk things over. Find a civilised way to sort out their differences.'

'You don't always negotiate,' I say. 'You've been known to shout at Boris.'

He smiles. 'That's different. Boris is infuriating. I'm

exasperated, not angry.' His smile fades and his eyes look inwards. 'Obviously, words can't solve every problem. There was widespread panic during the spread of Hoffman's. Everyone, and I include myself, was terrified. Some people decided they didn't need to obey the law or keep to a moral code. They thought they were special because they were still alive, invincible, free to behave however they wanted. The rest of us were distracted by the need to survive. The only safe thing to do was to stay where you were, make no waves, not let anyone know you existed.'

I watch him. He's never spoken of this before.

'There were terrible things going on . . .' He hesitates. 'Sometimes you have to retaliate – you have no choice.' There's silence, a tension that pulses through the air. 'Hoffman's got most of them in the end, of course. The bullies weren't immune.'

I wait for him to continue. I don't want to interrupt his thoughts.

'There were looters – no police to stop them, no cavalry on the horizon. He didn't have a conscience. He was going to take whatever he wanted.'

He? Who's he?

'He was threatening your mother, you see. I couldn't stand by and let it happen. She was peeling potatoes – the kitchen knives were out. He didn't know I was behind him.' He shakes his head. 'What else could I do? They were desperate times . . .'

'What happened?' I'm seeing my father creep up behind a man, a Goliath, eight feet tall, wider than two men, who's pushing Moth up against the wall. Did Popi really do this, take on a monster to save Moth?

'It's harder than you think,' says Popi, 'stabbing someone. You need so much strength. Once isn't enough – he didn't react for ages. When he finally – finally – turned away from your mother and came towards me, he was roaring with fury. But his legs gave way in the end and he just toppled over – like a tree, chopped down. Only just missed me.'

This is hard to take in. My Popi, a man who believes in the power of the mind, a gentle, cultured man, the father who has been present in the background of my life for ever, ready with a guiding hand, a kind word, has killed someone, and I never knew. 'What happened to him?'

'It wasn't easy. We squeezed him into a wheelbarrow and on to the delivery lift, then out behind Idaho. I dug a hole in the dark – Moth wasn't up to it, she was traumatised – when there weren't any drones going over. You used to be able to tell in the dark, just about, some of them left traces, silver threads in their wake – you had to know what to look for – doesn't happen any more. Korean, I think. They were showing off. Then we tipped him in and I shovelled the soil over him. Don't know if the satellites saw us, but no one ever said anything. Maybe they weren't watching the screens at the right moment. Maybe the watchers had all died of Hoffman's.' He passes his hand over his face.

'We're not safe here any more, are we?' I say, panic making my voice tremble. 'Aashay could lead other people to us. We can't just sit and wait for them to turn up.'

'Moth and I have been discussing this – we've realised how uncertain everything's become, how tenuous our claim on Lucia—'

'What do you think we should do? Go to Brighton?' What am I saying? Leave the only home we've ever known?

Popi looks down at his hands. He's opening and closing his fists, stretching them out, turning them over and tracing the lines on his palms thoughtfully and meticulously. The fingers on his right hand are thicker than those on the left, unable to straighten completely. Is this the onset of arthritis already? He's too young. It's the hand he uses for sculpting, the hand that holds the instruments that express his deepest, most instinctive thoughts. 'We've always assumed there are a reasonable number of families around somewhere,' he says. 'Parents like us, but also more people in their twenties and thirties, with younger children.'

'Well, none of them live round here,' I say, 'according to Olisa. We'd have come across them, or at least seen signs. There are more families in Brighton, though. Hector's got a younger brother.'

Popi nods. 'But you'd still expect to some more children at the fair – babies, toddlers. Phil – do you remember him? He carved animals, small ornaments – he believed the children had been left at home, but I'm not convinced. Every adult we spoke to had an overwhelming desire for contact with a real, living child. They're over-emotional, desperate, irrational.'

He's right. Children seem to create a physical craving in most people, an irresistible urge to touch, lift them into their laps, cuddle them. How do Onyeka and Ogechi cope with all that attention? What happens if adults no longer have expectations about the future? Do they become more and more selfish? Take what they can, while they can? Like the man Popi buried outside Idaho, or the uncles and aunties. 'So what are you saying? You don't think there are many younger parents?'

'I'm not sure there are any. Remember how anxious the government was to have you tested when you decided to marry Hector? You represent one of the very few chances for another generation. You're even more valuable than we thought.'

This is a burden I don't want. What if something goes wrong? What if I can't do it for some reason? 'But there were some older children at the fair – teenagers. They'll all be parents in a few years' time.'

'Maybe. Moth and I reckon most of the young people belonged to only a handful of families – maybe five or six with post-Hoffman children. That's not very many.'

I've already worked this out. There was Lancelot's family – he was probably pre, but his sister was younger – and Olisa's daughters, who were definitely post. Apart from that, I saw at least two other teenage girls and maybe four boys playing football, including the three who came out with Boris when we were leaving. But it's possible they were older.

'The trouble is,' says Popi, 'you and Boris and Delphine represent a tiny minority.'

I don't want to be special, it makes me uncomfortable. We've just inherited genes that we might never have known about in a different existence. And Lucia, the rarest of us all, doesn't strictly belong to us anyway. Really, we're kidnappers ourselves and, like everyone else, we can't admit it.

'We have the children everyone wants, we live in an isolated position and we've just announced our existence.'

'We have to go to Brighton,' I say. 'As soon as we can. At least we'd be protected from the people with guns.' People like Aashay. 'Hector and I are heading there anyway, and Boris and Delphine wouldn't need much convincing to stay after the wedding.' It would probably be harder to persuade them to go home.

Popi alters his position on the end of my bed, leaning against the wall now and stretching out his legs. 'But . . . what if Lucia's original family are in Brighton?'

So that's our dilemma. We're in danger here; we'd be in danger there. 'We'll have to risk it. There isn't much choice.'

'It's the best place for you three – I just can't decide about Lucia.'

'You could always leave if there was a problem. Hector and I could come with you. Stick together.'

'Maybe. But once we're there, they might not let us go.'

How could they stop us? We're the Polanskis, the offspring of Moth. We don't follow orders blindly. 'They've let us live here up to now. Why shouldn't we come back if we want to?'

'Everything's changed,' says Popi. 'You're too valuable and there are too many threats to your safety. They'd need to protect you, and they wouldn't have the resources to do it here, miles from Brighton. In fact, I'm surprised they haven't made an attempt to persuade us all to come in already.'

'That's because they know we'll all be going there anyway, for the wedding. What about China? Surely they could help. We work for them. They owe us.'

'No, the Chinese wouldn't be interested. They've got their own problems with fertility, and they're too busy inventing, creating, planning colonies in space.'

I can't accept the bleak picture he's painting. 'We're alive, we have brains – the world should be prepared to help us.'

Popi's face seems to shrink and his eyes darken. 'Roza, they don't care – and they never will, even if we descend into anarchy and end up destroying each other. Look how much they'd save in aid. And drones.'

He's being unnecessarily gloomy. We're not living in the dark ages. People still have a fundamental goodness – we saw that at the fair. 'This is all Aashay's fault. None of this would have happened if he hadn't turned up.' He's the one we should be afraid of, the man from nowhere, Yankee Doodle, the man in the moon. *Where do you come from, where do you go?*

'I suppose we've been lucky to remain hidden for as long as we have,' he says.

Our luck has been manufactured. Rules about online contacts: talk to whoever you want, but never tell them where you are. 'At least the uncles and aunties have never revealed our whereabouts.'

'They don't know where we live,' says Popi. 'None of them ever came here.'

I've never given this much thought before, but it's true. The expeditions were always ours, never theirs. 'So how did Aashay find us?'

'Who knows? Contacts? Chance?'

Lights in a night sky?

'It's hard to believe he just came out of nowhere. He must have seen the signs of our existence, watched and waited.'

'Would it even be possible to hide from Aashay?'

'It's tempting to try to just disappear. Aashay wouldn't be an easy person to lose, but it's not impossible.' He's drumming his fingers on the end of my bed, tapping out rhythms on the floor with his feet.

I'm shocked to find that tears are rushing into my eyes. 'This has always been our home, Popi. It's so hard to think we can't stay here.' He leans forward and puts his arms round me, patting my back. I'm a child again, sitting on his lap, with the warm weave of his jacket making patterns on my cheek, soaking in his solid certainties, letting his arms – which used to feel so much longer than they do now – enclose and hold me with an unassailable strength.

'It'll be hard,' he says, 'but you'll be fine. Hector will keep you safe – and you'll feel more secure when you have your own children.'

If I have children, I'll spend my entire life fearing for their safety. 'This is the only home I've ever known. I thought you and Moth would always be here, living the same life, and I could come back if I wanted to.'

'Things change. It's inevitable.'

I lean over and find some shoes under the bed. 'If you and Moth don't come to Brighton, and we don't go with you, you'll be condemning Lucia to a life without a family. She'll die of boredom.'

Popi stands up and brushes down his trousers. 'Nevertheless, we should at least try to protect her until she's an adult.' He's suddenly brisk. 'The snow is due any time now, and then we'll be marooned until after the floods. So we should be safe for a while at least. We can postpone a final decision until the spring.'

'Hector might have some other thoughts.'

He nods. 'Good point.'

'Have you discussed this with the others?' Aashay introduced Boris and Delphine to new possibilities, and now they have to fold up all that hope and put it back into the cupboard.

'Only Boris. He feels very betrayed.'

Aashay in the art gallery, his eyes round with honesty and sincerity, his arms circling my waist, his presence solid and secure. Surely I'd have seen something, a kink in his smile perhaps, or a hesitation in his voice. 'We all do,' I say in a small voice.

Popi pats my arm. 'I know. Everyone's enjoyed having him around.'

No, I think, that's not strictly true. You've never liked him for longer than about half an hour. *I do not like thee, Doctor Fell, The reason why I cannot tell.* Popi was the only one who was never entirely sure.

'Come downstairs as soon as you're ready. We need to talk about this as a family.'

'Will Lucia have a say?'

'Of course. It's her future too.'

'We need to keep an eye open for Hector.'

'If he's going to be part of the family, we need him with us when we make decisions.'

I know exactly what Hector will say once he knows Aashay is involved.

21

But why is Hector taking so long?

The computers are all on, the four screens watching silently in my tech room, the enormous one in my leisure room. They remain blank, set to receive, their empty faces subliminally flickering, alert and ready, waiting for communication, unable to offer the information I want without input from Hector. While I'm staring at them, willing them into life, they start to wake up.

'Hector!' I say, with relief, before I've pressed the key to give him access.

But it's the face of Weishan from TU that flashes up, four different angles of him, his expression polite and hesitant, apologising for disturbing me on my holiday, asking if I would be able to discuss something with him for a couple of seconds. I listen to the beginning of his message, not taking it in, waiting for the end, in case Weishan knows something about Hector that I don't. But it's all technical, an emergency that can be dealt with by someone else. I close him down without responding. It's Hector I need, not work colleagues.

I prowl round the flat for a while before going downstairs, unable to make decisions, my mind whirling with images of Dan, dead on the floor of Grand Central, Hector lying injured somewhere else, my ears buzzing with his imagined voice: 'Nearly there, Roza. On the borders of the Promised Land. Don't leave before I get there – wait for me.'

I find the family sitting round the kitchen table, arguing. Popi is issuing instructions. 'I want you all to pack a go-bag, just in case we have to leave in a hurry. You probably won't need it, but it's best to be prepared.'

'Why would we leave in a hurry?' asks Delphine. 'Don't you think running away from the fair was enough? I didn't notice anyone chasing us along the M6.' She won't cope with packing. She's accumulated a vast supply of colour-coordinated coats, dresses, shoes, which she stores in the flat next door because there isn't room in her bedroom. 'How am I supposed to decide which dresses to leave behind?'

'You don't need dresses in a go-bag,' says Moth. 'Essentials only.'

'Great,' says Delphine. 'So when it hits forty degrees and we're all jogging along in jeans and boots, chased by hired assassins, it'll be OK to expire from overheating.' She sits back and folds her arms. 'I'm not going without proper luggage.'

'If you were fleeing for your life,' I say, 'you wouldn't care about clothes.'

'That's what you think,' says Delphine. 'Anyway, we're not.'

Someone is going to have to tell her about Dan.

'It's just in case,' says Moth, sharply. 'We don't intend to leave until spring.' Her face is pinched and pale. She's probably thinking the same as Delphine. How do we abandon somewhere we've lived for more than twenty years? How can we possibly decide what to take and what to leave? And if we did have to go in a hurry, which is hard to believe, could Lucia cope with the ride to Brighton? What if a blizzard started while we were travelling?

'What about Edward?' asks Lucia. 'And the chickens?'

'We've got all winter,' says Popi, after a few moments. 'We'll think of something.'

'You have to plan,' says Lucia. 'You're always saying you can't leave things to the last minute.'

'We could let them loose on the Woodgate Valley.'

'No,' cries Lucia. 'They'd starve.'

'They'd find food easily. Animals know instinctively what's safe to eat.'

Lucia stares at Popi, wide-eyed. 'But they'll drown when the floods come.'

He doesn't reply.

'Couldn't we put them in the trailer?' I say quietly. We have a good, reliable trailer – Popi built it a long time ago to fetch supplies from the drops.

'But what about the rest of the luggage?' asks Moth.

'Oh, I see,' says Delphine. 'You're expecting to have a huge trailer while the rest of us make do with a small go-bag.'

'The go-bag is for emergencies only,' says Popi. 'I've already told you that.'

'I'll pull a trailer if it means we can take the animals,' says Boris.

'And me,' says Lucia.

'It must be possible,' says Moth. 'Why don't you design us another trailer, Nikolai? You're good at that kind of thing.'

'I don't know why you're even contemplating leaving in a hurry,' says Delphine. 'None of us would survive the floods, never mind Edward and the hens.'

'We could head for high ground,' says Popi.

'It's not that straightforward,' says Delphine. 'It's not always a matter of high and low, hills or valleys. It's to do with blocked drains and saturated land and things we don't understand.'

She's right. Birmingham is on high land, but there are still floods. Water isn't predictable. It can come thundering down from above, or rise up through the ground. Streams become rivers, which become raging torrents. We're amateurs. We wouldn't know how to read the land, how to find safe areas. Even planning to move seems impossible. People only flee when they're terrified. I'm not frightened enough now that we're back in familiar surroundings, far from Grand Central. Delphine isn't frightened at all.

'It's not far to Brighton,' says Moth. 'We'd find a way, even if the weather deteriorated.'

'Or we could forget Brighton,' says Popi, 'and head north – the Yorkshire moors, the Lake District. It must be possible to go above the floods.'

There's a long silence.

Eventually Boris snorts. 'Are you serious?'

'According to Aashay,' I say, 'no one lives in the north.'

'He told me that too,' says Boris.

'Excellent,' says Popi. 'Just what we need.'

'It probably won't have occurred to you,' says Delphine, 'but there must be a good reason for that.'

'The weather,' says Boris. 'It's colder. You get even more snow.'

'No,' I say. 'That's all changed. They've got vineyards in Sweden now.'

'It's never consistent,' says Moth. 'Some places are warmer, some are colder, and every year is different. Swedish Chardonnay one year, iced water the next. Nobody understands the weather, not properly. It's unmeasurable and unpredictable.'

'Why would we believe Aashay?' says Popi. 'What he said about the north might not be true. It's probably a paradise and he wants to keep it all for himself.'

'I can't believe you're even thinking about it,' says Delphine. 'We're going to Brighton, just like everyone else.'

'The whole point of leaving,' says Popi, 'is to avoid people.'

'So suppose we go north and there's no one there,' I say, as if I'm seriously contemplating it, 'what would happen if we needed help?'

'It's not exactly as if we're familiar with the concept of a gang of useful pals waiting in the wings with expertise,' says Moth. 'What's the difference? TU would still be online, and presumably Brighton would still support us.'

'We're not hiding from Brighton, then?' says Delphine. 'Only everyone else.'

'What about the internet?' I ask.

'Brighton probably has a record of passwords,' says Popi, deliberately softening his voice, trying to calm the anxiety.

'Well, someone really should have thought of that before,' says Delphine. 'It would have solved a few problems.'

'Could the drops be redirected?' asks Boris. 'They have their uses.' We exchange glances. Like me, he knows we'll have to go, but he's only pretending to consider Popi's options. He's expecting to go to Brighton.

A bleakness is settling over us. We couldn't possibly go in a hurry, even in an emergency, out into the unknown without basic survival skills. Living off the land is not the same as a camping weekend in the spring when the weather's good.

It's the world the Weather Watchers want to create. But it's an intellectual exercise to them, not an immediate reality. They'll be sitting at their desks at home now, designing a system that works without assistance from Brighton, but when it comes down to it, they haven't a clue either. Their Cloud Cuckoo Land is just along the road from ours, nestling up nicely to the borders of Fairyland.

'We'd be all right if Aashay was with us,' I say. 'He's got the right sort of knowledge.'

It's a stupid thing to say, but no one contradicts me.

'Would our bikes be strong enough to pull Edward?' asks Boris. 'She's a substantial goat.'

'Depends on the trailer,' says Popi.

'We could start work on it now,' says Boris. 'Ready for spring.'

I wish Hector would come. Another set of brains with a different perspective would be useful.

'We could sleep in a tent,' says Lucia, cheerfully. 'Like Harry Hedgehog and William Weasel.' It's an adventure to her, a nice story. Nobody wants to explain that we may never come back.

We sink into silence.

'What exactly is wrong with Brighton?' asks Delphine after a while.

'Well—' says Moth, 'Lancelot's family might live there.'

'They don't,' says Delphine. 'They come from somewhere else – Wales, I think.'

We all stare at her.

'That's what he told me,' she says.

'Well, well,' says Popi. 'On their own, or near other people?'

She shrugs. 'How would I know? We didn't waste time discussing his neighbours.'

So there are other families living outside Brighton after all. 'Perhaps you should have mentioned this earlier,' I say.

'Why? Nobody asked.'

'OK,' I say. 'Let's go to Brighton.'

'But what about the kidnapping?' asks Moth, softly, turning to me and away from Lucia so she can't hear. Her face has lifted slightly and there's a lighter expression in her eyes.

'Let's just worry about one thing at a time,' says Popi. 'We can't cover every risk.'

'Boris and I have to go anyway,' says Delphine, suddenly cheerful. 'It's the law. No harm in getting there early.'

'Interesting,' says Moth, 'how you're willing to obey that directive, when other rules seem to send you into an apoplectic rage.'

'Nice word, Moth,' I say. ' "Apoplectic".'

Popi clears his throat. 'On the subject of the law . . .' he says.

I turn to him in surprise. Does he have a new revelation? 'Are you going to tell us we don't have to go to Brighton after all?' I ask.

'No,' he says. 'Not exactly. It's just that . . . How do you define a law? Bearing in mind that most families are already in Brighton.'

'Except Lancelot's,' I say.

'It's not much of a law, is it, if it only applies to a handful of people? We all know you'll have to marry by twenty-five, have children—'

'Maybe,' says Delphine. 'The children, that is.'

'The long-term future of the country depends on you, so Moth and I have never been too uncooperative.'

'Speak for yourself,' says Moth.

'But it's an agreement that you have to go to Brighton by a certain age, that's all. Not a law.'

There's a silence.

'And?' says Boris.

'Well,' says Popi, 'I'd feel nervous about breaking the law, but it's not impossible to break an agreement.'

'I can't really see your point,' says Delphine.

'Everyone knows about it,' says Boris. 'And it applies to all of us. Why is that not a law?'

'Mmm,' says Popi. 'OK, but I'm just saying that you shouldn't feel obligated . . .'

He's fighting a losing battle. Only he and Moth resent the twenty-five-year rule.

'Brighton would be heaps better than the middle of nowhere,' says Boris. 'Lots of people – safety in numbers – and Hector says they've got things we haven't even heard of. Their drops are much more interesting.'

'Actually,' says Moth, 'you could be right. We'd have to be careful, but having more people near by could be an advantage.'

'You don't like people, Moth,' says Boris. 'That's why you chose to live here.'

'Well, let's not make a decision,' says Popi, sounding more cheerful. 'There's plenty of time. We've got to get through the winter yet.'

So the original plan still stands. Brighton in the spring. The only difference is that we might all stay. 'Do they have spare homes for refugees?'

But where's Hector?

I go back up to my flat and place a chair in front of my window where I can sit and watch for him. Occasionally, I catch a movement in the corner of my eye, and use my binoculars to check, focusing on the roads and their immediate surroundings. But it's only a tree caught by the wind, a wild animal, perhaps, the shadow of a cloud.

It's now seven o'clock and the light is starting to fade, making it harder to pick out details. I've tried my POD over and over again, but there's never a reply. He must still be cycling. Why's he taking so long? What could have delayed him?

Someone knocks at the front door. 'It's Boris,' says Rex. 'Am I authorised to let him in?'

'Of course.' He doesn't normally ask.

Boris brings a chair over and places it next to mine. 'No sign?' he asks, sitting down.

I shake my head.

He peers through the window. 'It'll be dark soon.'

'I know,' I say, studying his profile. Unlike the rest of us, he's become calmer in the last few hours, as if he's discovered an ability inside himself to analyse and process information before making decisions.

He doesn't speak for a long time. 'I'm sure he's whizzy,' he says eventually. 'Something's delayed him, but he'll know where to find shelter. He's a resourceful kind of guy.'

'Hmm,' I say. Hector works at his computer all day, shuffling figures and getting excited by new permutations. He wears a suit, a tie, like a twentieth-century businessman. He likes discussions. 'We don't actually know that.'

Boris chuckles. 'Can't imagine what you see in him.'

Judging by his holo, which probably isn't fair in view of the failing power of my POD, Hector isn't Muscleman. I can't imagine he'd be much help if you wanted to carry a tree trunk upstairs. 'He makes me laugh.'

He should be here. The gathering darkness fills the room. I'm peering through drizzle, still cycling in my mind, struggling to see as dusk soaks up the view. Exhaustion is fogging my thoughts.

'Did you sleep this afternoon?' I ask Boris.

He shrugs. 'Everyone went to bed almost as soon as we got back. When I woke after about an hour and went downstairs, the others had all conked out. They woke up when the hot water beeped.'

'Was Lucia awake?'

'No, she dropped off under the coffee-table in the leisure room. She'd spent half the journey asleep and still zonked out the moment we were back. Hadn't even taken her coat off.'

'She's only little. She needs more sleep than the rest of us.' So for at least an hour no one had been awake. Could we have missed Hector's arrival? But he'd have waited. He wouldn't have received any of my messages, so he'd have assumed we weren't back yet. He'd hardly have turned up, found us missing and gone away again.

Boris stands and stretches elaborately, with much groaning

and sighing, then sits down again. The lights come on in the flat and the outside fades into blackness. All we can see is our reflections staring back at us.

'Turn them off, Rex,' I say. 'I can't see properly.'

Nothing happens. What's up with Rex? He's programmed for instant obedience.

'You couldn't see anything before,' says Boris. 'You only thought you could.'

I get up to switch off the lights manually, but Boris takes me by the shoulders and eases me back down – gently, not at all like the Boris I've grown up with. 'There's nothing you can do, Roza, except wait. He won't be cycling now. It's nearly dark and he's probably been looking for shelter for the last hour or so. You don't need to worry. He's not a fool.' Boris knows him better than I thought. He's played games with him. He must be able to understand his thinking.

'He'll be all right, won't he?' I say, wanting to visualise Hector in a waystation, but too tired to feel confident.

'What? Will Hector be all right? Get real. If ninety-nine point nine per cent of the remaining world population succumbs to a new version of Hoffman's, Hector will be one of the survivors. You know that, Roza, you just know it.'

I smile at his reflection in the darkened window. He's trying very hard to be a good brother.

'The others didn't see what we saw,' he says, after a while. 'It's harder for them to believe in it.'

'Popi does. He has no doubt whatsoever, but all this talk of go-bags makes me nervous. Do you think he's overreacting? Should we leave now?'

Boris shifts around in his chair, making himself comfortable. 'Really, our lives have been a doddle up to now,' he says. 'But I'm beginning to understand how lucky we've been. Even the uncles and aunties haven't felt like a real threat – they're just irritating – and we've never been in any real danger. Some of the guys I met at the fair – you know, the ones our age – have had a tough time.'

I don't want to hear the details. 'So you think we should go?'

He nods. 'Popi's right. There's stuff that's going to catch up with us. The sensible thing to do is to head out, escape while we can.'

'Boris!' I say. 'Since when have you been sensible?'

He moves his head, trying to avoid my scrutiny. 'It comes to us all in the end,' he says, and grins.

'You liked Aashay, didn't you?' I ask him tentatively.

He sighs and nods. 'We had some good times . . . I never thought . . . although I suppose he's the kind of person . . . you could see that at the fair . . . Hard to believe he had a gun, though. And that he'd use it.'

'He'd have kept it hidden. He knew about secrets.'

'You liked him, too, didn't you?'

I try to banish the memory of his touch, the irrational tension when he stood close to me. 'It was the excitement of someone different, I suppose. But I think I always knew he was dangerous. He made us naïve because we'd never met anyone like him before. If we'd known loads of people, we might have had more confidence in our ability to challenge him, find out what he was up to.' As soon as I've said this, I don't believe it. No amount of experience would have saved us from his charm. And we weren't the only ones. Everyone at the fair was under his spell.

But Boris likes this thought. 'Perhaps if we'd gone to Brighton all those years ago, after the virus, we wouldn't have been so easily fooled.'

'But we'd be different people.' Maybe Boris wouldn't have picked up Popi's good qualities if we hadn't been so isolated. I think of Hector telling me about his brother, his rows with their parents.

He nods slowly, as if I've said something very wise. 'Experience changes you.'

We sit quietly for a while.

'Well,' he says eventually, 'better get to bed. Catch up on some sleep.'

I watch him go. Boris, my brother, who is growing up.

I wave my hand in the air. 'Curtains!' I say.

They glide together, smooth and efficient. At least something's working properly. 'Good night, Roza,' says Rex. His macho voice cheers me. There's still one area of my life in which I can maintain control.

I toss and turn in a cycle of dozing and waking. Hector whispers to me throughout the night, his mouth close to my ear, and I keep jumping, expecting to find him leaning over my bed, smiling, triumphant with his arrival.

'Rise and shine, Roza, I'm here!'

'Why didn't you wait up? You knew I was coming.'

'I'm hurt. There were men with guns – an ambush.'

'Better late than never. Here I am. Real life. Right height.'

But every time I turn, force my eyes open and peer into the dark, he's not there. No breath on my cheek, no glitter of his eyes in the moonlight.

What if he never turns up?

He will, he will . . .

I lie still and look up at the ceiling, which I can't see. Has something happened to his bicycle? Is he walking up the M40 right now, cold and miserable in the dark, knowing how worried I'll be, but unable to let me know?

Could he have had an accident? Is he lying on the side of the road, seriously injured, waiting for a rescue that may never happen?

I've given up on the go-bag. How can I think of anything practical when I know Hector's out there, coming towards us, but inexplicably failing to arrive?

When the first glimmers of dawn creep past the edges of the blinds and illuminate my room with a soft half-light, I finally fall into a deep sleep and dream of monsters, guns and dead men.

Within seconds, it seems, Boris is by my side, shaking me awake. 'Come on, Roza. Rise and shine!'

I struggle to regain consciousness. All night, my mind has been jittering around, jumping between accusations and

283

complications, and now that it's time to wake up, I'm heavy and sluggish. 'What's going on?'

'We're going out to find Hector.'

I force myself to concentrate. Yes, that's the answer! We must go and look for him. I haul myself to my feet, nudge Boris out of the bedroom and stumble into the same clothes as yesterday. Cycling clothes, still slightly damp. As soon as I'm ready, Boris hands me a bag containing sandwiches, apples and a flask of water, and we leave as quietly as possible, creeping past the family flat and down to the cycle floor.

'Shouldn't we tell someone where we're going?' I say, as we pull our bikes out of the racks.

'It's all right,' says Boris. 'I've left a note.'

'Popi won't like it,' I say.

'Too bad,' says Boris. 'We owe it to Hector.'

I climb on my bike and discover with a shock that sitting down is painful. We've cycled too far in the last couple of days. But I follow Boris down the ramp into the clear, cold air without complaining. The sky is a delicate blue and there's no sign of yesterday's mist. A blackbird sits on the crest of the gateway to our blocks of flats, singing the same tune over and over again, keeping a careful eye on us as we approach. He flaps away when we go underneath. When I look back, he's returned to his perch and resumed his repetitive song, unconcerned by our brief visit. *Two little dickie birds sitting on a wall, one named Peter, one named Paul.*

'What if he goes a different way?' I ask.

'Did you discuss the route with him?'

'Yes, he was at Banbury, when we last spoke, so M40 north, M42 west, M5 north, A456 towards Birmingham. It's the most straightforward way, roads big enough to be still passable and no chance of taking a wrong turning.'

'No problem, then.'

There's a crispness in the air, a promise of autumn, and it's refreshing out here, just me and Boris. Everything's going to be fine. We'll meet Hector and he'll come home with us. Then he can help us plan to go to Brighton. *Fly away, Peter, fly away, Paul. Come back, Peter, come back, Paul.*

We stop at our drop site, the roundabout of Junction 3, before going on to the M5. It's a giant rubbish dump. Abandoned capsules are scattered over the central roundabout and along the roads in every direction, twenty years' worth of drops. They resemble coffins, battered by bad landings; some burst open on impact; others were damaged when we rolled them around, searching for the way in. They never tell us when they change the design. The older capsules are more solid, big enough to walk inside, relics from an earlier age when foreign countries cared about us and thought there were more survivors than there actually were. When we were little, we used to play in and out of the capsules while Popi and Moth did the hard work, but later they insisted we help them and the expeditions lost their attraction.

So much stuff we don't want. Fifty tins of butter beans, one brand-new shoe without its pair, plastic covers for phones that no longer work, manuals for cookers we don't possess. Compassion clearly has a limit. It must be hard to go on supplying people you'll never see, who'll never throw their arms round your neck with joyful gratitude.

'I'm not sure why they bother,' says Boris, staring around with distaste.

'That's what the Weather Watchers say.'

'Maybe they've got a point.'

'Yesterday you said it was useful. And some of it is.' I want to defend the aid-givers. We shouldn't discourage generosity. 'You'd struggle without shaving foam.'

He shrugs. 'The other flats in the blocks will go on supplying us for some time yet.'

Nearby, on open land, there are the rows of shallow graves dug by Popi, and more recently by Boris, full of the goods we couldn't use. The graves have got bigger as the unhelpful contributions increase. Why do they send us apples, when we've sent so many messages to tell them we have an abundance? It's fine to have one or two lemons, but their use is limited. They're not like oranges, which would be nice, but which they never send. And what do they expect us to do with all those pots of cinnamon?

Aid can't go on for ever. America has almost certainly lost interest, but want to believe in their own goodness. They expect us to continue to be grateful, so they bung in anything they can find to fill the space – ballast for the unfortunate. I would prefer to think they're still benevolent, that they really do care about us. I try not to give in to cynicism.

A thought occurs to me. 'You don't think Hector has crawled into one of these empty capsules? He might have thought it would be a safe place to shelter when it was dark. He could still be asleep inside one.'

'Call him and see.'

We shout into the emptiness. 'Hector! Hector! Are you there?' Hide and seek. Coming, ready or not!

Our voices echo around, but there's no response.

'He's not here,' says Boris, eventually. 'We'd see his wheels.'

It's a good point. 'Let's get on, then,' I say. Another hope dashed.

We cycle for hours, stopping occasionally when we see something promising: a gap in the undergrowth along the side of the road where he might have gone for shelter; a mound of clothing that becomes a twist of ancient, mangled rags; a shape under a bridge that turns out to be the branch of a tree, part of a window frame from a long-demolished house, or an old machine, rusted into a shapeless mass and lodged in a corner by the force of an earlier flood. We investigate everything. We don't rush, but we soon lose our initial optimism.

There's no sign of him. No footsteps in the mud, no flattened grass or bushes bent back to allow him to pass through. Every now and again we call, but there's never a reply.

At midday, we pull up by a bridge and drain our water bottles. I climb off my bike and sit on a concrete ridge. It's caked with mud, but I don't care. 'How can we have missed him?' I ask.

'I don't know.'

'What about waystations?'

Boris gets out his map and unrolls it on the ground between us. 'There's nowhere obvious,' he says. 'They're quite a distance from the motorway.'

I point at the map. 'I don't remember seeing this one – between Junctions 3 and 4 on the M5 – it's not far from our drop site.'

Boris frowns. 'That's odd. How did we miss it? We can check on our way back, but why would he stop there anyway? He'd be almost at ours.'

If he was in a waystation, he'd have used the router, contacted me.

We need to go home, but neither of us wants to be the one to give up. 'Come on,' I say at last, pulling myself to my feet and turning my bike round. 'It's getting late.'

Our journey back is torturous. I'm weighed down by invisible burdens: boots of lead; a rucksack full of stones. Every revolution of the pedals pulls my muscles tight to screaming point, takes us further away from the possibility of finding Hector.

Boris is struggling, too, although he pretends he isn't. Every now and again he summons a surge of power to prove he's not defeated, and races ahead for about a hundred metres. When he stops and waits for me to catch up, I drag energy from my diminishing supplies, determined not to slow him down. We don't talk. There's nothing more to say.

Maybe Hector's at Wyoming now, having a cup of tea with Moth and Popi, waiting for us. Perhaps this is all an elaborate game to prepare for his grand entrance. If he suddenly appears, if he thinks this is funny, I won't marry him.

A twisted road sign indicates the slip-road that leads to the waystation by Junctions 3 and 4 and we stop to examine the exit. It's full of rubble from a collapsed bridge. Nobody has been up there for a very long time.

We pedal home, still searching – ahead, behind, on both sides of the road, in the branches of trees . . .

I refuse to believe he's not going to come.

When we limp stiffly up the ramp to the cycle floor, pushing our bikes, we find Popi removing the wheels from a child's bicycle.

He glances up. 'Oh, there you are,' he says, as if we'd just popped out for a stroll. 'Did you find him?'

'He's not here, then?'

He shakes his head. 'Nope.'

I feel an overwhelming urge to sink to the floor and weep, but I don't. I would prefer to go to my flat and collapse in comfort.

'Do you want a hand, Popi?' asks Boris.

'Wouldn't say no.'

Boris bends down to examine the wheels, revived by the need for his expertise. 'The trailer for Edward?'

Popi nods.

Boris picks up a wheel and squints across the centre to see how straight it is. 'Nifty,' he says.

Popi smiles.

I leave them to it and start the long climb upstairs. The smell of freshly baked bread draws me into the family flat. Moth's in the kitchen, mopping the floor. Two loaves sit on the table, and the cupboard doors are all open, the china stacked neatly, the shelves disinfected. She sees me and stops, leaning on the mop. 'Oh, hello, Roza. Have a slice of bread. Was there any sign?' Neither she nor Popi seems annoyed that we went without telling them. They must have agreed to be understanding.

'No,' I say, sinking down on a chair, easing the pain in my legs.

'Oh dear.' She breathes deeply. 'It's all very odd.'

'What happens if Hector doesn't turn up?' I'm trying not to cry.

She sits down opposite me and covers my hand with hers. 'I don't know. Popi's had Delphine stationed on the roof with Edward and a telescope to see if she can spot him. She's supposed to be watching for invaders too. She's got a whistle to blow if she sees anything suspicious.'

I tear a piece of bread from the slice and stuff it into my mouth gratefully. 'Why are you cleaning? You never clean.'

'Well, I needed something to do while your father was messing around with bits of wood and wheels, pretending to be technical. I thought it might be nice to make everything clean and fresh so we can leave it in good condition.'

'But it's not going to stay fresh and clean. We've got to get through the winter yet.'

She smiles. 'It will encourage me to keep it nice.'

'Do you still think we should go?'

'Popi has decided.' She seems softer and younger than usual, almost mellow. Maybe it's the successful bread-making. When the machine refuses to knead correctly, or skimps on the proving, we end up with dense, solid loaves and everyone complains.

'What if Lancelot's family decides to move to Brighton too?'

A moment of anxiety drifts across her face, replaced almost immediately by a smile. 'Who knows?' she says. 'Maybe we should have a plan of action in place, luggage already packed, a rough idea of where to go, that kind of thing. It's not quite so hard if you have forewarning.'

'We've never travelled as far as Brighton before. Do you think we'll cope with the journey?' If Hector can't manage it, how would we?

'It's our only practical option.' Popi's voice makes me jump. I turn to find him leaning against the side of the door, his face weary. 'The trailer for the animals is going to be good. Boris had a couple of clever ideas.' He turns to Moth. 'Have you heard anything from Delphine?'

'Not a squeak. She's probably chatting to her new friends on Highspeed.'

'She's meant to be keeping a lookout.'

'Nikolai, she's a teenager, not a trained soldier. She'll be doing her best.'

'Hmm,' says Popi. He comes into the room and sits down next to Moth. 'I know you won't like this, Roza, but have you considered . . . Have you ever – that is, has it crossed your mind that Hector might not actually exist?'

I stare at him. 'Whatever are you talking about?'

He scratches his head, leans over and rubs his knees, then clears his throat. 'I just wondered – you remember Dan and his classroom of holos, children he created for his audience? It's easy to fool people if you really try.'

'Don't be absurd,' says Moth. 'Of course Hector exists. We've all talked to him. How could he not exist?'

'A computer-generated image can be very convincing,' says Popi.

Is this possible? Could Hector have been created by someone on the other side of the world for a joke?

'No,' says Moth. 'He's too real for that. He's clever, he's individual, he has interesting conversations and he reacts to us.'

Popi's eyes focus on the distance. 'I knew someone once – pre-Hoffman's – who bought a motorbike online. He showed me the picture on his computer – a manual with gears, real accelerator, real brakes, beautiful thing, none of your driverless . . .' He doesn't continue. The outcome is so obvious he doesn't need to spell it out.

'But what about his friends, his family?' I say. 'I've talked to them online. They can't all be computer-generated?'

Popi sighs. 'How can we be sure?'

'There are too many of them. All his colleagues at TU, people in Brighton, his family.' If we carry on like this, we're going to start thinking Brighton doesn't exist.

Moth rubs my hand. 'I'm sure they're all there, as real as us,' she says. 'There's no point in being so negative. Either of you.' She glares at Popi and he lowers his eyes, embarrassed. 'Something's delayed Hector, that's all, and he hasn't been able to find a router. You know how unreliable they are.'

'You're right,' says Popi. 'Just a moment of panic on my part. But he doesn't have long. The rains are due.'

I need the rain to hold off, to give Hector more time, to make sure he reaches us. But at the same time we need the rain to come as soon as possible to keep the family safe: from kidnappers, people with guns, Aashay.

Guns change things. Certainties become uncertainties.

I go back up to my flat, trying not to think of Hector wandering around, injured, perhaps, separated from us by miles of waterlogged highways. Just before I reach my landing, one of Aashay's cats catches my attention. I don't remember seeing it before, on the wall, just below eye level. It's sitting up, tall and cheeky, with pop eyes and wide whiskers. It's grinning at me.

22

I'm woken from nightmares about Aashay – engaged in a frantic version of the Stair Game, terrified that he's ahead of me and not behind – by violent claps of thunder directly above Wyoming, each new crash competing with the previous one. They're jostling for position in a contest of power, a crescendo of sound, rolling on and on with no mechanism to bring them to a halt, accompanied by a series of flashes that bathe my room with moments of penetrating brilliance, as intrusive as X-rays. Then the rain starts. Almost as ear-splitting as the thunder, a solid waterfall, a deluge that can uproot trees, topple wind turbines, sweep men to their deaths.

Aashay painted that cat before we went to the fair. Didn't he? Why can't I remember seeing it before?

This is the second storm in less than a week, so the ground is already saturated. By tomorrow, the entire area will be water-logged, all routes bleeding towards each other, starting to disappear under a layer of lying water.

If Hector is still wandering around out there, he won't be able to find us.

He's in danger of drowning. And there's absolutely nothing any of us can do about it.

If he exists.

If Aashay's here, in Wyoming, we're trapped with him and his gun for the entire winter.

I wave my hand to open the shutters.

'Are you quite sure, Roza?' asks Rex. 'It's still the middle of the night.'

'I want to see the storm,' I say. It's pitch black when the shutters first draw back, and rain is flinging itself wildly at the windows. An immense jagged line of lightning splits the sky in two, revealing the entire area. Water is already accumulating round the base of our flats, creating large puddles that are rapidly merging into ponds, then small lakes. Spouts of water are rising out of the inadequate old drains, flushing out the system.

Where would Aashay be? Hiding in one of the flats? Why haven't we seen or heard anything?

I close the shutters again and snuggle back into my duvet. We're safe for now at least. No one will be able to come and find us.

Hector, oh, Hector . . .

If he wasn't in danger before, he is now. Few people possess the necessary survival skills for conditions like these. I can only hope he's near high ground. Is he capable or tough enough for this?

I sit up again and listen to his last messages:

'*Roza, Roza, give me your answer true, I'm half crazy, over the love of you.*'

'You should see my muscles – they're expanding like balloons. I'm so blown up I'd float if I didn't have all my luggage.'

'*It won't be a stylish marriage, I can't afford a carriage.*'

Could a computer-generated image be so playful, so unpredictable?

'Not sure about this waystation. Over-used. I know that's what it's for, but you'd think they'd be more careful, wouldn't you? Everything's battered. Even the solar panels are looking wonky. Wondering if I should go up there and do some repairs.'

'*But you'll look sweet, upon the seat of a bicycle made for two.*'

'Almost there, Roza. Cherry-oh.'

Did he go up on to the roof and attempt to mend the panels? Did he slip? Is that why I haven't heard from him since?

No, that can't be right. He sent his last message just before he left – 'eight o'clock on the dot. Cherry-oh.'

'Setting off. Today's the day.'

293

That was Friday, and it wasn't the day. And now the rain has come, and it's early on Saturday and today won't be the day, either.

Last night, after Popi's suggestion that Hector doesn't really exist, I messaged his family to find out if he'd set off when he said he did. To see if they really exist.

His mother replied immediately: 'He left on Wednesday. We watched him go, waved until we couldn't see him any more. He was carrying plenty of food and drink. I made sure of that.'

His father added details: 'I checked the bike with him. All ship-shape and Bristol. Looking good when he left.'

His mother again: 'He's not as strong as he looks.'

Between the words I can hear their fear.

'Let us know as soon as he arrives.'

'If you find out anything . . .'

They're solid, I'm convinced of it. Their messages are too subtle, only half concealing a worry that can't be expressed. You have to be a real person to understand a subtext.

I slip in and out of sleep. I'm too tired for all this.

The rain doesn't let up. Water rampages through the drainage system, soaks into the aquifers, filling underground streams and lakes, until there's nowhere else for it to go except over the land. It spreads, strong and wilful, churning between our blocks of flats, through the pillars, dragging along everything that gets in the way: branches; entire trees; spare parts from the remains of collapsed pylons; broken arms snapped from the top of the last wind turbines. The debris pounds against Wyoming, the vibration of every collision booming up through the walls, a powerful accompaniment to the rain and thunder.

None of us can sleep. We creep around in the dim daylight hours, unable to find anything to say to each other, peering through the gloom, our faces pinched and tight with exhaustion. I'm constantly alert for signs of Aashay. But if he's here, he's leaving no trace.

'The cats are everywhere,' says Boris, when I show him the one on the stairs. 'That one was already there.'

Was it?

By the fifth night, my reserves of energy are finally depleted and I fall instantly asleep for the first time in ages. Almost immediately, it seems, I'm awake again. There's a persistent tapping on my door. Just loud enough to hear. For a few moments, it's part of my dreams, and I don't believe it's real. It doesn't stop.

I open my eyes and adjust to the lack of light. The readout on the ceiling is 5:30. Who could possibly be awake at this time? We're all too tired to go wandering around in the night. Is it Popi, here to tell me that we're leaving, that we have to build a boat, fight our way through the floods and navigate the M40 and the M25 towards Brighton and safety?

I sit up. 'Who is it, Rex?'

'I'm not sure, Roza. I'll let you judge for yourself.'

A screen appears on the ceiling. It wavers wildly, the edges uncertain, the light waxing and waning. This is how our technology will fail. From sharp to blurred, from reliability to uncertainty, from something to nothing.

Hector? Has he made it after all?

The face gradually comes into focus, too close to the camera, wide and distorted, eyes bulging, almost unrecognisable.

It's Aashay.

I jump up and find myself swaying drunkenly by my bed, still dazed with sleep.

I can't think what to do. He'll be reasonably certain I'm here at this time of night. But he won't be able to get through my front door if it's locked from the inside. I need to contact Popi, Moth, Boris. I fumble with my POD.

The message whooshes away. No one replies. No green glow, no comforting vibration on my wrist. They're all asleep.

What if I ignore him? Will he go away?

He must know I can see him. The winking eye of the camera will tell him I'm watching. That's why he's putting his face up so close, trying to communicate through the lens.

My pulse pumps deafeningly in my head. Does he have the gun?

How has he managed to hide himself from us for so long? Why? Has he been plotting with other people to kidnap Lucia or abduct Delphine?

I need to be prepared, fully dressed, in suitable shoes in case I have to escape. I pull on some trousers, my hands shaking. The right leg, the left – they're back to front. Try again – where's the vel? – my jumper's tangled, one arm caught inside – slower, more careful – it's on inside out – who cares? I grab my shoes, but keep them in my hand. I don't want him to hear me as I tiptoe into the hall.

I can't think. What do I do?

I can sense him. His essence seems to seep through the door, powerful and magnetic, the physical presence a formality that can follow later.

'Roza,' he says softly, his voice muffled by the intercom. He knows I'm here.

Why's he being so cautious? No one can hear him. Boris is too far away, his flat separated from mine by the landing.

I mustn't answer. 'What are you doing here?' I whisper.

'Let me in, Roza.'

'No,' I say, louder to give myself confidence.

There's a long silence. Has he gone? I need the screen to be transferred to the hall so that I can see what's going on outside. Will he just leave if I wait long enough? I should go back into my bedroom, where he can't hear me, and give the command. But I'm afraid to leave the hall, afraid to turn my back on him. I dither, turn towards my bedroom, come back, finally decide to go anyway. If he has a technique to get through the locked door, it can't possibly be that quick.

Back in my bedroom I ask Rex to transfer the image to the hall wall.

'Of course, Roza,' he says. 'Are you feeling threatened?'

Why can't he be a real person? He'd be so useful. 'Yes,' I say.

'Would you like me to double-lock the door?' he says.

No, triple-lock, please. 'It's already double-locked,' I say. He should know this.

'OK. Well, let me know if you want me to do anything.'

Reassuring. But oddly, unexpectedly, as soon as Rex suggests Aashay's a threat, I find myself wanting to defend him. I stop in the bedroom for a few moments to collect my thoughts, to make myself more rational. Am I overreacting? Aashay has always treated me with respect, looked after me, protected me – in the art gallery and at the fair. Do I seriously believe he would harm me? What am I actually afraid of?

The gun.

I return to the hall and watch him outside the door, safe in the knowledge that he can't see me. His image is blurred, wavering, as the power fluctuates. He's leaning against a side wall now, further from the camera, examining his POD. Who's he messaging? Reinforcements elsewhere in the building?

My wrist vibrates. 'Let me in, Roza. We need to talk.'

'What about? Have you got your gun with you?' I message back.

He leans forward, astonishment sweeping across his face. 'What are you talking about?' he says out loud.

'Dan. I'm talking about Dan.'

'What about him?' He doesn't seem to understand. He shakes his head slowly, confused. 'Explain.'

'You know.'

'No,' he says. 'I don't.' His image stabilises, and I can see him clearly. His wide-eyed innocence, his eyebrows shooting up his forehead into the dark waves of his hair. He's a small boy who's being accused of something he didn't do. Is this yet another act for my benefit? 'Let me in, Roza. We can talk more easily eye to eye.'

His voice is almost a smell, strong and pungent, too powerful to be limited by the microphone, more real than its electronic manifestation. 'No,' I say, hearing the certainty in my voice begin to fade.

He steps back, raising his hands slightly – that gesture again. I'm innocent. Whatever you're accusing me of, I didn't do it.

You've confused me with someone else. 'Has something happened to Dan?'

'You know.'

'So you keep saying, but I don't. I really don't. Tell me what's happened. Dan's an old friend of mine.'

'He's been shot. You shot him.'

He steps back, rigid with shock. 'No. That's not right. Why would you think that? Where?'

'At Grand Central Station.'

'No – I mean, what part of him? An arm, a leg, where? How badly is he hurt? Who's looking after him?' He seems genuinely upset.

I hesitate before answering. 'He's dead.'

Aashay gasps and leans back against the wall as if he's been shot himself. 'No – no, that's not possible. You can't be serious. I was talking to him only a few days ago – he was fine then. Were you there when it happened?'

Is he pretending? How can I tell? I don't know how to react to him. If he's got a gun, he's dangerous. But if that's the case, he's hardly going to tell me. We're going to be together in Wyoming for some time now. What can he do? Would he shoot us all if there was no way of escaping?

But why would he? He's never been intimidating to me, never given the impression that I'm under any threat from him. He's always been generous, friendly, anxious to help.

I close my eyes and press the pad to let him in, not watching myself do it, as if this absolves me from blame when it all goes wrong. I lean back against the wall, and take deep breaths.

Nothing happens at first. Then I hear the door glide open. He's being cautious. Not bursting in with guns blazing. The door stops moving, and I open my eyes. He's still outside, peering in at me. 'Can I come in?' he asks, oddly polite, almost tentative.

I nod but don't speak.

He steps in slowly. He's radiating heat and comfort, like a giant stove, the centre of a home, the hearth, the source of safety and nourishment. I want to resist him but I can't – his inner power source is irresistible. I'm drawn towards him, not wanting to – wanting to – not wanting to—– He puts his arms round me. I hold myself stiff and rigid for about two seconds, then collapse against him, my legs weak with relief. I'd forgotten how reassuring his strength could be.

'I thought you'd come to take Lucia,' I say, after a few seconds, abruptly pulling myself away from him, cross with myself for succumbing to his charm so easily.

He stands back and studies me. 'Why would I do that?'

'You must have known it's not safe to show people your children, that there's a danger of kidnapping. Why did you take us to the fair? Didn't you see the family resemblance – Lancelot's family?'

'Wah – steady.' He looks bewildered. 'Give me a chance. You're chucking accusations at me like we're playing basketball. One thing at a time.' He thinks for a few seconds. 'I don't know anything about kidnapping – where did you hear about that? What would be the point? Where would they hide? What kind of ransom could anyone pay?'

'They don't want a ransom. They want the children. I suppose it's stealing really, not kidnapping.' I hesitate. 'Hector told me.' But it's a mistake to mention Hector. I feel like two short planks. As if Hector's been misleading me and I shouldn't have believed him. I turn away and go into my leisure room.

He follows me and throws himself carelessly into the largest chair. 'Hector?' he says, in apparent amazement. 'What does he know—–' He sits up and looks around with a puzzled expression. 'Where is he?'

'He hasn't turned up,' I say, determined to keep my voice steady.

'Why ever not?' He laughs suddenly and loudly. 'Don't tell me he chickened?'

'No – we don't know. I haven't heard from him since before the rain started. We can't work out what's happened. His last message was from Banbury. Boris and I cycled a long way down the M40 trying to find him, but there was no sign, no sign at all.'

Aashay is silent. I'd expected him to mock Hector's lack of practical skills, or at least to look superior, but he's serious and thoughtful. 'That's all bit rum and Coke. He must have had an accident.'

'That's what we thought, but if he has, it's not visible from the road.'

'When it stops raining, when it calms down a bit— Don't suppose you've got a boat? If he's headed for high ground – there are places you can get to. I've been down the M40 loads of times – know it in the dark, backwards. In fact . . .'

He stops and I look at him hopefully.

'If he could make it to Nepton – if he gets in touch, suggest it. It's a waystation, a bit further from the motorway than usual, built in the days when they cared about scenery, well above sea level – usually misses most of the floods. He'd be hunky there. If he kept his wits and searched for high ground . . . It's an old village and there're people living there, mostly cobwebbies but they'd help him. No router, though – taken out by lightning a few years back, just a tangle – so no chance of making contact. Did he have much food on him?'

'He was OK when I last spoke to him. Isn't there supposed to be food in the waystations?'

Aashay widens his eyes as if I've said something ridiculous. 'Get real, Roza,' he says. 'You can't believe everything you come across. Food gets eaten. No one brings replacements.'

He sounds like Popi. I've been believing myths for most of my life. 'I'm not a child,' I say. 'I can work it out for myself if I'm given the facts.'

'Having said that,' says Aashay, 'some places are better than others and he's not short on luck – he got the girl, didn't he? But if he's found high ground, he'll be holed up for some time yet. You don't think he'd do anything crazy, do you? Like setting off on a marathon swim, or fancying himself as an engineer and building a makeshift raft that would sink a few miles downstream?' He shakes his head. 'No, he's not that sort of guy, is he? Not long on initiative.'

I experience a brief flash of annoyance at Aashay's assumption that Hector is incapable of being practical, but it's quickly replaced by the comforting thought that he's talking about him as if he's still alive. He's giving me hope.

'Can't imagine what you see in him,' he says.

'So where do you keep the gun?' I ask, now that I can watch his face and see his reaction.

His mouth drops open. 'What? Are you serious?'

'Well, somebody's got a gun. How can I be sure it's not you?'

He wants the details. When I describe finding Dan in the doorway in a pool of clotted blood, he bows his head for a few seconds, puts a hand up to cover his eyes and takes several deep breaths.

'Why didn't you tell us you knew him?' I ask, still unsure if I believe in his grief.

'I don't tell you everything,' he says, his voice deeper, more throaty than usual. 'Same as you don't tell me. You've never given me a list of everyone you've ever met.'

He's right. I'm being unreasonable. Although he must know as well as I do that his list would be pages long and mine would be laughably short. I allow myself to be persuaded that his emotion is real. 'How well did you know him?' I ask.

'We go back a long way. He was lonely, so I used to drop in if I was passing. He could monitor smaller branch lines through the routers – you might think you're hidden but you leave traces – so he had information about the distribution of people across the country.'

'You knew about us, then, before you turned up?'

He looks up at me, prepared to claim incomprehension. He wants to deny it, I can tell, but he doesn't. After a moment, he nods. 'Kind of. Just knew there was someone in the area, that's all. Dan played Scrabble. Good at it.'

'He told us he played with the other caretakers,' I say. If Aashay knows about the Scrabble, then at least some of his story is true. 'I think one of them was killed recently. Not Dan, another man.'

'Who told you that?'

'It was just a rumour – on the net.' I'm not going to tell him it was the Weather Watchers. He'll mock me for believing them.

'Hmm.' He seems annoyed, as if he should have known about it. 'Be cautious, Roza. Don't believe everything you hear.'

'What about the other travellers out there? People like you. Could one of them have killed Dan?'

He doesn't speak for some time. I wait, impatient for an answer but not wanting to interrupt his thoughts. Does this length of time mean he suspects someone or is he just going through options? 'He said nobody ever visited him,' I say. 'So he was lying.'

Eventually Aashay shakes his head. 'It doesn't make sense. Don't know why he'd say that. Perhaps he was exaggerating, trying to get sympathy.'

Well, if anyone understands about getting sympathy, it's Aashay.

'It must have been a robbery,' he says. 'Why else would anyone want to kill him? People liked him.'

'I thought he was going to kidnap Lucia,' I say.

Aashay half smiles. 'He wouldn't be interested,' he says. 'His networks were electronic, not physical – he'd never have been interested in a child. I think you must have misread him.'

'Well, someone on one of his networks was physical,' I say. 'A bullet isn't electronic.' How hard it is to establish what's true. Everything is subject to individual perceptions. Maybe Dan simply wanted to observe Lucia, watch her sleep, experience a memory of an old life, a time when things were more straightforward. 'I saw him,' I say, 'watching Lucia in the night.'

'No,' says Aashay. 'Kidnapping wouldn't have been on Dan's radar. He didn't have the right contacts.'

'So there are contacts, then. Networks for moving children around?'

A sudden draught startles me.

Did we leave the front door open?

There's a presence in the room. Someone has entered silently, crept up behind us— Before either of us has time to react, he throws himself on top of Aashay with a terrifying roar.

I scream and leap to my feet. Aashay jumps up and tries to swirl round in one swift movement, but he's not quick enough. An arm grabs him from behind, clamps itself round his neck, starts to choke him.

I recognise the shape of the arm, the glinting eyes behind Aashay's head, the unbrushed hair. 'Boris!' I shriek. 'Stop!'

His expression is closed, concentrating, while he squeezes. Aashay's face is going red. He's struggling to breathe. His hands pull at Boris's arms, his own arms rigid, straining to break the grip.

I attack Boris from behind, punching him, kicking him, trying to break his concentration. 'No!' I shout. 'Let go! Leave him!'

Slowly, slowly, I sense that Boris is losing his advantage. With a final massive effort and a long grunt, Aashay wrenches himself free. He overbalances with the sudden release of tension, but manages to throw himself sideways, rolling across the floor until he reaches the corner of the room. He immediately jumps to his feet and crouches, panting, his arms up in front of him like a shield, ready to continue the fight with the wall at his back.

Boris is still standing, breathing raggedly, furious. 'Now look what you've done,' he yells at me. 'He's got away again.'

'It wasn't him!' I shout.

Aashay rises to his feet carefully, not taking his eyes off Boris. 'The gun,' says Boris. 'Where is it?'

'He doesn't have one,' I say.

Aashay doesn't leave the security of the wall, but drops one hand and holds out the other to Boris, as if he expects him to come over and shake it. 'Boris,' he says, almost cheerfully, his voice dry and rasping.

Boris ignores the hand. 'Give me the gun,' he says.

'There isn't a gun,' says Aashay. 'Ask Roza. She knows. It wasn't me. I swear. Dan was a mate.'

Boris looks at me accusingly. 'He's done it again, hasn't he?' he says. 'Talked you into believing him.'

'We were only guessing it was Aashay,' I say. 'Because we'd seen him at Grand Central. We don't know for certain he killed Dan. It was only ever a theory.'

'I'd like to know who else would have done it.'

'It could have been anyone,' says Aashay, slowly lowering his arms. 'The country's a dangerous place. People pass by. It's hard to know who you can trust.'

'I wouldn't argue with that,' says Boris, coldly.

There's a long silence. Nobody knows how to proceed. Aashay wants to be conciliatory and Boris's conviction is weakening.

'Why don't we all have some breakfast?' I say eventually, now reasonably convinced they're not going to kill each other.

I leave them there together, eye to eye. I can hear Aashay murmuring to Boris and Boris replying. Their voices are low and tight. They're not shouting, or even disagreeing very loudly. And they're not fighting.

23

It rains and rains and rains. All we can see through the windows is water. It obliterates the roads, swamps the crops in the Woodgate Valley, swirls through the base of the machinery platforms, dislodging loose screws, anything not fully secured, every piece of equipment that was left out by mistake. It ploughs into Wyoming just below our lowest windows, the collisions booming though the building, like giant palpitations; irregular, unsettling, eroding our sense of security.

Nobody can decide whether or not to believe Aashay. Our thoughts and conversations bounce backwards and forwards like the water, alternating between huge waves of fear and gentler ripples of conciliation, echoing with uncertainty.

'He must be lying,' murmurs Popi, when we're gathered in the family leisure room, his voice barely audible above the sound of the television. 'Who else could have done it?'

'Sometimes you just have to trust people,' says Moth. 'Too much cynicism can be paralysing.'

'He's all shimmer,' says Boris. 'You can't work out what's real.'

'If it was him,' says Delphine, 'why's he come back?'

'Roza was convinced by him,' says Moth. 'Maybe we should trust her instincts.'

'No,' I say. 'I don't . . .' It's not fair to give me the responsibility. I can only believe him when he's there. When he goes, the questions start up all over again.

The door bursts open and we swivel round, like conspirators caught red-handed in the glare of a searchlight, expecting Aashay. Popi increases the volume on the screen. But it's Lucia, who's just been to fetch her book from her bedroom. 'Let's play the Stair Game again,' she says.

'No,' says Moth. 'That's for snow.'

'We could cheat,' says Lucia. 'Do it for rain instead of snow.'

'Then we'd spend all autumn and winter playing.'

'Yay!' says Lucia. 'We could have fun every day.'

But Moth won't allow it. She's remembering how Aashay first appeared.

'We need to settle for now,' says Popi. 'Pick up our routines and wait for spring. First thing tomorrow morning, I'm back at work on the sculpture.'

'But we won't be able to take it with us,' I say.

'No worries,' he says. 'I'll finish it, weatherproof it, and get it out there. It'll be a monument to our lives.'

The head's taking shape. A child of about five, her head tilted slightly so that you can see the soft roundness of her chin beginning to emerge. Popi worked on the eyes first, and they're gazing upwards – she'll be looking at the sky when she's outside, but at the moment she's examining the ceiling with a kind of naïve trust, as if she knows that everything will be all right one day, that security is just a helicopter ride away (or it will come floating down from the flat above). Her hair is still an unformed block of wood, so it's not yet clear if it will be thick and heavy, like mine, shaped into a plait, or light and wispy like Lucia's. Although the sculpture was originally me, I'm starting to think she's quietly metamorphosed into Lucia. Has Popi changed his mind or is it an unconscious decision? Now that everyone we encounter sees Lucia as the embodiment of childhood, it would hardly be surprising if he's been influenced too.

'How do we know there aren't other people hiding in the building?' says Moth. 'Someone else with a gun?'

'We could check the flats,' says Boris. 'It would be fun. We can all do it.'

'What about the other blocks?' asks Delphine. 'There could be someone hiding out there.'

'Doesn't matter,' I say. 'They couldn't get in here once the flood barriers go up.'

'What am I missing?' says Aashay's voice from the doorway. We all jump again.

Boris recovers first. 'We're going to search the flats,' he says. 'For intruders.'

Aashay grins. 'More people like me, you mean?'

'That's it,' I say. 'Anyone else who might creep up unexpectedly.'

'There's no one here,' he says. 'But if you want an extra pair of eyes, I'm your man.'

'You must work in pairs and all stay on the same floor,' says Popi. 'You're not to go anywhere on your own.' Uncertainty now pervades everything we do, restricting our freedom of movement. It's hard to dismiss the possibility that there could be a secret army hiding somewhere in the building, waiting for the nod from Aashay.

But we'd have heard something: loos being flushed; hot water heating up; footsteps on the stairs.

'If you see anything even slightly suspicious,' says Moth, 'you don't investigate. You come straight back here.'

'I'm coming too,' says Lucia.

'Only if you stay with me and Delphine,' I say, knowing she'll soon get bored.

'I'll have to change first,' she says. 'I want to wear my red trousers.'

We start at the top. Aashay leads the way up to the roof and personally checks behind the solar panels, in Edward's shed, round the back of the storage tanks. The rain has temporarily eased – it's just a thin drizzle now, and the surrounding country-side is transformed into an ethereal, shifting canopy of grey. We wander round, not really believing we'll find anyone up here, talk to Edward, check for eggs, then head back down to the flats.

It takes longer than we expect, two of us in each flat and one out on the landing in case a hidden occupant tries to escape when they hear us coming. We open every door, inspect every room, check behind curtains, under beds, searching for signs of habitation. Most of it is familiar territory. We've already hunted for useful things, raided the wardrobes for clothes, the kitchen cupboards for unperishable food, the bathrooms for soap and shampoo. We've investigated the secret, hidden places where people kept their most treasured possessions – old letters, mementos – and put them back where we found them, embarrassed by their intimacy. There used to be photos everywhere on devices that flicked between screens once every thirty seconds, revealing an endless supply of images to an audience who no longer existed. They displayed every member of every family, but mostly the children, over and over again, holding each one for a few loving moments, then moving on to the same baby in the same bath a second later with a different expression. Or at the seaside, held over shallow water by hidden parents, feet dangling, arms flailing, shy in front of the camera. If you watched them for too long, as I did when I was younger, babies started to lose their attraction.

In the early years of my life, the building was awash with these photos, but one day Moth and Popi went through and turned off every device, turned their faces towards the walls and let them fade into darkness. It took them a whole week.

'No point in squandering electricity,' said Popi, at the time. 'Better to preserve it.'

'In case the people come back?' asked my eight-year-old self.

I can still remember the sadness in his voice. 'No,' he said. 'In case we need it ourselves in the future.'

I meet Delphine on the landing of the 14th where she's been keeping guard while Lucia and I search one flat and Boris and Aashay race through three. They're either more efficient or more careless than us. 'There's nothing here,' she says. 'I'm not entirely sure I'd recognise it if there was.'

'Stray crumbs,' I say. 'Drops of water in a sink, a trail through the dust.'

She sighs. 'No sign of anything like that. We'd have come across it ages ago if there was.'

'Not necessarily. Someone could have moved in recently,' I say. 'Don't forget we didn't know Aashay was staying on the 17th. It was only when we played the Stair Game that I realised someone had been sleeping there.'

'I think he wanted to be found,' she says. 'This just feels like a waste of time, and there are so many other things I could be doing.'

'Well, you don't have to help,' I say. 'We're over halfway down and we can manage without you.' I should be working. TU are expecting a translation by the end of the week, but I'm reluctant to communicate with them because I would have to ask them if they've heard from Hector and I don't want to hear their answer. If they confirm his disappearance, it will become official and I'll have to face the possibility that he's never going to come, despite Aashay's reassurance about high land. His family will have contacted TU by now – his parents' right to information is greater than mine. They're related, they've watched him every day for the last twenty-seven years, from when he was a baby to the time he disappeared. I'm just the fiancée, never even met him in the flesh. I can't claim kinship.

'Would you mind?' asks Delphine.

'I'm sure the three of us will cope,' I say.

'Four,' says Lucia, at my side. 'You forgot me.'

'Can't imagine how,' I say, watching her hopping round me on one foot. She keeps wanting to explore everywhere, talking when we need to get on. 'Wouldn't you prefer to go home with Delphine?'

She considers. 'OK,' she says.

'Off you go, then,' I say.

'Are you sure?' says Delphine. 'You can't work on your own. In pairs, Popi said.'

'No probs,' I say. 'Two together, one lookout.'

Delphine and Lucia head off up the stairs. 'We're down to three,' I say to Boris and Aashay when they emerge from the nearest flat.

'We could do a flat each on every floor,' says Aashay. 'And join up for the fourth.'

'No,' says Boris. 'We'll work together.' He still doesn't entirely trust Aashay.

'You drew that cat on the stairs just below my flat, didn't you?' I say to Aashay as we clatter down to the 13th. 'Not long after we got back from the fair. I thought it must have been there before, but I was wrong, wasn't I?'

He grins and looks exactly like his cat. 'If that's what you want to believe.'

We carry on, losing some of our earlier zeal when each flat is as silent and abandoned as the last. Time has sealed them into an unbreachable past, and it becomes increasingly difficult to summon the will to penetrate beyond the entrances. We find more cats as we go, usually in hallways, just inside the front doors, as if Aashay has spent several days rampaging through the building with his paint pencils, determined to place his personal stamp of ownership on every available surface. His invasion ends close to each entrance, but it's enough to prove that he's been here, that he exists, and that he wants us to know.

'What's with the cats anyway?' asks Boris, as we meet on the landing of the 8th. He's been making it clear for some time that he finds them irritating. Every time he comes across another, he draws my attention to it wordlessly, rolls his eyes, sighs. He wants to emphasise their triviality, but at the same time he sees them as a threat, as if Aashay is marking out his territory, claiming ownership. It undermines Boris's own place in Wyoming, challenges his belief that he should be in charge.

Aashay stares at him, as if astonished by the question. He's a cartoon version of his own cartoons, his expression conveying barely suppressed superiority, a secret catlike independence, a mysterious other life. 'Why do you think the cats are there, Boris?'

Boris shrugs. 'You tell me. They're your cats.'

'Did you have a cat of your own, a real one, when you were a child?' I ask.

Aashay starts to speak, changes his mind. He looks away from us, out of the window at the water glistening in the late-afternoon light, and says nothing for some time, as if he's looking back at some deeply disturbing memory. He has too great a hunger for other people's compassion.

Boris has no patience with this. 'Oh, well,' he says, after a while, 'I was just asking.'

'No,' says Aashay, in a low voice. 'It's only fair you should know. You're right, Roza. I did have a cat once. Nice little thing. Black and white, long tail. He used to come and find me every night and we'd curl up together. Then one day, one day . . .' there's a long pause '. . . one day when I came back he was gone.'

'Cats do that,' I say. There are hardly any left now, only feral animals that slip in and out of the shadows, but Moth has told us about her childhood pet, Mango, a ginger cat, so I know a little about the way they used to wander freely, pursuing their own agenda.

'Pre-Hoffman's?' asks Boris.

Aashay seems annoyed by the question. 'Obviously,' he says, with a frown.

'Were you with your parents then?' I wonder how this fits into his story of childhood neglect.

'I can't believe you asked me that,' he says, with indignation. 'You know it wasn't easy for me.' He addresses Boris. 'My upbringing was bins compared to yours. We weren't all lucky enough to have parents like Moth and Popi. My dad was around – well, in the area – when I had the cat, but I wasn't exactly *with* him. It wasn't possible to be with people like him.'

'Did the cat have a name?' I ask, anxious to avoid his personal history.

He shakes himself, apparently brushing away an unpleasant thought. 'Don't be nutsy. It was a cat.'

In other words, he wasn't that attached to it.

'Anyway, I went out to look for him – asked around. He was a sociable cat, so they all knew him. People used to feed him and make sure he was OK. But there was a man who didn't like me much – his name was Tonto.'

Tonto sounds more like the cat than the man. Is he making this up as he goes along? 'Why?' I ask. 'Why didn't he like you?'

Aashay pauses for a few seconds with a look of surprise on his face, as if he can't understand why we don't already know this. 'Because I knew what he was up to.'

'What was he up to?' asks Boris.

But Aashay isn't interested in detail. 'Never mind,' he says.

Boris scowls, but lets him continue.

'I found the cat in the end. Tonto had taken him up to the roof of the block of flats where we lived, and when I found him, he was holding him out in front of him, like he was dirty or something, over the side of the building. He was waiting for me, and as soon as I was close enough, he dropped him. Over the side. Just like that. Thirty-five floors.'

Ding, dong, bell, Pussy's in the well. I can't decide if I believe him. 'Why would he do that?'

'Because I knew things about him and he didn't want me to tell anyone. "It'll be you next," he said to me.'

'How come he was waiting there, ready to throw him over, at the exact moment you turned up? Bit of a coincidence, wasn't it?' asks Boris.

Aashay shrugs. 'Can't say, but that's exactly what happened. No twisting.'

'So what did you do?' asks Boris.

'I rushed forward and pushed him over the edge of the roof.'

I can't believe what he's said. 'You killed him?'

Aashay throws back his head and laughs and laughs. 'No, of course not. You didn't really think I'd do that, did you? He was far too big for me. I was only a kid.'

We're silent for a while, not really understanding why this would make him draw cartoon cats everywhere he goes.

'Did you go and look for the cat?' says Boris.

'No point,' says Aashay. 'He'd have been as flat as a pancake. Come on, let's get on with the search. We're wasting time.'

We hurry through the rest of the flats until we meet Popi in his workshop in the leisure room of a flat on the 3rd. The girl's nose is taking shape. Mine or Lucia's? Would I recognise it if it was mine? 'All clear?' he asks.

'Everything's cosy,' says Aashay. 'We've been in and out of each flat together, so there's no secrets. Boris hasn't smuggled his gang in and hidden them anywhere. We're all squeaky.' He wants Popi to know that he knows he suspects him of something.

Popi sits back and studies him. 'What are you really doing here, Aashay?' he asks.

Childlike bewilderment washes over Aashay's face, a mask he can slip on and off whenever he feels like it. 'What do you mean?'

'We know a bit more about you than we did when you first came, so you can't fool us with that injured expression,' says Popi. 'I want you to tell me what's going on. Why are you here? It's a simple enough question.'

I hold my breath. Popi is rarely confrontational. When we were younger, Moth was always the one who disciplined us when a firm hand was required, never Popi. I'm embarrassed for him now, and nervous. What if he's misjudged the situation? It's hard to know how Aashay will react.

But Aashay squats on the floor opposite Popi and gives him his full attention. 'You're afraid I'm here to kidnap Lucia, aren't you?' He holds out his left hand and taps the index finger with his right thumb. 'Number one: nobody's kidnapping children. It's a myth put about by people who've got nothing better to do with their time than make up stories to frighten others.'

He's talking about Hector. He wants to discredit him.

He taps his second finger. 'Number two: I've never kidnapped a child in my life and don't intend to start now. I'm here because I like you. I admit when I first came I had the idea that there might be some good salvage in the flats, but when I observed you, then experienced your hospitality, I decided I didn't want to take anything. I'm here because I enjoy your company. It's no problem. I can find stuff elsewhere. It just means I have to travel a bit further north, but that's OK.'

He's talking very seriously, the glint of humour gone entirely from his face, and he seems earnest, genuine, thoughtful.

'But what about the family at the fair?' I ask. 'Lancelot's family. They all looked like Lucia. You must have known we'd see the resemblance – and other people would too.'

Slight disappointment settles over his face as he contemplates me. 'Too much imagination, Roza,' he says. 'It's easy to see things that aren't there, once your mind goes in that direction.'

He makes it sound so simple. 'But it wasn't just me. We all saw it. Didn't we?' I appeal to Boris and Popi, who are watching Aashay.

'It seemed obvious to us at the time,' says Popi, nodding slowly. He's qualifying it, as if he's beginning to doubt himself.

'Not to me,' says Aashay. 'And, believe me, if anyone else had seen it, you wouldn't have been allowed to pedal out of there like you did.'

He has a point. I try to believe him. I want to believe him. 'Did they ever lose a child?' I ask.

'Lancelot's family?' He thinks for a while. 'No,' he says at last. 'Not that I can remember. Of course, lots of people have lost family – the country's not a safe place – but, no, I can't recall anyone ever telling me they'd lost a child.'

I can't look at Popi or Boris for a while. Is everything my fault? Are we contemplating leaving because of my overactive imagination?

'So why are you here now?' asks Popi.

Aashay spreads his hands. Look, he's saying, my innocence is so strong, it's coming out of my fingertips, shining through my nails. I'm as transparent as water. 'I've been looking after you,' he says. 'Making sure you got back safely. Covering your tracks, going ahead, checking there's no one there to surprise you, doubling back in case someone's following.'

'I can't think how you managed that,' says Popi. 'I had a look-out on the roof all day after we arrived home and she didn't spot anything or anyone. Can you really move around so silently, so invisibly, that no one sees you?'

Aashay grins. 'Oh, come on, do you really trust Delphine? She's sixteen. The goat's up there – she likes the goat. And she'd have had her POD with her. Anyway, I'm good at it. I have alternative routes. I go where no one else goes. Or nearly no one else,' he says, looking at me. So he came through the city centre. 'Don't forget, I knew Dan. I know all the caretakers. And other people as well. I know who to trust.'

'What about the smuggling, then?' asks Boris, his voice sceptical.

'Smuggling?' says Aashay, as if he doesn't understand.

'We're not glass-eyed,' says Boris. 'Everyone at the fair knew about it. Why wouldn't we?'

Aashay smiles, but not warmly. 'And what exactly do you know?'

'Not much, actually,' I say. 'Only what someone told Delphine.'

We're all watching Aashay, waiting for him to enlighten us. 'Don't ask,' he says to Popi. 'You're right, I do have one or two – shall we say . . . clandestine operations going down, but they're my concern, not yours. The less you know, the better. Your priority is to protect your family, not to become involved in something that might endanger them. So I'm not going to tell you anything about that. My deals are nothing to do with you.'

He's very convincing. Now that we're talking about business, he's different, less open, less friendly, but somehow impressive. He knows what he's doing.

'Look,' he says, his voice gentler, 'I'm a good man.' He looks directly at me when he says this, holding my eyes with his, willing me to believe him. 'I'm here to help you, so take advantage. Don't spoil everything by meddling in matters that have nothing to do with you.'

Boris folds his arms and glares at me because he's not confident about glaring at Aashay. 'Hmm,' he says.

Popi stares at Aashay for a few seconds, clearly unsure how to respond, then turns back to his sculpture. He places his chisel almost parallel to the right cheek of the girl and slices a wafer-thin sliver from the side of the nose, smoothing it with his hand afterwards.

'So who killed Dan?' I say.

He frowns. 'I don't know. But I'll find out.'

'And where's Hector?' asks Boris.

He shakes his head again. 'That I don't know.'

Lucia bursts in, flapping her arms as if she's a bird. '*Goosey goosey gander*,' she chants, '*Whither shall I wander?*'

'Did you come down here on your own?' asks Popi.

'No,' she says, dancing round us, hissing like a goose. 'Delphine's just behind me. Moth wants you all to come back up for lunch.'

24

The rain keeps coming, ironing out the landscape, erasing the low hills first, then creeping up the steeper ones. I stand in front of my living-room window, watching the weather as I've watched it all my life, trying to analyse everything that Aashay has told us this morning. As soon as I'm no longer in his presence, I become more sceptical, more uncertain about what is true and what isn't.

He was plausible – of course. The only thing he wouldn't discuss was the smuggling, and that's not unreasonable. He doesn't owe us an explanation for matters that don't affect us.

I'm trying to be objective about our reaction to Lancelot's family. Once the suggestion was planted, did everyone react without considering the likelihood of it being true? If you think you've seen something, it's hard to pretend you haven't. We were all nervous, confronted with so many strangers, ready to panic if anything went wrong. I was the one who first saw the resemblance. I didn't tell Moth what I'd seen until she'd seen it for herself. Am I so persuasive that I can convince everyone to see something that doesn't exist? I was flustered by the encounter between Aashay and Hector, confused by my reactions to both of them. Did I transfer my confusion to everyone else? Did I give Moth's anxieties about Lucia a focus?

I lean forward on the windowsill, watching a piece of debris churning along with the tide of water, about to collide with the block of flats opposite. It looks like an old carpod. I didn't think there were any left. It hits the side of the building and I watch the waves it creates, the way it surges backwards and forwards, bouncing off the walls, coming back for another attempt to breach our defences.

My attention is diverted by something on the inside window-sill, just above the curve of the edge, that wasn't there yesterday. It's a cartoon cat, more meticulously drawn than some of the others I've seen, its face more serious, gentler.

Aashay's been in my flat. Without my permission.

Goosey goosey gander, whither do you wander?

I experience a sharp prickle of panic. It was obvious that he could get into empty flats, so why did I assume he would respect my privacy? When did he come? Was it at a time when I wasn't here or has he been prowling around in the night, watching me sleep, seeing me at my most unguarded?

Upstairs and downstairs, And in my lady's chamber.

'Roza.'

I jump and leap round. He's standing behind me. How can he move so silently, so lightly, when he has such a tangible presence?

He puts out a hand, but I don't respond. I take a deep breath, tight with shock. 'How did you get in?' My voice is artificial and high-pitched.

'The door was open,' he says. He's like a small boy, trying to justify himself, his face earnest with conviction.

But the door wasn't open. I know it wasn't.

I gesture at the cat on the windowsill. 'When – when—' Fear is gripping me, confusing my thoughts.

He ignores the question. 'I came to tell you something,' he says. 'I lied earlier, when we were talking to your pop.'

I just stare at him.

'I came back for you, Roza. That's why I'm here. Not for the others. Just you. It's you I've been watching, keeping safe, making sure you weren't ever in danger.'

I can't speak. My throat is restricted, my heart beating so fast I can hear it in my ears, drumming through my skull.

He takes my hand from my side and pulls me towards him. He puts his arms round me and I'm engulfed by his smell. I can almost hear the interior workings of his body: the sweat glands humming; the blood circling beneath his skin; the heart pumping on and on, never pausing, never doubting. His breathing

317

surrounds me, like a hot wind, steady, controlled. His face is just above mine, his lips coming down towards me . . . For a fraction of a second I'm ready to respond, and then hot fury ignites.

I twist my face away. 'It *was* you, wasn't it?' I say.

'What?'

'You killed Dan. That's why you were there when we came out. Keeping an eye on us, checking we'd gone before you went back in.'

He stays in the same position, his face only a few centimetres from mine. I begin to wonder if he's heard me. I don't have the strength to break away. He straightens up and rests his chin on my head. I start to make calculations. How can I let him believe he has control over me, even though he doesn't? When should I attempt an escape? Where can I run to?

'Dan was a threat,' he says at last. 'He could trace you through your PODs, pinpoint your exact position, and he'd have told the others where you were. You were right. He wanted Lucia. He had contacts, he knew the markets, and he'd have sacrificed you without a thought if it meant he could get his hands on her. I couldn't let that happen, Roza.'

I go limp. The markets? 'What do you mean, the others? Who are they? Are you talking about the people we met at the fair?'

I can feel him nodding. 'Don't underestimate any of them. Someone lost Lucia long before your Popi found her – you're her third owners, not the second. The people who were careless enough to lose her the first time – and the ones who lost her again – didn't survive. Where she came from originally isn't the point. She's a child and she's currency.'

Owners? He sees us as Lucia's owners?

I think of the people we met: Farzana, the Weather Watchers; Olisa, who has her own children, who gave Delphine the dress; Phil, who got on so well with Popi. I don't believe Aashay. 'You're exaggerating,' I say. 'Some of them are good. They'd have a conscience.' Unlike him.

I can feel his muscles tense, his irritation at my scepticism. Then he laughs. Once I would have felt a loosening of tension, assumed he accepted what I was saying, but now I feel an increase of danger. 'Don't judge everyone by your own standards, Roza. We're all out for ourselves, even you and your family. Let's face it, Lucia doesn't really belong to you either, does she?'

'You're judging us by your standards,' I say. 'Not everyone thinks like you.'

Unexpectedly, he loosens his grip and lets me step back, but keeps his hands on my arms, so that he can look directly into my eyes. 'Yes, they do,' he says softly.

'But you've admitted that you lied. Why should I believe anything you say?'

'I've told you the truth.' He takes hold of my plait with his left hand and runs his thumb backwards and forwards over one of the coils. 'Not your parents, not Boris, just you.'

My POD pings.

'Leave it,' says Aashay, his voice hard. His hands move behind my head again, pulling me gently towards him.

'Leave me alone!' I say, twisting to get away from him.

'Roza – what's going on?' Delphine is at the door of the room, agitated, staring at me.

I take the opportunity to escape from Aashay's grasp. 'Delphine!' I say, rushing to her with relief. 'Thank goodness you're here!'

But Delphine turns away, back to the door, not knowing how to react to Aashay's presence. 'You've got to come – now,' she says. 'We've found something on the cycle floor. You need to see it.' She concentrates on her reason for coming. 'Hurry! Everyone's down there!'

Everyone? What can possibly have happened? 'What is it, Delphine?'

But she won't tell me, and her urgency is frightening. 'Just get a move on,' she says over her shoulder as she half runs out of the flat, expecting us to follow. 'You'll see when you get there.'

Aashay doesn't attempt to restrain me, so I run down the stairs with Delphine, flight after flight. He follows us, his tread firm and controlled. I can't think clearly.

Popi and Moth are standing together on the cycle floor, by the wall furthest from the exit, with Boris holding Lucia, as if he's been told to protect her.

'Roza,' calls Moth, and her voice is slow, dry, odd. 'Come and see what we've found.'

There's a bicycle in the corner behind them, pushed up against the wall, a Pinarello Mercurio, black with red streaks on the crossbar and fork ends. Its tyres and panniers are caked with mud. It's wedged behind two other bikes, a Boardman mountain bike and a junior Apollo, one male, one female. We know every bike. We've spent hours here during floodtime, working our way through them, experimenting with sizes and saddles and gears. Boris used to ride the Boardman a couple of years ago, until he opted for his present speed bike. Delphine and I both used the Apollo for a while when we were younger, and we've given Lucia rides on it, although it's still too big for her.

I've never seen the Pinarello before in my life.

'Lucia found it,' says Delphine. 'She was just playing while Boris and I were testing brakes.'

There's a rucksack dangling from one of the handlebars. Navy, grey round the edges where it's worn thin, dark stains across the front. The vel is losing its grip on the corners of the opening and separating slightly.

Popi is running his hands through his hair. 'I saw it,' he says, in a strained voice, 'earlier, when I was looking for wheels for the trailer. But I didn't think it through – it didn't register.'

Nobody else seems to want to touch it, so I approach slowly and ease the rucksack from the handlebars, carrying it out on to the open floor. I know what it is. I've never seen it before, so I don't exactly recognise it, but I know where it's come from. I kneel down and open the flap with trembling hands.

There are clothes – men's clothes – compressed into tight, neat balls; two rolled-up ties, one in blue silk, the other in red and green tartan; two bottles of water, one half empty; plastic containers of apples and hard, dry-looking vitamin bars. And more personal things: a battery-operated chessboard; a gold pen, old, slightly battered, so typical of him, taking up valuable space with something that nobody uses any more; a wafer-thin cloth paper, folded immaculately into a small square. I unfold it. *Brighton to Roza*, it says at the top, followed by a list of directions. Names of waystations. Little comments and doodles: *on my way*; a picture of me printed from the net; *a bicycle made for two*.

Hector.

He's real! I always knew he was real.

I look round. 'Where is he?'

Nobody answers.

I go over to Aashay and shake his arm. 'Where is he?' I say quietly. 'You know, don't you?'

'No,' he says, with amazement. 'This is nothing to do with me.' He brings his hands up in that familiar gesture. Lucifer. Beauty and evil, companions, neighbours, nestling down together, snuggling up to each other for comfort.

It comes to him too easily. 'Yes, you do!' I gaze into his face, willing him to tell me the truth, my voice hard. 'You're pretending, the same as always.' I'm shouting. 'Where is he? What have you—?'

'Roza.' Moth comes over and puts a restraining hand on my arm.

'No!' I shake her off. 'He knows exactly what's happened to Hector. You've killed him, haven't you? Just like Dan.'

There's a silence. I can hear water sloshing in the storage room below us, the rush of new rainfall, wind whistling towards us over the low walls, whining through the open spaces.

'So it was you who shot Dan,' says Boris. 'Just as we thought.'

'Do you know what you're saying, Roza?' asks Popi. I can hear his attempt to regulate his voice, to be reasonable.

'Ask him,' I say. 'Go on, see if he'll tell you what he told me.'

Aashay doesn't appear to be discomforted by the attention. He's swaying comfortably on the soles of his feet, not smiling exactly, but his mouth soft and amiable, his eyes almost merry, as if we're having a pleasant chat, as if he's about to tell us a story, sing a nursery rhyme.

He's a cartoon, an exaggerated copy of a human being. Nothing he does or says is real.

'Think about it,' I say. 'Everything's going well for us, we're getting along fine, no problems, our lives organised and manageable – and then Aashay appears. Suddenly everything gets complicated. I wonder why.' I address his chest, no longer willing to look him in the eye. 'You've always intended to get rid of Hector, haven't you? As soon as possible. So when we all went to sleep after returning from the fair, you realised you had a good opportunity to intercept him without our knowledge. I'm right, aren't I?' I don't want to look at his face to find out, but there's a looseness about the way he's standing, almost as if he's about to burst into laughter. 'You were jealous of him. You couldn't bear the idea of us eye to eye.'

He still doesn't respond, as if he's waiting for something.

Popi comes over to stand close to me, offering support. 'Is she right?' he asks Aashay, almost politely. 'Did you shoot Dan? Have you done something to Hector?'

I'm beginning to imagine the way it worked. Aashay must have cut through the city centre after he'd shot Dan – and reached Wyoming before us. He might well have been there when we arrived, hiding until we all went off to sleep. Either he waited there or headed towards the M5 so that he could meet Hector. He would have greeted him, shaken hands, offered friendship. He's good at that. I can see them together, Aashay letting Hector go first up to the cycle floor, calling to him as they rode up the ramp, making a joke, then suddenly wrenching him off his bike and—

Oh, Hector. Why didn't you look behind you?

Not high enough to push him off the side of the building, but a gun, a knife? Or a violent blow to the head. He could have beaten him, kicked him, strangled him, if he didn't want to risk the sound of a gun going off. What chance did Hector have? Most people would struggle to defend themselves against Aashay – even Boris doesn't have the strength.

322

Then we all woke up and there wasn't time to dispose of the bike.

When Boris and I went to search for Hector, in all that open space, we should have been looking inwards not outwards, at home, not away.

Why didn't Aashay remove the bike later, when he was on his own? Did he want us to find it? Has he been waiting for it all to come out into the open, so he can justify himself? Or is he so arrogant that he doesn't care if we know or not?

'What's happened to him?' I ask. I want to be wrong, to give Aashay the opportunity to tell us it was an accident or that he regrets his actions. I want Hector to be locked up somewhere, alive, waiting for us to find him.

'You're quite wrong, Roza,' he says kindly. 'I don't know anything about Hector.'

'So who brought his bike here?' asks Boris, moving closer, flexing his fists. 'It would hardly have been one of us.'

Then, amazingly, Aashay turns away. 'You're all getting too worked up, jumping to the wrong conclusions. We'll talk about it later, when you've calmed down.'

'You're just going to walk away?' says Popi. 'Without a word of explanation? Nothing to defend yourself?'

'He didn't expect to get caught,' I say. 'He needs time to make something up.'

Aashay smiles and waves his hand in the air. 'Cherry-oh,' he says.

And then I know for certain. 'You *have* met Hector,' I say, grabbing his arm. 'Nobody says "cherry-oh" except Hector. You've had a conversation with him, made him believe you're a friend, said goodbye to him.'

Aashay stops and examines my hand on his arm. Then he looks up and searches my face, his eyes narrowed, his eyebrows crushed. He looks hurt, betrayed. 'If I've done anything,' he says quietly to me, 'which I think you'll find I haven't, it was for you, Roza.' Then he turns to everyone else. 'You're mistaken, all of you. Everyone's heard Hector saying "cherry-oh". Nothing odd about that.' He flaps his arm to release it from my grasp, to shake me off.

Goosey goosey gander—

But the only time he's been present when I've talked to Hector online was at the fair. Did he say 'cherry-oh' to me then? He might have done – I try to remember. I remember watching Aashay leave while Hector and I were still talking, and the next time I saw him, he was strapping boxing gloves on to Boris. He couldn't have heard.

'Just tell us what you know, Aashay,' says Popi, urgently. 'You owe it to Roza.'

Aashay talks quietly, so we have to strain to hear him over the sound of the wind. 'If you want him to turn up, you just have to wait. He'll get here in the end. The bike's probably nothing to do with him.'

'Don't be ridiculous,' I say hotly. 'This is his bike, his rucksack. We need to know where he is.' As I speak, I realise I've understood for ages that there would be no eye to eye with Hector. When Boris and I were cycling down the M40 looking for him, I wasn't expecting to find him.

'You should never have trusted Aashay,' says Boris to me. He must be having the same thoughts, and now he's directing his anger at me.

'Why did you let him into your flat again, Roza?' says Delphine. 'How could you?'

Upstairs and downstairs And in my lady's chamber—

'I didn't let him in,' I say. 'He has this way of coming and going wherever he wants. Locks don't seem to bother him.'

Moth picks up the rucksack and places herself in front of Aashay. 'Please tell us what's happened to Hector,' she says firmly. 'We can't stop you doing whatever you want to do, but you've known us long enough to understand that we mean you no harm. Surely you can show us some consideration – out of respect for our friendship. We were all very fond of Hector. We deserve an explanation.'

'You never met him,' says Aashay. 'How can you be fond of someone you don't know?' His voice is less breezy, less certain.

His eyes slip past Moth and I turn to see where he's looking. The door to the ground-floor storage room.

'Hector's down there!' I say. 'In the storage room. The only place we haven't searched.'

I head for the door, but Popi stops me. 'You can't,' he says softly. 'It'll be flooded.'

He's right. There are stairs behind the door, two flights down to the storage room that occupies most of the ground floor. It's intended for cold storage during the long, hot summers, but abandoned in the autumn. Vents open automatically when the temperature outside drops and the rain starts, so the whole area acts like a floodplain, a way to relieve the pressure without destabilising the building. We've been hearing the water the whole time we've been here, lapping up against the floor beneath our feet, rolling and booming with its self-induced current. If Hector's down there, he'll be under water, drifting around, banging against the ceiling, rotting . . .

'I hope he was dead before you put him there,' says Moth.

This is too horrific to contemplate. 'He was, wasn't he?' I say, my voice catching. 'Please say he was.'

'I can't believe you think I've had anything to do with Hector's disappearance,' says Aashay. 'Don't you trust me? You've known me long enough.' A stranger, who'd only just met him, would be utterly convinced. Honesty, openness are written all over his face. 'You probably don't appreciate this, but I've been protecting you for ages. The world is a dangerous place, and there you all were, wandering around as if you were the only people in the country, wide open, inviting attention. The number of times any one of you could have been abducted – I could have done it myself, but I didn't. Should I have left you like that, unprotected? You needed a guardian, someone to watch over you. That was my role. It's what I've been doing for longer than you can imagine.'

This can't be true. He's already told me that he knew of our existence, but that was all. He's never suggested that he's been watching us for so long. Have we been existing in a sinister world of hidden threats, walking safely because Aashay was always ahead of us, clearing our pathways? A secret master puppeteer with our interests at heart, manipulating strings in the background, wandering through our flats when we were out, observing us silently . . .

There I met an old man who wouldn't say his prayers . . .

He's making it up, exaggerating, creating yet another story. I can't recognise the world he's just painted. But I can't deny a niggling doubt that distrusts our analysis of the situation and still wants to believe him – even now.

'So,' says Moth, after a few seconds, 'a self-appointed guardian. How thoughtful.' She doesn't believe him.

'Curiously,' says Popi, 'we've done a pretty good job of looking after ourselves. It really wasn't necessary for you to spare the time.' There's a hard edge to his voice that he doesn't disguise.

'And you didn't think you should have mentioned this earlier?' asks Moth. 'At least put us in the picture.'

'Maybe I should have,' he says, nodding urgently. 'But I liked your innocence. It made me' – he pauses – 'it gave me something to believe in. So I just kept watch.'

'What changed then?' says Delphine, also sceptical. 'Why did you reveal yourself? Why did you take us to the fair?'

His eyes slide over to meet mine, then he shrugs slightly. 'It was all going to change, wasn't it? Roza was going to marry Hector, everyone was going to go with them to Brighton. Nothing lasts.'

What changed was me – that time we met in the art gallery. I've wondered why he revealed himself at that point, but perhaps he simply decided it was time we talked. He probably wasn't anticipating such a powerful current to flow between us any more than I was. I recognised that something had happened, but it was hard to acknowledge. He wouldn't have had the same inhibitions. So, from his point of view, Hector was going to spoil everything. He needed to disappear. If Hector hadn't set off from

Brighton, and if I hadn't responded to Aashay as I had, none of this would have happened.

'So what are you hoping to achieve now, Aashay?' asks Popi, more assertive, prepared to take charge. 'Are you trying to turn the clock back? Do you want us to carry on in exactly the same way for ever, while you continue to act out your role as protector and benefactor?'

Hector was dying while we slept; his body's been below our feet all the time, unseen, unattended. If we'd known, if we'd found his bike earlier, could we have saved him?

There are tears in my eyes now, hot and angry, spilling over my cheeks. I grab Aashay's arm and stare into his face, making him look at me, searching for an admission of guilt, a sign of regret. But there's nothing. Just blankness. 'How could you do that to Hector? What did he ever do to you?'

The colour in his face drains away, leaving it frozen and life-less. He seems finally to understand that he's gone too far, done the unforgivable. Unbelievably, it's as if, right up to that moment, he's just assumed I would think like him.

'We can't let him get away with this,' says Boris, his fists clenched. 'If he can kill Dan and Hector, he could kill us all, one by one.'

'Ah,' says Aashay, softly, turning away from me with a smile. 'The boy wants another fight. Not a quick learner, then?'

They stand there, eye to eye, as if they're alone.

Too many films, Boris. You're not superhuman.

Suddenly, unexpectedly, Aashay reaches inside his jacket and pulls out a gun. The gun that killed Dan. At the same time, he swivels round, glides smoothly to one side and grabs Lucia, pull-ing her off her feet. There's a moment of stunned silence, then Lucia screams, an ear-piercing sound that echoes through the open space. 'Let me go!' she shrieks. 'Moth! Roza! Make him let go!'

Nobody moves, terrified of escalating the situation. Popi raises his hands, trembling slightly, and pats the air as if he's trying to contain it, to calm a sudden breeze. 'Come on, Aashay.

Your quarrels are with us, not Lucia,' he says, into a brief silence between her screams.

'There's a market for children,' says Aashay, still calm, still in control. 'If I'm leaving, I might as well take her with me. Get something for all my efforts.'

None of us knows what to do.

He moves carefully along the wall, the low wall where we once stood and watched the first Lucia swept away in the floods. Boris edges towards him, his hands flexing, but Aashay is watching him carefully.

Lucia stops screaming and struggling and settles into a more passive whimper.

'Please, Aashay,' says Moth, her face white and clenched, 'let her go. She's never done you any harm.'

'I've done everything for you,' says Aashay, 'and all you do is accuse me of things I'm not responsible for. Instead of showing gratitude, trusting me, you betray me.' His eyes flicker towards me again, but I look away quickly.

'Why don't you take more time to think about what you're doing?' says Popi, approaching him from the opposite side to Boris. I can hear the effort he's making to keep his voice calm. 'You can't leave yet, not while it's still flooded, so there's no need to act hastily.'

But Aashay doesn't want to be reasonable. He keeps an eye on Boris, whom he obviously considers to be the greatest threat, and pushes the gun against Lucia's neck. We all freeze. 'Back off, Boris,' he says. 'I could throw her into the floods, if that's what you want, or I could run an online auction. I know at least twenty people who'd give anything for a child. Anything. And plenty more will join the queue when word gets around. There's no shortage of reward.'

'No!' I say. 'You don't mean that – you don't!' There must be some goodness in him somewhere.

He meets my eyes. 'I'm a good man,' he said to us, not long ago, and I know he believed it then. Is he remembering that conversation too? I lock my eyes on him, willing him to soften, but his face is set and impenetrable.

Lucia starts to squirm, kicking wildly, pummelling him with her small fists, embarking on a deafening scream.

'No!' shouts Moth. 'Don't move, Lucia!'

Aashay tries to tighten his hold on her, but she's wriggling too violently, a slippery, rubbery, uncontainable alien creature. 'Keep still!' he yells, raising a hand to hit her.

She leans over and bites his other arm. The hand holding the gun jerks away and he yells with pain and fury.

At that moment, Popi hurls himself at him, taking Aashay by surprise. Boris leaps from the other side, almost simultaneously. As they make contact, the gun is knocked out of his grasp and falls to the ground.

Moth and I throw ourselves forwards. Moth grabs Lucia and I grab the gun. There's a brief scrabble, while Aashay attempts to keep hold of Lucia and defend himself against Boris and Popi, but Moth and Delphine wrestle her away, freeing her with a jerk that sends all three of them skidding backwards and landing heavily on the concrete floor.

I move away from them as quickly as I can, refusing to let anything distract me. I lean over the wall, raise my arm and throw the gun as far as possible, with every drop of energy I possess, determined that it won't come washing back towards us. It falls obligingly into the water with an insignificant splash and sinks. Only then do I turn back to help the others.

Boris is attempting to restrain Aashay, holding his arms and clinging on, but Aashay throws him off with a roar of fury and turns to confront him, light as a cat. Boris hurls himself back at him, kicking, clawing. The rest of us scramble out of their way, shocked by their ferocity. Their first fight, in our kitchen, was playful in comparison to this, just a game. This is real violence, real anger.

'We have to stop them!' shouts Moth to Popi.

But what can Popi do? If Boris can't defeat Aashay, none of us can.

'Delphine!' yells Moth. 'Get Lucia out of here! Up to the flat. Lock yourselves in.'

But locks don't keep Aashay out.

Delphine doesn't move. Like the rest of us, she is transfixed with fear and horror.

Popi edges up behind Aashay, shuffling backwards and forwards to keep up with him, trying to get close, then makes a grab for his ear, attempting to twist it, wanting to inflict pain. Any small act that might distract him, cause him inconvenience. We have nothing to lose. Either we stop him here, now, or he carries on deciding for himself what is right or wrong, accumulating power, growing stronger and stronger. I throw myself at him, following Popi's example, reaching for his ponytail, grasping it in my hand and yanking it.

We simply don't have the strength, even together, and Aashay tosses us away as if he's brushing off flies. He's Gulliver, a giant, repelling the little people as if we're nothing more than an irritation. He's Samson, bringing down the house of the Philistines.

I slide across the rough concrete floor, my knees bleeding and thudding with pain. I take a deep breath and drag myself back to my feet. We need a weapon, something to raise the odds in our favour. But all I can see round us are bikes.

Close by, Popi is pulling himself creakily to his feet, and hobbling back towards the fight, lining himself up with Boris. Boris tries to push him out of the way, to protect him, but Aashay attacks them both frenetically, his fists moving so fast it's impossible to keep track of what's happening. Popi falls first, thumping on to the floor, and Boris follows, rolling aside just as Aashay attacks him with a fist. The fist hits the concrete floor with a sharp crack.

It gives me hope. He can be weakened.

Lucia is crying again, loudly. The sound is high-pitched, excruciating.

'Delphine!' screams Moth. 'Get her out of here!'

But Delphine is heading towards one of the cycle racks. I follow her direction with my eyes and see what she's seen. A metal bar dangling from a loose screw. 'Help me!' she shouts.

I join her, rotating it, twisting it backwards and forwards. Then Moth is next to me. The three of us apply every drop of energy we can muster, heaving, panting with frustration, until finally, with a metallic shriek, it breaks away.

I grab it and rush over to where Aashay has sent Popi flying again and pushed Boris up against the side, bending him backwards over the top of the wall, through the open space. He's hitting him viciously, determined and intense. He doesn't see us approaching. Without allowing myself time to think, I raise the metal in the air behind my head. It's heavy, it swings more wildly than I was expecting, but I force it over my head and down on to Aashay's shoulders with a huge clash.

He turns with an angry cry, springing away from Boris, blood welling out through his jacket on to his back, but still not weakened. He's unstoppable. Even with our combined efforts, we're incapable of defeating him. We can't generate enough power. I stare at him, struggling to keep hold of the metal bar, but it's too heavy and falls to the floor with a clatter that rings through the air.

When he sees that I was the one who hit him, he stops, genuinely puzzled. He studies my face.

In that moment of silence, Moth staggers forward and confronts him. 'Stop it,' she croaks, her voice weak and tearful. 'We don't have to do this. We can sort everything out.'

But Popi, our gentle, reasoning father, the man who doesn't believe in violence and has to do this once before, the man who would always prefer to talk, picks up the piece of metal, charges up from behind me, and whacks Aashay in the face so hard that the force sends him staggering against the wall. He's knocked backwards, his feet leaving the safety of the floor.

He struggles to maintain his balance, blood pouring down his face, finally weakened. He scrabbles with raised hands, as if there's a bar above him to grab hold of, but they're grasping at the air, unable to find anything solid to hold. He hovers on the wall, his feet flailing over the cycle floor. He forces his head up and looks directly at me, his brown eyes peering through a veil of blood, his face bewildered. I see deep sadness, immense hurt.

Moth darts forwards. 'Quick!' she shouts. 'We can save him.'

But she's wrong. He can't be saved. Popi raises the iron bar once more, swings it round, and slams it across Aashay's chest. Delphine and I take a leg each, push furiously—

So I took him by the left leg and threw him down the stairs.

He tries to throw himself back up, twisting his body upwards with a terrifying strength, scrabbling with his feet to make contact with the wall. He's still looking at me.

His legs slip away, scraping against the bricks. As he lets go, he tries to heave himself into a more upright position, struggling to gain enough momentum to pull himself up. Then, slowly, slowly, slowly, he topples backwards, the wrong way, down into the rushing waters below.

Nobody speaks. We lean over the wall, all of us breathing heavily, and watch. Even he's not powerful enough to resist the sheer force of the water. It's not like the time we watched the first Lucia disappear. It's not an accident. He nearly destroyed us. We've defeated him, but in some ways, he's managed to defeat us, too. He's forced us to become brutal.

There's a loud throbbing sound, something different, in the distance.

I still believe he can survive, scramble to safety, but when his head comes to the surface, his mouth opening and shutting, then sinks down under the surface again, I realise he can't swim. He keeps coming back up, but for shorter periods. Is he shouting, screaming, asking for help, still protesting his innocence? We can't hear him against the roar of the wind and the rain. His body slams against the side of the opposite block of flats, submerges, comes back to the surface, drifts towards us. The rain is still coming down in sheets, a deluge, an impartial executioner. He disappears, re-emerges. He's looking at us. He's looking at me. He can't be. He's too far away. He's blinded by water, he's drowning. He sinks below the surface again.

It's the last time. We stand there and watch, searching for evidence that he is still alive, but he doesn't emerge again.

The throaty rumble in the distance becomes a roar, cutting through the deluge, overwhelming, deafening.

My face is wet with tears, wetter than if I was out there in the floods, wetter than the rain itself.

25

The new sound grows and grows until we're paralysed by its enormity. None of us can move away from the wall, only held up by the security of the bricks beneath our hands. I'm still terrified that Aashay will come crawling up the side of the building, and drag himself on to the cycle floor, prepared to confront us all over again.

The noise is overwhelming. I can't think.

Lucia shakes my arm and points upwards. She's shouting, but I can't hear her.

It's a helicopter. Hovering in the space between Colorado and Montana. A giant insect, parting the rain as it approaches, hugging the surface of the flood waters, buzzing with an angry intensity. As it gets closer, it expands and fills the sky. My mind feels as if it's shredding, unable to withstand the sound. I've never seen a real helicopter before. I didn't think there was enough fuel in the country to get one off the ground.

It stops moving forwards and hovers just above us, its blades scything through the rain, sweeping it away with nonchalance, furrowing the surface of the flood water. A powerful wind tears at us, threatening to blow us off our feet.

Has it come for us?

There's a man in an open doorway, dressed in a sleek black suit, staring out and gesturing. A disembodied voice comes from the helicopter, loud enough to penetrate the rain. 'Stand back!' it booms.

Blindly obedient, we take a few steps away from the wall.

'Stand back!' it orders again. The man is waving furiously at us to move much further away.

We shuffle in the opposite direction and watch as a line comes snaking from the helicopter and hooks over the top of the concrete balcony. They tug it from their end, jiggle it, operating a remote that locks the mechanism into place. Then a man takes hold of a wheel-type device and slides towards us, followed by four others.

The first leaps on to the floor and comes over to where we're standing. He pulls his headgear away from his ears, and puts a hand up to flatten his blond-grey hair. The wind from the helicopter blades immediately ruffles it into a confused mess. 'Good afternoon,' he shouts. He's followed by a woman in a face mask. Her eyes are Chinese.

Popi recovers first. 'Good afternoon,' he shouts back. I'm impressed that he can still manage politeness. 'We're the Polanskis. Who are you?'

'We're from Brighton. We're here to rescue you.' He herds us all to the other side of the cycle floor where we can hear each other, gesturing at two of the men to help Boris, who's half lying against a wall, unable to get to his feet. 'I'm Howard Cush, from the government.'

'You've brought a helicopter?' asks Popi. 'All the way from Brighton?'

'Actually,' says the Chinese woman, her voice muffled by the face mask, 'some of us have come from China. From TU.' She looks vaguely familiar. How could I possibly have seen her before? 'The helicopters are ours, on stand-by in Brighton. We make them available to your government.'

'We have to wait for Chinese authorisation,' says Howard Cush. 'They provide the fuel.'

'You know that,' I say to Popi. 'It's our health-care agreement with TU.'

The Chinese woman glances around, sees me and comes over, putting her hands on my shoulders and smiling. 'Roza,' she says in perfect English. 'I'm Fang, your work colleague. I am delighted to meet you at last.'

I can't believe this. She's barely out of her teens. The skin that's visible behind her mask is pale and translucent, studded with acne. Her hair is long, wavy, luxuriant. I've always believed the Chinese were older than they looked, enhancing their screen images to bring back their youth, but now it seems they've been going the other way, pretending to be older to give themselves gravitas.

'But' – I'm struggling to speak – 'what are you doing here?'

'I flew over last Friday, when we lost contact with Hector,' she says. 'He was one of our most brilliant young scientists. A clever, clever man. You know this, of course.'

'Of course,' I say, pretending, but suddenly furious with Hector. Clever, yes, but brilliant? He should have given me a clue. It's not right that I didn't know this.

'We were monitoring him,' says Howard Cush. 'He was valuable to us, too.'

'All our workers are important to us,' says Fang. 'You are important, Roza.'

I'm still gaping at her. 'Have you come here for us? Because I work for you?'

Fang looks round to include Boris and Delphine and Lucia. 'Your family has enormous potential,' she says. 'Brains are a valuable commodity.'

'You've been monitoring us?' says Moth to Howard Cush. 'After you agreed to leave us alone?'

'Oh, come on, Moth,' says Delphine. 'You're as pleased to see them as I am.'

'We've been keeping a closer eye than usual, Mrs Polanski,' says Howard. 'It was only when we spotted Aashay Kent on the roof earlier today that we realised he was here. We thought he was heading east – not sure how he managed to fool the satellites – so we hadn't initially connected him with Hector's disappearance. But Hector's POD wasn't just disabled – something serious must have happened to him – and Aashay Kent was close by. It was too much of a coincidence. That was when we made the decision to intervene.'

So we've never been alone. When we were searching Wyoming for someone hidden, someone hidden was watching us.

When I was very little, pre-Hoffman's, Moth took me to the

Sea Life Centre in Birmingham. Apparently, I ignored the sharks, the rays, the big stuff, and spent the whole day watching the clown fish – little orange creatures with wide white stripes and narrow black ones, their flippers round and comical, as if they were toys. I don't remember the visit, I was too small, but I've often imagined it. I even considered going to find out what had happened to the Sea Life Centre when I first went through the barriers, but cycled past eventually. It could only be bad.

Now I feel that we've been the specimens in a modern-day aquarium, on display to anyone who pays the entrance fee, a spectacle for strangers. Aashay hasn't been the only one watching us. How much could they see? Do they have cameras? Can they see inside our flats, listen to our conversations? Do they know about the two Lucias? Did they watch us kill Aashay, witness us taking on the role of executioners? Are they interested in our defence?

'If you've been spying on us,' says Popi, 'you presumably know we're all intending to come to Brighton after all.'

Howard shakes his head. 'We can't read minds.'

'Not to worry,' says Popi. 'You'll get there in the end.'

Boris coughs and spits out a tooth in a pool of blood. Moth rubs his back. 'Hold on to the tooth, Boris. If we're going somewhere with a dentist they can put it back in.'

'Looks like we were just in time,' says Howard Cush.

'No,' says Delphine. 'You're late. Half an hour earlier would have been good.'

'There has been much debate about whether we should have stepped in, at least to warn you, when Kent first turned up. But the majority favoured non-intervention unless you were in immediate danger.'

'Clever,' I say. 'Wait until something happens, then step in, only to find we've all been massacred.'

'Unlikely,' he says, looking round at us all. 'With your record of resourcefulness.'

'A warning might have been helpful,' says Moth, angrily.

Howard looks at her and almost smiles. 'But you're the one

who's always insisted on self-sufficiency. Some of us really admire your determination to manage your own lives, to instil strength of character in your children. It's created much debate, much controversy.'

'Oh, wonderful,' says Popi. 'Now we're the subject of an experiment.'

'If you were going to do something, you should have done it sooner,' I say. 'Do you know what happened to Dan – at Grand Central?'

He nods. 'We do now. Once you and Boris had gone back there. It took us by surprise.'

'Not omniscient, then,' says Popi, grimly satisfied.

'And Hector?' I ask Fang.

She sighs. 'His POD just stopped.'

I point at the floor. 'He's underneath us, dead, lost! You're too late!' I'm shocked to find myself shouting, while hot, fat tears unexpectedly cascade down my cheeks. 'If you had the means to stop it all, you should have—' I run out of words.

Lucia comes over and takes my hand. 'Don't cry, Roza,' she says. 'They're here to help us.'

'Look, folks,' says Howard Cush, 'there'll be time to debate all this later. Right now, we have to get you out of here.'

I wipe away the tears with my sleeve. 'Supposing we don't want to come?' I ask. 'You weren't here when we needed you. We saved ourselves. Why should we leave now?'

'You get more like your mother every day,' says Popi, patting my shoulder.

'I would strongly advise you to come with us,' says Howard Cush. 'The loss of Hector confirms our suspicions. Kent is a dangerous man.'

'Not any more, he isn't,' says Boris, his voice distorted as he struggles to move his mouth.

'No,' says Fang. 'We know.'

Has a roomful of people in Brighton been watching satellite pictures as they directed the helicopter towards us? Have they all seen what we did?

'Make no assumptions,' says Howard Cush. 'He's a survivor. He'll resurrect, spring back up and start a new racket, which we won't discover until it's at least a year down the line.'

Why does this send a tiny dart of excitement down my spine?

'Will we be able to come back here?' asks Delphine.

'Unlikely, I'm afraid. We've located a house for you in Brighton. You'll be safe there.'

'I've heard they kidnap children in Brighton,' says Moth.

Howard Cush frowns. 'We're very careful with our children, ma'am. They're our future.' He looks round at us. 'You are our future.'

'Why does that not fill me with joy?' says Moth, who will never say the right thing at the right time.

'What about my things?' says Delphine. 'Can I go and pack them?'

Howard Cush studies her for a moment. 'Delphine, right?' She nods, oddly undisturbed by his gaze and the way he identifies her so easily. 'We can't wait,' he says. 'Our fuel supply is limited. We have to get you on board right now and head for Brighton. Let's start with Lucia.'

'No!' says Moth, stepping in front of Lucia. 'She's not going anywhere without me.'

Howard Cush is taken aback by her ferocity.

'My wife is not to be thwarted,' says Popi. 'She thinks you'll go off without the rest of us once you've got Lucia.'

'If you have the slightest intention of stealing Lucia,' says Moth, 'you'll have to contend with me first.'

'That won't be necessary,' says Howard, 'We can only transport one of you at a time, so we'll take you first, then Lucia. Will that do?'

Moth nods. She doesn't have much choice.

'Look!' says Lucia, as we make our way back to the helicopter. 'There's a man steering!'

We can see him through the glass at the front, juggling with an upright stick, holding it steady against the gusting wind.

'You'll never entirely eliminate the need for human intervention.' Howard is shouting to make himself heard. 'The guys on the computers can't manoeuvre in these conditions.'

We stand watching, hair and clothes whipping around us, as they run a capsule down the wire, strap in Moth, then wind it back up to the helicopter. Lucia goes next, then they send over a cot for Boris. He's in pain and starting to lose consciousness. They want me to go after Boris, but I insist they take Popi first. I don't trust them. They might make the mistake of thinking artists are expendable.

I stand on the cycle floor and watch the capsule taking Popi, loose strands of hair that have escaped from my plait buffeting my face. The roar of the helicopter makes it hard to think. We're abandoning our home. I might never come back. Only a few days ago, we were agonising about leaving – and now we're just going, turning our backs on everything familiar without protest. I was expecting to be married, to leave here and go to Brighton. Now my choices have evaporated. Hector no longer exists – he's just a dead body in water. And someone else is making the decisions.

We always thought we were alone, but we weren't. Are the people who debated our situation a committee of big brothers or kind uncles and aunties? Have we been looked after or controlled?

They've come back for Delphine. I'll be the last.

Edward! The hens!

I don't want to leave Popi's sculpture. I love the hugeness of his carefully crafted girl, the dimpled knees, the ankle socks, the roundness of her legs as they emerge from the flare of her skirt. Will he feel able to start again, find new wood and recreate his masterpiece?

I could just refuse to go. They don't have much time to argue with me, not enough fuel. I could hide in one of the flats, exist here on my own, surviving on the crops from the Woodgate Valley. It wouldn't matter if the machines all stopped. I could pick apples by hand, dig up a few potatoes. I wouldn't need drops. I could explore further afield, find the Weather Watchers and help them create a new world. Maybe I could rescue Hector's body from the storage room, bury him properly. Maybe Aashay will wash up here in the spring. He's bigger and heavier than the first Lucia, and he won't drift out to sea so easily. It's in his nature to resist, dead or alive.

I don't have to go to Brighton.

The capsule is gliding back along the wire towards me. Fang is balancing it with one hand and holding out the other to guide me in. She smiles at me, a friend.

'No!' I say.

She looks at me, still smiling, perplexed.

I sprint towards the stairs and run, expecting to be followed, but hoping to take them by surprise. I take two stairs at a time: 8th, 16th, 23rd, pausing every few flights to recover my breath. Each time I stop, I hear footsteps pounding up from below and the sound gives me renewed energy, a determination to beat whoever is following me. When I finally reach the roof, Edward and the hens are huddled into their separate sheds, terrified by the sound of the helicopter.

I unlatch the doors and prop them open, my fingers fumbling in the rain. The chickens flutter away, but Edward stands still, her head on one side, confused by this suggestion of freedom.

'It's all right!' I yell. 'I've come to save you.' I heave all the sacks of grain out of the rain and into the shelter of the sheds, then punch holes in them so that the contents spill out. I take the plastic sheets off Edward's supply of hay and twigs from the Woodgate Valley. There's enough to last them through the winter – there must be. I look round for something big and heavy. There's a water tank, half full, near the door. That's what I need. I get behind it and start pushing, throwing myself at it, kicking it, unable to move it more than a few centimetres.

Two of the men from the helicopter burst through the door. We face each other. 'Help me!' I scream. 'We have to wedge the door open.' To their credit, they don't hesitate, and together we wrestle the tank forward until it's standing in the doorway, giving the animals an escape route. The opening faces outwards so they

341

can still drink from it, and the pipe remains in place on top, ready to catch the water from the shed guttering.

I unfasten Edward's chain from her neck and ruffle her head gently. 'Best I can do,' I murmur, into her ear. She nuzzles my cheek and I resist the urge to cry. Do goats eat hens? I won't think about it.

One of the men puts a hand on my arm and pulls me firmly away.

'Thank you,' I say. I wouldn't have been able to do it on my own.

Then we're tumbling back down the stairs, so fast I'm afraid I'll fall over my feet.

The roar of the helicopter increases as we descend. It's waiting. They haven't gone without me. Well, they wouldn't, would they? They'd hardly leave their own people.

There's a catch on the fire door into the bicycle floor, which I lock open.

Edward and the hens have a way out. At least they'll have a chance. They can descend the stairs, go down the ramp and out to fend for themselves. Can goats swim? Or hens? Maybe they'll wait for the waters to subside in the spring.

'Please!' calls Fang. 'You must come!'

I glance at the helicopter, hovering dangerously close. I can see Lucia's face, just inside the doorway. Her face is split into a giant grin. She knows what I've done.

The wind from the helicopter blades is stirring the water into waves large enough to crash over the walls of the bicycle floor and soak us. The throbbing of the engine fills the air, blasting through the space, sweeping away everything familiar.

I take Fang's hand.

Acknowledgements

I would like to thank the following: Chris Morgan, Pauline Morgan, Gregory Leadbetter, Helen Yendall, Julie Boden, William Gallagher and anyone else I might have forgotten who has contributed to the development of the novel; Laura Longrigg, always so wonderfully cheerful; Carole Welch and Lottie Fyfe from Sceptre, Hazel Orme, the copyeditor, and Celia Levett, the proofreader. No research to acknowledge this time – the really useful thing about setting a novel in the future is that you can make it all up.